THE CHINESE PROVERB

HUNTER GRANT SERIES

TINA CLOUGH

THE CHINESE PROVERB

Copyright © Tina Clough 2016

PAPERBACK ISBN 9780473379261

All rights reserved. No part of this book may be reproduced, stored in a retrieval system, or transmitted in any form or by any electronic or mechanical means including photocopying, recording, information or retrieval systems, or otherwise, without prior permission in writing from the publisher, with the exception of book reviewers, who may quote short excerpts in reviews.

Disclaimer

Most locations in this book are real places, but details have been changed to avoid comparisons with real businesses and individuals. The characters are the author's invention and are not based on any particular persons.

Lightpool Publishing

www.lightpoolpublishing.com

Cover design by Tara Cooney Design

A catalogue record for this 5x8" edition is available from the National Library of New Zealand

To order copies of this book please contact Publishers Distribution Limited orders@pubdist.co.nz

THURSDAY

I woke with a jerk of panic, my heart was pounding, every nerve jangled. Adrenaline had flooded my system and the only way to break the spell was to get up. I lit the camping lantern and went into the main room to put more wood in the stove and make a cup of tea. Scruff opened his eyes and looked at me without raising his head.

I rarely dream about Afghanistan these days. When I first left the army I regularly woke from a nightmare where dust swirled around me, and I smelt blood and burning diesel. I would wake in a panic, my hands trying to wipe splatters of blood off my helmet visor and only slowly realise where I was. This time I felt sure I had heard a high-pitched scream of pain or terror even after I opened my eyes; the dream had unnerved me more than usual.

A sudden downpour drummed like hailstones on the tin roof. I sat down by the fire with my laptop and forced my mind to concentrate on the proposal I was writing and after an hour I was calm enough to go back to bed.

In the morning I woke up feeling bleary and unmotivated. It was still raining, but less violently and by lunchtime it had slowed to a drizzle. I put on a weatherproof jacket and rubber boots and set off to inspect the track. The roar of the stream could be heard from a kilometre away, a distant throaty rumble. The ford would be impassable for another couple of days at least. Scruff ran around, sniffing out new scents, looping in figures of eight. Then he raced ahead and disappeared around the next bend.

Abstracted and on auto-pilot I walked down the muddy track through the dense New Zealand bush thinking of the security proposal I was putting together for a client in Venezuela. Last night's downpour had made deep ruts and the mud was slippery. At the last bend I got a clear view of the stream. The noise was deafening, and I could hear boulders rolling in the streambed. The ford was below at least a metre of water and the torrent rushed over the larger rocks in cresting waves.

Heading back uphill I whistled for Scruff a couple of times. Halfway up the track I heard him barking a long way off; that special bark that said, "you have to come and see this, I can't leave it". I left the track and made my way in the direction of the sound, calling back a couple of times to get a response to guide me until I saw him between the trees.

He was in his guard position, sitting erect and with his front paws together. He ran towards me and then straight back to where he had been sitting and nudged at something. I went closer and saw an arm and a shoulder and the back of a dark head. A boy's body, nearly completely covered with brown fern fronds and leaf litter, lay in a shallow depression. I caught my breath and took an involuntary step backwards.

It was the first dead body I had seen since I left Afghanistan and here in this peaceful and remote location it shocked me. Why was he here and how had he died? There was little I could do about it with no cell phone coverage and my only connection to the rest of the world blocked by a raging torrent. Then I noticed that Scruff was not sniffing the hand, he was licking it.

'Stop it, Scruff,' I said with a feeling of disgust, but he continued licking.

'For God's sake, come here!' I went forward to grab hold of his collar and the hand moved minutely, a small twitch and my heart leapt in my chest.

Kneeling beside the boy I tore at the ferns to uncover him, shocked at how cold and wet his skin was. I rolled him over and saw a thin face and thick black hair cut short with jagged bits sticking out. He was probably no more than twelve or thirteen years old. His jeans were made for a much bigger person, tied at the waist with a rope made from plaited strips of fabric. The checked shirt was made for an adult man, and he had no jacket, no shoes. He was starved-looking and filthy. I tore my jacket off and manhandled the limp wet body into it and zipped it up with his arms inside. I put my woollen beanie on him and tugged it right down. Long dark eyelashes fluttered once and then the face was still again. I gave the beanie another tug to cover as much of his head as possible and lifted him.

I knew we must be close to the big curve in the track halfway to the cabin and set off diagonally uphill. After ten minutes' hard going I laid my unconscious burden on the edge of the track. It would be quicker to run up and get the car than to carry him all the way to the cabin and every minute was precious. 'Stay! Guard!' I said to Scruff and ran up the track. I looked back at the first bend and smiled. Scruff was lying beside the boy, stretched out along his body. 'Good boy!' I called and his tail wagged in response.

Twenty minutes later I carried the boy inside and laid him on the old sofa. The first objective was to get the cabin really warm. I tucked a blanket tightly around him and piled more wood on the fire. I put two pots of water on the stove top and went out to the shed and started the generator. Three of the six fuel containers were still full; enough for a few days. The rain was falling steadily from the dark sky. Back in the cabin I lit the lamps and checked the fire in the cast iron stove.

Those wet clothes must come off right away, I thought,

something warm for him to wear, a sleeping bag. And some bottles of warm water to tuck in around him.

I got a T-shirt, a jersey and thermal leggings from the bedroom and laid them on the arm of the sofa. I cut the wet knot in the plaited rope that served as a belt, eased the wet jeans down and discovered with a feeling of shock that this was not a boy, it was a girl, or rather a young woman. She was excruciatingly thin; her hips were sharp ridges of bone, her stomach concave. There was a barbaric-looking piece of metal around her left ankle, and I left it, just patted her legs dry with a towel. I pulled the leggings on her with some difficulty, over feet that made me cringe; cut and bruised and filthy from walking barefoot over rough country.

I had never seen anyone in this state before. She had been wet for so long that it was impossible to properly dry her spongy skin. If I rubbed too hard it would tear and peel off. I unzipped the jacket and rolled her this way and that to get her arms out of the wet shirt that clung to her in damp folds. Pity clenched my throat as I looked at her bare body. I imagined that if I were to run my fingers down her ribs it would make a noise like when you run a stick along a picket fence. Her back was covered in diagonal marks, some looked like scars.

The first sign of consciousness came after I had dressed her. I was rolling her onto the unzipped sleeping bag to fold it around her. Black eyes opened briefly, looked at the ceiling and closed again. She moved a hand from under the cover and touched her face and then let it drop back. I held her hand between mine for a moment, willing it to absorb some warmth before I tucked it in. The water heating on the stove would soon be warm enough to do some good. I took three empty wine bottles with screw tops from under the bench and put them beside the stove. I was acutely aware that the girl might die of hypothermia before I could achieve anything. I lifted her upper body from the sofa and sat down, holding her half-sitting against my chest with my arms around her, hoping to warm her chilled body with my own body heat.

By the time the water was warm enough she seemed a little less cold. I put socks on the bottles and arranged them around her in the sleeping bag with one at her frozen feet and zipped the bag right up to her neck. I wondered how long it would be before she woke up properly and what she would tell me. I must have something hot ready for her to eat and drink; getting warmed up from the inside is supposed to be the best way. I studied the shelves above the bench and a can of chicken soup caught my eye. It would be nourishing, provided she did not choke on it. Five minutes later I had fished out the pieces of chicken and cut them into tiny pieces and the soup was heating on the stove. Scruff jumped on the sofa and stretched out alongside her. The girl worked an arm out from the sleeping bag, put her hand on Scruff's body and lay still again. I touched her hand; not warm but less deeply chilled than before.

I sat beside the hot stove reading and keeping an eye on the girl. An hour later I felt her eyes on me and looked up. She closed her eyes and lay still, but I knew she was awake. I took the saucepan of soup from the stove, poured some into a bowl and went over to the sofa. She might be from south-east Asia; her features indicated one of the countries in that region. Vietnamese, perhaps?

'How are you feeling?'

Her eyes stayed shut, but I knew she had heard me. I hitched the three-legged stool closer with my foot and put the bowl on it. 'There's a bowl of hot soup on the stool right next to your head. Why don't you have some?'

Her voice was a surprise, quite dark and husky, not the sort of voice I would have expected from such a waif. 'No.' Her eyes remained shut.

I went back to the stove and sat down again, glancing across now and then. I never caught her looking at me and after a while I had to say something.

'Why don't you want some warm soup? You're very cold, you need something warm to eat.'

'I am going to die,' she said and opened her eyes. 'I don't need to eat.'

For once in my life, I was speechless; trying to brush her statement off was not an option. I studied her closed face.

'Why are you going to die?'

'Because Master will find me – and I won't go back.'

It was a statement with such dark implications that at first I could think of nothing to say. But then I thought, to hell with it, I'll just go on talking and asking questions until I can make sense of this.

Making an effort to sound relaxed and unconcerned I asked, 'What's your name? My name is Hunter.'

She looked at me with black eyes that gave nothing away. 'My name is Slave.'

Whatever was behind this was way outside my experience. I walked across to the sofa, and she flinched, pulling the sleeping bag round her as if she thought I was going to attack her.

I kept my voice calm and even. 'Don't be afraid, I'm not going to hurt you. Please try the soup now, it will do you good.'

I picked up the bowl, felt it to check it was still warm and held it out to her. Slowly she eased herself into a sitting position and Scruff moved a bit but stayed beside her. She glanced at him.

'He's not growling.'

'No, why would he growl? His name is Scruff. He found you and he's been keeping you warm. Are you frightened of dogs?'

She made no reply, just slowly lifted the spoon and tasted the soup. She had another spoonful and then a third. I got the pot from the stove, and she held out the bowl for me to top it up. Progress, I thought, maybe we're getting somewhere now.

'Why did you say you are going to die?'

She looked at me in a considering way as if to estimate if I was intelligent enough to make it worth her while to explain. When she spoke, her voice was flat and without emotion.

'Master will find me and take me back and I can't go back. So, I must die. I can't get off the island and I have nowhere to go. I was trying to die when the dog found me.'

She had not told me anything new, but I had a strong premonition that this was something I was not equipped to deal with. I changed the subject.

'Slave is an unusual name.'

'I had another name, but he changed it. My mother called me Dao. '

She hesitated and added, 'It means peach.'

'And then?' I said, 'What happened – for your name to be changed?'

She lifted the bowl and drank the last of the soup from it, looking at me over the rim. It reminded me of those advertisements for starving children in Africa on TV a few years ago.

'Master decided I should be called Slave.'

Maybe it was best to leave that subject for now; it might be a minefield. Clearly everything would have to be elicited from her one small piece of information at a time. What kind of man calls himself Master and renames a girl Slave? It implied abuse, enslavement, perversion. I was uncertain if I could handle a discussion about it without causing her distress. Maybe this was a job for a professional who knew how to deal with traumatised people.

'Well, I'm going to call you Dao. I don't like the name Slave. How old are you?'

She was silent for a long time, looking inward as if she was debating with herself.

'I'm not sure. My mother left when I was twelve. After she had gone there was nobody to tell me when it was my birthday and I'm not sure now. I didn't keep track of it.'

It was impossible to guess her age; she could be twelve or

twenty. She was obviously tiny anyway and now she was so starved she looked like a child.

'Do you know what year it was when your mother left?'

Her eyes moved from my face to the floor. 'I don't know. I'm sorry.'

I said casually, 'There's no need to be sorry – it's not important.'

To my surprise she said seriously, 'I always have to say sorry if I can't tell Master what he wants to know, or I get punished.'

'There is no need to be afraid – nobody is going to punish you here.' I tried to sound cheerful and decisive at the same time. She said nothing, just wriggled down, put her head on the pillow and suddenly she was asleep again. I made myself a late lunch and worked on the proposal for a couple of hours, consulting my lists of available personnel with the right army experience. Late afternoon I was reading beside the fire with a glass of red wine beside me when she opened her eyes. Without moving she looked at me and then her hand reached out and touched Scruff's shoulder very lightly. He raised his head and looked at her and his tail wagged twice.

'I like him,' she said. 'I am scared of Master's dogs. They growl a lot and show their teeth – they're very dangerous.'

This was a safe opening, something we could talk about for a few minutes. 'Why do they growl at you? Surely they know you well, don't they?'

'They're tied up with chains and I'm not allowed to touch them and if I go too close they growl. Master got them to stop me trying to run away – he says that if I run away he will let the dogs loose and they'll find me and tear me to pieces.'

'What a nasty thing to say – I'm sure he wouldn't really do that, would he?'

She said in a matter-of-fact way and with no change of expression: 'I think he would. He thinks I would tell people about him if I could. Since my mother died he has been very careful to stop me running away.'

I bent down and put some more wood in the stove. The cabin was warm, and it was nearly completely dark outside. I got up and pulled the curtains across the little windows before I sat down again.

'I thought you said your mother left?'

'She's dead.'

Once again that brief look of assessment, weighing up how much to tell me.

'He told me she had left, and for years I believed him, but I know she's dead.'

I changed the subject to something I hoped was comforting.

'Would you like something else to eat now? I'm going to make sandwiches with ham and cheese and relish and have a cup of coffee – would you like some?'

'Yes, please. Do you want me to do it?'

'No, I certainly don't – you're not well. You've been very cold and wet, and you look as if you're starving. You just stay there and keep warm. We'll talk about what to do when you feel better.'

Her face told me everything: black eyes stared at me in disbelief that someone would look after her, that she did not have to do any work and that we would talk about what to do. I knew with cold certainty that she had been enslaved and abused, isolated and starved of kindness, possibly for years.

While we ate she told me about a few things in response to casual comments I made. When I said something about the cabin being nice and warm now she wrapped her arms around her body and smiled for the first time.

'I love it – it's so good. It gets really cold in the shed at night.'

'Did you live in a shed? What kind of shed?' I was trying hard not to sound outraged, hoping to keep her talking without taking fright.

'I sleep in the big shed. Master lives in the house – I'm allowed in the house to work, but I'm not allowed to sleep there.'

I was about to ask another question when she started unwrapping the sleeping bag from her legs.

'Where are you going? Do you need to go to the toilet?'

She nodded.

'We have to go outside – I don't have a proper toilet, just an outhouse. Hang on and I'll find something to put on your feet.'

The only thing I had that might stay on was a pair of neoprene booties. They were far too big, but better than anything else I could think of. I helped her zip them up, gave her a jacket and picked up the flashlight. The cold, damp night air welled into the room when I opened the door, and she shivered inside my big jacket. Scruff leapt off the sofa and walked beside her to the outhouse.

'Take the torch inside with you. I will wait here.'

When she came out Scruff got up from beside my feet and walked beside her back to the cabin, close enough for her to touch him. Dao got back in the sleeping bag and Scruff lay down beside her again. I hung our jackets up and put more wood on the fire. It was evening now, and I thought she might like to go to sleep.

'Are you going to be all right sleeping on the sofa?'

For the first time there was a flash of irony, a wry smile.

'I've slept on the floor since my mother left. This is very nice. Is Hunter your real name?'

'It is – my parents were fond of unusual names. I have two sisters – Willow and Plum. Do you want to go to sleep now?'

'No, I'm not sleepy.' Again, that little glint of irony. 'I rested when I lay on the ground.'

I hesitated only for a moment. This might be the perfect opportunity to find out some facts. She was warm and fed now and she was beginning to loosen up.

'Would you like to tell me a bit more about that walk? Like

where did you walk from, and how long did it take – and where were you hoping to get to?'

While she considered this I made us cups of tea and got out the last packet of chocolate biscuits. When I put the cup beside her she had her hand on Scruff's neck, still silent.

She's not going to tell me anything more, I thought. She doesn't trust me enough. She's very cautious and wary – God knows what she has been subjected to.

But then she started talking, the way someone might if they had not told a continuous story for a long time. Short sentences and without any of the flow most people get into when they tell a story.

'I wasn't hoping to get anywhere – not to any particular place. I was just trying to get somewhere to lie down and die. Far enough away so he didn't find me before I died, because if the dogs found me they would tear me to pieces. But I had to leave.'

Her hesitation was clear to see. She looked steadily at me, silent and still. I knew she was holding things back. She was deliberating with herself about what and how much she would tell me. She drank some of her tea and looked at the biscuits.

'Take one, Dao. You don't have to ask, just help yourself.'

She picked one up and started talking again.

'I had to leave. I thought he was going to kill me. I had made him very angry, and he said he was going to sell me, but I thought he might just kill me. Safer for him.'

'Why was he so angry?'

'I discovered something – I went somewhere I wasn't supposed to and he heard the bells and found me.'

She saw my look and explained.

'I have to wear the bells when I go through the bush to work in the gardens.'

'Bells? He made you wear bells?'

'Yes, they're very noisy. They're on a chain that goes around my waist with a padlock, and I can't take it off. It's so he can hear me working and so I don't go somewhere I'm not allowed. But that day I did. I tried to hold on to the bells to stop them making any noise, but he heard them clanging. So he knew I was in the wrong place, not where I should be. He was very angry, and I got punished – worse than usual.'

'How? What did he do?'

'He whipped me, he always whips me. But this time he wouldn't stop, he was so angry, and he beat me a long time, harder than he usually does.'

She looked at me and I tried to look calmly interested despite my growing rage.

'So that night I decided to try to get loose. The bangle is fastened to a chain and the chain is attached to a metal loop on the wall in the shed. I thought I might be able to get the loop to break off, but I didn't have to.'

Her skinny face lit up. 'It was really lucky! I was standing up in the dark trying to unscrew the loop from the wall. And I pushed really hard, and my hand slipped, and I nearly fell over – I had tripped over the pickaxe. It's usually hooked over a piece of wood in the roof where I can't reach it. There are never any tools I can reach when I'm chained to the wall, they're all up high. He doesn't want me to try to get away. So, I used the pickaxe to hack the loop off my bangle. That's how the chain gets locked onto me at night – he padlocks the chain to the loop on the bangle.'

White hot fury flared in my mind. She had been chained to a wall at night and slept on the floor. She had been forced to wear bells and been beaten and whipped. I felt a violent urge to strike my fist hard against something, but I stopped myself from displaying my anger. Instinct told me that the trust we had established could disappear in a heartbeat. I kept my voice calm and steady.

'Is the bangle that thing on your leg? Can I have a look at it, please?'

She eased her legs out of the sleeping bag and pulled up the much-too-long leg of the thermal leggings. I walked across to the sofa and sat down on the edge and looked at her ankle. The 'bangle' was a flat strip of brass, quite thick and crudely soldered closed in two places. I could see where the padlock loop had been attached; a lighter mark with the remains of solder round it. I reached out to touch it and she flinched.

'I'm not going to hurt you – I just want to look at it.'

I held it away from her skin and turned it. There was a wide dark mark round her ankle and one long narrow scar up the inside of her leg.

'You've worn this for a long time, haven't you? What made that scar?'

She bent forward to look where I was looking.

'Oh, that – that's where he burnt me with the soldering iron when I moved – it was when he was putting the bangle on. He did it on purpose – he likes hurting me.'

She seemed quite detached, and I wondered how damaged she was. Maybe she was emotionally numbed from long abuse and brutality. Or else she had developed that calm façade as a coping mechanism to help her survive.

'Why do you call it a bangle?'

She shrugged. 'I know it's not a bangle, but when he put it on he said he was giving me a present, a nice bangle to wear. He was just being nasty.'

He was being more than nasty, I thought, he's a controlling sadistic monster and I will find him and deal with him.

I put one finger under the shackle and felt the mark round her ankle. The depression looked like a bruise, but maybe it was a permanent scar.

'Don't worry about it, I'm used to it now,' she said, as if I was the one who needed comforting.

'Well, it's coming off – stay here with Scruff, I'll be back in a minute.'

I took the torch and went out to the shed to look for tools. Before I started working on the bangle I got my phone and took some photos of her ankle with the bangle attached. I only had a hacksaw and the rusty old bolt cutter that had been in the shed when I bought the place. She watched without comment while I carefully pushed the folded edge of a towel between the shackle and her ankle.

'This bloody thing is coming off even it takes all night. Tell me if I hurt you.'

She nodded without comment, and I started working. The only way to fit the jaws of the bolt cutter around the metal band was to insert them nearly sideways. I knew I was hurting her when I applied force, but I had to do this. Fury burnt with a clear flame in my mind. This symbol of her enslavement had to come off. The first break in the shackle felt like a small victory over evil. The bolt cutter had done the job, but now I had to start again. It would be impossible to force the thick metal band open while it was on her ankle, so I had to make a second cut on the opposite side.

Throughout she made no sound of pain or protest. I was hurting her, but she never flinched. I thought grimly of the conditioning that had turned her into a stoic, the fear of further punishment if she cried out or cringed. Or was it her determination not to give Master pleasure by showing pain? When the shackle fell apart in two halves she reached forward and picked up one of the pieces and looked at it for a long moment. Then she held it out to me. 'Thank you! Please throw it away. I don't want to see it again.'

I put the pieces on the bench, but I had no intention of throwing them away. They were evidence against the man she called Master and I would keep them. I had made up my mind about what I was going to do, but I would not tell her until I was sure I had her full confidence. The stage of trust we had reached now was very new and might not last if she thought I was going to do something that alarmed her.

I crouched beside the sofa to look at her leg. The mark was hideous, like an ugly branding. I lifted her foot and checked the skin was not broken.

'I didn't think you'd be able to get it off.' She looked at her ankle and smiled. 'It's lucky that you have such big hands, Hunter.' She held her own hand up as if to compare it to mine.

'Dao,' I said, imitating her gesture. 'It's lucky your hands are so tiny – you would look very silly with hands as big as mine.'

She laughed then, a real laugh of amusement, maybe it was her first genuine laugh for a long time.

'It makes me feel different – not having the bangle on my leg. Thank you.'

'Tuck yourself in again. Tomorrow we'll get you properly cleaned up.'

I had a feeling that she should drink a lot and eat high energy food, so I made a cup of hot chocolate and put it on the stool beside the biscuits. 'I'm sorry I hurt you when I took that damn thing off – drink this, it will make you feel better.'

I sat beside the fire, watching her, thinking that I had never before been able to change things so radically for someone by doing such mundane things. But instead of making me feel I was doing something good I felt I had taken on a heavy burden of responsibility.

'You said before that you were on an island, but which island? Do you know what it was called?'

'This island,' she said as if confused by my question.

'This is not an island – we are on the mainland.' I watched her expression change as this sank in. 'I drove here in my car, from Auckland. It takes about two and a half hours.'

She leant her head back against the sofa and closed her eyes. This time the silence lasted minutes and I could tell she was struggling with strong emotions.

When she lifted her head her eyes were full of tears.

'He said we were on an island – he tricked me so I wouldn't try to run away!'

Tears ran down her cheeks. I got up and fetched a handkerchief from the bedroom. I handed it to her and stood beside the sofa looking down at her, wondering how far I dared probe.

'If I had run away when my mother left, I mean when she died, before he started putting chains on me – I could have got away.'

Once again I felt she was leaving something out. Her hesitation was visible, and I saw the very moment she pulled back and closed her mouth on whatever it was she had nearly said.

She was devastated. She was twisting the handkerchief into a knot while she was talking; tense and frightened even to talk about it. 'After he caught me – when I went where I wasn't supposed to – he said he was going to sell me. He knows I wouldn't try to get away from an island, I can't swim, and I don't like the water. And the man on the boat wants me – and I think Master would give me to him and he would use me for a while and then he would throw me into the sea.'

'Who is this man on the boat? And how would he use you – do you mean sexually?'

'Are you asking if he will fuck me?'

'Yes, that's what I mean. Who is he?'

'He's one of the men who come now and then, in boats – there are two of them. One is called John and he's horrible. He tries to touch me when Master isn't looking and now Master is going to give me to him – or sell me.'

'Listen Dao – let's draw a line between the past and the present. Don't speak about Master as if you still belong to him. Don't say, 'Master is going to sell me'. Say 'he *was* going to sell me' instead. From now on he can't do anything to you – it's in the past. You are safe here.'

I demonstratively walked around the room checking that the door was locked and the windows secure. Her eyes followed my every move, but she made no comment. I put a couple of logs on the fire and closed the damper a bit to make them last.

'I'm going to sleep in the bedroom, and I'll leave the door open so you can talk to me if you need me. And I'll leave this camping lantern turned on all night so you can see after the generator shuts down, probably in about an hour.'

I put the lantern on the table and turned it on; it would shed enough light for her to see everything in the room and I would be able to see her on the sofa.

Half an hour later she appeared silently beside my bed. I had just put my book down and turned off my light.

A tense whisper. 'There's someone outside.'

I got out of bed and turned the light on. She was terrified. 'Where is Scruff?'

'He's on the sofa.'

'In that case there's nobody anywhere nearby. Scruff can hear things that we can't and if anyone comes close to the cabin he will bark. Possums come around at night and he tells me every single time. Are you frightened that Master would turn up?'

She nodded and replied in her normal voice, 'I thought he might have come to take me back.'

'There isn't much chance he would find this cabin in the dark. If he was trying to track you he would be doing it in daylight when he can see where he is going. The door is locked and nobody can get in. How big is he and how old?'

She looked at me as if I was mad, but after thinking for a moment she said, 'I think he's maybe fifty, older than my mother, than she would be. He's shorter than you and a bit fat – quite fat.'

'Does he do a lot of heavy work?'

Again that look, as if I was crazy. 'No, he does nothing – or not very much. I do, I mean I did all the work. When the men from the boats aren't visiting he just sits there and watches films on his computer and smokes cigarettes and drinks beer. He has a lot of disks with films. Or he goes fishing.'

'OK, so I'm taller and younger and stronger and if he turns up I'll knock him down. Do you think I could do that?'

'You could – but if he brings a gun?'

'What sort of gun does he have?'

'I don't know what they are called – they're just guns. One is long and black, and one is black and very short, sort of smaller all over, you know – the kind you hold in one hand. And then there's one that looks a bit like the long gun, but the back end is made of wood. That one has two barrels, instead of one and they're a lot shorter.'

'OK, that's good to know. Now let's get some sleep.'

I lay on my back looking up into the dark ceiling, thinking of those guns. One rifle and one handgun, calibre and types unknown. Plus, a sawn-off shotgun. He was well armed, and it was good information to have.

Three times during the night I got up to check on her and to put more wood on the fire. Each time her eyes opened as soon as I set foot in the main room, and I wondered if she got any sleep at all.

2

FRIDAY

I woke before dawn. I had slept in my clothes to be prepared for anything and now I felt uncomfortable and a bit seedy. I closed the door to the main room and got the pack of baby wipes out of my bag. Willow had introduced me to them, and they would be very handy now for Dao to use.

In the main room the sofa was empty, and Dao was waiting beside the door. We made another trip to the outhouse with Scruff once again walking beside Dao. Back inside the cabin she stood beside me watching me make porridge. Not right beside me, but close enough to indicate that she was not physically frightened of me.

'Did you sleep at all?'

She was looking better than yesterday, even if she had not slept a lot. She was still wafer thin and fragile-looking, but more together in some nearly indefinable way. Perhaps freedom was beginning to make a difference already; perhaps it was getting the damn shackle off her leg.

'I was so comfortable.' She hugged herself, just as she had the night before. I had a mental image of her in some cold shed with nobody to keep her warm and only her own arms to provide comfort.

'I have slept on the floor for a long time, since just after my mother left.'

I was intrigued by the way she referred to her mother as having left, but she had told me that her mother was dead. Perhaps saying she was dead was a way of blocking out the fact that her mother had abandoned her to live alone with the man she called Master.

For the first time she initiated a new conversation. 'You asked me how long I had been walking and I think it was four days. I have counted the nights in my head, and I think I'm right. It took me a long time to get so tired and hungry that I thought I could lie down to let myself die.'

I didn't look at her, just continued stirring the porridge. 'Can you get a couple of bowls from over there, please?' I nodded at the open cupboard. 'And two spoons. And you'll find brown sugar in the glass jar on the shelf next to the table.'

I had decided to avoid any reactions of outrage or pity. I would simply accept each statement as calmly as possible. Normality would become the default position we reverted to each time she revealed another atrocious fact about her life.

We had porridge with long-life milk and brown sugar and then toast made on top of the hot stove and cups of tea. She ate everything I put in front of her, silent and keeping her eyes on her plate, rarely looking up

'You're very quiet, Dao,' I said. 'Is something wrong?'

'I don't know if I'm allowed to talk while we eat.'

'Were you not allowed to talk? Or did you always eat on your own?'

'I ate on my own, in the shed. And I thought you might like me to be silent.'

I tried to strike a balance between sounding relaxed and making a firm statement.

'It's up to you if you talk or stay silent. There's no rule about it. Everyone in my family seems to talk all the time, particularly at mealtimes.'

'Have you got a family?' She said in surprise. 'But where are they?'

'You'll meet them when we get back to town. I don't live here – I just spend a few days here now and again. I have parents and two sisters – one of my sisters is married and has two children.'

Dao got up and started putting things on the bench. 'We will leave as soon as we can drive through the creek,' I said. 'And then we'll have to start thinking of how to find someone you know or who knew your mother, relatives or friends that you can go to.'

I got up and picked up my plate and mug. 'If you want to have a wash you can go into the bedroom and close the door. You can take a bowl of warm water and have a wash with a towel and there's a packet of baby wipes if you prefer those. I've only got an outside shower here and there is no hot water for it, so at this time of the year I don't use it.'

I showed her the baby wipes and pulled one out of the packet for her to see.

'These are nice,' she said and rubbed it over her hand. 'I'll use them instead of the bowl of water.'

I did the dishes while she was in the bedroom, but when she had not come back out after ten minutes I knocked on the door.

'Are you OK in there?'

No answer, so I knocked again and opened the door. The room was empty, and the window unlatched, just pushed closed from the outside. For a moment I stood there, looking at the window and thinking back over what I had said that might have caused her flight. Going after her right now wasn't necessary. She was barefoot and Scruff would find her. It must have been when she realised that I did not live here, and I said we would find someone who knew her mother that she could stay with. Perhaps she imagined that if we found people who had known her mother the Master would be able to find her. Her intense fear of the Master seemed to prevail whatever I said or did to make her feel safe.

The thought of the swollen stream changed my mind about the need to go after her quickly. What if she tried to cross the stream? She had said she could not swim, and she was frightened of water, but when someone is in flight mode there is no telling what they might do.

I unclipped the Remington shotgun from under the table, put three cartridges into the clip and inserted it. In the back of my mind circled Dao's description of the man she called Master and his dangerous dogs, and I wanted to be prepared. I called Scruff and went outside to have a quick look around the shed and in the outhouse, but as expected there was no sign of Dao.

'Find!' I said to Scruff, but he simply looked up at me with his head tilted to one side as if asking a question. I went inside for the sleeping bag and held it in front of him.

'Where is she?'

Scruff sniffed the bag and looked at me again to make sure there was no misunderstanding before he started tracking. He disappeared behind the cabin, so I tossed the sleeping bag inside the front door and ran after him. Outside the bedroom he turned around several times, going back and forth. Then he set out away from the house, straight into the bush. He was running fast with his nose close to the ground. I followed, but it was impossible to keep up. There were trailing supple-vines, fallen trees and obstacles that Scruff leapt over or ducked under, but for me they were barriers that slowed me down. Moisture hung in the still air and the forest was full of the scents of damp earth and rotting vegetation.

Thank God she's gone in this direction, I thought as I clambered over yet another fallen tree trunk. At least she won't reach the stream before Scruff finds her. If he gets too far ahead of me he'll let me know as soon as he finds her – and then I'll find them both.

But it took a lot longer than I had expected. When I finally heard Scruff barking it was from over to the west, at a forty-five-degree angle from his initial path. Now and then I whistled, and each time Scruff barked twice and soon I saw them. Dao sat with one knee bent against her chest with her hand around the ankle and the other arm round Scruff, who was leaning against her.

I knelt beside her. Tears were running down her cheeks and she looked at me without saying anything. I realised that however composed and strong she had seemed the previous evening, when she told me without expression about the whipping and about being burnt with the soldering iron, she was not able to cope on her own. It was scary to think that by default I was responsible for her. I had no idea of what a girl in her situation might need, or if I might say or do something and unintentionally damage her.

'Have you hurt yourself?'

'I'm sorry. I had to leave and then I hurt my ankle.'

There was no point talking about why she had left. The main thing was to get her back to the cabin and warmed up again and then I would think about what to do for the best. The painfully slow trek back took well over an hour. I thought grimly that perhaps the exertion counteracted the cold for both of us. With a broken branch as a support on one side and me on the other Dao hobbled towards the cabin. I lifted her over obstacles and helped her every step of the way, but suddenly her strength gave out. She stopped and swayed, and when I looked at her face I could see that she was at the end of her strength. I bent down and put an arm behind her knees and lifted her up the way you do a sleeping child and carried her back to the cabin. Her eyes were closed, and she said nothing.

Inside I put her down on the sofa and said, 'stay here' and got dry clothes from the bedroom. Without ceremony or concern about her modesty I stripped the damp jersey and then the T-shirt off her. I pulled a dry fleece sweatshirt over her head and threaded her arms into the sleeves the way you would with a passive child. I lifted her legs and said, 'and now lift your bottom' and repeated the process with the thermal leggings. The ankle made me flinch when I saw it. I pulled a pair of my track-pants on her, put a dry sock on the uninjured foot and straightened up. She looked like a child dressed in adult clothes. Since we got back she had said nothing at all. I looked into her unreadable black eyes and thought to myself that she and I had a lot of talking and explaining to do, but first things first.

'Right, now we need to get you a hot drink and find a bandage and some painkillers. Then we'll think of what to do next. You'd better roll those sleeves up so you can use your hands.'

I found painkillers in the first aid kit and an elastic bandage. I put them on the stool beside the sofa while I got a glass of water.

'Take these,' I pressed two capsules from the foil package and put them beside the glass.

She looked at them and said the first words she had uttered since we started the trek back through the bush. 'What are they?'

It was a perfect illustration of her situation. She was ignorant of so much and things did not always make sense to her. She had spent years in isolation, most of the time alone with a brutal man and no other input. In a way she was like a 'wilderness child'. I would have to consider everything I said and did in the light of her lack of knowledge.

I held out the little cardboard box. 'They are pain killers, and they'll make your ankle feel a little better, I hope – just put them in your mouth and swallow them with a lot of water. You can read what it says on the packet if you want to.'

Dao shook her head and swallowed the capsules. I watched her, wondering if she had run away from me or from the situation I had put her in when I mentioned taking her to town and finding someone who knew her. I must try to work out what was in her mind so I could predict her reactions.

In a different part of my brain my common sense was protesting: 'You don't know anything about girls, and to all intents and purposes she is a child, you are taking on something you don't have the skills to deal with, you could damage her, you have to ask for advice, what about the proposal deadline, you don't have time for this and it's not your business'.

But I knew it was too late; if she wanted to stay with me I would make myself responsible for her. And without thinking consciously about it I had decided that I must deal with Master. I dismissed my mind's warnings and started thinking of what to do about her ankle. I put on water to heat for a cup of tea and sat down at the end of the sofa.

'I don't know what we should do for the best. We have to try to work it out together.'

There was nothing other than cold water to cool the swelling. I had no fridge and no ice. Keeping the ankle strapped and elevated was the best I could do, but as I was about to lift her foot up and reach for the bandage I thought of something. 'Hang on a minute.'

I went out to the car and searched the glove box and the compartment between the seats and found the tube of anti-inflammatory gel I had used on a sore wrist a few months ago.

'Now we can start.'

I spread the gel around her ankle and rubbed it in as gently as I could. The swelling felt like a water-filled balloon under my fingertips. I searched my memory of images from the Army's first aid course many years ago: keep the foot at as much of a right angle as possible and wind the bandage in figure-eight loops alternating between the foot and the leg to give stability. When I had finished it looked quite stable and tidy.

'How does it feel?'

'It feels much better now. Thank you.'

She paused and then she said, 'I'm sorry – I didn't mean to be a problem.'

I pulled the trouser leg down and felt her toes; they were icy cold. I folded the other sock into a shortened version of the original and pulled it halfway up her foot until it met the edge of the bandage. When I pulled the sleeping bag back over her legs Scruff jumped up. I said 'careful Scruff' and lifted the sleeping bag to show him the bandage. He sniffed it and watched as I covered her legs again.

When I returned to put a mug on the stool Scruff was back in his place beside Dao.

'He understood what you told him,' she said. 'He's clever, he was careful not to lie down on my foot.'

We talked about Scruff and his clever ways and what good company he was. In the back of my mind, I tried to figure out how to find out more. I wanted as much detail as she could give me about Master and 'the island' before I decided what the next step should be.

'We need to talk about what's going to happen next,' I said. 'Let me tell you a bit about myself and what we'll do when we leave here. Then you can tell me some more about yourself. How does that sound?'

'It sounds good,' she said, her pointy little face serious and intent. 'I would like to know about you.'

'OK then – I was in the army for years, the British army and now I work for a company in England. I do it via email and something called Skype which you probably don't know – I'll explain it later. Sometimes I have to travel to other countries but mostly I live in my townhouse on the North Shore in Auckland.'

It was hard to assess what needed explaining. I had no idea of how long she had been captive, how old she was when she first went to live on 'the island' or what she might not know.

'I live alone, apart from Scruff of course. My father is a potter, his name is Rob, and my mother is called Glenda –

she's a doctor. They live in New Plymouth, but they come to Auckland quite often. And I have two younger sisters – Willow who is just a couple of years younger than I am – and Plum who is twenty-one.'

'What is a potter?'

'It's someone who makes pots and things out of clay – pottery.'

She nodded and looked past me as if she was reaching into the past. 'Ah, yes I remember now, I'd just forgotten the word.'

'Do you mean that you used to know, but you hadn't heard it for a long time? Or did you know it in another language, but not the English word?'

'Oh no, not another language, I don't know any other language. I think I have a lot of words that I used to know, but I haven't heard them for a long time – and I haven't used them either. Master doesn't, I mean didn't let the men on the boats talk to me and I was only allowed to reply when he spoke to me.'

She had that inward look again, as if she was looking into the past.

'When my mother was alive we talked very quietly when Master could not hear us, but since then I've had nobody to talk to – not really talk to.'

Then she smiled, as if she was sharing a secret. 'I used to have conversations with myself inside my head, I would pretend I was two people and argue with myself and sometimes I won and sometimes the other person won.'

I made pasta with sauce out of a sachet and tomatoes from a can while I mentally rehearsed the things I wanted to ask her. I put her lunch on the stool next to the sofa and sat down at the far side of the table, so we could see each other. After lunch I put water on the stove for coffee and spoke casually to her while I was moving around tidying up our plates.

'Dao, do you mind if I ask about a few things now so I can work out how I can help you? I can't do any good if I don't know enough and I want to make some notes, so I don't forget things.'

'No, I don't mind, but...' she hesitated for a moment. 'I know so little – it might not help you.'

I made mugs of coffee for us and sat down with my notebook, but my search for information was derailed within minutes. The questions that I had hoped would take us logically from her earliest memories to the time she ran away deviated into side issues. There was no point in interrupting her; everything was grist for the mill. At the end of the afternoon, and after a toilet visit and a cup of cocoa, I had three pages of random notes.

'One thing I've wondered about, Dao. How did Master get you to believe you were on an island? I presume you arrived by car, or did he pick you up in the boat from somewhere when you first arrived?'

'I never thought about it until my mother died. When he started chaining me up he said I couldn't get away – apart from by swimming because we were on a big island. When we first got there he picked us up from the bus in a little town, and then he parked his truck, and we went to the house by boat. So, I believed him.'

'That's enough for now,' I said. 'You need a break – would you like something to look at, a book or something, while I write up my notes?'

'Have you got books?' Her voice was full of happy surprise and her eyes lit up. 'I would love a book – I had some books, but I left them behind.'

'Yes, I have lots of books in town and you'll be able to sit and read for months if you want to. I don't leave many books here because the cabin gets damp when it's empty during the winter. But I have an interesting magazine that you might like to look at.'

There were obviously going to be difficulties if I kept her with me, but I had made my decision. Now I must establish her age before discussing the future. I typed my notes into a document on the laptop, occasionally asking Dao about some detail. She sat on the sofa with her legs up and Scruff beside her, reading a *New Zealand Geographic* magazine I had picked up from my mailbox when I left for the cabin. After a while I noticed her deeply absorbed in something.

'Have you found something interesting? What is it you're reading?'

She looked up and said simply, 'Everything, I'm reading it all,' and lowered her eyes to the page again.

When I looked up to tell her I had finished she was asleep with the magazine closed around her finger to keep her place. I removed it and put a match at the place she had reached and went outside to start the generator and bring in more firewood. It was nearly dark now, but the cabin was warm. The curtains were pulled across the windows and the stove radiated heat like a small furnace. There had been no real rain since early morning and now a stiff breeze rustled the forest canopy. The cloud cover was breaking up fast and I thought things looked hopeful.

There was one spot up here where I could use a cell phone, but it was a half hour trek up a hill on the far side of the valley. It was annoying not to be able to check the forecast. I thought we might be able to get out the next day if it did not start raining again. I made a mental note to bring new batteries for the radio next time.

I plugged the laptop in to charge while the generator was running and sat back to study my notes, a shocking picture of brutality and cruelty and a smaller section with details of her family. There was a mass of questions I wanted to ask Dao, but I needed to think before I made any further plans. We would continue talking the next day, either in the car on the way to town or here, if we had to stay another night. And I must find out how old she was. I could not offer her sanctuary and look after her if she was a minor.

We had a simple meal and once again I let Scruff out to do his evening run alone. I sat on the end of the sofa with Dao's leg across my thigh and unwound the bandage from her ankle. It had improved, but it was still swollen, and the skin was very pink. I prodded gently with my fingertips, watching her face to see where it hurt most, but she showed no signs of pain.

'No pain?'

She looked back at me quite calmly. 'Oh yes, that hurt.'

'You didn't say anything. Can you point to where it hurts?'

'I don't – I mean I didn't like to show Master when things he did to me hurt – because he liked that.'

She pointed out where my touch had hurt, and I stored the information away for later. I put more gel on the ankle and wrapped it up again and went back to sit beside the stove with a glass of wine.

I continued a random conversation, hoping that further details of her years on the island would emerge. She was talking quite freely now and once or twice she volunteered a longer coherent story of what her life had been like. The first clue about the timeframe came when she told me how she had found a newspaper.

'I hadn't had anything to read since my mother died, when Master made me live in the shed. He took all my things away and I never saw them again, all my books and my jigsaw puzzles and pens. So, when I found the newspaper I took it and hid it. If Master had found it he would have taken it off me – and he would have punished me. This was before I found the book boxes in the laundry cupboard. I wanted something to read, I didn't care if it was a newspaper or what it was, I just wanted to read something.'

'Where did you find it?'

'One of the men – you know, the men who come on the boats – he threw it away. So, I took it.'

'But how did you manage to keep it hidden?'

'I tucked it inside my shirt after Master put the bells on me and took it with me to the gardens. I took the whole paper apart and folded each page really small and then I hid them under a couple of buckets that I used to leave upside down beside the gardens. I only took one page at a time back to the shed – in the pockets of my pants. I was always scared he would feel paper when he took the bell chain off me. I hid the pages in a lot of different places where they would not get wet. I made sure I remembered where they were so I could get one out now and then when it was safe. Sometimes I read a page when I knew Master was on the radio because then I could hear him, and I knew exactly where he was. He always closed the door, but I could hear his voice.'

She smiled at how cleverly she had tricked Master. 'I had some pages hidden in the shed where I could reach them when I was chained up. I read them when he went to town to get supplies. I had a good hiding place that he didn't know about. But I didn't want them all in one place in case he found them.'

I noted the information about a radio and stored it away to find out more details later.

'I'm glad you had something to read. Was the paper interesting?'

'Oh yes, very interesting. I read each page lots of times, every single word and then I buried it to get rid of it. And then a bit later I would get another page out and read that many times – until I ran out of pages. It lasted for ages and some pages I kept for a long time and read them again later – the really interesting ones.'

I was getting excited now, this might be the clue to her age that I needed. 'What do you remember best of what you read in that paper?'

She thought for a while, her hand absently stroking Scruff's head.

'Well, I remember a lot of stuff about the new pope. My mother had told me who the pope was, because the people in the flat beside us believed in him – they went to a special church on Sundays. So, when I read in that paper that there was a new pope I was interested in how they do it. You know – how they lock themselves in and vote and make a special fire, so people see the white smoke when they have decided who the new pope is. And people come from all over the world to stand outside and watch for the white smoke. And then he comes out with a special hat on and blesses them all– I've forgotten what the hat is called, a pointy hat.'

I was surprised both at the amount of detail she remembered and how much more fluently she was speaking now, as if her vocabulary was being revived with every conversation we had. A few minutes later I was sure we had it sorted. Pope Benedict would have started his papacy only a few months after Dao's mother left.

'Do you think it was a new paper?' I wondered if it might have been old when she read it. 'Could it be a newspaper he had had on the boat for a long time and then he just decided to get rid of it?'

Dao thought for a moment before she replied as she often did, either from a wish to be as accurate as possible or trying to find the right words. It made me feel as if my comprehension was being assessed.

'No, I'm sure it was a new one. I saw it in the rubbish hole in the forest when I walked to the gardens – it was lying right on top of his bag of rubbish. I had seen him bring it ashore from the boat – a yellow plastic bag. He'd been sitting on the deck reading a paper after he arrived that morning. I took it only a short time later and it was still sort of clean and white. You know how newspapers go yellow when they're old?'

I nodded and she continued. 'Master had newspapers in the house. He sometimes bought one when he went shopping. But I didn't dare touch them in case he noticed one was missing. I just used to read the little bit that showed when they were folded – you know, when I was cleaning the house. But they sat there for ages and the old ones went that dirty yellow colour.'

Finally, we had established something concrete and useful.

'This is really good, Dao,' I said. 'If you were twelve when your mother left I think you're probably no younger than twenty and no older than twenty-two years old. I think the pope you read about was Benedict and he became pope about ten years ago, I think – about 2005 or 2006. But whenever it was it proves that you are definitely not a minor.'

She looked like a young teenager, and it was hard to reconcile the way she looked with her age. I must be careful not to treat her as a child. She looked at me, uncomprehending and a bit worried. 'What is a minor?'

'It's someone who is under the legal age for making decisions about themselves. If you were a minor and I took you back to town to stay at my place the authorities could take you away. They might put you into the care of someone they think would be better at looking after you.'

She responded immediately, without any thought or hesitation. 'If they give me to someone else I will run away.'

And I had no doubt that she would; her determination was impressive. But why would she run?

'Well, we don't have to worry, because you are not a minor and nobody can make you do anything you don't want to do – and that includes me. You can leave any time you like and nobody can force you to do anything.'

She had that inward look again. I was sure she was assessing how much more she would tell me. 'Hunter,' she said seriously. 'I can tell that you don't think Master would really kill me, but if he finds me he will. I know he will! I know things about him that are so bad – he'd rather kill me, and risk being caught than let me tell anyone.'

Her face was a mask of calm, but I sensed an increasing urgency behind it. She was definitely holding things back; there had to be more to this than what she had told me so far.

'I do believe you, but I don't think he will find you – particularly once we've left here. And I won't let him take you away.'

'No, I know you will stop him taking me away, but he

might just come in and shoot me dead and that would be it. That's all he needs to do.'

There was the slightest tremble of fear in her voice. And her logic was irrefutable. We looked at each in silence and then Scruff growled. Dao looked at me in alarm and I said, 'Steady, Scruff'.

He jumped off the sofa and ran to the door, his hackles rose and he growled. He ran over to the window, standing up against the windowsill trying to push the curtain aside to see out, barking furiously.

Dao was shrinking back into the corner of the sofa, her face white and terrified. I pointed to the bedroom.

'He's heard something. Go into the bedroom. Stand behind the door and stay there – no light.'

She limped across the floor and disappeared into the bedroom. I grabbed my LED spotlight off the shelf by the door, picked up the gun and took the key out of the lock. Outside I locked the door while Scruff raced ahead of me barking furiously. I stood still for a moment and swept the intense white beam from left to right; nothing there. I followed Scruff around the corner, sweeping the light from side to side. He was way ahead of me, running into the bush, silent now. I aimed the light in the direction he was running, but stayed where I was and listened. The wind was quite strong, and I heard nothing. I continued around the cabin, shining the light in wide sweeps as I went. Then I heard a dog in the distance and then another. Two dogs, perhaps three. Someone had been here or very close. Maybe he had left the dogs a bit further away and explored quietly around the cabin and then taken off when Scruff started barking inside. I whistled for Scruff to come back. If someone was out there in the dark with dogs I did not want Scruff involved in a fight. He is not very big, and I had no idea what kind of dogs Master had.

Scruff returned, nose still to the ground. I stood still and let him do his thing. By the outhouse he picked up the scent again and traced it first back towards the bush and then around the front of the cabin, then around the corner. Whoever had been outside had come right up to the house. I circled the cabin again and checked the windows. There were no gaps in the curtains, nowhere someone could have looked in and seen us. I wondered if our voices would have been audible. I went inside, taking Scruff with me.

Dao had stayed behind the door in the bedroom. Her face was rigid with fear.

'There was someone outside,' I said. 'They've gone now. I want to check if our voices could have been heard from outside. Come back into the other room.'

I held her arm as she limped back to the big room and made her sit down on the sofa.

'I don't think we were talking very loudly, do you?'

She shook her head. 'No, we were just talking like we are now, just normal.'

'Talk to Scruff for a couple of minutes, perhaps a bit louder than we did before. I'll go outside and check.'

She looked alarmed and I said quickly, 'It's OK. I'll be close to the house all the time. And Scruff will be in here with you. You can lock the door from inside.'

It was clear that she was terrified of letting me go outside, but she nodded and moved towards the door, ready to lock it behind me.

Outside I stood beside the door and heard nothing. I moved over to the window on that side and listened intently; still nothing. I went around the corner, no sounds from inside. I returned to the door and knocked.

'It's me, you can unlock the door now.'

She stood beside me as I took my boots off and locked the door. She held herself the way people do when they are too scared to move freely, shoulders rigid and tense.

'Did you talk to Scruff the whole time I was out there?'

'Yes, I talked all the time and a bit louder, like you told me.'

'Well, I heard nothing, not a thing. The wind is rustling the trees and even standing right by the window there was no sound. Your voice is a lot softer than mine. If they heard anything it would only have been my voice.'

No comment, just that watchful expression and her eyes never left my face.

'So whoever it was could have heard my voice, but they wouldn't know who else was here.'

She said nothing and her expression did not change, but I knew she was terrified. I had never had anyone come near the place by chance before. And who was out in the forest in the dark on a night like tonight? Anyone else but Master would either have walked past or knocked on the door.

'Look, Dao. I have to be honest, it's no use pretending. It seems like an incredible coincidence when we had just been talking about him, but it could have been Master. I heard dogs in the distance and called Scruff back. I didn't want him involved in a fight, especially not if there were several dogs. We'll leave in the morning.'

I went around making sure the curtains were properly across the windows. Dao limped beside me every step I took, never more than an arm's length away.

'Sit down here at the table while I reorganise the place a bit. But first I have to go outside for a minute. I won't let anyone get to you, I promise. Scruff, stay with Dao.'

I put on my boots, picked up the gun and the torch and went outside again. I filled the generator tank and locked the shed and stood for a moment at the cabin door, listening to the night noises.

Inside Dao sat at the table with Scruff beside her and watched as I swung the sofa around and pushed it over to within a metre of the wall beside the bedroom door. Whatever happened I had to be in a position where I would see an intruder before he saw me or at least at the same time. If he broke in through the bedroom window I would hear him and by the time he got to the door to the main room I would see him before he saw me. If he came in the door from outside or through one of the two windows in the main room I still had the advantage; I could see them all from where the sofa was now. The only way to do this, without risking damage to Dao or myself, was to shoot him the moment I saw him. I would worry about his dogs and the general consequences later.

'You will sleep on the floor between the sofa and the wall. I will sleep on the sofa. That way he has to deal with me first.'

I took the mattress from the bed and put it between the sofa and the wall and threw the sleeping bag and a pillow on it. Still, she said nothing, just watched everything I did. I took the shotgun from the corner and put it on the floor alongside the front of the sofa and put more wood on the fire.

'We're not going to have any lights on tonight. I'll give you the lantern, but you're *not* to turn it on unless I tell you to.'

'I want you to be behind the sofa too.'

'I can't. I need to be able to move fast if something happens. You will be just behind me, but you can't be right next to me.'

If anything happened I had to be able to strike fast and worrying about Dao would be a distraction. The sofa would not stop a bullet, but I thought it would be a reasonable barrier for shotgun pellets. It had a solid wooden back, and she would be at floor level. If someone shot at me from the window the trajectory angle should prevent her being hit, provided she stayed down, and their aim was not low.

'If there is trouble I want you to stay down, don't get up – stay flat on the mattress whatever happens. Promise?'

She nodded; she was very frightened, but I had to be brutally direct. If we were attacked I had to be sure that I could get the intruder before he got me and then Dao.

'It could have been Master. Maybe his dogs picked up your scent from this morning. But if he couldn't hear your voice he might have thought that I had someone else here. And that you had walked around the cabin and then back into the forest. You would have made scent tracks around the front door and the outhouse. Then you made a new set when you ran away this morning. If his dogs led him here and then away again he might think you'd come here, found the place empty and moved on. And that I had come along later, after you had gone.'

I hoped she believed me. I halfway believed it myself; it was a logical theory and fitted the facts. I was prepared for trouble, but I knew I would have only one chance to get it right. I dozed off, woke up, listened, dozed again. Scruff would bark if anyone came near, but the urge to listen carefully anyway was compulsive. I was glad I had the shotgun. When I bought the Remington Versa Max I had nothing particular in mind, I was just so used to always having a weapon with me that it seemed a natural thing to do. It is a semi-automatic 12-gauge shotgun with a clip that takes three cartridges and now it felt really good to have it.

Nothing happened in the night. At intervals Dao would say 'Hunter?' very quietly and I would reply 'OK, I'm here.'

3

SATURDAY

Again, we got up early, both exhausted. After a quick breakfast I backed the station wagon out of the shed and drove us down to the ford. The creek was still quite high, but lower than I had expected; we would be able to get across very soon. I turned around with some difficulty on the muddy slope and headed up-hill again.

'Now listen, Dao' I said when we were back inside. 'We'll leave as soon as we are ready – even an hour from now the water level will be lower. I want you to sit in my armchair in the corner by the stove until we're ready to go.' The corner provided good protection from two sides, and I would be going back and forth through the door, able to see and intercept anyone approaching.

I sorted out the bedding and restored the place to its normal appearance. If Master came back to have another look there would be no sign of anything unusual. The gun was never far from me as I moved back and forth packing things up and putting them in the car. When we left I put the shotgun on the floor behind the passenger seat, where I could reach back and grab it quickly. Normally I would never travel with the gun loaded, but this was not a normal day.

We forded the creek with ease. Scruff stood on the back

seat with his head out the window, barking madly as he always does when we drive through the water. Dao turned in her seat to look at him.

'Will he try to jump out?'

'No, he just loves driving through the water.'

There was no sign of anyone along the track or on the farm road. When we turned left onto the main highway I relaxed and tried to think of something that would make us both feel a bit more normal.

'Ask me about anything you see that seems strange. You've been away from normal life for so many years – a lot of things will be new. Or you might not have noticed them when you were a little girl. You might as well start learning right away. There is a book of road maps in the door pocket if you want to see where we're going.'

'OK, I will.'

By the time we had reached Auckland's North Shore I had explained a lot of things, with varying degrees of accuracy and detail. She noticed my cell phone in the dashboard sleeve lighting up as messages and missed call signals started coming through and one thing led to another. We talked about solar power panels, cell phones, speed cameras and road signs, the word 'deviation' and how cruise control works. She asked me to explain who could remove a minor from someone's care and what minors could and could not do, and that led us to the court system and what prosecutors are and then barristers, oaths and jurors.

I was amused and impressed. She was like the proverbial sponge; absorbed whatever you told her and then thought of the next thing. She had been starved of conversation and information for a decade, during the years when young people learn about the world and now she was making up for it. She seemed to feel safer and more relaxed in the car than she had at any time since I found her.

At the house I drove into the garage and helped Dao upstairs to the living area and then brought my luggage up.

'Let's discuss what you would like to do and what I think we might do.'

All she said was, 'OK'. This seemed to be her standard response when she thought someone was telling her what to do. I knew now that it did not indicate agreement, only that she would obey. So now, for the first time, I decided that I must make it clear that she had the right to make independent decisions about herself.

'Do you want to make up your own mind about where you sleep, or do you want me to decide?'

'I want to talk about it.'

'Let's discuss it then. Instead of you limping around the house I'll tell you how it's laid out. Upstairs, on the floor above where we are now, there are two bedrooms, mine and a slightly smaller one and a bathroom. On this level you can see everything – it's just one big living space with the kitchen and laundry behind that low wall behind you – and a toilet. On the ground floor we have the garage, a small bedroom plus the hall and a toilet with a shower. You can sleep in the smaller bedroom upstairs or in the little bedroom downstairs.'

'I want to sleep in your room.'

'Well, I'm afraid you can't because that's where I sleep.'

I didn't quite know what to say. What if she simply did not understand about males and females and normal sleeping arrangements? She knew what 'fuck' meant, but did she have any idea of the normal social protocol?

'You said I could make up my mind about what I want to do and I don't have to do what people say – and I want to sleep in your room.'

She looked at me to check if I was following this train of thought. 'With you.'

'You can't, that's not what people do. Girls don't sleep in the same room as older men unless they are married to them, or they have a relationship.'

I saw that the last bit made no sense to her. 'People might think I'm taking advantage of you,' I added, trying to clarify things. 'They might think that I was using you for sex instead of looking after you.'

'Who are those people? And how would they know?' Dao asked seriously. 'And I'm not talking about fucking, I am just saying I will sleep in your room with you. How old are you?'

I was at a loss now; her logic was perfectly clear to her and in the cabin she had felt we were in the same room because the door was open at night. Aha, I thought, that's the answer.

'If you sleep in the little bedroom upstairs and we leave the doors between us open, then we'd be just as we were in the cabin. Would that be all right?'

'OK. How old are you? You don't look old.'

'I am thirty-eight. Are you scared of being on your own?'

'No.'

I could see her processing the pros and cons of going further.

'I wasn't before. But now I'm scared of being far away from you in case something happens.'

My mind filled with apprehension. I had done nothing to deserve such unconditional trust. How would I wean her away from me, where would she go and how would she cope? It was overwhelming to suddenly be responsible for someone I had only known for three days.

I got some bread out of the freezer, thawed a few slices in the microwave and made us sandwiches and coffee. Dao sat on the sofa with her lunch and some books, and I sat in my armchair by the balcony door, checking my phone and laptop to see what I had missed. Most of it I could ignore. People were used to me being away and the only deadline I had to meet was for the proposal for the Venezuela client. The proposals I construct are for a very special kind of service which we blandly call security. In reality it amounts to suggesting the right number of armed men, the right type of vehicles and communications equipment to keep someone in a dicey part of the world safe. Some of our clients are dictators and some are drug cartel bosses. They use us because we know how to get hold of well-trained mercenary soldiers that cannot be bribed to betray the man who pays them.

I fired off an email to the London head office and told them the proposal would be with them in a couple of days and that this time I would only be available for video conferences as I could not leave the country for a while, even if the client requested it. I did not explain why. I never offer explanations unless people ask for them and in my experience most people do not.

Before I made the most important call I gave Dao some sheets of paper out of the printer and asked her if she could draw a plan of 'the island'.

'It would be very useful. Put everything on it that you can think of, every detail. I have to make a couple of phone calls now.'

For once Charlie answered the phone right away.

'Hunter!' she said and laughed. 'I thought you'd fallen down a deep hole or something. Or did you lose your phone? I've left a couple of messages.'

'I got stuck in the cabin, the creek flooded, and I couldn't get out. Listen, could you come over tonight for a couple of hours? I've got an urgent problem and I might need some help.'

'OK, I can be there by six if you promise to feed me. Kristen is at her dad's place sorting out some business stuff and she's going to be late. Have you got any food in the house?'

Charlie and I go back a long way. We spent nearly three years all up on overlapping tours of duty in Afghanistan. She is a great helicopter pilot and a tough nut in every way; there is nobody I would trust more. These days she lives in Auckland with her long-standing partner Kristen.

I walked upstairs to my bedroom while I talked; no way did I want Dao to hear this conversation. 'There's nothing edible in the house, we just got back – could you bring three take-away meals please? I've got cold beer in the fridge.'

'Three? Is someone joining us?'

I closed the door and went over to the window. Scruff was in the courtyard, asleep on the warm tiles by the table, enjoying the winter sunshine.

'I found a girl in the forest, nearly dead. She's run away from some bastard who's kept her enslaved for years. She's staying here for the moment.'

'Shit!' said Charlie. 'Really? How old is she?'

'About twenty-one, I think – give or take a year or two.'

I gave her a run-down of what I knew and hung up, absently looking out the window. Inside my head I relived the scene where I had last seen Charlie flying, the scene I sometimes dream. The smell of burning diesel, thick dust swirling as a helicopter lands; sounds muffled and distant, someone drags a body off my legs and a voice says 'Shit – we'd better get this one out fast'. I raise my head and see a large piece of metal sticking out of my thigh. There are broken bodies strewn over a large area with the wrecks of vehicles and a crater in the road where something has disintegrated, leaving no trace of what it was.

Next I rang my sister Willow and told her the story. She is a lawyer and the smartest in the family by a long way. And the most ethical too, so I had to be careful how I handled this.

'I want you to represent Dao,' I said. 'I'm going to need some legal advice. You can do some work while you're on maternity leave, can't you?'

'I can do private jobs, no problem. My practicing certificate is up to date. Sounds as if the first thing we need to do is find out a bit more about Dao and her parents. Get everything you can from her; full names, dates of birth, where was she born, were her parents married – everything she can remember. I'll come round tonight after the twins have gone to sleep. Plum's not going out, she can babysit – Matt's doing

44

the Singapore-London run so he won't be home for a few days.'

I went back downstairs and found Dao at the dining table with several sheets of paper in front of her. 'How is it going?'

I was expecting something basic and not very sophisticated, but she surprised me. The paper she handed me was a plan full of details and there were words here and there in a child's cursive writing: 'big shed', 'house', 'dogs', 'garden', 'generator shed'.

'This is very good - you draw very well.'

'I like to draw - I used to draw on the floor in the shed. The floor is earth, very hard but I had a long nail I'd found, and I used it to draw - and then I would rub it out with my foot before Master saw it.'

When I passed the paper back to her she looked at it with a frown.

'I have to fix it, the big shed is not really parallel to the house as it looks here - it's at an angle of about five degrees, perhaps a little bit more.'

'How do you know about degrees of angles?'

She had not done any schooling for a long time, not since she was twelve. She said nothing, just shrugged and put the paper to one side.

'Well, it's a very good plan - exactly what we need.' I looked over her shoulder to see what she was drawing now, but she put her arm over it.

'I'll show you when it's finished. I haven't got it right yet.'

I was still standing there looking at the plan, thinking of ways of dealing with this, when the phone rang. I looked at the number before I answered, but I knew I had better take the call. Vivian was my live-apart woman friend, mostly on, sometimes off. A smart blonde schoolteacher with a highly developed instinct for being seen in the right places and with the right people. God knows how we had lasted so long; we shared very few interests. She had left a few messages while I had been away, and I could not leave her dangling too long.

'Hi!' she said in her usual breezy way. 'You're finally back! You missed the most entertaining dinner. Did you get my message?'

'I got all your messages, thanks – just read them. Sorry I couldn't reply. I was trapped by floods at the cabin.'

Vivian had never been to the cabin. She is not an outdoors sort of girl unless outdoors means a champagne lunch on a terrace.

'But I'm back now. So, you've had a lot of fun?'

Most things Vivian tells me are full of exclamation marks and this was no exception.

'The most brilliant fun! That dinner party at Mark's that you missed turned into a riot. One of their friends got drunk and had an almighty row with his wife when she told him he'd had too much to drink, and they should go home. He threw the car keys at her and said she could take her boring self off home, but he was staying.'

She laughed; this was her territory. 'And she threw the keys back and hit him in the forehead and he bled like a pig all over Maria's new white sofa – total uproar!'

'Well, it was lucky I wasn't there then,' I said mildly. 'That's exactly the sort of thing I dislike most. It sounds as if I was better off in my little cabin in front of the fire.'

It pays to remind Vivian at regular intervals that we are totally different, just as a reality check. Spending the night at her place now and again is fine but we could never live together.

'So!' she said, not daunted by my reply. 'Do you want to come to that exhibition opening I left a message about? On Tuesday? Everyone will be there.'

'Sorry, but I can't afford to do anything but work for a little while.'

I had to put her off until I got things sorted out; my priorities lay elsewhere for the time being. I had to make it sound good too or she would try to persuade me to do what she wanted. Much easier to avoid being nagged at by whatever means came to hand.

'I've got a job that can't wait and it's going to take me a while. I didn't get enough done at the cabin. I'll call you when I've caught up with things.'

She knew better than to try to persuade me when it was about work. We had stopped seeing each other for a while a few months earlier when she tried to make an ultimatum about the future. She knew any relationship we had would be on my terms.

When I put the phone down and turned around Dao was leaning against the banister at the bottom of the stairs, and she looked tired.

'Let's go upstairs now,' I said. 'You must want a shower. My friend Charlie is bringing dinner over a bit later.'

I helped her upstairs and showed her the bathroom, got a couple of towels out for her and found a spare toothbrush.

'Look, this towel rail can be yours. There's shampoo and stuff in the shower and there's a nail brush so you can scrub your feet. Is there anything else you think you need?'

She shook her head.

'I haven't used shampoo or warm water for years – this is lovely, thank you.'

She was looking around the bathroom. 'Do you have such a big shower because you're so big?'

I wondered if she was familiar with showers and how they worked. 'Do you need help with the shower?'

A fleeting look of mischief crossed her thin face. 'Those people might think it was wrong.'

It took me a moment to understand that she was quoting my words back to me and it was unsettling to realise how easy it was to underestimate her. She looked like a child and sometimes spoke like one, but she was a fast learner.

'I mean, do you know how the shower control works or do you want me to show you? Perhaps you would like a chair to sit on, so you don't have to balance on one leg to scrub your feet? That ankle will take a while to get better.'

'I know how the shower works. We had one at home and I cleaned Master's shower but he never let me use it – not after my mother died. I don't think I need a chair – thank you.'

As I turned to go she said, 'Can I have a bath one day?'

'Of course, you can do whatever you like. A bath would get your feet cleaner probably. I'll give you a clean sweatshirt to wear until tomorrow.'

It was hard to imagine what I should offer her to wear instead of panties. She had not had any when I found her and she had just worn leggings or the track pants since. Somehow it seemed to matter a lot more now we were in town than it had in the cabin. In the end I compromised.

'I haven't got any underpants for you – you're so little that nothing I have would fit you. Will you be OK without any just for tonight and then we can get some tomorrow? I can give you a pair of clean track pants and a T-shirt.'

'I haven't had any clothes that were mine for a long time, just old ones of Master's that he didn't want any more. I'll wear clean track pants if you have some.'

She spent half an hour in the bathroom. I made the bed in the guestroom, found a clean elastic bandage, and got some clothes for her. She came out of the bathroom with a towel wrapped around her, pink and warm from the shower, just as I was putting the clothes on her bed. I was leaving her to get dressed when I thought of her back.

'Do you mind if I have a look at your back? I saw you had some marks when I took your wet clothes off in the cabin. I want to take a photo of them – do you mind?'

'Why?'

'Because it is proof of what he did to you. Just like when I took pictures of your ankle before I took the shackle off.'

'OK.'

I ran downstairs and when I returned with the phone I found

her standing in her bedroom with her back turned and the towel round her hips. I went in and turned her by her shoulder at the same time as I walked around her. I wanted to get the light from the window on her back and I was trying to be discreet at the same time. And just like the first time I saw her back I had one of those red-hot impulses to punch something really hard.

'What does it look like?' she said, and I realised she had never seen it.

'Bloody awful – I will kill the bastard!'

I ran my hand over her back. 'I'm not sure they are scars – they might be welts and calloused areas because you got whipped so often. Maybe they will go away now that nobody is beating you.'

She limped back to the bathroom without covering herself. I followed and saw that she was trying to see by twisting around in front of the mirror. I reached into the drawer on one side of the basin and got out the folding mirror I sometimes take with me on trips.

'Here, use this.'

She turned around, looked in the mirror and said calmly, 'I thought it would be like that – I can feel it with my hands when I reach around.'

Discretion was no longer on the agenda. 'How far down did he whip you?'

She let the towel drop and turned around.

'That must have hurt!'

Nothing I said could make up for it, but I could make sure the Master got what he deserved. I took a deep breath, photographed her from behind and left her to get dressed.

'Come down when you're ready. You're not worried about meeting Charlie, are you?'

She shook her head. 'Not if you are there too. What are you going to say my name is?'

'What do you mean, what will I say? I'll just say your name is Dao.'

'I didn't tell you my name is Dao. I said my mother called me Dao. My real name is Susan Johnson.'

My mind came to a sudden halt as I realised once again that I could make no assumptions at all about her.

'I was going to ask you what your full name is, my sister Willow wants to know. I thought Dao was your real name. Would you like me to call you Susan?'

'No, please call me Dao – it makes me feel good. I don't mind if everyone calls me Dao, it's not a special name, it's just what my mother called me. At school I was always Susan. And …'

She stopped talking, but I was curious now.

'And what? Do you have more names?'

She had that far-away look on her face again.

'No – I was just remembering the funny names my dad made up, sort of mixing up Dao and Susan. Sometimes he called me Daosan and sometimes Susao, just to be funny – I hadn't thought of that for years and years.'

I went down and found an unopened piece of brie cheese which I put on a plate with some crackers. Then I sat down at the dining table to add more details to the fact page about Dao. I had just printed three copies when she came down the stairs looking like a child dressed in adult clothes. The track pants were rolled up in thick rolls so she could walk without tripping and the T-shirt was like a tent. She had the roll of elastic bandage in her hand.

'I don't think I can do this – not the way you did. Can you do it again, please?'

She sat on a dining chair, and I wound the bandage around her ankle. 'God, that looks mad, Dao,' I said. 'Those clothes are so big. Wait here.'

I came back with the big scissors from the kitchen. 'Now stand up.' I lifted her to stand on the chair, unrolled the trousers legs and cut them off just above her feet. 'That's better – at least you won't trip.'

I stood back and took another look. 'Hang on, we can do

better than that – stand still.' I walked around her cutting the T-shirt hem off at a reasonable level and then the sleeves. When I lifted her down she looked at her feet and then at me and started to laugh.

'You are so funny, Hunter! You've ruined your clothes.'

'Doesn't matter – at least you look a bit better now.' I picked up the cut off pieces and went to throw them in the kitchen bin.

4

SATURDAY EVENING

When Charlie arrived, Dao stared at her with surprise written large on her face.

Charlie said, 'Hi there! You must be Hunter's found girl. How are you?'

Dao said nothing and looked at me. 'What's wrong, Dao?'

She stood on tiptoes and whispered, 'Is it a girl or a man?'

I leaned down and whispered back, quite loudly, 'It's a girl.' I was not surprised that she was confused. Charlie has that androgynous look, and her hair was shorter than ever.

Charlie grinned and biffed Dao gently on the upper arm. 'Don't worry, Dao – I'm a real girl, I just like to keep my hair short, a bit like yours. Did you cut it yourself?'

Dao's face closed and she said nothing, and I had to come to the rescue again.

'I think Dao's had to keep her hair short from necessity Charlie. She had her first warm shower and shampoo for several years less than an hour ago.'

We sat at the table and ate Thai food. Charlie drank beer, I drank wine and Dao drank water. Charlie set out to charm Dao as only she could, with a mixture of friendly interest and casual chat. Before long Dao was talking to her nearly as easily as she did to me. Willow arrived and we went through the routine again but much quicker. Willow is so calm and unhurried that you would never guess how sharp and decisive she is. Now she drew Dao into conversation about her parents and other things she remembered that Willow needed to know. They had the plan Dao had drawn in front of them and Willow was making notes as they talked.

Charlie and I sat in the chairs by the window, keeping our voices low while I told her what I wanted her help with.

'I want to find that location – the place where she was kept that we call the island now. I've had a quick look at Google Earth, but I don't know how far she had walked or even from which direction. She could have walked in circles for days for all I know.'

Charlie was slouched in her chair with the beer bottle resting on her thigh, looking as if she was half asleep, but I knew she was listening and thinking.

'And there's something else that I haven't mentioned yet. I don't want Dao to hear me talking about it, but there's something she's not prepared to tell me – or not yet anyway. And it's something important, something that scares her.'

Charlie looked a question at me without saying anything. That's one of the best things about Charlie. She lets you finish before she chips in with her contribution.

'Two or three times she's nearly started telling me something and each time she's stopped herself at the last moment. My gut feeling is that it's something really bad. What she's told me already is bad enough, but this other thing – whatever it is – it must be so scary that she can't bring herself to talk about it, or she doesn't trust me.'

Charlie nodded and glanced over at Willow and Dao at the dining table.

'I noticed the way she clamped down when I commented on her haircut. No comment, nothing. Do you think there's another whole layer of abuse – you know, so bad she can't bear to say the words? Or do you think it's something else altogether?'

'I've no idea – could be either I suppose. But it would be great if you could fly me up there one day soon when you have no jobs. And I might need to hire you as a bodyguard too if things get bad. I can't leave Dao alone and if anything crops up I'll need an extra pair of hands, or an extra gun. That man wants her dead and he's well equipped, at least three guns and some vicious dogs.'

She didn't even look surprised. 'So, you're going after this guy, are you? Before you do anything about reporting him?'

'That's right. I want him first and then the law can have him. Just being sent to prison is too good for him.'

This was becoming a personal campaign and Charlie was the only person I was prepared to tell. We share memories of the war we had fought. We never talked about it, but those things stay with you, and a sound or a word can bring up images in your mind that flood you with a mixture of fury and pity. A child's mutilated body behind a fallen stone wall in a village where the men had been slaughtered and the girls and women raped and then killed. Atrocities committed against innocent civilians and those responsible long gone. Abandoned vehicles rigged as bombs and improvised explosive devices turning roads into minefields; an indiscriminate brutality that can never be forgotten. And the same extremists getting away with it, time after time. It leaves a crease in your soul that a return to a quieter life can never smooth over. To find the same kind of brutality in a different form in my own country was shocking. At least this time I had a chance to make someone's suffering come to an end and close a chapter in a definitive way.

Charlie was studying my face as I was thinking and now she leant forward and said quietly, 'You're going to kill him?'

There was no indication that she was surprised or making a judgement, it was just a question.

'I'll do what needs doing at the time – I certainly want to make him experience fear and punish him for what he's done.'

'OK – I'm booked for tomorrow and then I haven't got anything until Thursday, but after that I'm busy for a couple of days with a film crew. Let's go Monday. And you need to get Dao some clothes that fit her – she can't go around dressed in your chopped-off gear in public, she looks mad.'

'I know – we'll do it tomorrow. Can I borrow one of your handguns?'

I knew she had a couple. When she first left the army and came to live in New Zealand she set herself up as a bodyguard for a time, looking after international VIPs – organised through the company I work for.

She nodded, thought for a moment. 'I've got a B endorsement on my firearms licence, and I still have the two pistols that I got when I was doing those special jobs, you know the escort duties. It's legit to carry them concealed as long as they aren't loaded.' She laughed and drank the last of her beer. 'But we know that unloaded guns aren't much use, don't we? And I never got caught, but you have to be careful.'

'OK, that's fine. It's impossible to move around in town with a shotgun – I need something smaller and more convenient, something that doesn't show.'

She grinned. 'You're on. I didn't realise this was so serious – or potentially serious anyway. Just like old times but without the dust and the donkeys.'

Joking aside, I knew she would go out on a limb for me without any hesitation. 'But seriously Charlie – this guy came snooping around the cabin late last night. I have no idea how persistent he'll be, but he knows damn well that if Dao has survived and tells her story he's history. So, I've got to move fast before he disappears – or kills her.'

'But how would he find you – and her?'

'He could ask around at the farms up there, pretend to need to locate me for some reason. I don't know – but the fact is that he tracked her after several days, was prepared to spend all that time and effort. It must mean something. Whatever the reason he wants to find her, or perhaps kill her.

As I said, I think there's more to this than meets the eye and I'm not about to leave anything to chance.'

Willow rose from the table at the other end of the room and came towards us. She looked her usual cool blonde self, but I sensed something else, some sort of puzzlement or concern.

'Dao and I have done what we can for the moment. I've got a lot of information to work with now and I'll spend as much time as I can tomorrow and Monday researching things. Dao says you made some notes at the cabin, Hunter. Do you think they would be useful to me?'

I got up and we all moved back to the table. Dao was sitting where she had sat since dinner. I looked closely at her; there was a slight tension behind the quiet façade. What had she and Willow discussed that had unsettled both of them?

'I printed some copies before you came. Pour another glass of wine and we'll have a look. Dao, do you mind if they see the notes?'

She shook her head. 'No, I don't mind. But I'd like to go to bed now if that's OK.'

She was looking at me as if I had to give her permission. She went upstairs followed by Scruff and we read the notes in silence.

FACTS ABOUT Susan Johnson aka Dao

Scruff found Dao in a wet hollow in the forest where she had been lying in the rain for a day and a night covered with branches and ferns. She was dressed in a man's shirt and jeans, no shoes and no underwear. She had walked for several days. She was unconscious and very cold. She had a brass shackle round her left ankle.

- *Dao's father Philip Johnson died in an industrial accident when she was eight. When Dao was ten her mother took a job as a live-in housekeeper for a man on* an isolated property on the Northland coast. After some time there she told Dao she thought the man was doing something illegal.

- When Dao had just turned twelve, her mother left and all her belongings disappeared. Dao was no longer allowed to live in the house and had to sleep on the floor in a storage shed. A shackle was soldered around her ankle, and she was chained to the wall at night and when the man was away. She did all the work around the place: cooking, cleaning, washing, tending the garden and growing vegetables. The man demanded that Dao call him Master and said her name would be Slave. She thought they were on an island, but now realises he made her think this so she would not try to escape after her mother left. Dao can't swim.
- The gardens are separated from the house by a belt of native bush. The man allowed Dao to go there, but padlocked a chain with bells around her waist so he could hear that she was there and working.
- Dao has worn only old clothes of Master's and has had no shoes since she outgrew what she had when her mother left. She has not been allowed to use the shower in the house and has eaten left-over food in the shed. The schoolbooks from the Correspondence School and all her belongings were taken away.
- Periodically a couple of men come to 'the island' by boat – separately. One of them wanted Dao and Master told her he would sell her to him. Dao thinks that the man would use her sexually and then throw her into the sea to drown. She decided to escape and find a place to die before Master's dogs found her 'and tore her to bits' – which is what she has been told the dogs have been trained to do.
- The house is a hundred metres from the beach, there is no jetty, but there is an aluminium boat with an outboard motor. The boat is pulled up under a big tree and

padlocked to a post. Master has a radio set and there is a radio aerial that is lowered when not in use. There are two sheds and dog kennels.

- *Dao was born in New Zealand, and she thinks her father was too. The Johnsons lived in a rented flat in a suburb whose name she cannot tell me. This suburb has a big green and red supermarket (New World) with a primary school in the same road and a park with red slides and a skate-bowl, a 'pretty building with a domed roof' and a cell phone tower beside the school playing field that she remembers because there was 'a lot of arguing about it'.*

- *Dao has told me that her mother is dead, though she refers to her as having left. I have not pushed her to explain why she thinks her mother is dead.*

- *She hurt her ankle when she tried to run away from the cabin the morning after I had found her and removed the shackle. She fled because I said I would take her back to town and we would find someone else to look after her and sort things out.*

Willow put the paper down on the table and looked down at it for a long moment and sighed. She ran both hands through her blonde curls and shook her head like she always does when she is working through a problem. 'It's hard to believe, Hunter. You don't really expect to come across this sort of thing in real life – even if you know that it happens.'

'What do you think about her state of mind?' said Charlie. 'I suppose I mean her mental health. Is she OK or really damaged? She's so damn calm looking it's hard to say what goes on in her head. And she's awfully skinny.'

I wanted them to understand Dao and see her through my eyes. If they were going to be effective in helping me sort her life out it was important that they saw her as I had learnt to.

'From a physical point of view, I think she's basically OK. When I stripped her wet clothes off she was unconscious. She was frozen, bluish grey. Her skin had been damp so long that I hardly dared use a towel in case I rubbed her skin off. I put her on the sofa and just peeled all her clothes off and got her into the warmest things I could find. I wrapped her in a sleeping bag – she was still unconscious. I put wine bottles full of hot water around her and Scruff helped warm her up. She has a terrible mark round her ankle from that bloody shackle. And there's a long scar on one leg too – that bastard burnt her with a soldering iron to punish her. I have photos of the shackle before I took it off and of the scar. I still have the shackle – as evidence. I got it off with bolt cutters.'

I paused to think. What would make them actually grasp how brave she was, how strong and fierce? 'When I offered her warm soup she said, 'I don't need to eat, I am going to die' and she meant it. She had considered her situation, concluded it was intolerable and decided it would be better to die on her own terms than stay where she was. That takes unbelievable strength of mind – because she wasn't in a state of mental dejection or despair. She had decided this from a logical point of view, determined to exercise the only form of control over her own life that was open to her. And to get away from a tyrant who enjoyed hurting her. Or that's how I see it, anyway.'

Willow's eyes were fixed on mine, and she nodded. 'It's heroic – and how very lucky that she did not die. Heaven knows what she might achieve in life if she's given a chance – so strong spirited and focused.'

'Since she warmed up she has had a good appetite and seems fine,' I continued. 'She was malnourished and in terrible condition from her trek, but I don't think there's anything much wrong with her.'

Both women were silent, their eyes fixed on me and waiting. I cut a piece of cheese and put it on a cracker and tried to sum up the rest. 'So she is mentally very strong, and emotionally too – considering what's she's been subjected to. But she's terrified of Master finding her, or his dogs for that matter. Really terrified, not just scared but literally fearing for her life. And she trusts nobody. I truly believe she would rather die than be enslaved again or betrayed to any degree at all. She is prepared to make herself die rather than give Master the satisfaction of killing her. I didn't believe this at first, but I do now – it is not posturing or looking for attention. It's a reasoned conclusion she has arrived at – as I said, the only way she can retain control over what happens to her.'

Willow turned the stem of her wine glass slowly between her fingers. 'Well, it's quite clear that she trusts you. That was obvious when we talked. But there's something I can't put my finger on – something she knows or something that has been done to her that frightens her very much – maybe she needs time to be able to talk about it. I couldn't get to the bottom of it and I wasn't going to push – I need her to trust me too.'

'I know – I told Charlie just now that I'm sure there is something she hasn't told me yet. She has very nearly started telling me a couple of times and then she's decided not to – literally closing her mouth to stop it coming out.'

Willow reached out and took a cracker and absentmindedly broke it in half, then into smaller pieces. I knew what she would do with it; she has been doing it since she was a child.

'I think we should inform the police tomorrow and let them start doing whatever they think is best. And I'll find out all I can about Dao's background, where and when she was born, find her suburb and her school and all that sort of thing. Possibly the Vietnamese embassy knows something about her mother – she told me her mother came from a town called Donghoi – I have no idea how to spell it. We might need a medical certificate for the police that Dao's mental state is fragile, and we'll stipulate that you have to be present as a support person when they talk to her, even though she isn't a minor, not just me as her lawyer. What do you think?'

Charlie's eyes were fixed on me and I knew why. She was

wondering how on earth I would persuade my strong-minded and law-abiding lawyer sister not to report it; without precisely explaining the reason.

'Yes, that's exactly the sort of thing I had in mind – we need to find out all we can,' I said trying to sound as reasonable as possible. 'But I want a bit of time before we involve the cops, Willow. This man, who calls himself Master – he's hell-bent on finding Dao and if he does he'll kill her. As I said, I completely believe Dao - he wants her dead. He might still be at the so-called island, and I want to find the place and see if I can get a look at him. If we wait or if the cops start making enquiries he could just vanish. I want a few days to make sure and then we'll report it. We can say Dao hadn't revealed very much until then or whatever is necessary to explain the delay.'

Charlie spoke before Willow had time to reply. 'I think you're right, Hunter. If he takes off we have nothing, don't know what he looks like or anything. Who knows if the place belongs to him or if it's rented? Let Hunter get on with it for a few days, Willow. We'll use the chopper to find the island and see what we can see, get some pictures and go from there.'

Willow's voice was a notch harder than before. She looked me straight in the eyes and raised her chin. 'You can't do that, Hunter! It could compromise your credibility and I can't represent you if you are committing me to lying. No way!'

I had expected opposition, but this was serious. 'Now, hang on,' I said before she got any further. 'Isn't the most important thing here that Master doesn't get away scot-free? Isn't that what Dao needs to know so she can get on with the rest of her life? Can you imagine what will happen if one single iota of this gets to him before the cops do? He'll vanish – that's what will happen.'

Willow stood firm. 'It's the same principle that applies to criminals – I can't represent someone as 'not guilty' if they have told me they are guilty. Lying, even by evasion, I can't do it. You don't understand what you're asking!'

She put up a good fight for doing the right thing straight off but in the end she gave in. She did not say it, but she was worried I would take the law into my own hands. I did my best to convince her I would do nothing of the kind, but with Charlie alongside me she probably feared the worst. But in the end she gave in, motivated mainly by the wish to make sure Dao would not be left wondering when Master would catch up with her.

'OK then – but you've got to promise not to do anything illegal, Hunter. Don't think you can take the law into your own hands! I can tell how angry you are, but you can't start dishing out punishment instead of letting normal processes do the job – or you'll end up in trouble yourself.'

The cracker in front of her was reduced to little crumbs now and she was pushing them around with her fingertips and shaping them into lines.

'OK – I'll be careful, I promise. And you said you can do this while you're on leave? Officially, like Dao is a formal client?'

'Oh yes, that's not a problem. But I'm truly concerned about your part in this. I can see that she's developed a strong bond with you, but can you cope with taking her on? I mean, this isn't going to be fixed and go away in a week, is it? It could be a long time before she's OK to function on her own.'

Her gaze was locked on my face, and I knew I had to be honest with her. No point pretending it was going to be plain sailing or that I did not have my own doubts.

'I know – it could be a long process and possibly hard work. I might have to keep her and help her for a long time, but I feel responsible. And I like her – she's interesting and smart and she deserves a chance to have a normal life. I don't know what it is about her, but I think I understand her mind, what drives her.'

Willow smiled and her fingers created a crumb pyramid on the table. 'It's going to be hard work at times, but it might be rewarding too. At least she's lucky she was found by someone with the means to support her – and no family to get jealous of all the time she will undoubtedly take up.'

Charlie agreed. 'She could have been found by someone who would have handed her straight to the authorities and they couldn't match what you're prepared to do. How safe is this house – you have an alarm system I suppose?'

Willow's eyes swivelled from Charlie to me with a look of suspicion. 'Why? Is there something you haven't told me?'

So, I told her about the incident during the night and what my conclusions were.

'Christ, Hunter! What did you do? It's so isolated up there in the forest.'

'Got the shotgun loaded and set us up in a defensive position as well as I could. Tried to make sure I'd be able to get him first if he broke a window or smashed the door in – you know, just sensible stuff. And Scruff would have warned me if anyone got close.'

Willow said nothing, just looked at me with an expression of horror; to her it sounded like complete anarchy. I could never explain to her that to me it was second nature; it's what you do.

'Where is Scruff?' said Charlie, looking around.

'He's upstairs with Dao. He's appointed himself her personal bodyguard and keeps her within line of sight at all times. And yes, I do have an alarm system but I'm going to beef up security here. Willow, if I can get Dao to agree, could she be at your place when I go flying with Charlie on Monday? And can I borrow Matt's new camera and that long lens he bought?'

'Of course – Matt's away for days, he's doing the Singapore – London run so he won't be back until next week. Of course, you can borrow the camera – he left it at home this time. I've got to go now but let me know for sure about Monday.'

She emptied her wine glass and picked up the fact sheet and her own notes. By the stairs she paused and pointed.

'I saw the gun sitting there when I arrived, but I thought you just hadn't put it away again after coming back.'

'Sorry Willow – I know you hate weapons, but from now on the Remington is going to be where I can grab it fast if someone breaks in. I have no idea how persistent that bastard is or how far he'll go to track Dao down. I'm not taking any chances.'

'Is it loaded?'

'Of course, it's loaded. No point threatening someone with a gun if you can't act on the threat. And if he breaks in armed I'll need to shoot him before he gets to Dao. It won't be a case of negotiating.'

Willow shivered. 'God, Hunter – be careful! You're not in the army now. Please try to remember this isn't a war zone – or not yet.'

'I know I can't guard against every eventuality, but at least I can make her feel safe when we're at home.'

At the door she turned around and looked seriously at me. 'And be careful, Hunter – she could easily develop a sort of saviour attachment to you. The Chinese say that if you save someone's life you are responsible for them forever.'

I hugged them both and closed the door behind them thinking of what Willow had said. I had to admit that she was right. But there were too many issues that needed my attention and I had to concentrate on the urgent things. The philosophical aspects could wait. It was after eleven when I went upstairs deep in thought.

Dao's light was on, and she was lying down with a book open beside her. Her eyes were open and as soon as she saw me in the doorway she said, 'Can I see those notes you made please?'

I had made a mistake, treated her as if she was a secondary participant in this, when in fact she was the main character.

'I'm sorry, Dao. Of course, you must see them. I just didn't think of it – that you hadn't seen them. It's more as if we wrote those notes together and we both know what's in them. I'll go down and get a copy for you right now.'

'No, no – it's not like that, not at all. I just want to read them. We did write them together, sort of. I'm not upset about it – I just want to see them.'

I went down and got my copy and gave it to her. I said goodnight and put the shotgun just inside my bedroom door where I could grab it fast if things turned bad. When I came out from the bathroom I looked in at Dao who now appeared to be asleep with the bedside light on. Scruff was under her bed. He looked at me without lifting his chin off the floor and wagged his tail. I left the light on in case she woke up in the night and went to bed wearing my only pair of PJ pants. Too tired to read I turned off the light and scrunched up the pillow.

Ten minutes later a small voice from the other bedroom said, 'Are you there, Hunter?'

I got out of bed and went to stand in her doorway again. 'There's nobody in the house apart from you and me and Scruff. The door is locked and it's perfectly safe.'

'OK.'

At half past one in the morning I woke to find her standing beside my bed, supporting herself with one hand against the wall and looking down at me. I sat up. 'What's wrong?'

'I couldn't hear you breathing, and I had to see that you were still here.'

I sighed and turned the bedside light on. 'Go back to bed, Dao, I will be right here all night. There is no need to worry.'

At three I woke again. Dao was sitting on the chair beside the wardrobe, just sitting there in the half-dark with Scruff on the floor beside her. I got out of bed and turned the light on. Her face was drawn and worried; she said nothing, just looked at me. I had no idea how to handle this. Her fixation that she was only safe if I was visible to her was getting me down. Was I going to have to be right beside her all the time?

And for how long? Would I be able to persuade her to go to Willow's place? Any minute now I'm going to have an anxiety attack, I thought. Not that I ever had one before, but I was beginning to feel haunted.

Aloud I said, 'Are you scared?'

She considered before she answered. 'I'm not scared when I can see you – or hear you. I feel all right then, but when I can't I'm scared that Master will come in the door with the dogs, or through the window. I'm sorry. I don't mean to be a problem.'

It was clear that she had not finished, that she was still thinking.

'I thought I could just sit here. I won't make any noise.'

'No Dao, it doesn't work like that. I won't be able to sleep if I know you are not in bed. And you need your sleep. We would both be exhausted tomorrow.'

Her face was a picture of internal conflict. I could tell that she wanted to please me, but it made her feel very insecure to be in her room.

'OK,' she said and got up, leaning one hand against the wall. 'Is it OK if I go down to the big room?'

That threw me; I tried to figure out what it might mean. Why would sitting in the living room be any better than being in her bedroom? Surely it would be worse; it was on a different level. I wondered if it was related to whatever it was she had not yet told me. Perhaps she thought I would not be able to keep her with me; was she keeping open the option of 'going away to die'?

Will she wait until I'm asleep, I wondered, and then go down one more level, out the front door into the night – because she would rather do that than not feel completely safe? Is this her way of dealing with yet another intolerable situation? She's already done it once. Would she rather die on her own terms than be caught in a situation where she is powerless? And if safety is completely linked to my presence then I have no option but to do what's needed. I have underestimated how terrorised she is by her fear of Master. What she feels makes little sense to me, but it's real for her. I keep getting fooled by her apparent composure, the very thing I warned Willow about.

'Come around to the other side.'

I took her arm and walked her to the other side of the bed and held the duvet up. 'Hop in!'

She got in without saying anything and watched me as I went back to my side. I grabbed the fleecy blanket that hung on the back of the chair and lay down on top of the duvet pulling the rug over me.

'Now go to sleep like a good girl.'

I reached up to turn the light off and saw her dark eyes fixed on me.

'It's all right, Dao, I'm not angry – I'm not an angry person. I'm just tired. We're OK now, aren't we?'

'Yes. Thank you, Hunter.'

5

SUNDAY

I knew from the way the light was falling in through the skylight that it was much later than my normal wake-up time. The other half of the bed was empty. Dao was sitting on the bed in her room with the book of road maps she had taken from the car the day before.

'Good morning – what are you looking at?'

'I'm trying to see if I can find where the island is – well, I know now it's not an island, but that's how I think about it. I am trying to figure it out from the sunrises – you know, the directions.'

She looked at me as if she expected me to tell her not to waste her time or laugh at her. But I was impressed with the initiative. 'What have you discovered so far? Do you need any help?'

'You said Whangarei was not far away and I found that, it's on this side, east.'

She turned the book to show me and pointed. 'The house must be in a little curve of beach that faces that way – not one of these bays that are at an angle and face a different direction. But I don't know how far I had walked when I lay down in the forest, or which direction. Can you show me where your cabin is?'

'It's a good start,' I said. 'But I have something even better for us to take a look at later today – we'll check out Google Earth. Have you ever used a computer?'

She shook her head. 'We didn't have one at home. Master has a laptop, but I've never used one.'

'OK, let's have breakfast and feed Scruff, and then we'll go and buy clothes for you.'

She looked troubled but said nothing and I went to get dressed. Downstairs I sat her down at the table and went to make breakfast.

'Porridge again, I'm afraid – we're right out of bread now,' I said from the kitchen.

'I like porridge – I can do it in the mornings if you like.'

When I carried our bowls to the table she was busy drawing again. I leant over to put a bowl in front of her and realised it was the drawing she had left unfinished the day before. It had a crease down the middle. She had probably folded it and kept it in the road atlas.

'Are you going to show me?'

She handed me the paper and said apologetically, 'It's still not quite finished – it doesn't look right.'

At the top half of the paper she had drawn a boat in precise detail with a name on the side at the front in tiny letters: 'Sea Breeze'. Below that was the outline of a man's face; a long narrow face with a moustache, slightly hooded eyes and pronounced curved lines both sides of the mouth, big ears. It was basic and unsophisticated, but I could see that with more detail and a bit of shading it would be recognisable as a particular person. Beside the boat she had written a note in brackets (= Easy Rider).

'Dao, this is good – I'm impressed. Is it Master?'

She took the paper back and put it on the table and looked at it.

'No, it's the man who comes on that boat. He's the one who wants to buy me – his name is John, but I haven't written it down yet.'

'Why does it say, 'equals *Easy Rider*'?'

'That's the other name of the boat. He has another white board with the other name painted on it and sometimes he puts that over the *Sea Breeze* name – when he's trying to make it look like a different boat.'

Just as I was about to ask her why he needed two names for his boat she pulled the bowl towards her. 'I really like the brown sugar and the way it melts -it makes the porridge lovely.'

I left my question for later but made a mental note to be sure to ask her. Trying to make a boat look like a different boat was a suspicious thing to do and it had to be significant, but would she know why?

In the kitchen after breakfast, while we were tidying up, I asked casually, 'How did you get on with Willow and her questions last night? Could you tell her anything that would help her find out some more about your parents? I don't even know what your mother's first name is. All I know is that their surname is Johnson.'

'Only Dad and I were called Johnson. My mother liked her own surname – she used to say that she didn't need to borrow someone else's. My dad always laughed and said she could have it for free, it was nothing special. I'd forgotten that till now. My dad's name was Philip and my mother's name was Lucy – he used to call her Lucky Lucy.'

'Do you remember aunts and uncles or grandparents?'

'Dad had relatives in the South Island, but I don't think I ever met them – or maybe when I was very little, and I can't remember it. But not my mother – she had no family in New Zealand at all. She came here after she met my dad, just her – nobody else.'

We were in the car on the way to the shopping mall when she suddenly said, 'My dad's brother is called Stuart and his wife is called Nora.'

I stared sideways at her in surprise, and she laughed at my expression.

'They sent us a photo that we had on the fridge and my dad wrote their names on the white edge at the bottom 'Uncle Stuart and Aunt Nora' – I've just remembered.'

But when we got to the mall the mood changed.

'Hunter, I don't want any clothes,' she said when I had parked the car.

'Well, you must have some – you can't walk around in those huge things. I thought you'd like to wear something that fits you after all these years of wearing men's clothes.'

She looked at me, silent and stubborn, and made no move to get out of the car.

'Tell me why,' I said. 'There must be a reason.'

She hesitated and then she said, 'I haven't got any money,'

I had to smile. 'Of course, you don't – how could you? Bet that bastard never paid you for all the work you did. But lucky for us I've got plenty.'

'But you shouldn't be paying for things for me!' She was genuinely concerned, not just being polite.

'Listen, Dao,' I said seriously, looking straight into her eyes to make sure she knew I meant it. 'I have nobody who needs me, no wife, no children. I have more money than I need and nobody to spend it on. Now you're part of the household and that means I pay for things for you.'

She thought for a moment and decided to accept my reasoning and I drew a sigh of relief. The fewer complications we had the better.

People in the mall stared at us and when I saw us reflected in shop windows I had to admit we made a strange-looking couple. The height difference for a start, at least a foot, and then Dao's lumpy haircut and her bare feet, not to mention the huge clothes she had on and the fact that she was limping. People probably thought I had picked up a street kid somewhere and beat her up.

We went to the big red store that sells everything and I grabbed a trolley. It was a strange situation, to be shopping for someone who had nothing and needed everything.

'I don't know how we should do this, Dao. You need lots of things and God knows I have no idea what they are. Let's get lots of clothes and shoes and whatever we see and pile everything into the trolley. Then we'll put you in a fitting room and you can try them on.'

We spent half an hour throwing things in the trolley: shoes, socks, jackets, pants, tops, nightwear and underwear. But when I suggested a skirt I met complete resistance, no skirts. I wondered if the scar around her ankle was the reason, but I said nothing. Just as I thought we had finished I remembered all the girl things Plum brings when she comes to stay, toiletries and hair things and a brush. Dao went into the fitting room with three changes of clothes, and I persuaded the attendant to let me feed more things to her at intervals. Half of it was too big, even though it was the smallest adult size and I had to go and find replacements in the children's section.

We left exhausted, with Dao dressed in jeans and a T-shirt with a hooded striped jacket over the top. Apart from the haircut she could have been any young teenager out with an uncle. She had taken the bandage off her ankle so she could get her new shoes on, and though she was still limping she was moving a lot easier.

'We have to get your hair tidied up,' I said as we loaded a mass of carrier bags into the car. 'Let's go back into the mall – I'm sure there must be a hairdresser in there somewhere.'

We went into the first shop we saw and got directions to the nearest hairdresser. I sat in the waiting area and read the newspaper while they cut Dao's hair, hoping they would do a good job. I hoped she would feel a lot better if she looked good. And it was worth it. The girl who came back out had a short haircut with a spiky fringe and looked a hundred times better.

'Very pretty,' I said. 'Let me take a photo of you and send it to Willow and Charlie. They won't believe it's you – proper clothes, new hair style and everything.'

I took three photos from different angles and showed them to her. She studied them carefully before she picked which one to send.

Just as I had suggested we should find a café and have lunch, my phone rang. I stood in the busy mall with one finger covering my free ear trying to hear the voice at the other end. Even with the sound up full it was hard to hear, and the voice kept cutting out.

'Hunter, it's Mac ..... just saw it from ...... tell you right away....'

'Sorry, can't hear – you keep cutting out. Can you try again, please?' I shouted, hoping my voice went through to him. I tried to think what it might mean. The only Mac I know is the farmer whose access road I use to reach the track to the cabin. He's been helpful a few times; he keeps an eye on things and gets a bottle of whiskey for his troubles at Christmas. He had only ever called me once before, when a section of the track collapsed after heavy rain. We found a café and were halfway through lunch when he called again.

'I was in my paddock across the valley from the bush,' he said. 'Never used the phone from there before – the reception was terrible. I rang to tell you I spotted a small truck coming down your track, too far away to see any details. But when it went around the steep bend, just after where your track crosses the creek, I got a glimpse of a couple of dogs on the tray. Can't say I've ever seen a strange vehicle up there. Thought you might like me to go up and have a look? Unless it's someone you've lent the place to?'

'No, it's not anyone I know. I would let you know if someone else was going to be there. Could it be hunters?'

'They'd have to be bloody cheeky to go through two of my pasture gates to get to the track itself, very unlikely.'

'OK, I'll drive up now. I had someone come around on foot the night before I left, someone with dogs.'

I thanked him and put the phone down. Dao's eyes were fixed on mine, anticipating danger.

'That was the farmer out by the main road. Someone's been at the cabin and I want to go up and check it out. I'll drop you at Willow's place – I should be about five hours, back in time for dinner.'

'No, I'll come.' Once again that non-negotiable look on her face.

'That's not a good idea. If it's Master again we're in big trouble. I can handle it much better if I don't have to worry about protecting you. You have to go to Willow's place.'

'No. Just take your gun.'

'That's not enough. The minute he sees you he'll shoot and then it's over. It's too dangerous, Dao – you can't come.'

'I'll go into the back - under that cover you pull over, so he can't see me.'

She saw me hesitating and leapt at the opportunity. 'It's OK if he can't see me.' She paused and stunned me with her clinching argument: 'If he kills you, someone has to be able to say who did it.'

I gave in, very reluctantly. Her focus and courage amazed me. Was she hoping she would see me shoot him? Forty minutes later we were on the motorway heading north. I took the Remington, loaded. We brought Scruff, who was delighted with another long ride so soon. The phone rang again when we were half an hour away from the turn-off to the farm. I stopped and took another call from Mac.

'I went up and had a look, Hunter,' he said, sounding quite alarmed. 'Someone's broken in and it looks as if they've gone through every single thing in there. Can't imagine what they were looking for. You didn't leave a gun there or anything valuable, did you?'

'No, never – just some ammunition. I'm on my way, nearly there. I'll check in with you before I drive up.'

'Now you get into the back,' I said to Dao when I had finished with Mac. 'Keep really quiet when I stop and talk to Mac – the fewer people up here who see me with a girl, the safer you are.'

She climbed into the far back of the wagon and made a nest among the shopping bags and shoeboxes. I pulled the luggage cover over and made sure it was fastened properly before I shut the tailgate and locked it. Visions of Master shooting me and opening the back played like a movie in my mind.

Mac was watching out for me and came down from his house as we turned in the farm road.

'Do you want me to come up with you?'

'Thanks, Mac – I'll be fine.' No way did I want to endanger yet another person. The fewer people I had to worry about if things went wrong, the happier I would be. 'I've got tools up there so I'll be able to do something temporary – unless the door is shattered or something?'

Mac smiled grimly. 'No, not shattered. It will be weatherproof if you can nail a board over to keep it shut. The edge is splintered where they forced it and the lock is stuffed, but nothing too drastic. Same thing with the shed. Bloody mongrels!'

I thanked him and promised to let him know if I found anything interesting. As we drove through the ford Scruff went crazy with excitement and I heard Dao laughing. Instead of cheering me up it made me feel more worried. How could I have let her persuade me to bring her? There was a remote chance that someone was higher up on the hillside keeping an eye on the access track. We could be driving straight into a dangerous situation. I stopped under some big trees just after the ford.

'I'm going to lock you in the car and have a look around, before we drive up. I'm taking Scruff. Don't do anything at all, just stay where you are. Are you all right?'

'Yes, I'm fine. I won't do anything silly.'

'That's all very well, but our ideas of what is silly might differ. Just don't do anything at all – do you understand?'

'OK.'

I took the shotgun and did a circuit up the hill to one side of the track and back down on the other, letting Scruff roam. He gave no indication of anyone being around, so we went back to the car and drove up the hill.

'Stay there for a few minutes,' I said to Dao and locked the car.

The cabin door was pushed shut, but quite badly damaged on the lock side. A long shard of wood had broken away and there were light-coloured crush marks in the weathered door jamb from whatever tool had been used, possibly a tyre lever. The shed door had been forced open and hung crookedly from one hinge.

Inside the cabin it was clear that someone had gone through things very thoroughly. The table was strewn with stuff taken off the shelves. Crockery and cans of food in an untidy mess, the contents of the drawers emptied out, cutlery on the floor. The drawers had been thrown to one side and in front of the little bookshelf magazines lay tossed in an untidy heap. It was impossible to see if anything had been taken, but it looked like a search. It must have something to do with the hunt for Dao. Someone was trying to find out if she had been there and maybe who I was.

I went back outside and let Scruff out of the car. He ran around a bit like he always does when we first arrive, around the shed and the back of the cabin. He displayed no signs of sensing that anybody was nearby, and I watched him for a couple of minutes before I opened the tailgate to let Dao out.

'Someone's been having a good look – maybe trying to find out who was here. Come inside while I have a proper look.'

I put the Remington on the table where I could reach it fast if I needed to.

'Sit in that chair by the stove again while I tidy up a bit. Are you scared?'

All she said was 'yes' and I made no comment. After a few minutes she said, 'Where did you put the clothes I had on when you found me? And the bangle, I mean the shackle?'

Clever girl, I thought, you're no slouch when it comes to processing information.

'The clothes are in the rubbish bag we took back to town and the shackle is in the glovebox in the car. It's evidence, so I kept it.'

She threw me a glance and said no more about it. There was nothing to be gained from looking around further; whoever had been there had not come to steal. The way the magazines and the contents of the drawers in the bedroom had been tossed about made me certain they had searched for something that would tell them who owned the place.

Dao stood up suddenly and Scruff got up from the floor, alert and ready. 'You know that magazine you gave me to read? And it was still in the plastic bag they had sent it in? It had your name and address on the bag. Did you throw the bag in the rubbish?'

She was right. In my mind's eye I saw her sitting on the sofa wrapped in the sleeping bag, ripping the bag open and my hand reaching out for it. But then what?

'I don't know – I think I put it on the table when I took it from you. But what did I do with it after that? I can't remember putting it in the rubbish bin.'

We checked the mess on the table and under it. I looked in the pile on the floor by the bookshelf, pushing things around and turning them over. There was no plastic bag anywhere. I was really worried now, because I had no recollection of throwing it in the rubbish. Some last-minute odds and ends from the bench and the table had gone into a carton when we packed up in a hurry to leave, but I couldn't remember the bag the magazine had come in. Had I seen it when I unpacked that box in the kitchen in town?

'We'll have to check the rubbish sack and that box when we get back to town.'

We tidied up a bit and I found a couple of boards in the shed to nail across the doors to keep them shut. While I worked endless speculation cycled through my head. If

Master had found my name and address, would he pursue me to try to find out if Dao had been or was still with me? Would he try to gain access to the house, or would he just watch the place? How far would he be prepared to go in town where there would be people watching?

We did not discuss it, but I knew Dao was as aware of the danger as I was. I stopped briefly at the farmhouse and told Mac that we had found nothing missing and that the doors were nailed shut.

'Strange,' he said and shook his head. 'You'd think the only point in going up there would be to steal, or maybe camp out in the cabin for a while. Can't imagine what they were after. I'll keep an eye out for that truck, and I'll put a padlock on the last gate. Let me know next time you're coming up and I'll give you a key for it. Do you want a cup of tea before you head back?'

'Thanks Mac, but I'd better get on the road – it will take me a couple of hours to get home and I've got things waiting to be done.'

Once back on the main road I stopped and let Dao back into the front seat. After a few miles she said hesitantly, 'I wish I could see the photo again, the one I liked that you sent to Willow and Charlie. But maybe they will show it to me – on their phones.'

I passed the phone to her. 'Have a look if you like – I can talk you through how to find it.'

'You said you sent it to them.'

I kept forgetting how little I could take for granted.

'Ah, I see what you mean. Well, what happens is this – you take a photo, and the phone saves it. When you send the photo to someone else they only get a copy, the original one stays on your own phone. If you want to, we can download it to the laptop and have it there as well.'

There is going to be a lot of catching up, I thought. She has missed out on all the digital knowledge we gradually absorb as things develop and a lot of other things as well. It will be a long road however quickly she learns.

When we got back to town it was dark, the early winter evening was chilly and bleak. There was a lot of stuff I needed to do tonight and the break-in at the cabin had moved home security to the top of my list. I stopped at the shopping centre and bought pizza for dinner. As soon as we had eaten I put a bowl of ice cream and my tablet in front of Dao, along with paper and pens.

'I'll show you how to start using the tablet and then you can try whatever you like. Ask me if you get stuck – I just have to make some calls.'

'What if I ruin it? I don't know anything about it, I might do something wrong.'

'You can't ruin it – just mess around and try to find things on the internet, check out Google Earth – anything you like. But tell me if you need some help.'

I showed her how to get on the internet and how to open Google Earth and left her to it. The plastic bag was nowhere – the carton was on the kitchen floor and yielded nothing, so I went down and checked the rubbish sack in the garage – not there either. If Master had found it he knew where I lived. I rang Charlie.

'What's the surname of that guy in the New Zealand unit you were friends with that first time in Afghanistan - the technician who whistled all the time, Paul somebody? I need to get hold of him. I think someone said he has set up his own security business or something like it, after he left the army. I need someone to help me fast.'

I told her about the break-in and what it might mean.

'Bugger! You'd better have some extra protection then. I have Paul's number on my phone. I see him now and again – it was probably me who told you about him. He's got his own business installing alarm systems – he said he's doing really well. I'll text you his number. But listen, Hunter – you'll have to be careful when you come and go from the house too – it's not just about preventing anyone getting in.'

'I know – Dao was in the back of the wagon with the luggage cover over her just in case someone was still up there. We won't be taking any risks.'

I went upstairs to call Paul. Dao was apprehensive already and I did not want her listening to me describing all the potential danger points to Paul and discussing solutions. He made it easy, clearly he knew all there was to know about home security and after half an hour we had it mapped out.

'I've only got one job booked for tomorrow and I'll put them off for a day,' he said. 'I could be at your place at half past seven to check it out and then go and get all the stuff we need. It should be done by the end of the day. But listen, Charlie said you're working for some security outfit based in London – why don't you do it yourself?'

'Not your kind of security – more to do with personnel and weapons and stuff like that.' I knew he would get the drift; I heard him chuckle at the other end. 'Ah, I get it. Is tomorrow OK then?'

'We're out most of the day tomorrow. If you come over first thing I'll give you a key and show you around so you can come back after you've got the bits you need and let yourself in.'

Dao was still at the dining table with the tablet pushed to one side and sheets of paper strewn in front of her. A revised plan of the island was the first thing I noticed; the shed was now at a slight angle to the house and some details had been added. On the sheet with the drawing of the motor launch called *Sea Breeze* the man's face had been subtly enhanced; I would recognise him if I met him. On the third sheet there was another boat at the top, smaller with no cabin. And at the bottom of the page a man's face, a fat and unshaven man with a mouth that turned down at the corners. This must be 'the other man' who came visiting by boat. The word Mint was printed beside him and at one side of the paper she had drawn arms with tattoos.

I picked up the fourth sheet of paper and studied it. No boat on this one, just a face. Was this the man she called Master? I glanced at her face, and she said, 'That's him – Master.'

She would have left him to last, the one who would have been the hardest to draw. The face surprised me; he looked ordinary and harmless. Just an ordinary man in his forties or fifties, slightly overweight with a bald or shaved head and a moustache. There was nothing in his features that indicated brutality or cruelty. The name on the drawing was not 'Master' as I had expected, but 'Bramville' printed in neat schoolgirl letters.

'Is that his real name? I didn't know that you knew his real name.'

'My mother used to call him Bram and the men from the boats too. My mother asked him once what his real name was and he said Bram was short for Bramville – he said it was too long and fancy, spelt like a French place.

'You're good at this, Dao. I think I will recognise these guys if I come across them. We'll take them over to Willow's place and she can scan them into her computer and make them part of her file.'

'I haven't quite finished. I need to add the tattoo on the back of Master's neck.'

She pointed at the back of her own neck. 'He's got one right in the middle at the back – you can see it when he wears a T-shirt.'

The name should make him easy to identify, I thought, very unusual, sounds like a surname. Wonder if Willow can trawl through the birth registers just by one name?

Dao pulled the paper towards her and drew a small image between two vertical lines and held it up to show me.

'That's what it looks like – it's black, about this big.'

She held her thumb and forefinger a couple of centimetres

apart. It was a swastika; exactly what I would have expected from that nasty piece of work. By now it was nearly nine o'clock. Dao looked exhausted and I was tired after two interrupted nights.

'Let's go to bed now. Tomorrow you'll spend the day with Willow while Charlie and I go up the coast in her helicopter and try to locate the island.'

Dao's face was mutinous, but I gave her a serious look; this time there were no options.

'Did Master – sorry, I mean Bram – did he have a dishwasher?' I said to change the topic. 'Do you know how to operate one?'

She came around the corner, still silent and I showed her how to start the dishwasher. As I turned the kitchen light off she said, 'Who is coming here in the morning?'

She must have heard some of my conversation with Paul. 'It's a guy I know from the army. He's going to install some extra security in the house. Do you understand what that means?'

She shook her head.

'See that little white thing with a red dot up in the corner there? That's a sensor – if I move it will blink. It picks up anything that moves if it's larger than a cat and has what's called body heat. If the chair fell over it wouldn't react at all. If someone breaks in when the system is activated the sirens go off both inside and outside and it comes up on a computer screen at the place where they monitor the alarm. Then they call to check if I'm at home and if I am not they send one of their guards to see what's going on and call the police.'

She was one step ahead. 'But if they ring here first the burglar could answer the phone and pretend to be you.'

'He could try – but there's a password he needs to know. If he couldn't give them the password they would ring the police right away.'

'What is the password?' She looked at me as if she was testing me.

'Bamyan.'

I knew she would remember it like she did everything she was told, but the word would mean nothing to her. For me it was a significant word, the name of the place where my recurring nightmare scene had happened in real life. The place where I had lost close friends, and everything had changed.

On the way upstairs to bed she surprised me. 'I am going to sleep in my room tonight,' she said decisively. 'I must learn to be braver.'

'You don't have to – I don't mind if you sleep in my room. I don't want you to lie awake all night worrying and waiting for trouble.'

I knew the day's events had alarmed her. The tension in her stance had been nearly palpable when I told her about the alarm system changes. The decision to 'be braver' seemed strange in the circumstances, but I made no further comment. We went to bed, and I read for a while, but she stayed in her room and after a while I turned the light off. In the middle of the night, I woke and realised that she was back in my room, asleep on top of the duvet beside me with nothing over her. I got out of bed and covered her with the rug from the chair and went back to sleep.

6

MONDAY

The next morning, I found her in front of the bathroom mirror. She was looking at herself with an expression of intense distaste.

'I wish he hadn't cut all my hair off!' she said and clutched her head with both hands.

This was news. I had imagined that she had been forced to have her hair very short for years, since her mother died. 'When did he cut it off?'

'Not very long ago, to punish me. First he whipped me and then he cut my hair off, all rough.'

She turned around to face me and I saw the exact split second when she stopped herself from saying whatever it was she had nearly said. Instead, she smiled. 'But it looks a lot better than it did before. I had never been to a hairdresser before – it was really nice.'

I knew the moment had passed and wondered if I was ever going to find out what lay behind those bitten-back words.

The doorbell rang at half past seven and I did a tour of the two lower floors of the house with Paul. He knew his stuff all right and asked a lot of questions.

'I'm on a contract with a security monitoring company,' I

84

told him. 'I will call them and say you're working on the system. I've written down their number and the security code word in case you need it and the code for the panel.'

Paul looked over his notes and suggested a few changes and left with my spare key. I was interested to see that he had a perfectly plain white van with no windows in the rear. No sign-writing or anything that identified what his business was. I raced upstairs to make sure there were no signs that two people had slept in my room. Not that he needed to go up there, and it did not really matter. But because Dao looked like an underage teenager I would rather he had nothing to speculate about. I had introduced her as the daughter of a friend who was visiting and had to keep things consistent with that.

At Willow's house the front door was unlocked, and we found her standing in the kitchen reading the back of a packet of baby cereal.

The twins were in the recessed breakfast area that Matt had partitioned off with a little picket fence. The whole space was theirs, full of toys and cushions and no furniture apart from a table in the corner. Willow and Matt called the space 'the cage' and the twins spent a lot of time there.

'Perfect, really,' Willow said to Dao who was gazing at the twins with cautious fascination.

'They can see me wherever I am – in the kitchen or at my desk in the dining room. I can see and hear them, and now that they've just started to crawl I can safely leave them when I go to the laundry or into the garden or whatever.'

Today the twins were asleep on their sheepskins in the cage, relaxed with arms and legs flung out as if someone had casually dropped them.

'They do look comical,' I said. 'Do other people's babies do that?'

'Do what?' said Willow. 'Sleep?'

'No, I mean sleep like that, wherever they happen to keel over – on the floor?'

'God, no! Other people's kids get carted off to their room and tucked into a tidy cot and the door is closed and if they cry some adult goes in and worries in case they are wet or dirty or need burping. So much hard work goes into it, you wouldn't believe it.'

She turned to Dao and laughed. 'We decided to treat them like little animals, and they've been behaving accordingly ever since. But don't tell anyone – we'd probably get reported for child neglect.'

We sat at the table with a cup of tea and I put the drawings that Dao had done in front of Willow. Dao was half-turned away, still looking at the twins while I watched Willow's face as she turned the pages.

'My God, I wasn't expecting anything like this. You'll have to tell me who these guys are, Dao. Did you do one of Master?'

Dao turned back towards Willow and pointed to the last page.

'That's him – that's his real name.'

'I'll probably ask you a bit more about that later on,' said Willow. 'I did some research yesterday and found out bits and pieces, but we'll leave that until the end of the day when Hunter comes back. I imagine Charlie is waiting?'

'She's expecting me in half an hour, so I'd better get going. Where's Plum? Is she still asleep?'

Plum is our much younger sister, the tail-ender. Willow and I used to call her a foundling when she was little; we are both tall and blondish and Plum is just like a plum, short and round and dark. She lives in the little garden flat at Willow's place which means a long commute to Auckland University. She would be better off living closer to the city centre, but she likes living with Willow and Matt.

'No, she's helping our neighbour in his warehouse this morning – wrapping and packing. She'll be back after lunch some time – she wants to meet you, Dao. Hunter, the camera bag is on the floor beside the hall table and the long lens is in the separate cylindrical case.'

Dao looked at me, borderline ready to stop me going. I ignored the look, smiled and walked towards the door.

'I'll see you two later,' I said and left.

Charlie was doing pre-flight checks when I arrived. Somehow or other she had managed to raise the money to buy a Eurocopter Squirrel AS350, a truly top-class machine. I remembered her telling me all about it when she first got it; how many armed forces and rescue services use it, how it was great for high altitudes and the only helicopter ever to touch down on the top of Mount Everest. She had chosen the single engine model and opted for four passenger seats instead of six. 'Leaves lots of room for luggage,' she had said with a grin. Some of her clients were wealthy people holidaying in New Zealand. 'You should see what some of those women bring for a couple of weeks' stay! Leaves Kristen for dead. Not to mention the golf clubs.'

'Just hang on a minute, Hunter – nearly finished,' she said now and I stood to one side and watched her ticking things off on a list, focused on the task as usual. There is nothing of the casual chopper cowboy about Charlie. She still follows army regulations and seeing her now in camo pants and a sweatshirt made me smile, as did the thought of the difference between the big grey Chinook she used to fly and this little white bubble.

'Like a toy compared to what you used to fly. I'm glad it's not a Robinson.'

'Of course, not – I have no desire to burn if I crash,' she said over her shoulder, crouching down to inspect something under the body of the helicopter.

Then she turned around and grinned. 'Don't know if I told you – last time I met Paul for a beer he sang me a new version of I'm glad *I'm not a Kennedy*? He calls it 'I'm glad it's not a Robinson' – very funny. But you'd be amazed if I told you the price of this toy! Not to mention what it costs me to insure it.'

'But you are doing OK?'

'God yes! I'm earning good money, doing what I like and around here I'm surrounded by blokes – what more could I wish for?'

This last statement was an old joke from our army days. Charlie is completely immune to male attraction and has never had eyes for anyone except Kristen for as long as I have known her.

The day was slightly overcast, but it looked as if the forecast rain might hold off. Charlie assured me we would find clear sky on the north-east coast. We cruised across the northern suburbs discussing tactics.

'OK then, how about we head way north of where she could possibly have set out from. Then we fly back slowly along the coast until we reach a point too far away for her to have walked from to your cabin. That should cover it. You haven't worked out how far she had walked, have you?'

'Not a clue – we'll have to check every little bay. What's the range and speed of this thing?'

'Cruising speed about two hundred and fifty kilometres per hour,' she said. 'I can do about six hundred and fifty kilometres, or maybe close to seven hundred – depends on the weather. The tanks are full.'

I watched the suburbs thinning underneath us. 'I wouldn't think she had walked very far – no shoes, rough ground, rain and wind – not to mention not having any food. But it's anybody's guess.'

Charlie passed a map over; folded to show the area we were interested in. 'I've checked out some good landmarks so we'll know when we're in a line with the cabin, or nearly – I can't identify exactly where the cabin is, so it's a rough guess. How far do you think it is from the cabin to the coast in a straight line?'

'Perhaps five or six kilometres.'

She leant over and pointed at a spot on the map. 'Let's

turn and start looking when we get to this little estuary here –
I marked it with a cross.'

We found it easily and Charlie turned and flew slowly
south along the meandering coastline. I took the first version
of the plan that Dao had drawn out of my pocket and
smoothed it out on top of the map - and then suddenly there
it was. We had come over the top of a little headland and
there in front of us was the bay.

'That's it, but don't slow down – fly past.'

'OK, will do.'

I craned my neck and got a good look as the bay slid by
under us.

'Exactly as she drew it – every detail right. And the big
shed is about five degrees off being parallel with the house.'

'What's that?' said Charlie. 'Five degrees – how?'

'I'll tell you later. Let's carry on for ten minutes or so
before we turn around, so it doesn't look as if we are spying
on him. I don't want to alarm the bastard. When we come
back I'd like to be just out from the shoreline so I can take
some photos. And we need the exact GPS coordinates.'

'I love my work,' said Charlie. 'Look at the view outside
my office window.'

Green hills sloped down to little slivers of sandy beaches,
cliff escarpments here and there and a huge blue sky like a
dome above us. Below us the glittering sea stretched to the far
horizon and the sun cast a shadow of the helicopter that
undulated over the swell just to one side.

'I am so lucky, you know. I did those secret bodyguard
jobs for a couple of years, quite boring having to be out of the
country for weeks on end with some of them. But it gave me
the money to pay about a quarter of the price for the Squirrel
in cash. And I met some very famous people – and some
infamous ones.'

'We are both lucky. And we would still be lucky, even if
we had to clean toilets for a living – compared to some.'

She knew what I meant; there was no need to explain. We

had both lost friends in that unforgiving conflict and seen others mutilated and crippled and I had nearly lost my right leg. We were lucky indeed.

I got the camera ready as we retraced our course at a slower speed, a bit lower and not directly overhead. I had Matt's long lens on the camera, and I knew I would get close-ups with great detail. I twisted in the seat so I could shoot sideways and even backwards as we flew past the place. And there it was again: a small bay, just a little shallow indentation in the coast with an uninterrupted view to the eastern horizon. A small white house with a green roof sat about a hundred metres back on an open grassed area that merged into the sand of the beach. A large, nearly square shed, new-looking and with a couple of corrugated clear plastic panels in the roof, placed closer to the water. There was some native bush with big trees behind and to the side of the clearing and a large-canopied pohutukawa tree at the northern end of the beach. Dog kennels behind the house, a clothesline and a smaller shed.

A man came out of the house and looked up at us with his arm shading his eyes and I hung over the back of my seat to get as many shots as possible before we were out of range. Just as I was turning forwards again I saw the garden Dao had mentioned and took some pictures of that too. An extensive plantation, separated from the house by a rise with a wide belt of scrubby bushes and trees. There were several large plots cleared among the trees, hard to see from the air but marijuana seemed a likely crop.

'Done!'

'Was that the gardens? Wonder if he's growing pot?'

'I'm prepared to bet it isn't just potatoes and cabbages. But I haven't asked her yet and she might not know, her general knowledge is very limited.'

'Let's find the cabin,' said Charlie. 'Now that we've found what we came for we have loads of time. I'd like to see how far it is from where she started.'

Finding the cabin took a while. We had to backtrack and find the main road so I could navigate by the route I take by car, find the two turn-offs after the main highway and then the farm track and finally the bush track across the creek and up the hill.

'I'd better call Mac and tell him it's us up here,' I said. 'After that intruder he'll wonder what's going on when he sees us circling this low over the bush.'

Mac laughed when he got my call.

'I'm standing on the terrace watching you right now. Heard the chopper circling low over your hill and wondered what the heck was going on. Not that I can see your part of the bush, but I knew it was just near the cabin. What are you doing?'

'An old army friend is showing off her new chopper and we thought we'd have a look at the cabin. It's nearly impossible to see from the air – it's well hidden under the trees.'

When I put the phone down Charlie rolled into a steep turn, gained altitude and pointed towards the distant glitter of the ocean.

'Look over there – you can't see the actual bay that you call the island but it's straight ahead of us now. So, it's east-north-east of the cabin, about eight kilometres away.'

We contemplated the steeply undulating landscape in silence. A succession of hills stretched like deep corrugations all the way to the coast, some densely forested. There were occasional open fields and not much else. It was hard to imagine how Dao had walked that far over such difficult terrain without shoes. She would have been forced to walk around ravines and sheer drops. She must have walked two or three times the straight-line distance.

'Let's go back and fly down the coast from the north again – a bit inland from the coast this time so we're not straight over the house. I want to see where the nearest road is.'

We found the road without much trouble and traced it

back from the coast to the nearest junction. It was a gravel road, little more than a track that just touched the next bay north of 'the island' before it straightened out northwards. I marked it on the map.

'I don't know how Dao is going to feel when she finds out how close she was to that little road. She spent years thinking they were on an island and now she'll know there is a road just a couple of kilometres north of the place. She could have reached it easily. He must have a vehicle parked somewhere there – he goes up the coast for a few minutes in his boat, hops in his truck or whatever he has and drives away to do his shopping.'

I felt Charlie looking sideways at me. 'You're really fond of her, aren't you, Hunter? You really worry about her?'

'I do – she's my responsibility now. That Chinese proverb Willow mentioned got it right – if you save someone's life you become responsible for them.'

Charlie reached over and patted my leg. 'Just be a bit careful, comrade – we don't want you falling in love with her and things getting all complicated.'

'Oh, for God's sake, Charlie! Of course, I won't – it's like being fond of a child. She's been abused and maltreated and isolated. She needs help and support, that's all.'

'Yeah, I know – but she is actually a young woman and she's very smart and pretty. I can see how lovely she'll be when she stops looking like a skeleton – trust me mate, I have a good eye for that sort of thing. Be careful – for both your sakes.'

'And she's not my style at all – you've met Vivian, haven't you?'

This was a deliberate red herring; I would never live with Vivian; it was just a convenient and mostly entertaining friendship with sex as an added-value component. It successfully side-tracked Charlie who has a very low opinion of Vivian. But as we talked about other things I admitted to myself that she was right. I was getting very fond of Dao, intrigued in more ways than one. She was smart and challenging and as Charlie had pointed out, she was attractive now and would be more so when she put on some weight. Fortunately, she regarded me as an uncle or older brother, because anything else might be a disaster. The process of integrating her into normal life needed no emotional distractions.

Back in town we went to a café for lunch and spent an hour discussing security and speculating about what the worst-case scenario might be. Charlie was puzzled by my insistence that Bramville would try to kill Dao if he could.

'But why would he, Hunter? I don't get it – so she got away, and she could tell people about him, but then what? Surely that's not enough to make him want to kill her? It doesn't make sense. You say you really believe he might – but on what grounds? Who would kill someone for something they could just deny or explain away? It's a bit drastic, isn't it? And by now she would have told the story anyway, it's way too late.'

It was hard to think of a convincing argument. My own conviction was based on a whole raft of details and impressions and some of them would seem pretty flimsy to someone else.

'It's hard to describe why – I'm not really sure myself what it is that makes me believe it. I know Dao's fears could be the result of long-term brutality. But it's more than that. You know I said there's something she's not telling me? She nearly came out with it again – yesterday. It was on the tip of her tongue. And I think it's something relating to Bramville, something she knows that is so dangerous for him that he would kill her to stop her giving evidence. Whatever that is, it's the reason she feels sure that, if he catches up with her, he will kill her. I've been trying to imagine what it is – I've got a mental list of possible reasons, but it's all just speculation.'

Charlie drained her smoothie with a long slurping noise and looked seriously at me.

'You know what? I'm not saying it's impossible, but I don't think it's probable – not at all.'

She held up her hand when I started to respond. 'No, hear me out, please. I was going to say that I think the whole killing threat is nothing but Dao's fear of that brute of a man – she imagines he's capable of absolutely anything, because he's had her under complete control for so long. But it makes no difference. I will be there to back you up if you need a bodyguard for you or for her. And if something nasty really needs to be done I'm up for that too.'

She grinned. 'Two is better than one, even just for planning. So, let's make some plans about how we're going to react if something happens. Let's go to my place now and I'll give you that gun and the ammo.'

Having her as back-up was the best support I could have. There is only so much one person can do and having Charlie would be like having a clone, who knew the same things I did and who would not hesitate to use whatever she could lay her hands on if things got tricky.

Charlie and Kristen live between Remuera and Mt Wellington; I've never quite figured out exactly what they call it. It's halfway between the Ardmore airport where Charlie keeps the Squirrel and Kristen's office in the city. Seeing Charlie in her house is a study in total contrasts. Her partner is a sophisticated city woman, and the house is elegant with modern art on the walls and exceptionally tidy. Charlie looked comically out of place in her army style gear and boots.

She led me though the house to the spare room and opened the wardrobe door with a flourish. The gun safe was a featureless black monolith, its only detail a keypad lock.

'What do you think of that? I had it installed last year – isn't it great?'

'It looks like a seriously serious piece of gear,' I said. 'I don't know what I expected, but not this – looks like something some Texan gun nut would have.'

'That's exactly what it is. One hundred and forty-five kilos of 14-gauge steel,' said Charlie proudly and ran her hand over the matt surface. 'The gun-safe equivalent of an armoured vehicle – or a bit better. And it's got a re-locker system too. It's a super-safe safe.'

'What the hell is a re-locker?'

Charlie is a fiend for technical stuff; I knew she was dying to tell me.

'If you try to drill out the lock or cut it out with a blowtorch there's a sheet of glass inside the door that shatters. Which trips a wire that releases a spring-loaded bolt that locks the door – re-locks it. But the bolt isn't where the first lock is, it's in a so-called random place, so you don't know where to start attacking it next.'

She studied my face for a reaction, and it must have been what she hoped for.

'Impressive, eh? It's also got concealed hinges and it's bolted into the concrete floor through the base – you'd practically have to demolish the room to get it out.'

She grinned and unlocked the door.

'And what if you forget the code? You'd never get into it again, I suppose?'

'Can't forget it, mate, it's the date of our anniversary. The thing I can't do is move house.'

The door swung silently open and revealed one shotgun, a rifle and two handguns.

'Kristen was concerned about always having guns in the house – well, she went crazy to tell you the truth. She hates guns – so last year I got this instead of having them in the locked cupboard in the front hall. She knows nobody can get into it and take the guns and shoot us while we sleep. I think she's got used to it now. I put it here so she wouldn't see it all the time.'

She took out one of her two Glock 36 semi-automatics and handed it to me.

'Hold this, will you?' She reached into the shelf at the top and pulled out two magazines and a box of ammunition.

'This model only takes six bullets, so I'll give you two mags and some spare ammo. And a holster, if you want one.'

She had two holsters, and I took the one that fitted on a belt so I could wear it at the side or at the back. The Glock was new to me and it seemed small and light in my hand, deceptively harmless.

'What made you decide on the Glock? Was it the weight – lack of weight I mean?'

'No, I just like the way this model has short recoil, and it doesn't take up much room. This slim-line model is one of the shortest, easy to carry without being obvious and very light. You could conceal a longer one, but I can't, not enough room on my body without looking loaded down. And my hands aren't that big. I'm very comfortable with this gun.'

She took the other one out, tossed it from one hand to the other.

'Not much weight to worry about. And Glocks are very reliable, the most popular law-enforcement pistol in the US, so it's got to be good – you know how many people they shoot every year.'

She laughed and closed the cabinet.

I borrowed a plastic supermarket bag and put everything in it, stowed the gun under the front seat and drove home. Paul had just finished and was ready to leave.

'I was just about to call you,' he said. 'I want to show you a few things and we need to load the software on your phone and laptop so you can see what's going on.'

We did a complete tour of the house again, inside and out as Paul pointed things out. The front and back of the house now had movement-activated LED lights and video cameras. Two extra sensors inside in addition to the ones I already had, two video cameras inside and all angles taken into account.

'Now listen,' he said when he had shown me how neatly

the little hard drive box fitted into the pantry. He was ticking things off on his fingers and he only just had enough fingers.

'The outside lights come on when someone approaches closer than three metres from the wall and the entire span of the wall is covered – nobody can get to the doors without triggering the light. When someone triggers the light the cameras start recording and you get an alert on your laptop and your phone rings; you can set a special buzz signal, so you know that's the call. And you can see what's happening from either device.'

He walked over to the balcony door and pointed. 'The wide-angle camera out there captures the entire width of the courtyard. The back and front of the house are independent, so you can turn one off and have the other system on. I was going to put infrared beam gates on the stairs, but I changed my mind – couldn't find a neat way of mounting them without spoiling the decor. I've put a double sensor up instead of a single on both lower floors – one beam looks diagonally across the stairs, about halfway up and the other covers the room. If the sensors pick something up, the camera starts recording and your phone rings. If you arm the alarm system when you go out, just like you always did, then the sirens become involved if there is any kind of breach, otherwise not.'

We went through it again and I checked it on the phone and the tablet.

'This is great,' I said. 'Exactly what I wanted. How much do I owe you?'

He shook his head. 'Don't know yet – I'll send you a bill when I get my account from the supplier. They invoice me once a week for everything I've picked up. You'll get mate's rates, but it won't be cheap.'

He grinned at me and waved his arm in a sweeping gesture.

'There's a lot of security gear in this place now – one day you have to tell me why all this is necessary – it's not as if you have anything worth stealing, eh? Let me know if anything needs tweaking and keep that dog of yours under control at night or you'll be up all night checking who's coming up the stairs. And by the way, I have put in a continuous power supply pack so you don't have to rely on a battery that doesn't last forever.'

'Is that one of those battery things that charges continually?'

'Yeah, a pretty good one – it will keep the system running for days of activity if there's an outage. I'll come and check it once a year.'

Just as I was closing the front door behind him he turned around. 'And no need to worry, Hunter. Nobody finds out what I install and where - it's strictly between you and me.'

I closed the door behind him and went to save the pictures from Matt's camera on my laptop. I spent a moment looking at the shot of Bramville, studying what I could see of his face under the shadow of his raised arm before I left the house again.

The traffic was full-on as I headed for Willow's place and it took twice the time it usually does. On an impulse I had made a detour on the way and bought Dao a cell phone.

'I want a phone just like this one,' I said and handed mine over to the spotty young guy behind the counter.

'I want a different coloured back or one of those covers, red perhaps. And can you load that app on it – the one people call 'find my phone' or something like it? Do you do that sort of thing?'

'I can do anything,' he said with utter self-confidence. 'I'll have to put in a fully charged battery, of course, so it works right away. The one in the box isn't charged, but I have some out the back. I use them when people bring in phones with flat batteries and claim there's something wrong with the phone.'

He was back in a couple of minutes and started assembling the phone. 'I can leave this battery in and keep the one from the box, if that's OK? You can check the whereabouts of this phone from yours or from your computer – I'll show you how it works.'

Half an hour later I left the young wizard to close the shop and returned to the car with everything set up.

MONDAY EVENING

By the time I got to Willow's it was dark. I let myself in and heard voices from the kitchen. Willow was doing something at the counter with Plum and Dao watching and Scruff asleep in a corner. The cage was empty; the twins must be in bed already. I watched for a minute before I spoke and Plum turned around, looking happy and animated, as she usually does.

'We're teaching Dao how to make spinach and feta quiche. We've had a great afternoon, haven't we, Dao?'

Dao smiled back at Plum, but she looked tired. Willow gave Plum a little push with her elbow.

'Pour Hunter a glass of wine and one for me too, will you? I'll just pop this in the oven and then you girls can do the salad and the dressing. I've got a few things I want to discuss with Hunter.'

The dining table was covered in papers and files. Willow opened a manila folder and handed me a printout.

'I printed out the addresses of all the New World supermarkets south of the Harbour Bridge. It's impossible to say if they were all there ten years ago, but I'm sure most would have been. I think it might be easiest to use Google Earth first off and see if Dao recognises the shopping centre.

Once we've identified the suburb we should be able to find the school and maybe even the place where they lived, perhaps the GP clinic they belonged to. And once we know which electorate they lived in I can trawl through the old electoral rolls and check the Johnsons. But I might be able to use what we know of her parents already and check with the Registry of Births and find out if she was born in New Zealand. We must get a birth certificate for her – she'll need that for all sorts of things. And the school will have records as well.'

She lowered her voice and leaned towards me.

'Just a couple of things before the girls join us. How much are we going to tell Plum? I told her that Dao is the daughter of an army friend of yours and that she's been living on an island with her mother, being home schooled, very isolated. I told Dao that I was going to say this before Plum came back. Do you know what she said?'

I shook my head.

'She said, 'but that is a lie' and I had to explain that a lie of convenience was the only way to protect her so her story doesn't leak out. I said we'll just have to ask Plum to forgive us later on. I'm sure she has serious doubts about my ethics now. Anyway, she agreed it was a good story and Plum hasn't expressed any great curiosity for details so far, so that's all good. But while Dao and I were alone here this morning I asked a few questions – things I thought you would not have thought of.'

'Such as?'

'I said, 'how did you get on when you had a period?' and she told me that she had been forced to improvise. But she's never heard of tampons and she's basically as ignorant as a five-year old. So I've promised to take her shopping and show her what she needs and where to find it in the supermarket. She knows about sex though – and that's the second issue.'

She drank some wine and looked at me with a slight frown.

'When I tried to make sure she had some basic knowledge of reproduction – seeing she has been in cold storage since the age of ten, lots of gaps in her knowledge – she said, 'I know about fucking' and I stopped asking questions. Do you think he abused her? What if she's pregnant or has some venereal disease?'

'I don't know. She said the same thing to me, when she told me about the man Bramville was going to sell her to – she said 'he'd fuck me' or something like it. I must talk to her. I suppose she should have a pregnancy test – I know about those test kits you can buy, so that's not a problem. How about you buy one when you buy whatever you are going to get and then we have it if it's needed?'

'OK, I will.'

But now she was smiling, and I could see that she had saved the good bit for last. She is, after all, the sister who saved the best sweet for last even as a three-year-old. She took another sip of wine; she was trying to stop herself from grinning.

'Now brace yourself, Hunter. We're going to have to find someone who knows about maths. A lot of maths, possibly university level. But as you know, my ideas on the subject are a bit vague.'

Plum and Dao came over from the kitchen and Willow looked at Dao.

'Are you going to tell him about the books, or do you want me to?'

Dao sat down beside me. She looked away into the corner of the room, she was very uncomfortable. 'Please, Willow – it's nothing to make a fuss about.'

'You just let me be the judge of that. I think it's incredible and if I'd heard it from someone else I would never have believed it – never.'

Plum was staring at Willow, intent on what was to come; this was news to her too. Willow took great pains to tailor the story to fit what she had told Plum about Dao's background.

'It turns out that in the house Dao lived in on the island there was a storage cupboard in the laundry where the previous owner had left some boxes of books. When Dao was twelve or thirteen she started looking through them and found dozens of maths books. And Dao loved maths – she had been in an accelerated maths programme at school from the age of six, before she lived on the island. Must have had a great teacher. So she started working her way through these books on her own. There was nobody with the knowledge to help her and she never asked. She just worked away with her library of what I'm sure were both high school and university texts. And of course, she got stuck sometimes, because she was a child. When she came up against something that stopped her continuing along a certain path she would put the problem aside and start a different topic. Sometimes she found another book later on with some fact that explained what had stopped her earlier and she could continue a process she had abandoned. She never talked about it, just thought of it as a hobby to keep herself entertained. She says the first two books took her months to read – well, the very first step was trying to understand which book even to start with. And when she says read she actually means learn.'

Dao said nothing, just sat there looking as if she was mentally divorcing herself from the story, trying to avoid being the centre of attention. Plum, who usually has a comment or an opinion on every possible topic, was completely silent. I noticed how carefully Willow was phrasing it; no indication that getting the books without Bram noticing must have been very hard. I made a mental note to ask Dao later how she had managed this. Willow smiled at my expression, glanced at Dao and continued.

'Anyway – over the years since then Dao has learnt – or as she modestly says 'thinks she has learnt' – most of those books and she has two favourites. Dao, tell Hunter what they are called, I've forgotten the names.'

Dao spoke reluctantly, not looking at any one of us. 'They

were just two that I thought were interesting. I would like to continue with some of the things I found in them. One is called *Equations that changed the world* – it's full of lovely things.'

Her gaze shifted from the middle distance and settled on my face. 'Like Euler's Formula, you know the polyhedron equation? That is so clever – beautiful. And the other book I liked was quite simple, but it was sort of clever too and fun. It was called *Linear Algebra 101* – I think those were the best ones.'

I sat for a minute with my gaze locked on her face, trying to digest this. And at the same time, I registered how her way of expressing herself was changing day by day, becoming more adult, more assured.

'Holy cow – I don't even know what linear algebra is. Not to mention the poly-what's it thing, never even heard the word before. It certainly sounds like university level stuff to me – 101 usually means the first paper for the first year of study. You're right Willow, we need to find out more about this – it is way beyond anything you or I can help with. Dao, are you the only one in the family who's good at this?'

I saw that she understood the way I had phrased the question. Plum had no idea she had no family and Dao's brief reply fitted right in.

'Yes, I'm the only one who likes maths. I've liked it since I learnt to count and write numbers.'

Plum finally opened her mouth. 'It's awesome, I can't imagine how you did it – just by yourself. I couldn't do it. The pain I had to go through to get good enough grades to get into architecture school, special coaching and hours of grief – not something I'd call fun.'

I emptied my glass and rose.

'We'll have to discuss this later. Obviously we have to find someone for Dao to talk to so she can continue her studies, if that's what she wants – but for the moment we must go home. Thanks for everything.'

Plum was disappointed. 'I thought you'd stay for dinner – there's plenty of food.'

'Sorry, but we'll have to take a rain-check. Dao's exhausted – look at her – she hardly got any sleep last night. And I've got to get a proposal away either tonight or tomorrow or I miss a deadline. But we'll have dinner with you another day, perhaps when Matt's back?'

In the car Dao said, 'You lied – about me being so tired.'

'That's true – but sometimes it's a simple way to be able to do what you want to without upsetting anyone. But you do look tired, and I didn't want us to spend the whole evening there. You and I have things to do. And I really must do the last checks of that proposal and send it away.'

After a simple meal we sat down together on the sofa and started searching for Dao's suburb. She had the tablet, and I had the laptop. Between us was Willow's list of New World supermarket addresses.

'And when we've found the right supermarket and your school you might find your house too. And Willow thought finding your family doctor would be useful.'

We did a quick Google Earth tutorial about how to search for specific addresses and how to rotate the camera views and then Dao was off, looking up addresses and checking them out. We shared the list, she started from the top and I started from the bottom and after ten minutes she found it.

'Look, Hunter! I found it – this is the place.'

She moved closer and held up the tablet. 'Here's the supermarket and a bit further down the road is the school.'

She rotated the camera view, and we were looking at the gate to a primary school. She panned left a fraction and handed me the tablet.

'See – there's that cell phone tower, the one they made all the fuss about. That little building next to it, under those trees – that's the changing shed beside the swimming pool.'

We sat there for a moment, absorbed in the image. How easy this had been compared to my first idea of driving past every supermarket in the southern suburbs. And it was good that Dao had found it herself. She took the tablet back and got busy again, sitting back into the corner of the sofa with the tablet on a cushion on her knees. I watched in silence, sure that I knew what she was doing but not wanting to spoil her pleasure. Ten minutes later she straightened up.

'There! That's where we lived.' She pointed at a row of two-storied council houses, each one quite narrow. 'That one there, second from the left – that was ours.'

She had traced her route to school backwards, remembering corners and crossings and she had found it. Her face was triumphant.

'Well done,' I said. 'You got the hang of that very quickly. It's a great piece of technology, isn't it?'

But she was hardly listening, off again on another search. I left her to it and went upstairs to try to think of a way to keep Scruff from going down the stairs in the night without having to keep the bedroom door shut. Maybe something as a barrier at the top? Nothing useful came to mind and I was interrupted by Dao calling out from the living room.

'I found our doctor – in the street behind the shopping centre.'

I joined her in the living room, and we discussed what Willow would be able to find out from the doctor and the school.

'But come along now and let me show you what Paul installed today.'

We started downstairs in the courtyard and continued up through the house, as I explained all the surveillance equipment and how we would be able to see what was going on. We finished on the top floor with Dao limping quite badly again after all the stairs.

'Now, how do you think we're going to stop Scruff from going down the stairs and triggering the infrared beam and waking us up?'

Dao smiled at Scruff who had followed us every step of the way.

'We close the door,' she said. 'You don't need to hear what's happening in the house if you have the laptop or the phone beside the bed. The warning, what's it called – the alert? – would wake you up and you could take the gun and stand at the top of the stairs and shoot him.'

So, I had been right earlier on, she really wanted me to kill him. I tried to make light of it.

'What a bloodthirsty girl you are. OK, let's have the door closed.'

It was still a bit early to go to bed, even for tired people. This might be a good time to find out more about those books and how she had managed to keep her studies secret on the island. It had been in the back of my mind since we left Willow's house. The whole thing was so incredible that I really wanted to know.

We made mugs of tea and sat down in the living room again.

'So, tell me about those books, Dao. Where did you really find them and how did you manage to keep them secret?'

She cradled her mug between her hands and spoke very quietly. Her eyes had an inward look; she was reliving the past in her mind.

'When my mother left I had to do everything she had done. I washed everything in the tub in the laundry at the back of the house – there is no washing machine. And there's a big cupboard there, like a wardrobe but with shelves inside with lots old stuff – probably from the person who lived there before. The books had some other person's name in them. On the floor under the bottom shelf were four boxes. And one day I decided to have a look. They were full of books about mathematics!'

Her focus was back on me now and she smiled. 'So, every time it seemed safe I took one or two and I hid them inside my trousers under my shirt. It was lucky I had to wear those huge clothes because I could hide things and they didn't show. I had a hiding place in the shed. And after a while I had quite a lot of books out there and I sorted out the ones that seemed to be easiest and then I put some of the others back. I kind of got the boxes sorted so they were in the right order. You know - the most difficult-looking books in one box and so on. And at the same time, I had to try to figure out which ones belonged to the same kind of maths. I had to sort of list them in my head and try to keep them in groups. Anyway, that's how it started and over the years it kept me going. That and singing, it kept me sane.'

She had not mentioned singing before, but right now I wanted to hear about the books.

'How on earth did you manage to hide books in the shed? How come he didn't find them?'

She smiled with quiet triumph. 'He thought he was clever, and I was stupid, so sometimes he didn't check things properly. There was a big wooden crate, huge, next to where I slept, and it had two thick wooden boards sort of running across under it so it sat a bit off the ground. I think it had been there for a long time. It was half-full of bits of rubbish – bits of metal and all sorts of things. So, I pushed the books way in under it and then I would lie on my front and reach in with an old broom handle I had found in the crate and kind of hook them out when it was safe. And he never discovered.'

'Did you read in the evenings after he'd locked you in? Did you have a light in the shed?'

'No, but I used to read after he chained me up, when it was light enough. There are some parts of the roof that are made of plastic, nearly clear – and they let in a lot of light. I was in there from straight after I had finished tidying up in the kitchen, so it was early, plenty of daylight left – at least in the summer. And in the morning I always woke up early. I knew I would hear him coming – he coughs in the morning, for ages. So I just had to be careful about not having my pencil and or any paper where he could see them. I just shoved everything in under the crate.'

'So, you had paper and a pencil – I wondered about that.'

She nodded. 'Yes, I did – some anyway. I took paper bags and scraps of paper and smuggled them back to the shed, anything I could write on. The inside of the cereal boxes was good. I flattened them and had lots of space to write. And when I ran out I wrote on the dirt floor with that long nail I had found. I had two pencils, well one at a time – I stole them from his desk. He had an old mug full of pens and pencils. I used to take my pencil into the kitchen and sharpen it with the vegetable knife and then I'd put the shavings in my pocket and throw them away somewhere so he wouldn't see them in the bin.'

Willow was right; the whole thing was mind-boggling. Dao had managed to carry out serious study under very difficult circumstances with minimal resources and only her determination to learn to motivate her. It was possibly the most stunning enterprise I had ever come across.

In my mind's eye I saw her as she had looked when I carried her through the forest to the track after Scruff found her, a skinny waif at the very end of her endurance. And as I sat there looking at her and thinking back it struck me that if she had died that day nobody would ever have known what she had achieved. Somehow that thought had an impact that has stayed with me ever since.

'Dao,' I said. 'Let's do something special one day this week, anything you like – to celebrate what an incredible girl you are. And you really are – very clever and very special. Think about what you might like to do.'

There was only a second's hesitation, she hardly needed to think. 'Can we have dinner in a proper restaurant? One where you sit at a table with candles, and someone comes and serves the food?'

'Of course,' I said, surprised by the idea and wondering

what had led to it. 'Is that something you have always wanted to do?'

'I used to lie in the dark in the shed and think of what I would do if I ever got away – you know, the nicest things I could imagine. And eating in a restaurant; a real restaurant like I had seen on TV when I was little, that was one thing. It would be so different from eating alone in the shed. But what I most wanted to do and I used to dream about it – guess what it was?'

I thought I knew, but it would be cruel to spoil her pleasure. I shook my head and she laughed and said, 'Showers – hot water and soap and shampoo. Sometimes I would dream I was standing in a shower with warm water running over me, just standing there all warm and clean. Lovely! And now I do it every day.'

Just then the phone rang. It was Nigel, my neighbour on the left side. We had moved in at the same time and they took my mail in when I was away. Nice enough people, but boring.

'Hunter,' said Nigel. 'Something a bit odd happened today and Margie says I should tell you, just in case. I knew the guy with the white van was OK because I saw you talking to him outside early this morning. When I went out to get the mail at eleven the white van was back, but there was a man on the other side of the street. Just standing there under that big tree on the sidewalk looking across at your place – there was something about the way he just stood there, it looked a bit unusual. So I checked again when I got inside and he was still there. He was talking on the phone now, but still looking at your place.'

'Perhaps he wants to buy my house? But seriously, what was it that worried you? What kind of man was he? Could you describe him?'

'He had a baseball cap on so I didn't get a good look at his face, but I would guess he was in his thirties or forties, quite skinny. A bit scruffy, looked like a workman on his way to work, only it was the wrong time of day. And he took a couple of photos of your place before he moved on. I was standing well back from the window watching him.'

'Don't know anyone who fits the description, but I'll be a bit careful. The guy in the white van is an old army mate of mine who came to put in a new alarm system. I suppose you saw him putting up new outside lights and all sorts of things?'

I knew Nigel would have noticed. He's retired and his wife still goes out to work so he has plenty of time to keep an eye on things. I did not want him to think I was in some kind of trouble.

'Yes, I saw him putting new lights up both back and front. You're not in trouble, are you? I mean some kind of threat or whatever?'

'No, nothing like that but I had a break-in at my cabin, and it reminded me that I must get things fixed here. I was going to do it when I bought the house, but I never got around to it.'

I thanked him and ended the call. When I turned the room behind me was empty. I switched off the lights, picked up the laptop and went upstairs. Dao was standing by the window in her room looking out into the dark with Scruff beside her. She turned around when she heard my steps. I could not read her face, but she looked sad.

'Are you OK? Is something wrong?'

'No, nothing is wrong. I just can't believe it all yet.'

She sighed and dropped her shoulders. 'Hunter, it's so strange. Sometimes it doesn't feel real. I thought the only way I would ever get away was by dying – that's what I have believed for the last couple of years. I thought I would be there forever, that life in that place was all I was going to have. Until I decided to go away and die – and that is how it would have been. I would be dead if you hadn't found me. I'm very lucky.'

I nodded and said nothing. We both knew it was true and there was no need to discuss it. After a minute I held up the laptop. 'I want to show you something.'

We sat side by side on the bed and studied the alarm controls on the screen together.

'Let's say we activate the outside lights, so they come on if someone approaches – and the cameras record everything that moves close to the house, so we don't have to worry about that. I think that's right. And then we set this zone here, see the blue square that says 'level one' – we click on that, and the ground floor is covered. And it includes the extra sensor beam across the stairs to the living room.'

I was pressing icons as I spoke. Dao was leaning over, looking at the display. Everything I activated turned red on the floor plans.

'What about cars on the street? Do they start the cameras?'

'No, Paul said the sensors on that side will pick up things moving on the pavement, but not on the road. But when the camera records – because the sensor picked something up or because we set the camera to record continually – then it takes in everything right across to the other side of the street.'

'And at the back? Can the camera see the whole courtyard – or further?'

'The sensor would pick up someone coming over the wall into the courtyard, either from the neighbours' courtyards or from the lane behind us – and the light will come on as soon as someone lands in the garden. But supposedly it does not react to small things like cats.'

We put Scruff in my room and took turns to use the bathroom. I checked the Remington and leant it into the corner by the wardrobe where I could reach it if I had to go downstairs quickly.

'This is weird,' I said. 'I've never slept in here with the door shut. It feels strange. And mind you don't let Scruff out if you go to the bathroom in the night.'

I was on top of the duvet with my laptop, putting the final touches to the Venezuela proposal and Dao was in the bed, sitting up studying something on the tablet.

'What are you reading?'

'I found a thing about fractals.'

'What are fractals? Is it another maths thing?'

'Yes.'

She looked up and realised this was not a satisfactory answer.

'It's a geometric thing – you can use fractals to describe patterns. It says here *patterns on a progressively smaller scale.*'

She paused and thought for a moment. 'You could change a complex crystal shape or some random shape to a smaller scale. It's very hard to explain. It was mentioned in one of those books on the island, but I didn't understand what it was then. So I'm reading about it now – it's quite difficult.'

'God, it sounds awful. Do you understand it?'

'I sort of do, when I read it, but not properly. Not enough to explain it to someone else. I've only just started reading about it. And there are so many words I have to look up – I don't know enough words. Like this one – iteration? I must look it up. They talk about recurrence too and I know what that means – I think they might mean the same thing. But it's good to be able to look up words – before I just had to either figure it out or else just go on without really knowing what it meant.'

Her new phone was on the floor on my side of the bed; I had not told her about it yet. I picked it up and handed it to her.

'I got this for you – I thought you should have your own.'

Her face registered surprise, a short moment of hesitation and then excitement.

'Thank you!' She held the phone gingerly as if she thought it might break. 'But why are you giving it to me?' And she laughed. 'I don't even know anyone I can call.'

'Of course, you do. I've loaded my number and Willow's and Charlie's and Plum's. That's four people you can call. And you can go on the internet, search for things with Google – all sorts of things.'

She was stroking the phone with her forefinger, smiling and happy.

'I like red – it's my favourite colour.'

I went back to working on the proposal and half an hour later I sent it to London for forwarding to the client and turned my light off.

'You'll have to plug that in to charge soon,' I said.

'I will, in a minute,' she said and in seconds she was lost in the world of fractals again.

I half went to sleep, vaguely aware that she turned the light off some time later. We both woke with a start when my phone buzzed, and the screen of the tablet came alive and glowed in the dark. I sat bolt upright and grabbed the phone to silence the alert. The security display showed that the light in the courtyard had been activated and the camera was recording. I pressed the rear camera icon and with Dao leaning over my arm we watched a man in dark clothes scrambling over the top of the courtyard wall and disappearing into the lane behind the long row of town houses.

'Shit! I didn't expect something to happen so soon. Let's check that recording from the beginning.'

We watched it again: the man is caught in the strong light that comes on as he drops to the ground inside the wall; he takes a couple of steps towards the house before he turns. He leaps up to grab hold of the top of the wall, drops down, tries again and climbs up using his feet and disappears from view. A skinny man wearing a baseball cap that shadows his face and makes it impossible to see his features.

'Do you recognise him? Even I can tell it's not Bram.'

She shook her head. 'It's not him. I don't know who it is. Can we see it again? Didn't you say there was some way of seeing things closer up?'

'It must be someone quite fit,' I said. 'That wall is over six feet tall and he didn't have too much trouble getting up. He looks like he's about six feet himself.'

We went through the recording another couple of times using the zoom function. The intruder seemed to land very heavily as he dropped from the top of the wall but he did not lose his balance. He looked athletic and lean. The way he got back up over the wall was fast and assured, even though he had to try a second time. A fit man and strong. Dao was certain she had never seen him before. Once again I had a feeling that she was about to tell me something, that she was finally going to open up and confide in me. But she controlled the impulse and said nothing.

8

TUESDAY

G oing back to sleep had not been easy and it seemed like no time at all before Scruff woke us wanting to go for his morning session in the garden. I disarmed the alarm on the ground floor, took the Remington and went down to let him out into the courtyard. I left the gun just inside the door so Nigel would not see me with it and followed Scruff outside. I studied the place where the intruder had landed when he dropped down from the top of the wall and saw nothing. Not that footprints would have told me much anyway. The paved edge and the grass looked just like they always did. The only sign he had been there was a scuff mark on the wall where he had pushed with his toes to get up and over.

Upstairs I found Dao standing in the middle of the living room, still in her PJs, her face set. 'Hunter, I'm going to leave.'

'Why? Where would you go?'

I put the Remington in the corner by the stairs and turned to face her. Her stance was that of someone who is steeling themselves to face opposition.

'This is very dangerous now. They know where I am, or at least they know where you live, and they might have seen me – or they just think they know I am here. If I leave and if there is nothing here that shows I was ever here you could let them see that and they will stop. They don't want you, they want me.'

She had worked out a plan and made a decision; her character and strength of mind amazed me.

'I've got a much better plan, Dao,' I said as if there was nothing to worry about. 'You stay here, and we'll see what happens. We have the alarm system, so nobody can take us by surprise. But what we'll do is postpone any outings that aren't necessary – dinner at a restaurant will have to wait. And every time we go out you'll be in the back of the station wagon under the luggage cover before we even open the garage door. And we'll just carry on with life.'

She was about to protest so I added in a voice that made it clear that the discussion was over.

'I know I said you can do what you like and make your own decisions. But this is different. I'm not letting you go anywhere without me, Dao – that's final. I know how to fight, I'm armed, and you are going to be right beside me from now on – not with Willow or anyone else, apart from possibly Charlie.'

To my surprise her expression changed from determination to some emotion close to despair. There was silence for a long moment; she was struggling to make a call one way or the other. And then she sighed, and her voice held a note of defeat.

'I have to tell you something, Hunter. There's something you don't know and it's really bad. I will tell you now and you'll understand that I have to leave.'

'Let's get dressed and have breakfast first and then you can tell me. If it's really bad we need to sit down and have a proper talk about it - and that might take some time.'

What I was trying to do was return us from this moment of intense stress to something resembling normality, creating the impression that we could cope with anything. Hopefully having showers and making porridge would do the trick.

Neither of us spoke while we got breakfast ready, but I could see that now she had made the decision to tell me she could hardly wait to start.

'OK, let's sit down and have that talk now,' I said when we had cleared the table. 'I'll go and get the tablet and set the cameras recording continuously, just in case someone is watching the house.'

Dao sat on the sofa, staring at her hands. I sat at the far end of the sofa instead of in my usual chair. Perhaps whatever it was would be easier to say if she did not have to look at me while she was telling me.

'I took something from Bram,' she said suddenly. 'And that's why he wants to find me and kill me. I suppose he wants it back, but he will kill me anyway, because ....'

She paused and thought for a moment, organising her story to make sense and started again.

'The night I ran away I took his black book with me. I had taken it earlier that day and he hadn't noticed it was gone. He would have discovered it was missing when he went to town the next day. He takes his laptop in a special bag when he goes away for the day. He keeps the black book in the bag all the time, or nearly all the time, and there's a funny lock with little numbers on the bag. But that day he had been doing something with it – I'd seen him through the kitchen door. He had just put it back in the bag and he said 'Christ!' and rushed out of the room very fast. He left the bag on the table with the zip half done up. I was just outside the kitchen door disconnecting the gas bottle so I could swap it for a full one from the shed. The stove is gas, you see. I heard him slam the bathroom door.'

She paused and looked into the middle distance without focus, reliving the scene in her mind.

'I went into the kitchen and unzipped the bag. I took the black book and put it in my trouser pocket and then I closed the zip halfway again and went outside.'

She turned sideways to look at me; her face had a frozen look. Even talking about it made her terrified.

'I was very, very scared – I knew if he saw that the black book was gone before he locked the bag and put it away, then he would kill me right away. He would never have risked me escaping after I had looked at it. Even though he doesn't know I can remember long numbers by heart. But I knew I had to get away that night. He leaves me chained up for the day when he goes off, he doesn't even let me out first thing to have a pee – he lets me out when he comes back so I can make his dinner at the end of the day.'

She's gone back to talking about the island and Bram in the present tense, I thought. Stress and anxiety probably – perhaps once she's got this off her chest things will settle down again in a more lasting way.

'So, if that was the night you got away – and provided he did go off to do his shopping the next morning – then he would not have discovered that you had escaped till he came back the next afternoon?'

She nodded. 'Yes – or perhaps he would discover that the book was gone when he was in town, if he opened the bag. But it still gave me lots of time to go really far away.'

'And what did you do next – after you took the book?'

'I ran to the big shed where I sleep and hid the book under the crate. And then I ran back and picked up the empty gas bottle and took it to the little shed at the back of the house. I waited till I heard him flushing the toilet and then I walked back with the full gas bottle – quite slowly, so he saw me coming back towards the house.'

'And he didn't look in his bag for the book?'

'No, he didn't. He'd already put the laptop in and he just closed the zip and put the bag on the floor.'

The details of her flight came back to me. She had tried to break the chain from its attachment on the wall that night and found he had left the pickaxe where she could reach it. So instead, she had hacked off the chain from where it was locked on to the shackle around her ankle. I had no idea how she had got out of the locked shed, but it was getting to the stage when nothing she said or did would surprise me - maybe there was a window she could open. But what had she hoped to achieve by taking the black book?

'Does he call it the black book?'

'Yes – he's always muttering to himself. Like he'll be doing something and say 'and then I'll go and do this and then I'll put the laptop in the bag and write up the black book' and stuff like that. He's sort of reminding himself of things. So I've heard him talk about the black book lots of times.'

'Did you know what was in it?'

'No, but I knew it was very important and I thought it was to do with the thing that worried my mother – she said he was doing something very bad. And if I was right about the black book, then he would really hate to lose it. I just wanted to punish him for what had happened that week – and particularly what had happened that day. And once I had the book I had to disappear.'

The logic of her flight was clear to me now. She had not escaped on a random day when the opportunity of the pickaxe made it possible, she had to escape that particular day or it was all over.

'You took an incredible risk, Dao. What was it that happened that week that made such a difference?'

She was silent for a long time, and I waited without comment. Was she going to censor what she told me or was she trying to get things into the right order? Then suddenly she started up again. 'There were some other things that happened a bit before that, quite close together but not really connected. Do you want me to tell you the whole thing?'

'Yes please, tell me all of it. Even things you think might not be important. I need to know all the facts.'

Another silence: I waited. She turned sideways in her sofa corner and pulled her legs up and talked very slowly, as if to

make sure I would understand the importance of what she
was saying.

'The first thing that happened was that the Boss came to
the island. I used to hear Bram talking to him on the radio. I
don't think Bram was expecting him – he had never been
there since I had been on the island, perhaps he'd never been
there ever. He was very angry, and they had a terrible
argument, shouting and swearing. I knew who he was
because I heard Bram call him Boss.'

She looked at me, thoughtful and intent, and probably
considering how much she would have to explain.

'I didn't hear all of it. This is how it was – I saw him
coming around the corner of the bay in a boat, just a little boat
with a motor on the back. He was wearing a helmet that
covered his whole face. I didn't know who he was or what he
was going to do, so I ran and hid at the edge of the bush for a
while. Then I heard them shouting and I went back very
quietly and stood behind the shed, so I could hear.'

She was choosing her words carefully, still speaking very
slowly.

'They were standing between the shed and the house –
and they were shouting really loudly. Some of it was about
my mother and me. Bram was scared, I could tell from his
voice. The Boss had been told about my mother and me and
he was so angry. He said 'I told you last time, no more bloody
women here! Are you stupid?' Or something like that. And
Bram said, 'they're harmless, just good to do a lot of the work'
and the Boss said, 'I saw the girl but where's the woman?' He
meant my mother. He thought my mother was still there. And
Master said, 'she's long gone' and then he kind of laughed
and said, 'and there's no risk she'll be talking' and the Boss
went crazy. He yelled 'for fuck's sake, you've done it again,
you stupid bastard, haven't you? And what if the girl gets
away? We'll all go down if any of what she knows gets out'.'

Her expression had not changed, but I heard the tension in
her voice.

'After a while they went inside and closed the door and I couldn't hear any more, just their loud voices – not the words.'

I thought back over what she had told me. 'But who could have told him you were there?'

'I don't know. Perhaps John or Mint had talked to people – you know the two men who came sometimes on those boats I drew for you? I'm sure they all work for the Boss.'

This was news. Nothing had been said about anyone working at anything until now. I made a quick decision. She was on a roll of telling me things in chronological order and it was probably better not to interrupt. We had to finish the Boss story before I started asking questions about other things.

'What sort of helmet was he wearing? Can you describe it?'

'Very strange, black and shiny – ugly.'

'Like a motorbike helmet?'

'Oh no – much bigger.'

She thought for a while but found no words to describe it. 'I can draw it.'

I got my notebook from the dining table and a pen. She sat for several minutes, thinking, with the book on her knees and then she started to draw. I watched, fascinated by how fast she was drawing.

She had worked it all out in her head and then simply put it on paper without hesitation. Her hand stopped moving and she looked at it for a moment before she added some small detail and passed it to me.

'Darth Vader!' I said in surprise. 'He's a character in a film called *Star Wars* and he wore a helmet like that. You can buy those helmets and the black cape – just like he wore in the film. People wear them to fancy dress parties and at Halloween.'

'It was really scary, Hunter,' she said seriously. 'I heard the boat and looked out to sea and there was a big man with a big black head, and I didn't know who he was.'

'I would have been scared too. It's always scary when you can't see someone's face and you don't know who they are. Can you remember what he was wearing – or anything else about him? Like his voice or his hands, was he wearing rings? It would be good to know if you could recognise him again. And what sort of boat was it?'

'The boat was quite small, just a bit bigger than Bram's boat but the same kind, grey metal with a motor on the back, but just a little motor. The Boss is tall and big, but not fat. He was wearing jeans and a dark shirt.'

She paused again, thinking back. 'He had no shoes – well he might have had, but he had to jump out of the boat into the water so he could pull it up on the beach, so he had probably taken them off. I can't tell you what his voice is like because he was shouting, and that helmet made his voice sound really strange.'

'So, he didn't take the helmet off while he was talking to Bram?'

'No, he still had it on when he came out of the house – when he left. He had a tattoo on his arm – I saw it when I looked out from behind the shed, before they went into the house. They were standing sort of sideways to me and looking at each other. I could see his left arm, his sleeves were rolled up.'

Now I pricked my ears up; this was getting interesting. 'Could you see what the tattoo was?'

'It was just a word – I could draw it for you.'

This time it took much longer, and I sat quietly watching her hand move. Again, she thought for a while before she started, getting the image straight in her mind and she drew very fluidly with a look of total concentration on her skinny face. She looked at what she had done, checking it looked just right and handed the book to me.

'I think that's how it was – I hope the curly bit is the right way around.'

The word on the page was Norton and it was written

exactly like the motorbike logo including the curving line and after it the word (blue) in brackets.

'Your memory is amazing – you've got it exactly right.'

She looked at me, confused. 'How do you know it's right? You've never seen the Boss.'

'Norton is a brand of motorbike, very famous. The way they always write the name is just like this, even that swirly line – perfect. And I presume it was tattooed in blue?'

'Yes, dark blue. It was on his arm about this far up from his hand.'

She showed me on her own arm, about halfway to the elbow. 'It went across his arm, like a line of writing on a page.'

'It's a good thing to know. Something that identifies him a little bit and it's there forever.'

'I'm glad I dared take a look. When I looked around the corner, just a tiny bit, I could see the Boss but not Bram. And I knew the Boss couldn't see me because of that horrid helmet. He could only see straight ahead. So I stayed like that for a few minutes, because I could hear Bram's voice much better if I wasn't right behind the shed. That's how I remember the tattoo – I was looking at it for quite a long time. But as soon as they moved I hid properly again.'

'And then the Boss left and a day or two later something else happened?'

I knew that we were getting to the very heart of this whole business now. The things she had so nearly started telling me several times were emerging at last.

'After the Boss had been Bram was really strange,' said Dao. 'He didn't do anything the next day, he just sat around staring at me while I worked. Even while I was fixing things in the generator shed – he sat on the back doorstep and stared. He had never done that before. I think he was trying to make up his mind about something – about me. And then in the afternoon he told me to go and work in the plantation, that's what he calls it – my mother called it the gardens. And I found my mother's bones.'

My mind came to a complete halt; I felt as if someone had physically knocked me down, all thought suspended for a moment.

'You found your mother's bones? Do you mean you found her body?'

'Yes, I did – I found her bones in the forest. Buried – but not very deep down. I saw something white sticking out of the ground, not very far from the path so I went to have a look because it hadn't been there before. It was a bone. I think the rain had washed away some of the slope and that's why it showed – the last time I went on the path I hadn't seen it. I dug and she was there, her bones. Everything had rotted away, her clothes and her body. Her skull had a big piece out of it, above the eyes and there was a crack down to the hole where her eye had been.'

She stopped talking for a moment as if she was picturing the scene. I sat in frozen silence, not daring to interrupt or distract her.

'Her hair was still there and the red comb that she always pinned her hair up with, so I knew it was her. I didn't see everything because Bram came and found me before I had time to dig all of her up.'

Before I had pulled myself together enough to speak she continued. She twisted further around and wrapped her arms around her knees – it was as if a dam had burst and she was relieved to be able to tell me.

'I'll tell you how it was, Hunter – I was allowed to go through the bush to dig the gardens and do the weeding. If I stayed on the path. But when I saw the bone I went off the path and down the slope among the trees to have a look. I didn't realise it was a bone at first, just something white. I tried to keep the bells quiet – I've got to wear bells when I'm in the gardens so he can hear me. You know I told you before how he puts the chain round my waist and locks it so I can't take it off.'

I nodded, shocked and fascinated at the same time.

'I tried to hold on to the bells to keep them quiet when I left the path, in case he could tell I hadn't gone all the way to the gardens. But I couldn't hold the bells and dig up the bones at the same time. They kept clanging and he must have heard I was too close to the house and not in the gardens – so he came along and found me.'

'What did he do?'

'He punished me, he was really, really angry.'

'He whipped you?'

'Yes, but I knew that he might kill me too, well I was sure he would kill me. Because first the Boss had been so angry about me maybe getting away and now I'd found out he had killed my mother.

'And then what happened?'

I still had a feeling that she was holding back, that there was more to come. God knows there seemed to be endless layers to this story; perhaps I would never know it all. But to my surprise she continued talking.

'After I found my mother's bones I thought of the argument he had with the Boss the day before and I began to wonder what else they had said – you know, after they went inside the house. I knew the Boss was worried I would get away and perhaps he made Bram tell him about killing my mother. Or perhaps that's what he meant when he said, 'you've done it again'. Maybe Bram had killed someone else before? I thought that maybe the Boss had told Bram to kill me too. And now Bram was really angry about me finding my mother – perhaps it had made him decide he really would get rid of me.'

'I can't imagine what that must have been like, Dao – just terrifying. You've been through far worse than most people do in a lifetime. I'm really pleased you decided to tell me.'

I got up from the sofa and stretched. She was very tense now and what she had just said had added nothing; she was repeating what I already knew. Perhaps a normality break might be a good idea, doing something unthreatening and domestic.

'Would you like another cup of coffee? I'm going to have one.'

Dao nodded and got up and followed me to the kitchen and we talked about ordinary things like what we must remember to put on the shopping list and checked that Scruff's water bowl was full.

'Listen, Dao,' I said when we were back on the sofa. 'There's one thing I don't understand – those two boats that come and go from the island – what are they doing? You said you think they work for the Boss.'

'Well, it's about those packages. Bram would say 'we're going to have a delivery today – you have to keep out of the way'. And I'd go inside the house and do some cooking or cleaning or washing. The boat would come, always the same one, the bigger one called *Sea Breeze*, with a big round container made of blue plastic on the deck – like a barrel. They would take it to the shed on the wheelbarrow – I think they checked the packages and counted them and then put them back in the barrel. And Bram would sit on the veranda later on when the boat had left and make notes in his black book. Once they left the lid off the barrel and that night I saw the packets from the corner where I slept. I climbed up on the big crate, because the chain was just long enough, and I could see into the barrel over at the other wall. The next morning when Bram came to unlock the chain he noticed that the lid wasn't on – he got really angry and put the lid on straight away.'

She realised she had got side-tracked and stopped to collect her thoughts.

'The other boat would come more often, sometimes every few days. That was Mint – he would give an envelope to Bram first and then Bram gave him a few packets from the shed and then they'd have a beer, or lots of beers. But I never knew what was in the packages. He and Bram would go into the big shed and come out with a few of those packets and take them to his boat, so I never saw them close up. I was never allowed near the shed when the men were in there.'

'What do those packages look like? How are they wrapped – cartons, paper?'

'They are wrapped in something grey first and then in plastic, sort of all tight and hard around the edges – you know, no room inside, very tight. Or maybe the plastic is grey? Why, do you think you know what they are doing? My mother was worried about it. She said Bram was doing something that wasn't legal, and she didn't want to get mixed up in it and we would have to leave.'

'I think she was right, Dao. I think it's either drugs or materials to make drugs that come in those packets. And it sounds as if each package is what's called shrink-wrapped in plastic – probably in case water gets into the barrel. I imagine the barrel is dropped overboard from cargo ships from Asia. A lot of ships come down that coast on the way to Auckland. And the barrel would float just under the surface and maybe it had some sort of beacon on it – a little light and a radio transmitter and the man on *Sea Breeze* goes and picks it up and takes it to the island. And then the other boat takes the stuff from the island to someone who has ordered it and paid for it.'

'What are drugs?'

Once again I had overlooked how limited her general knowledge was. I spent the next ten minutes explaining about the trade in illegal drugs, and how much money is involved. She asked why people use drugs and we talked about what happens when people get addicted.

Dao looked thoughtful. 'That black book has lots of numbers in it. On the first page some very long numbers – rows of figures with dashes between. And then pages and pages of lists of dates and numbers which I thought was how many packets had been delivered and how many had been taken away. I read the book on the second day after I escaped because I thought I might memorise it all and then throw it away, so I didn't have it on me if the dogs found me. I didn't want him to get it back.'

She was on a roll again; finding new consequences and conclusions, linking what she knew with what I had told her about the drug trade.

'I think Bram did it like that on purpose, or the Boss decided – instead of one boat picking the barrel up from the sea and then taking a few parcels away now and then, he got those two men to do it separately from each other. You know what I mean – they were never there at the same time, those boats. It's only Bram and I who know who both of them are.'

She was right. That was the reason they were chasing her and prepared to kill her - and probably me too. She was the only eyewitness, and she could link all the key players.

'Yes, I think you are right – the Boss is making sure those two men don't meet. Each person only knows the next person in the chain – the people at the bottom of the chain only know Bram and he's the only one who has met the Boss – and even he doesn't know what the Boss actually looks like. And I suppose the Boss only came to visit Bram because he'd heard a rumour that there were women at Bram's place and he came to check it out for himself. Those guys who come on the boats, John and Mint – I bet they've never met him.'

Dao nodded and said sadly. 'Yes, he's safe from them, but not from me. I took Bram's black book and if he has told the Boss…'

She paused and a shudder ran through her. 'I know too much now, more than anyone apart from Bram and the Boss.'

'Yes, you do.'

There was no point trying to pretend she was wrong. She was a crucial witness and now that I knew what was going on I felt sure those men really would kill her if they found her. The Boss was likely to have links to gangs and organised crime which meant he could always find a paid killer. I had read enough about gangs involved in drug manufacture to know that it is big business with a turnover of millions and that they react with extreme brutality to any threat against their operations.

'And where is the black book now? Did you really throw it away?'

'No, I didn't. I learnt some of the numbers by heart, just because I wanted to – it was something to do. I hid it in a tree.'

I tried to picture this – in a tree? She saw my expression and for the first time since we got up that morning she smiled.

'You look funny – like you've never heard of a tree?'

'You'll have to tell me what it means? Did you find a tree with a hole in it or something?'

'It seemed a good idea. Bram was always telling me the dogs could track me by my smell and I knew the black book would smell of me, so I decided to find a good tree and reach up as high as I could and put it there and then they wouldn't find it.'

'Where is this tree?'

I thought of the distance she had travelled, probably in big curves and sometimes backtracking through the bush on bare feet. She had walked well into the evenings, as far as she could in the dark. Finding that tree might be impossible.

'You know where Scruff found me? In that hole in the ground? The tree is not very far from there, perhaps a hundred metres. I was so tired and cold then – I couldn't walk any further. I chose a tree that had lots of branches and lots of leaves – well, they don't look like ordinary leaves really, just little dark brown things. And it has thousands of round seed things all over it, grey seeds. Do you know what I mean?'

'Must be manuka, I think. A big one?'

'Yes, tall and with lots and lots of branches, little branches all tangled. I tied a fern stem around the plastic and then I threw it high into the tree and it caught and stayed there.'

'Where did you get plastic? Was the book wrapped in plastic?'

'Not when I took it. But when I ran off in the night it was raining. I didn't have any rain clothes and I knew the book would be soaked as soon as I was – and I hadn't had a look at it yet. So, I climbed into the rubbish hole in the forest and found a plastic bag, a little grey one. And I kept the book wrapped in that.'

My mind was working overtime now. This was fantastic news. I needed to talk to Willow and get hold of Charlie, as soon as possible.

'Listen, there are lots of things we need to do and I think we've got to move quickly. If you listen to my call to Willow, and then to Charlie, you'll find out what I'm thinking, and I won't have to say it twice. I'll put the phone on speaker function, so you can hear what they say, and we can both talk to them.'

We sat at the dining table, side by side with the phone on the table between us. First I called Charlie and asked if she would fly us to the cabin.

'This afternoon if you can, I'm in a hurry and it would save a lot of driving. We had an intruder here in the night, or an attempt at intrusion. We're definitely a target.'

'OK, can do. What time can you be at the airfield?'

'I've got to talk to Willow first about the legal angles. Say about an hour and a half? Dao and Scruff will be coming too.'

'OK, no problem. Do I bring the Glock?'

'Can't do any harm. We'll be there about one.'

Willow answered the phone after five rings when I was just about ready to give up.

'Hi, it's me. We've got a lot of news, most of it not so good and we need to talk to you. It will have to be over the phone – we're not coming anywhere near you for a while and you're not to come here either.'

I told her about Paul installing new alarm systems, about

the man watching the house from the street and the man in the courtyard.

'Good heavens, Hunter – that's bad news. How is Dao taking it?'

'You can ask her yourself – she's sitting right beside me and we're on speaker.'

I nodded at Dao, and she leant forward, hesitating slightly. 'I'm OK, Willow. Just a bit scared someone will try to get into the house. But Hunter's got his gun and he'll shoot him if he can.'

'God forbid! We don't need any complications. But listen, I did your shopping this morning. How do I get it to you if I can't come to your house?'

I thought briefly. The less time we wasted the better.

'We'll come past your place. Put the bag in your letterbox – it's not very big, is it?'

'No, it will fit in the letterbox, I think.'

'We'll come over shortly and just stop for a second and pick it up and drive on. Charlie is flying us up to the cabin again to pick something up. And now we're getting to the serious stuff, Willow. I'll send you an email in a few minutes and tell you the story Dao has told me this morning. I think we have to inform the police right away – for several reasons. So, if you could do whatever has to be done as Dao's legal representative we'll be in touch when we get back – possibly not until tonight.'

'Heavens!' said Willow again. 'This is getting worse by the minute. Well, send me the details and I'll get on to the police and I'll fill you in tonight.'

It was nearly eleven now and I had to get that email away before we did anything else.

'Dao, can you make us some sandwiches to take with us for lunch? Make quite a few. And if you look in the bottom cupboard beside the pantry you'll find drink bottles there. Fill a couple with fruit juice from the cartons in the fridge. And

Scruff's water bottle, the one I had in the car with a top that turns into a bowl? Bring that one as well.'

I heard her talking to Scruff in the kitchen while I tried to sum everything up in an email to Willow. By the time I had finished Dao had a row of sandwiches lined up and the bottles filled. She had investigated the drawers under the bench and found a plastic container.

'Is this enough?' She pointed at the row of sandwiches. 'I've made us some with peanut butter and some with cheese.'

'Great, let's put them in that box and put the whole lot into a supermarket bag. I'll just go upstairs and get your jacket and a couple of things.'

I ran up the stairs, had a quick look on my phone at the morning's video footage from the security cameras and got Dao's jacket. In the garage I grabbed my old army camo jacket with pockets big enough for a handful of ammunition.

'Now, then – you have to travel in the back. At least until I'm sure nobody's following us. I don't think Scruff can be under the cover, he'll just try to get out.'

I got a sleeping bag out of the storage closet in the garage and spread it in the far back of the station wagon.

'Here you are – let's hope you don't feel sick. If you do just shout and I'll stop and let you out.'

I backed out of the garage, set the alarms and headed towards Willow's place. We drove the long way around her block and there was nobody behind us. I stopped briefly to let Dao get into the front seat and took the bag out of the letterbox.

As we continued towards the airfield Dao said, 'Have you got a pen in the car – and something I can write on?'

'I think there's a pen in the glove box. Don't know about paper – you might have to improvise.'

'What does improvise mean?'

'It's when you use whatever you can find, if the perfect thing isn't available. So have a look and there might be a map or something you can write on the back of. What are you writing, anyway?'

She was taking things out of the glove box and putting them on her lap. The very last thing was an old ballpoint pen. She held up a folded envelope.

'Can I write on this – it's empty.'

'Sure – but you haven't told me what you're writing.'

'I'm going to write some of those numbers from the black book. Just in case we don't find it.'

'You're kidding! Do you think you still remember them?'

She was already writing and said absently, 'I think so.'

I kept quiet, intrigued and waiting. I remembered her comment that morning when she had said that Bram did not know that she could memorise numbers. I had planned to ask her what she meant and then so many revelations came out that I forgot. Every now and then I glanced over to see what she was doing. She had written one number or one line of something and then she sat for several minutes, just looking down at the paper, not writing anything. Perhaps she can only remember the last number she learnt, I thought, and now she's stuck.

We were close to Ardmore now and as I stopped at an intersection with heavy traffic, I noticed that she was writing again. It was just like when she drew Darth Vader's helmet, first getting it lined up just right in her mind and then putting it on paper without hesitation. But numbers were very different from an image. I could not even begin to imagine how she did it. By the time we were at the airfield she had finished. She looked at what she had written, folded the envelope and put it in her jacket pocket.

'How did it go? Did you remember some of them?'

'Most of them, I think. There's one I think is wrong, but I can't see it so I'm just leaving it as it is, but I've marked it.'

'What do you mean by saying you can't see it? Do you actually see those numbers, like a written list in your head?'

She did not respond until I slowed to a stop behind the

hangar. When she turned to face me I could see that as usual it was important to her that I understood her explanation perfectly.

'Once I have seen a long number, even if I didn't try to learn it by heart, I can often see it in my head – like a picture. As if I had a photo of it and once I see the photo I can read the number. It doesn't always work.'

'That's very clever,' I said, genuinely impressed. 'I think it's called photographic memory, but I've never met anyone who could do that before.'

She shrugged; her usual response to compliments that she was unsure how to deal with.

'It's just a habit. I had so little paper to write on when I was doing maths. Sometimes I tried to solve things in my head while I was working, and if it was a complicated problem I had to be able to see the whole thing inside my head.'

My god, I thought, there seems to be no end to the surprises she springs on me today. I can't wait to see how many she's written down and how it compares to the black book – if we ever find it.

9

TUESDAY AFTERNOON AND EVENING

Charlie greeted Dao like an old friend and let Scruff lick her hand, then turned to me and noticed the Remington. She punched me hard in the upper arm as she often does; knuckles first. Over the years I have had many bruises to show for it. For a small woman she delivers a nasty punch.

'That looks familiar – so we are expecting real trouble?'

'Not really, but I'm not leaving anything to chance now. I know a lot more today than I did yesterday – and things are more dangerous than I thought earlier. I'll fill you in on the way. We brought lunch; Dao made lots so you can have some too.'

'Ok let's go. But I can't have Scruff in the front, Hunter.'

Charlie realised that Dao had never been in a helicopter before and took great pains telling her how it worked and how she could make it turn and rise. I sat quietly in one of the back seats with Scruff beside me and called Mac to warn him we were coming.

'Hi, Hunter,' he boomed as he does when he's on the phone, his voice coming through far too loud. 'What's up now?'

'My friend's flying me up again so I can get some stuff

136

from the cabin without spending hours in the car. I just thought I'd warn you, so you don't worry if you see the chopper landing. I think we can land on that little flat just above the ford, don't you?'

I knew we could but Mac's the sort of man who likes to hand out advice and instructions.

'I'm sure you can – shouldn't be any problems with trees. Just watch out it's not slippery after the rain – that area slopes a bit. You don't want the chopper sliding into the creek!'

His laugh nearly deafened me, and I held the phone away from my ear. I finished the call in time to hear Dao say, 'Can we do that now, just like you said?'

The next moment we rose straight up, very quickly, turning as we went, and Dao laughed and turned to look at me.

The two in the front pointed things out to each other and talked about what they saw, and I sat in the back with my hand on Scruff's neck, thinking of what I had learnt since I got up that morning and trying to second-guess what might happen next. There were too many unknown factors to make a definitive plan of any kind; but I went through various scenarios and tried to prepare myself for the worst.

Charlie circled above the flat area just up from the creek, checking the slope and the trees around it.

'I'm not so happy about those big trees on the uphill side,' she said. 'I'll put us down on that slight incline a bit closer to the drop-off to the creek. It looks muddy, so watch it when you get out – could be slippery.'

We landed without incident and stood beside the helicopter looking around.

'How much space do you actually need to land?' I was looking up at the rotor; it was hard to judge.

'It's nearly eleven metres across – I like to keep well clear of branches, even if the open space looks OK,' said Charlie. 'Trees move in the wind and branches don't always move the way you think they will. But this is fine – plenty of room.'

We walked up the track until we were at the point where I had first heard Scruff's bark that fateful morning. It seemed impossible that it was only six days ago.

'I think this is where it was. I went towards his bark, more or less in this direction.' I pointed uphill. 'Let's start and see if I recognise anything on the way.'

It is very difficult to recognise where you have already been or to retrace your steps in the New Zealand native forest. People learn this when they leave a walking track to answer a call of nature and end up lost for days and having to be rescued – sometimes they are never found. The native bush is more like rainforest and jungle than anything else. Dense undergrowth fills the spaces between taller canopy-type trees and your line of sight is very short. Not to mention that it all looks the same, giant ferns and long vines, scrubby bushes, small leaning trees and the trunks of giant trees. It was well over an hour before I found the place and then it was mostly thanks to Scruff, whose memory cells suddenly fired at the sight or smell of something familiar. He took off ahead of us and when we caught up he was sitting beside the hollow where he had found Dao.

'This is it,' I said and pointed at the depression in the ground where dead fern fronds lay tossed to one side along with broken branches.

'This is where you lay, Dao. And all I could see under that pile of debris was the back of your head and one hand.'

It was a chilling thought that the margin between her dying and being found had depended on a small dog refusing to come when he was called. She looked thoughtfully at the hollow for a minute and then she shook her head.

'I can remember giving up, too tired to walk any further – and very cold. I know I pulled some dead branches over me to hide me a bit, but I can't remember you finding me.'

We looked at each other in silence; there was no need to comment further. Dao turned in a 360-degree circle, looking carefully at the surrounding bush. Charlie and I kept out of the way as she walked a short distance, stopped and turned again and then shook her head. She took quite a while to orientate herself and find the tree she had tossed the book into.

'It looks so different in the daylight,' she complained, looking around with a frown. 'When I got here it was nearly dark and all I thought of was hiding the book and lying down – I was nearly asleep on my feet. I never thought of having to find it again.'

But eventually she found the tree and it was obvious why she had selected it in the first place. A tall manuka tree with matted tangles of branches and twigs; perfect for catching something thrown up. It was not strong enough to support my weight. Charlie climbed up as far as she could, as agile as a monkey, but even she could not reach the book.

'It's far too high to reach from here and I can't climb any higher. Find me a long stick Hunter? I think I might be able to tip it off – it's lying on a little bunch of matted twigs.'

She poked at it with the stick that I passed up to her and eventually the little book fell down right on top of her. She came down a lot faster than she had gone up and handed it to Dao. It was wrapped in a grey plastic bag and it still had the fern stem wound tightly round it.

Dao stood there holding the little parcel, looking as if she had no idea what to do next.

'Well,' said Charlie finally. 'Are you going to have a look at it?'

I had explained my new sense of urgency to Charlie as we walked through the bush and how Dao had tried to remember the numbers from the black book. Now Dao handed the book to me and pulled the folded envelope from her pocket. I un-wrapped the notebook and opened it, holding it so Charlie could see. The first page was nearly blank, just three numbers that were obviously bank accounts in different banks.

Dao read out the numbers she had written, and I checked them against the book.

'Well, look at that —perfect score, Dao.'

'I bet he gets paid in cash,' said Charlie, 'and he has accounts in different banks so he can split things up – so they don't get suspicious about how much cash he gets. I've read about how drug syndicates deal mostly in cash, huge amounts.'

Dao looked at me. 'Those envelopes,' she said. 'You know, the ones I told you Mint gives to Bram when he comes. That's how the Boss pays Bramville – somehow he gets the envelope to Mint without having to meet him and then Mint brings them to the island. Don't you think?'

'I think you're right. It's very clever,' I said. 'The whole operation is divided up into water-tight compartments – the Boss is doing every single thing possible to protect himself and stay anonymous.'

The next page had half a dozen initials; each set followed by a phone number. Dao had one number wrong. When I told her, she smiled. 'See, I knew I had that one wrong, it's the one I marked.'

I leafed quickly through the rest of the notebook. The main part of it was some form of bookkeeping about deliveries and dispatches. Page after page in tiny writing, with dates in the margin and initials or some sort of shorthand code, and then the inward and outward numbers. He had started out very neatly with ruled columns for 'in' and 'out' but the last couple of pages were just scribbles. Every now and then he added up the columns and I spotted question marks here and there where his numbers did not balance.

'Look at this,' I said and held the book out so we could all see it. 'I guess these numbers are the packets he's got in and then sent out. Look, big numbers of packets come in at intervals and then small numbers go out more regularly with various initials,' I said. 'I imagine the Boss would check the stock levels regularly – he wouldn't want Bram setting up a little business of his own on the side. We know they were in radio contact.'

Charlie nodded. 'And the initials are the people who bought the parcels, I suppose. And they paid big money to the Boss and he paid wages to Master.'

I thought of the dark world of drugs and how an innocent girl had got caught up in a situation that had ended in deadly peril. Standing there in the filtered sunlight among the trees and surrounded by birdsong the whole scenario seemed unreal. But I knew that as soon as we got back to town reality would snap back into place. The importance of the black book was immense. If Dao had not taken it to punish Bram, this ace would not be in our hands now. Without it things would have looked very different, all guesswork and no facts to build a case on. I put the book in the map pocket of my jacket and picked up the Remington. We made our way back to the track and continued uphill to inspect the cabin. It was just as we had left it; the door boarded up and no signs of any further visits.

Lunch became a minor celebration. We ate our sandwiches sitting on the large rocks by the creek and talked about what else we might do. We had a chopper and a pilot and could do some sightseeing; in the end we left it to Dao.

'Can we fly from here to the island?' she said to Charlie. 'I know you can find it and I want to see how far I walked.'

So that is what we did. Charlie flew slowly over the steep hills towards the coast and she and Dao chatted about what they saw, and how Dao might well have wandered about in circles.

'I walked across some fields but not the ones with cows and horses,' said Dao. 'I don't know a lot about big animals. And that creek, I followed it for a while one evening in the dark, the last evening I think – and now I can see it's actually Hunter's creek. The worst parts were those deep valley things, the very narrow ones. They're so steep - I couldn't go down and then up. I had to walk around them.'

From the air the bush-clad ravines looked like narrow dark creases between the steep hills, where the bottom could only be guessed at, hidden by dense vegetation.

As we got closer to the coast Charlie turned to look at me. 'Hunter, I think we could fly over slowly and not too low and just continue straight out to sea and then curve to the south-west. We don't want to raise any suspicions – or what do you think? If he sees the same chopper for the second time in a couple of days he might panic and run.'

'Sounds good to me. I'm just about to call Willow and find out what we should do with the black book and what the cops said.'

I watched Dao from behind as we cruised quite high above the island and out to sea. She leaned to one side to look down, said nothing and then straightened up and looked forward. I wondered if she had noticed the little road just north of the island.

By six thirty we were back at home. Willow had set up an interview appointment with the police for the next morning and we had arranged to meet in the city at nine. She would bring the folder with all the documentation we had collected; my original fact sheet, her own findings about Dao's parents, the photos of the island and Bramville as well as my last email about the deliveries to the island. The final addition was the black book which I planned to scan, page by page, before I handed it over.

We talked to Willow on Skype after dinner, another new adventure for Dao. We talked through the day's events, what was in the black book and how the new security system was working.

'I've got to look at today's video footage on the hard drive,' I said. 'I haven't checked it since we left this morning. And I'll scan the black book tonight, so we have copies of everything – I'll email them to you. Anything we need to do in preparation for the interview tomorrow?'

'No, just turn up, but don't go in until I'm there, will you?

I don't want anyone questioning Dao unless I'm present. Why don't you go and do that scanning, Hunter – and check your CCTV footage and let me talk to Dao. I want to make sure there are no surprises tomorrow.'

I spent some time with the scanner before I sat down and checked what the cameras had caught during the day. The one at the front showed an old grey Toyota Corolla parked on the other side of the street for half an hour, with a man reading a paper and occasionally glancing at the house. It was impossible to say if he was the man who had come over the garden wall but he might be. He was thin and he looked tall, but his face was in shadow. When Dao came to tell me that she had finished I remembered the shopping Willow had done and went and fetched it from the car.

'Here you are.' I handed it to Dao who was sitting on the sofa with a book. 'This is the stuff that Willow got for you – she said you had talked about it.'

I was on my way to the kitchen to make a cup of coffee when Dao spoke behind me.

'Hunter, there's something else in here, not just the things we talked about.'

As soon as I saw the little box in her hand I remembered my conversation with Willow. It had gone right out of my mind and now Dao was holding a pregnancy test kit, staring at it with a mixture of confusion and apprehension.

'Sorry, Dao - I forgot to tell you. Willow said she would get one of those and I was supposed to talk to you, but I forgot with all the upheaval since. I'll explain it now.'

Her look told me that nothing I had said made any sense. I sat down beside her, desperate to do this well.

'Dao, you told me Bram had said he'd give you to that man with the boat, John – and that you knew he 'would fuck you'. Those were the words you used. Do you know what it means? Did Bram do it to you? I don't think you learnt that word from your mother.'

She turned her face away from me.

'He fucked me, but not often. Just now and then – when he'd been drinking with one of the men from the boats.'

'Where?' I said, just for something to say, to give her a chance to pull herself together.

'He used to lock me in the shed when they were drinking and then, when the other man had gone back to his boat, he would come and get me out and take me to the house and do it there.'

Her voice was barely audible.

'When did he start doing this? Did he do it when you were still young, a child?'

'No, he started a while ago, perhaps a year ago, or a bit more.'

She was still looking away from me.

'You know about being pregnant, don't you?'

She nodded without saying anything.

'Do you know what rape is?'

She shook her head, again without saying anything. Her hands were clenched into fists.

'It's when a man forces a woman to have sex, when she hasn't said that he can – by using force or threats. It's a crime and people end up in prison for it. I'm sure you didn't say he could have sex with you. You let him because you were scared of him, or he forced you?'

She spoke so quietly that I could hardly hear the word. 'Both.'

'So, because you have been raped by Bram it's another thing he's done that is illegal and we must tell the police tomorrow. When did he do it last?'

I was thinking of the possibility that she might be pregnant. She thought for a moment, and I wondered if she was trying to remember or if there was something she did not want to tell me.

'He hadn't done it for a while, a few weeks – but he tried the day I found my mother's bones. After dinner he grabbed me and said I owed him for being bad and going off the path. He laughed, he said whipping wasn't enough and having my hair cut off wasn't enough – I had to pay him an extra fee.'

'A fee?'

'That's what it's called. When I was bad he used to say that because I had no money I had to pay the fee by doing something – or him doing things to me.'

'And the fee that day was rape?'

She looked straight at me now and spoke with more force.

'But that day I hurt him – when he tried to rape me. And it didn't happen.'

I stared at her. 'What did you do, how did you manage to stop him?'

'I had my writing nail in my pocket – it was just chance. I'd put it there in the morning when he unlocked the chain, I didn't usually have it with me. So, I took it out and had it in my hand and when he got me on the bed I stabbed him in the thigh, very hard several times – fast and really deep. There was blood all over the bed and he was very angry, screaming and jumping around. Then he slapped me really hard and said he would sell me to the man from the boat next time he came. He said, 'your name is Slave and anyone can own you and he wants you.' That's when I knew for sure I had to leave as soon as I could. There were too many things that had made him angry, and he was scared of the Boss too. I knew something bad would happen.'

I thought of the way he had tried to dominate her and reduce her self-esteem to nothing. Cutting her hair off had been a particularly nasty act of vengeance. I could imagine her with long black hair, and I understood how her self-image had suffered when he chopped it off. The cruelty of that man, the way he had tried to crush her indomitable spirit and reduce her to the condition of a slave; it made me furiously angry, but I had to push it to the back of my mind for now, I had to act calm.

'Your hair will grow again, and you'll be just the way you

want to be. Nothing bad will happen to you if I can prevent it.'

I picked up the little box and held it out to her. 'This is a test kit so you can check if you're pregnant. I think we need to make sure before the police interview, don't you?'

Her face froze in shock. She leapt to her feet, looking around as if she was about to run. 'No! No! I can't be – I couldn't bear to have his baby!' She was crying now, beside herself.

I got up fast and put my arms around her, holding her tight against my chest. Her whole body was trembling in the grip of panic.

'Don't worry – it will be OK, you don't have to have anyone's baby,' I said. 'If you're pregnant we'll have it stopped. It's OK, we'll fix it.'

'Can they do that? Can they take it away?'

'Yes, it's easy. But let's hope you're not pregnant. We'll read the instructions and then you can do the test and we'll know.'

Gradually she relaxed and stood limply leaning against me. I turned her around and pushed her gently to sit down.

We studied the leaflet inside the box, and I made us cups of hot chocolate, thinking that a bit of extra fluid might be a good thing in the circumstances. We talked about our trip to the cabin and what fun flying was and gradually things felt calmer. Half an hour later Dao picked up the test kit and disappeared upstairs, saying nothing and not looking at me. I sat there and waited, unable to read or think of anything apart from how the impact of a pregnancy and an abortion might totally upset the sense of security that we had achieved in the last week. But she came down the stairs and said, 'It's OK, it's negative.'

I got up and took our mugs to the kitchen and said over my shoulder, as if nothing had happened: 'Time for bed?'

It seemed as if a return to our fragile sense of domestic routine was the most important thing just then. Dao went up ahead of me and I turned things off, picked up my book, the phone and the laptop and headed upstairs. Dao was sitting on the bed in her own room, leaning into the corner with a book on her lap.

I went into my bedroom, turned the light on above the bed and took my PJ pants into the bathroom to change. When I came out Dao was still on the bed in her room, reading.

'Aren't you going to sleep yet?'

'No, I'll just sit here for a while.'

Something was wrong. She had come to some conclusion that I did not understand. I wanted to ask her, but there was a tone to her voice that stopped me.

'OK, I'll leave the light on beside the bed.'

I read for half an hour and then tried to sleep, but it was impossible. I got up and looked into her room again; she was still sitting on the bed dressed in her PJs.

'Why are you still up? I can't go to sleep because I don't know what's wrong. Please talk to me.'

I sat down on the edge of the bed. 'Let me have a look at your ankle.'

Without waiting for her to say yes or no, I lifted her foot onto my lap and looked closely at the now nearly unnoticeable swelling and the scar from the shackle.

'It's amazing how fast this got better,' I said. 'You heal quickly.'

I was determined to get a response. I had to find out what was wrong, but she just said, 'That's good,' and continued reading.

So, it's a contest of wills now, I thought with some amusement. But I will outlast you if I have to sit here all night. You have no idea how stubborn I can be, little found girl.

I stayed where I was, sitting straight up with her foot across my lap and my hand around her ankle, rubbing it gently with my thumb and saying nothing. She lasted a long time, much longer than I had expected, but finally she broke.

'Go to bed, Hunter – you need your sleep.'

A direct quote of something I had said to her; I made no reply and continued to sit there. A few minutes later she sighed, sat up straighter and put the book down.

'Hunter, I can't sleep in your room anymore. I'm just going to read till I'm tired and sleep here.'

I knew what this meant; she had to be totally exhausted to sleep in her room alone. She would have to stay awake a long time to get tired enough and by that time it might be morning.

'Does this have anything to do with the fact that Bram raped you?'

Her eyes flicked to my face for the first time since I had come upstairs, then away again.

'Well, yes – in a way.'

'In what way?'

'It's hard to explain,' she said reluctantly. 'It's as if I've become a dirty person now that you know. And I can't sleep in your room – it feels all wrong.'

'Did you feel really bad about this all the time – before you told me about it? But now that I know it seems worse somehow?'

I was guessing, trying to get her to tell me how she felt. She nodded and looked past me without focus. I thought she was probably replaying scenes of abuse and threats and applying guilt or blame to herself. I had heard of this, of rape victims feeling guilty that they have been raped and blaming themselves for what had happened to them. I had never understood it. But here it was, right in front of me, and somehow or other I had to deal with it. This was right out of my range of experience, but common sense and affection would have to do the job.

'Dao, listen – you have been a prisoner since you were a child and kept enslaved by an adult man. He has mistreated you and tormented you and you hate him for it. What he has done to you only touches you in the sense that he harmed you. I know he deprived you of a normal life and made you live in fear, but it hasn't touched your own person, the thing that makes you who you are.'

I found it hard to express what I wanted to say. Inside my head I had a clear image of the concept but putting it into words was a different matter.

'I don't know if I'm any good at explaining it, but this is what I believe. Inside your head and your heart is the real you – your own self, or your soul, whatever people might call it. It's what your character depends on and your whole personality. Nothing can touch it unless you let it. You could be bitter about the years that have been taken from you, and that would affect your own self, but the person who did those things to you can't change your inner person. The fact the Bram is a dirty, nasty beast does not change your own self – whatever he's done to you.'

We were both silent. I had run out of words and Dao was either thinking of what I had said, or it made no sense and she had dismissed it. I lifted her foot off my thigh and stood up.

'I'm going to bed now. Don't stay up too late or we'll never get any sleep.'

I left the bedside light on and lay down on top of the duvet with the blanket over me, closed my eyes and waited. Ten minutes later she got in quietly on the other side of the bed and turned the light off.

'Is Scruff in here with us?' I said without opening my eyes. 'Did you close the door?'

'Yes, he's here on the floor on my side – and the door is shut.'

'Good, now we can go to sleep.'

A few minutes later a quiet whisper, no louder than a breath. 'Thank you.'

Just before midnight the doorbell went and at the same time the alert signal buzzed on my phone. I grabbed the phone and checked the camera at the front of the house. My neighbour was standing outside with a jacket over his PJs and a policeman beside him. Dao was sitting up, confused and frightened.

'It's OK. Stay here!'

I ran down two flights of stairs with the phone in my hand; only just remembered to disarm the system before I got to the ground floor. As soon as I opened the door Nigel started talking. He was on a high of excitement and urgency.

'Hunter, Margie got up to get a drink of water and she saw a man in our garden, and she called to me to come and have a look and I rang the police. When I looked again he'd gone but just before the police car came I saw him in the lane behind the wall. I could just see the top of his head. There's another police officer trying to catch him right now.'

The policeman had patiently waited for Nigel to finish. 'Can I come in, please?'

I held the door open, and they both came in.

'I noticed your security cameras and I thought you might have got him on your CCTV? And if so, I'd like to have a look at him.'

'I'll have a look at the recording,' I said. 'The camera picks up movement on my side of the wall, so if he had come here the alert signal would have woken me.'

I turned the light on and we stood in the hall while I checked the recording using my phone.

'No, he didn't make it into my garden – must have gone over your back wall, Nigel. What did he look like?'

'Well, I only got a glance, but Margie said he was a tall guy, slim with a baseball cap.'

I presumed he had told the cop about the guy, who had watched my place from the street, but neither of them said anything about it and I made no comment. The less complicated this became in the middle of the night the better, as far as I was concerned.

The cop said, 'He was apparently standing just by the wall that separates your gardens, looking as if he was about to climb over.'

I smiled and made an effort to sound unconcerned. 'He must have changed his mind. Perhaps he saw you watching and took fright.'

Telling the cop that the guy had already been here was not on the agenda. It would take half the night getting the details down and then I would have to repeat it all in the morning when we went for our interview. I returned upstairs to find Dao still sitting bolt upright in bed with the Remington across her knees. From where I was standing I could not see the safety button beside the trigger guard. She could have pressed it when she lifted the gun, in which case it would fire at one pull of the trigger.

'Very slowly Dao – lift your hands off. If you pull the trigger it will fire. If you held the trigger pulled it would fire several times.'

She raised her hands in the air and laughed a bit shakily. 'Good!'

I went to her side of the bed and lifted the gun off her knees from behind, checked the safety and put it back beside the door.

'Have you ever fired a gun?'

'No, but I know how to do it, I think. If it wasn't you coming upstairs I was going to shoot them as soon as they were in the doorway. Would it have worked?'

'Probably – because it's a shotgun and it scatters lots of shot so from close up it's very hard to miss the target. And if you hit them full-on from close range it makes a terrible mess. You don't really want to do that.'

'I might have to,' she said. 'If they'd killed you first I would have to.'

'Well, that didn't happen, so for now we can stop thinking about it. Let's try to go back to sleep now.'

I turned the light off and told her about Nigel and what he had seen.

'So we'll continue the way we've been doing things since this became serious. You have to be under the luggage cover in the car and you have to stay away from the windows. If they never see you they might decide you're not here after all.'

There was no point in talking about it any further. There was nothing we could do apart from take precautions, be alert and use our defensive resources to best advantage.

I was just dropping off to sleep when Dao spoke again.

'Did you ever kill anyone, Hunter?'

'Yes.'

'Did you shoot them because they had done something bad and because you didn't like them?'

'It was my job. When you're in the army you don't have a choice. The enemy of your country is your enemy and it's your job to stop them.'

I thought back to my days in the army; the close friendships, the shared experiences and what I had eventually learnt about myself.

'But in the end I decided that the army was not for me. I had to live a life where my own judgement of right and wrong determined what I did, not something based on political decisions.'

'But you would kill someone now – if you had to?'

'Go to sleep, Dao. It's very late.' And then I thought of why she might be asking. 'I would kill these guys who want to kill you. If they come near you, yes - I will definitely kill them. I'm not going to let them get to you.'

Nothing more happened that night but neither of us slept very well. Awareness of danger hovered like a dark presence in the back of my mind. It felt like a very long night.

10

WEDNESDAY

Next morning, I went into the bathroom first. 'If my phone rings, could you answer it, please? It might be Willow wanting to check some fact with you.'

I had just turned the shower off when my phone went in the bedroom. I opened the door a crack and heard Dao say, 'Yes, he's here, but he's in the shower.'

Short silence.

'My name is Susan. Who are you?'

Longer silence.

'I don't think I need to tell you anything. You can ask Hunter, if you want to know.'

Short silence.

'Bye.'

I came out of the bathroom. Dao was standing in the door to her bedroom with my phone in her hand. She looked quite calm.

'Who was that?'

'A woman called Vivian. She's very angry.'

'Is she now?' I was amused and wondered what had been said at the other end of that brief conversation.

'That was quite a long reply she gave you. Was she rude to you?'

Dao's eyes flashed black sparks. I had never seen her angry before.

'She was very rude! She asked who I was and what I was doing here. And I didn't think it was any of her business. She's not my boss.'

She handed me the phone. 'I'm sorry if I was rude to her. But she asked if I had stayed the night and if it had been fun. I think I know what she meant.'

'You are probably right. Don't worry about it.'

'What if she's angry with you too? Does she come and stay the night with you – you know, do you and her …?'

'She's a friend and we do things together. But she's never spent a night in this house.'

I thought of my reluctance to let Vivian properly into my life, the feeling that once she was in she would try to take control. She had tried to invite herself for a weekend stay a couple of times, but I had ignored her suggestions. Visions of having to change my habits had made me cautious. Sleeping with her now and then was one thing, but there would be no sharing of lives. I had lived alone for long enough to know I preferred it to anything else.

Dao was studying my face, trying to figure out what I was thinking. I smiled and said, 'I must get dressed – and you too. We have that police interview this morning.'

'What should I wear? I don't know what to pick.'

Amazing, I thought, how fast she has developed this concern about what to wear. But the next minute she proved me wrong.

'I want to look grown up. They won't believe me if they think I'm a child, Hunter. Don't laugh – you know you have said it yourself several times. So help me choose!'

'You look a lot less like a young teenager now you've got a nice haircut.'

I looked her over and discovered something else.

'And do you know what? I've only just noticed – you're

putting on a bit of weight. You aren't as skinny as you were a week ago. Very nice!'

But I did help her. She had organised her wardrobe with her usual attention to detail and sense of order. Everything was on hangers in tidy groups, jeans and pants, tops and jackets. We selected clothes that would make her look less childlike, but it was hard to make her look like an adult. We would have to go shopping again once this was over and get some smarter things for her to wear.

Willow rang while we were having breakfast. 'Just a quick question, before I rush off to the childcare place. Do you think Dao has told you everything now? I don't want any surprises coming out during the interview – do you think there are still things that she holds back?'

'I think it's all out now. Hold on a moment.'

I held the phone against my leg and spoke very quietly to Dao.

'Do I know everything now? Or is there more stuff you haven't told me? Willow needs to know before we meet the cops.'

She looked me straight in the eyes, no hesitation. 'You know everything. There is nothing more.'

'Willow, she says there's nothing else now, I know the lot. But she told me a couple of new things last night and I haven't had time to fill you in. We'll talk when we meet in town.'

'OK. If we get to a point in the interview where you realise there's something I haven't been told about, just take over and fill in. I mean if you can tell she's not going to tell them all the details herself – she might need prompting when we get to the unpleasant bits, and you know it all better than I do.'

We left at half past eight and I stopped four blocks away from the house and let Dao get into the front seat. The traffic was still full-on. I hardly ever travel at that time of the day, and I had misjudged how long it would take to get across the bridge and into the centre of town.

'Dao, can you call Willow and tell her we might be ten minutes late?'

Out of the corner of my eye I watched her make her first call from the new phone and listened, quietly amused, to the conversation that followed. I could imagine what Willow said at the other end.

'Hi Willow, it's Dao. We're a bit late, there's a lot of traffic. Hunter says we'll be at least ten minutes late.'

'We are just at our end of the bridge now.'

'No, he didn't. We left early but we got stuck behind buses and trucks.'

'OK, bye.'

I looked sideways at her and grinned.

'Did she suggest we left too late?'

'Yes,' said Dao. 'But it's not your fault that all those buses got in the way.'

'Thank you for defending me. Willow always arrives earlier than she has to. She thinks I always leave too late.'

Ever since I bought the phone I had debated with myself whether I should tell Dao that I had put that 'find my phone' app on it. Now seemed like a good time to do it.

'There's an app on your phone – it's called 'find my phone'. It uses something called GPS data and if you lose your phone you can check from another phone or from a computer and see where it is. I asked the guy in the shop to put it on your phone. Remind me to show you how it works when we get home.'

She thought for only a moment before she asked the pertinent question. 'So, if I get lost and I have the phone with me you could find me?'

'Exactly! And if it gets stolen we can see where it is, that sort of thing.'

'Have you got it on yours?'

'Do you think I should?'

I glanced sideways at her, and she was looking straight at me, black eyes steady, face revealing nothing.

'Yes, you should. What if your phone got lost?'

'I do have it on my phone too. I'll show you how to check where my phone is from yours when we get home.'

She was levelling the playing field, telling me without saying it that I was as likely to lose my phone as she was. And perhaps she was letting me know that if I could check where she was, she should be able to do the same. Life with Dao was nothing if not interesting.

'I presume Willow told you what to expect from this interview?'

'Oh, yes. She told me exactly what's going to happen. She said they will record what I say, and she only wants me to answer questions, she will do the talking and if she wants me to say nothing – if they ask something they shouldn't – then she'll just say that I'm not going to answer.'

I thought about the various things that might happen once we got there and what she should be prepared for.

'Listen, Dao – they will want to talk to me about how I found you and I will tell them. They need to know everything, even things that upset you and that you might not like to tell a stranger. Remember how you didn't want to tell me about being raped and taking the black book? It's very important that you don't hold back anything at all.'

'I know. Willow says that the more they know the better it is. Then they can charge him with a lot of different things, and he'll get more time in prison.'

'Right – but I don't know if they might want to talk to me separately from you. And if they do I will ask them to finish talking to you first with me present and then they can talk to me on my own.'

She looked at me as if I was one step behind, but kindly. 'Of course, Hunter. If they want to talk to us in different rooms I'll just say that I won't talk until you come back.'

She would too, I thought and smiled inwardly. I can just

see her sitting there – face calm, not fidgeting, looking into the distance, completely mute. They'll never get a word out of her unless she wants to talk. She might be the size of a shrimp, but my god, that fearless determination is king-size.

There was no time to fill Willow in on the whole rape story. Finding a place to park turned into a race against time and then we had to walk quite a long way. Willow was in the foyer talking to a cop, trying hard not to look impatient. All I had time to do was whisper 'he raped her' as we were shown into an interview room and sat down along one side of a table. I made Dao sit between us, hoping it would make her feel safe. Two police officers came into the room, a middle-aged woman and a younger man. The female officer introduced herself as Marcia Jones.

'I will do the actual interview and Constable Greek is here to observe.'

I had never been in a police interview room before and instantly noticed the clichéd reaction of feeling guilty for no reason. Willow introduced us and opened her briefcase. She took out a folder and put it exactly in the middle of the table as if she was indicating that it was still hers, but she might hand it over to Marcia at a later stage. Marcia did not reach out to pick it up.

'As I told you when I called, I represent Susan Johnson, who is sometimes called Dao. Hunter Grant is the person who found her, or rather his dog did, and he has been looking after her since. In this folder is a collection of papers which I would like to show you before we start. I have electronic copies of all these documents, and I will leave this folder with you.'

Marcia nodded, still silent. Willow opened the folder and listed each paper as she put them in front of Marcia.

'We have a fact sheet compiled by Mr Grant detailing how he found Susan and her condition at that stage, another fact sheet with what we have managed to find out about her parents and general background. A plan of the place where Susan was kept confined, drawn by her, as are the next sheets with drawings of boats and faces. We then have a number of aerial photographs of the place where Susan was kept, which we all refer to as 'the island'. The photos were taken from a helicopter by Mr Grant, and the exact coordinates have been signed off by the pilot. There are two photos of the man Bramville, who held Susan captive, also taken from the helicopter. The last item is a black notebook that belongs to Bramville. It appears to contain details of bank account numbers, phone numbers and some kind of tally of drugs or materials to make drugs. This book was retrieved yesterday from where Susan had hidden it in the forest when she fled.'

The constable was staring at Willow as if he had never seen a lawyer before. Marcia's eyes opened a fraction wider in surprise and she was about to say something, but Willow sat back, crossed her legs and started out on a new tack without pausing.

'When Mr Grant first told me about finding a girl in the forest neither he nor I knew anything other than the fact that she had been kept against her will. But just yesterday Susan, who as you can understand is seriously traumatised by years of enslavement, told Mr Grant a whole lot more and it seems likely that the place where she was held is part of a drug operation. And I realised the urgency of talking to you.'

Marcia finally spoke. 'Thank you. I can see that the material you have got together is going to be very useful.'

She looked at Dao and smiled. 'I believe you are usually called Dao. Would you like me to call you that, or do you prefer Susan, or would you like me to call you Miss Johnson? You are welcome to call me Marcia – I find it's easier to talk about difficult things if we are not too formal.'

'Call me Dao, please.' She sounded completely calm, but I saw the white-knuckled hand on her thigh under the edge of the table.

'And are you quite comfortable for Mr Grant to be present while we talk?'

Dao looked at her and said without the slightest hesitation, 'I will not talk to you if he is not here.'

The slightest raising of eyebrows was the only sign that Marcia was surprised by this uncompromising statement. She had been making sure that I was not some sort of predator or an interfering do-gooder, but Dao had made it clear I was necessary for her peace of mind.

'Of course – that's fine, Dao. You are entitled to have a support person.'

We proceeded from there and two hours later everything, but the rape had been discussed. Marcia looked at Dao and said, 'Well, I think we've just about finished. Is there anything you want to ask or anything you want to tell me?'

Dao looked at me as if to say 'Please say it for me!'

I turned to Marcia.

'The one remaining point is the sexual abuse Dao was subjected to.'

Marcia's nod told me that she had wondered about this. Maybe she had been just about to ask.

'Dao has been raped repeatedly for at least a year, by Bramville.'

More questions, some very difficult for Dao to answer. She never flinched, but nearly every time she replied she glanced at me, as if looking for assurance that nothing would go wrong. I felt for her, but there was nothing I could do. Marcia had offered to talk to her about it without the constable or me in the room and Dao had replied, 'No, just ask. I want you to know.'

The only point when she nearly broke down was when Marcia asked if she had ever consented to any form of intimacy with Bramville. Dao's whole body stiffened, her face outraged and shocked. I had no idea what would happen or what she would say. I had to clench my teeth to stop myself from objecting. Willow reached out and took hold of Dao's hand. Dao answered in a voice full of revulsion.

'No, never! Never! I hate him, he's cruel and evil and he

has whipped me and punished me for years. I didn't want him to touch me, it made me feel sick and that's one thing that made me decide I had to die.'

'What was the other thing, Dao? Was it finding your mother's bones?'

Dao nodded, her eyes were full of tears now and she pulled her hand from Willow's and wiped her eyes. I reached for the box of tissues on the table and put one into her hand.

'When I found those bones I knew I had to leave, I knew he might kill me because he was still angry that I had stabbed him with the nail. He said he would sell me, but he would have killed me.'

She stopped and blew her nose. 'And it didn't matter what he decided to do – I had to get away to die on my own, I refused to die at that place.'

'Why do you say that you had to die? Did you not think you could run far enough to escape and find help?'

Dao replied patiently, as if she thought an explanation should have been unnecessary, that the person asking the question was possibly a bit slow or had not listened.

'Bram told me we were on an island and that my mother had left me with him. When we first arrived, he took us there in his boat. So, when he said it was a big island and the only way to get away was to swim – or go in a boat – I believed him.'

She glanced at me, and I nodded reassurance and she continued.

'And he said there was no way for me to hide on the island because he had the dogs, and they would track me and tear me to pieces. What I decided to do was to go as far as I possibly could and then lie down and die before the dogs found me. I thought if I didn't eat or drink it would not take long. I didn't want to drown - I don't like the water.'

Willow looked at me over Dao's head. I saw that she was close to tears, but she cleared her throat and said, 'Marcia, I think my client has been through enough for one day. She needs to go home now and rest.'

'Just one more thing,' I said, determined to make sure they knew the kind of monster they were dealing with. 'Just to illustrate the kind of man Bramville is I want to quote what he said to Dao when she stabbed him with that nail and interrupted another rape. He said 'your name is Slave, and you can belong to anyone. John wants you and he can have you'. He needs to be stopped.'

Marcia thanked us and as she got up to open the door for us she spoke directly to Dao.

'You have been very brave talking about all this. We will probably need to speak to you again, but we'll come to your place, so you don't have to come here again.'

She smiled and gestured at the bare and functional room, 'It's not exactly like home, is it?'

Dao smiled back, but without real warmth. She looked tired and I wanted to get us out of there as soon as I could. Outside we parted from Willow, who hugged Dao for a long moment before she headed for her car. Dao and I stood there, lost and disorientated.

'I feel as if I've been run over by a bus,' I said. 'You must be exhausted.'

'Two buses,' she said. 'I want to go home.'

It was the first time she had referred to my house as home. At least the security of the house was now a fixed part of her world. But coming back into the house was oddly awkward. We both seemed out of joint somehow, as if our relationship had been skewed by the interview. Dao went straight upstairs and after a while I followed. She was standing by the window in her room, quite still and apparently calm. I went and stood beside her, looking down at Scruff in the courtyard and not at her. It was not the right moment to remind her not to stand by the window.

'What are you thinking about?'

She said nothing for a long time, and I stayed silent,

hoping that she would need no further prompting. Finally, she spoke, but without turning her head to look at me.

'It feels different now that other people have heard me talk about it. It's hard to explain. It feels as if it has made me a different person.'

Not for the first time her insight struck me. It was very surprising for someone so young, a girl who had grown to adulthood without guidance. Her physical stance spoke as loudly as words; she was deliberately distancing herself from me. I must find a way to help her to be comfortable with me again.

'I can understand that. To lay your personal experiences out on the table like that in front of people you don't know - very difficult. But for me it changes nothing about who and what you are. When we left the police station we left those people behind, now it's us again. I'm sure you will feel unsettled like this again – there are bound to be more interviews and perhaps a court case. And each time you might feel as if it has changed you. But when we walk away from those places and come home then we're back to being our normal selves again.'

I turned to look at her and she took a step closer and leant for a moment against my chest.

'You are right, Hunter. It's so good to be at home again.'

I had just stepped into the bright light of self-awareness. I had pretended even to myself that the strong bond of affection I felt for her was only what I would have felt for a daughter. I must never let her suspect that what she thought of as the safe affection from a parent or a brother was anything different. I had made a commitment to support her and care for her and I would. There could be no indication from me of anything different.

11

WEDNESDAY AFTERNOON

We had finished lunch and were sitting quietly reading with Scruff at Dao's feet. She had just looked up from her book to ask me what preposterous means when the sound of glass breaking downstairs made me jump to my feet. A second later the phone alert went off in my pocket. I threw the book to one side and headed for the shotgun and the stairs, shouting at Dao to get out of the way. I had no time to turn to see if she obeyed. Someone was running fast along the ground floor hallway toward the stairs. Feet pounded on the wooden treads of the staircase. I hoped Dao was safely upstairs.

I raised the Remington and trained it on the point where his head appeared a fraction of a second later. He was looking straight ahead into the room, not scanning 180 degrees as anyone experienced would have done. He carried a sawn-off shotgun in one hand, completely the wrong grip for fast action. No way could he fire before I did. A stupid man thinking he was clever because he remembered to wear gloves.

Just when he put his foot on the floor of the living room I shouted 'freeze'. It took him completely by surprise. He swung around, but he didn't raise the gun fast enough. The barrel of the Remington was pointing directly at his face from an arm's length away. He froze, a look of surprise and fear on his face. We stood there for a short moment, not moving, just staring at each other. He was quite tall and skinny, but fit-looking, like a long-distance runner. He was obviously not weapons trained and not very clever or he would never have come charging up with his gun in one hand like that.

Dao appeared behind him. She had come silently out from the kitchen on bare feet and was standing no more than a metre from him. I tried not to look directly at her.

'Eyes forward – don't turn around! There is another guy standing right behind you. I want you to bend down sideways and put the gun on the floor. Just put it down now and my mate will pick it up and take it into another room. OK? And use one hand only.'

Now it was critical that he did what I said. With Dao so close I would not be able to fire without hitting her too. Getting him to quietly put the gun down was vitally important or things could get messy. I could possibly aim at his feet and lower legs and maybe get shot for my troubles. And risk Dao's feet getting sprayed with pellets too. Or I could swipe the barrel of my gun hard across his arms and then tackle him when he dropped his weapon. I hoped that Dao would take the hint and not show herself, just pick the gun up and take it into the kitchen. He must not see her.

His eyelids twitched and for a second he looked as if he might charge me, but then he bent down and put the gun on the floor with one hand, over to one side. I nodded to Dao over his shoulder.

'Paul, pick it up carefully. I don't know if it's loaded. Take it away and stay with it. I'll deal with this.'

Dao stepped closer and bent down just behind him. She pulled the gun towards her and lifted it very slowly with both hands and walked quietly back to the kitchen. I heard her open a cupboard door, then silence. So far, so good.

'OK, now turn around and walk into the living room in front of me, look straight ahead.'

He did what he was told. When he was halfway to the end of the room I said, 'Stop there. Lie down on your front, arms out at right angles. Don't move – I will have the gun on you at all times.'

I walked backwards until I was level with the opening into the kitchen and glanced in. Dao was not in sight.

'Hey, Paul,' I said, looking at the open broom closet door. 'Open the bottom drawer beside the dishwasher. I think there's a plastic bag there with a bunch of black ties inside. Hand it to me, please.'

She came out from behind the open door, got out the bag of plastic cable ties and put it in my hand. I whispered, 'stay here' and walked towards the man on the floor.

'Now put your hands behind your back.'

I knelt on the small of his back with one knee, so my weight prevented him from getting up, and put the Remington on the floor beside me. A minute later I had fastened a cable tie round his wrists, tight enough to be pretty uncomfortable. I got up and shoved a foot hard against the side of his ribcage, rolling him over until he rested on his side, so I could see his face.

'Fuck you!' he said, squinting up at me. 'Man, that hurts!'

His right arm was twisted and caught under him, and there was nothing he could do to lessen the pain.

'Not as much as being shot at close range with a twelve-gauge,' I said. 'Now, before I ring the cops I want to know a couple of things. What are you after and who sent you? I know you were here twice at night after sitting in your car watching the house. I've got the video to prove it. So it's no use pretending you're a common thief.'

He looked surly and stubborn. 'I'm just looking for stuff to sell.'

'You're lying – I'm not a fool. You're after something and I want to know what it is. Who sent you?'

'Nobody sent me – I'm just after stuff to sell. I need the cash.'

'OK, you've had your chance.'

I put my foot on him and rolled him back to lie face down again. I took a couple of steps back, got my phone out of my pocket and dialled 111.

'I have an intruder in my house. I've disarmed him and tied him up. Could you send someone to take him away?'

The operator said, 'OK, they'll be with you very soon. Did you say you've disarmed him?'

I knew that mentioning weapons would make things more complicated, but I wanted him to be arrested for breaking in armed. At least they wouldn't let him out on bail.

'Yes, he's harmless, lying on the floor, tied up. Don't for god's sake get the armed offender's squad out, there's no need. Just send a car to remove him, please.'

I walked backwards until I was level with the kitchen and spoke very quietly to Dao.

'I will go to the left of him and make him look at me. I don't want him to see you. Go downstairs, open the front door and leave it open, then go upstairs and stay in the bedroom with the door shut. Don't make any noise. Where is Scruff?'

She nodded and whispered, 'OK. Scruff is here, I've told him to be quiet and stay still.'

'Where is that shotgun?'

She swung the broom closet door shut and pointed; it was lying on the washing machine.

'OK, just wait till you hear me tell him to look at me, then go down.'

I took the sawn-off shotgun and put it on the dining table. Standing on his left side I pointed the Remington down at his head.

'Turn your head and look at me.'

He managed to raise his chest just enough to turn his head. He stared at the gun in an upward squint, not knowing what to expect. He was sweating now, either from pain or nerves.

Dao returned from the ground floor, went briefly into the kitchen and reappeared with Scruff. They walked along the wall to the stairs and disappeared. Scruff's claws made a clicking sound on the wooden stair treads, but I would never have known Dao was there. After that I heard nothing else, the silence in the house was total.

I put the Remington in the broom cupboard, closed the door and went back to the living room. A few minutes later I heard a car stopping outside and footsteps in the hall. A voice called out 'Police – anybody home?'

I went to the top of the stairs. 'Come up to the first floor.'

Two police officers came up the stairs, both with guns. They took in the scene in one sweeping glance around the room: the sawn-off shotgun on the dining table, the man face down on the floor and me standing there empty-handed.

The older man said, 'What's happened here?'

I had decided to let them take the guy away with as little fuss as possible. I would only tell them the basic details and then call Marcia and give her the full story. That way the intruder would hear nothing about Dao and for the time being the local cops would be left with the impression that I had been alone at home. It was a gamble, but worth trying.

'I was sitting here reading and this guy broke in and came charging up the stairs with a sawn-off shotgun.'

I was applying the principle of minimum detail, minimum risk of stuffing up and contradicting myself. 'He must have come over the wall into the courtyard at the back. The first I knew about it was the sound of breaking glass downstairs.'

The older cop looked hard at me, suspicious and prepared to disbelieve everything I told him.

'And how did you disarm him?'

'I was running towards the stairs and just tackled him. I mean, I didn't know he was going to be armed. But he's an idiot. He came up with the gun in one hand – there was no chance he could change his grip fast enough to shoot me. He made it really easy. I got the gun off him and made him lie down and tied him up. And then I rang 111.'

A child could have seen that he did not believe me. He looked me up and down very slowly and deliberately with narrowed eyes. He was an old hand, and he knew there was something else going on. To pacify him I decided to add a bit of credibility.

'I was with the army in Afghanistan – I'm used to dealing with situations. And this guy was easy compared to most of what we came up against. I don't think he was expecting to meet anyone who knew a bit more than he does.'

They took him away after getting my name and details and inspecting the broken glass in the courtyard door. A couple of times the older man asked me for more details, but I stuck to my minimal story and promised I would come down to the station and make a statement a bit later.

'I just need to cover that broken window with something first and get a glazier in.'

I did not tell them about the video footage or the alarm alerting me when he broke in. They would probably be angry when they found out how much I had kept from them, but my first concern was to protect Dao. I went upstairs and found her sitting cross-legged in the middle of my bed, looking at the door.

'It's OK now. They've taken him away. Thanks for being so helpful down there. You understood why I called you Paul?'

'Yes, of course. That was clever. Now he still doesn't know that I am here.'

'Someone sent him – he's just a stupid guy with no clue how to take a house with a gun and get away with it. Either the Boss or Bramville hired him – or forced him to do this. But he didn't see you so that's all good. But next time make sure you don't stand in the line of fire. A shotgun scatters shot, lots of little pellets, so stand well to the side.'

I sat down on the edge of the bed, looked up the number

to the Central police station in the city and made the call to Marcia.

'Hi, it's Hunter Grant. I came in with Dao this morning. Have you got five minutes?'

'Well, you struck it lucky,' she said. 'I'm due in a meeting in five. What can I do for you?'

'We've just had a break-in here – a guy with a gun came storming in.'

'Christ!' she said. 'Tell me what happened.'

I told her the story and she listened without interrupting.

'So, you can see what this means,' I said when I got to the end. 'I'm going to be in hot water with the local officers when they discover that I've tricked them. But I thought the most likely reason that guy broke in was to get to Dao. And I didn't want him to be able to confirm that she's here in my house. I had to leave all that stuff out of what I told them while he was listening. But if you could get in touch with the local station and fill them in I suppose they'll understand. Dao and I can talk to them or to you any time.'

The only thing I had not told her was that I had used a gun to stop him. I would have if she had asked, but she did not inquire.

'OK,' she said. 'I'll call them and fill them in and explain why. Better make sure they know not to mention Dao to anyone at all outside the station. But they have to know there's potential for more trouble. Do you want to go somewhere for a while? Is there somewhere safe you could take her?'

'Not right now. I'll think about it. We could always go and stay in a motel somewhere for a while.'

'I think it might be a good idea,' she said, and she was serious. 'God knows how big this operation is. I've just been on the phone with the drug and organised crime people. They're on the way up there with the Armed Offenders Squad to raid the place as we speak. The main thing right now is to secure the place and make sure no evidence is destroyed or removed. It's a lot of stuff all at once – murder, drugs, enslavement, sexual abuse. These guys won't hesitate to do all they can to prevent Dao talking or being a witness – and so far they don't even know if you've got her or if she's dead. But she's certainly the key person in all this.'

'I know. She's a vital link – her and that black book. Once Bramville realised that she had taken it he must have completely freaked out. And if he told the Boss I imagine all the stops will be pulled out.'

'Exactly,' she said. 'Heaven knows Bramville might have left already, but at least we've got a good description. And I'll want that video footage you have too. I'll talk to you later, got to go now.'

I turned around to say something to Dao, but she was asleep, curled up just behind me. I covered her with the rug and looked at her for a moment. Her calm and quick understanding in a bad situation had impressed me. No screaming, no hysterics. And she had no idea how special she was. I must make sure to tell her. I left her with Scruff and went downstairs.

Nigel spotted me from his balcony later on when I was talking to the glazier in the courtyard. We were discussing security glass with embedded wire-mesh when Nigel's voice cut in from above.

'What's happened, Hunter? I saw a police car outside a while ago.'

'Someone broke in. No harm done – I'll come over and talk to you in a moment.'

I hung around until the glazier finished writing up the measurements and went back upstairs. Dao was sitting on the bed with the laptop.

'Have they gone?'

'Who?'

'Those men you were talking to. I thought I'd better stay here.'

'One of them was a guy who came to measure the glass.

He's gone away to cut it and then he'll come back and fix the door. And he's going to replace the window in the bedroom down there too. We're having glass with wire-mesh baked into it. Not pretty, but very safe. The other voice was Nigel from next-door; he was talking to me from their balcony. I have to go over and reassure him - he saw the police car and he wants to know what's going on. I'll lock you in and set the ground floor alarm while I'm at his place.'

'Can't I come?'

'I would rather you weren't seen outside. But OK, so long as you understand that I'm going to lie to Nigel. He's an old gossip and I don't want him to know anything about who you really are. So I'll make up some story and you just have to fit in with it. But it would be best if you and Scruff stay here instead of going outside. I don't think anyone else is going to turn up this soon.'

But Dao surprised me as she often did.

'Is the garden door safe – I mean is there just a big hole where the glass was?'

'No, the glazier fixed a sheet of thick plastic stuff in it for now. It looks like white glass but it's a really thick plastic material, a bit bendy. Very hard to cut a hole in, I would think.'

'OK, make sure you lock the doors and set the alarm for that level. Then you'll hear the alert on your phone if someone tries to break in and you can come back fast. Where is the gun?'

That made me smile. 'Never mind the gun. You don't know enough about guns to use it. Just sit tight for ten minutes.'

'I've been watching You Tube things about shotguns while you were talking to the glass man. There are lots of them and they tell you exactly what to do and what's dangerous. I do know a lot now. Where is the gun?'

'You're not having the gun. We'll discuss this later. Maybe

we'll go to a practice range one day so you can try firing it, but not yet.'

I went downstairs, checked the back door was locked and went out the front door. I stopped to set the alarm and walked across the grass to Nigel's house. The visit took less than five minutes. He wanted me to come inside and have a cup of coffee. I think he was bored, and some company and excitement would make his day, but I stood on the doorstep and talked to him so I could keep an eye on the street.

'Sorry, Nigel, I can't – not today. I've got the daughter of an old army friend staying with me for a couple of weeks. She's thinking of going to university here and her parents are out of the country.'

'But what happened, Hunter? Could it be that chap who came into our garden, do you think?'

'Could have been – I don't know. The cops took him away but I don't know what will happen next. He smashed the glass in the garden door and stuck his hand in and turned the lock knob. So I'm getting the glazier to put in that security glass with metal wires – and he's replacing the bedroom window with the same stuff.'

'I never thought of it before but those courtyards with the high walls all around, they're made for burglars,' said Nigel. 'If they can scale the wall they're in and nobody can see them from outside. What if he'd had a diamond cutter? He could have been inside and up the stairs taking you by surprise before you knew he was even there. I think we might do something about our glass at the back too.'

I did not mention that we now had the ground floor alarm zone activated all the time. There was no point in having him speculating about what went on in my life.

'I only saw the police car driving away, you know – I never saw who was in it. Tell the police that Margie and I might recognise him.'

'Sure, I'll let them know when they call me.'

Dao and Scruff were still upstairs in the bedroom. Scruff

opened his eyes without lifting his chin off the floor, wagged his tail once and closed his eyes again.

'Dao, you might be a girl warrior, but you are also a thief.'

Her head snapped up and then she saw my face and relaxed.

'The black book? Is that what I stole?'

'No, the black dog – the one that used to be my dog and followed me around everywhere. You have stolen his affection and now he hardly notices if I'm there or not.'

She looked so guilty I had to laugh. 'Don't worry, I'm kidding. I don't mind. But one thing I would like to know – how did you get him to stay in the kitchen and not follow you when I had that guy at gunpoint? And how did you stop him barking when it all started?'

She got off the bed and Scruff sat up, waiting to see what she was going to do. She put her fingers across her lips and said 'shush' very quietly. He watched intently. She pointed to the floor just in front of his feet and said 'stay!' still without raising her voice and then she walked out of the room and down the stairs. Halfway down she said loudly 'come on Hunter' and I followed her. We stood in the middle of the living room and waited. There was no sound of movement from the bedroom and Scruff did not follow us. Then Dao grinned at me and called 'Come, Scruff' and he came scrambling down the stairs, beside himself with joy. She rewarded him with pats and hugs.

'Wow,' I said. 'How the hell did you teach him that in no time at all?'

'I don't know. I've never taught a dog anything before, but he's so clever. It was just a way of playing with him when you weren't there. You know, when you were flying with Charlie and Willow was busy on the phone and when you were talking to Willow and Charlie down here or you were upstairs, talking to Paul. Lots of times when Scruff and I were waiting. It was just a game, but he picked it up so fast. Isn't he clever?'

12

WEDNESDAY EVENING

I was giving Scruff his dinner when I had an idea. 'Dao, let's go out for dinner, would you like that?'

'I thought we couldn't do that – not till we're safe,' she said. 'Or do you think the man who broke in is the only one – I mean, the only one who does that sort of thing, goes around killing people?'

'No, probably not. But I think you deserve a reward. We'll go to Antoine's in Parnell, it's one of my favourite places. I'll have to wear proper clothes to get in and I'm sure Bramville or any of those other guys would never go there.'

'What are proper clothes? Do I have any?'

She had me there; we had bought loads of casual things and nothing dressy. And then I thought of Charlie's partner Kristen.

'Let's see what we can do,' I said to Dao. 'We'll have to get organised soon if we're going out tonight.'

I rang Charlie and explained. She thought it was hilarious.

'I never thought I'd see the day,' she said, and I could hear the suppressed mirth. 'You, the hard man, turning into a personal shopper – for a girl! It's bloody funny.'

She started laughing and tried to say something else but I

cut in. 'Shut up Charlie – this is an emergency. Kristen is the size of a toothpick and so is Dao. Do you think they're about the same?'

She was still chortling away at the other end. 'Well, width-wise they might be – roughly, but Kristen is tall and Dao is very short. But I suppose it might work. Why don't you come over and we'll see what we can do?'

We left Scruff in the bedroom with the door closed and set out half an hour later. Dao was in the far back as usual, but I stopped before we got on the motorway to town and let her into the front of the car; I was fairly sure she had never seen the view from the Harbour Bridge at night. We drove on to the bridge and the lights of the city spread out before us with Sky Tower lit in icy blue light, its thin top spire glowing against the dark sky. Dao drew in a breath of surprise. 'Go slowly, please. Isn't it beautiful? Look at that tower!'

Charlie saw us parking on the drive and came out to meet us.

'Hunter, I still can't believe this. Are you having a mid-life crisis or something?'

The idea made me cringe. Was I having an earlier than mid-life crisis? But I put it in the back of my mind, and we followed her into the house. Kristen had just come home from work and Charlie had told her about our mission. Tall, extremely thin and as elegant as ever she said hi to Dao, lent forward to air kiss my cheek without touching any part of me, took Dao by the hand and led her away towards the bedroom end of the house. Kristen has an ambivalent attitude to me. On the one hand I think she likes me, perhaps because she knows that Charlie and I have such a long-standing friendship, but she is also afraid that I am a bad influence on Charlie, and it gets to her when we talk about the past and our friends from those days.

'Come into the kitchen,' said Charlie. 'You can keep me company while they do their girly stuff. Heaven knows

Kristen has enough clothes and stuff to stock a shop. Bet she's got dozens of things she's forgotten she ever bought.'

I sat on a stool and watched Charlie making something with pieces of chicken and a mass of ingredients. Everything she did involved grating or shredding or chopping. She's a great cook.

'Why don't you just put the chicken in the oven and roast it?'

I said it on purpose, knowing what her reply would be. It came out as ordered: 'Because that's not how I want to do it.' I'm sure she said it to her mother from the age of three.

She continued chopping something pale green that I did not even know the name of – some kind of grass by the look of it.

'So, how's it all going?' She put the little green bits to one side and started peeling a piece of root ginger.

I told her all the details about the police interview that morning and about the man breaking into the house after lunch.

'Shit, Hunter! It was lucky you were there with Dao and not on the top floor or something.'

'I know – very lucky. But her performance when I had that guy at gunpoint – she was as cool as a cucumber, no fuss. And then her asking where the gun was when I wanted to talk to Nigel – and telling me she knew all about shotguns because she'd studied the subject on You Tube – I ask you. Like some girl warrior. Could I do anything but reward her? And the only thing she's always dreamt of – aside from constant access to a shower and hot water – is to eat in what she calls a proper restaurant. Like she saw on TV when she was little. With candles.'

'Well if anyone can dress up your warrior girl it's Kristen,' said Charlie. 'When it comes to clothes… you have no idea.'

When Kristen and Dao came into the kitchen Kristen looked inscrutable, Dao looked slightly overwhelmed, and Charlie and I just stared.

'Good god Dao – you've got make-up on!' said Charlie. 'You look amazing, girl – fantastic.'

I said nothing. Gone was the twenty-one-year-old who looked like fourteen and in her place was an exotic-looking young woman in red and gold and black.

'Dao – I nearly didn't recognise you. Very pretty!'

Kristen looked Dao up and down and nodded as if she was marginally satisfied.

'It's an improvement, I think. But all we really did was to find a nice top to go with her black pants and some make-up and stuff.'

She turned to Charlie. 'Do you remember I said last year I wished I had never bought anything red and I was never going to again? After that horrible shop assistant said 'oh no, no, not for you' in that sort of revolted voice when I took something red off a rack. You were with me at the time.'

Charlie looked blank; clearly the event had not registered as significant.

'I've told Dao she can keep the top – I'll never wear it again after that comment and it's perfect on her.'

And so it was. A silky-looking red top with gold embroidery. Like a short, fitted jacket, slightly Asian-looking with a high collar and dozens of little buttons down the front.

Charlie and Kristen made me take photos of Dao on her own and with both of them on three different phones and then we left. I went to the far side of the car and opened the passenger door.

'I'll have to remember you're an adult now and not a little girl.'

She said nothing as I backed out of the drive.

'Are you pleased?'

She turned the question around and passed it right back. 'Are *you* pleased? Would you rather I looked like a little girl?'

Puzzled I glanced sideways, but she was facing forward. I had no idea what lay behind the question. I decided to adopt a safe stance.

'You look lovely. Do you want to look like that all the time? We can go shopping and you can buy make-up and whatever you want – or you can ask Kristen to take you shopping later on. She's the expert.'

The silence was deafening, and I was baffled. There was something going on in that clever head and I had no clues at all.

'Dao,' I said. 'Please tell me what's going on. We can't go out for dinner if we can't talk to each other.'

A shorter silence and then she gave in.

'I feel as if I don't know how to be with you now. I mean it – you know – what I asked. Which way do you want me to look? Like a scruffy girl or do you want me to be...'

She was lost for words. I had a fair idea where all this had come from. Certainly, Dao had not come up with this herself, so someone had voiced the question. When she went off with Kristen this had not been an issue, but now it was. Kristen had transformed her and commented on how she now looked adult and lovely. Perhaps she had made some comment about how I might react to the change. Or she might have tried to find out what Dao felt about me. I remembered Charlie's warning and thought she might have discussed it with Kristen. Whatever it was it had skewed Dao's relationship with me, or she thought it had.

'I just want you to be whatever you want to be,' I said casually, as if it was no big deal. 'Be different on different days if you want to. Dress like a scruffy girl and spend the day playing with Scruff or put on make-up and dress in smart clothes and look like a film star – it's all fine with me. It makes no difference to who you really are. I know you're still brave and clever Dao and the important thing is that you're happy and learning stuff and getting on with your maths or whatever you want to do.'

'Really? Is that what you really think? You don't think I'm just like a child?'

'Good god, no – I never thought of you as a child. You

look like a child sometimes, but that's your size and clothes, not you as a person. Inside your head you are too sophisticated and clever to be thought of as a child. What gave you that idea?'

And then we talked about other things and Dao remembered that I had not explained what preposterous meant and she had not looked it up. We had a quick lesson about dining in places with a menu; how you have several courses with plates of different sizes. Taking Dao to a 'proper' restaurant for the first time turned into a mixture of enjoyment and amusement. She was instantly charmed by the brick-paved courtyard and quietly followed the immaculate man who showed us to our table. He pulled out her chair and called her madam. She smiled at him and thanked him with a look of calm pleasure. Nobody in the world could have guessed that she was fizzing with excitement and that she had never been near a place like this before. When he left us to study the menu she leaned forward and said in a whisper, 'He called me madam!'

'So, he should – this is a very good restaurant and when you are here he is your servant. Whatever you say or do is right – even if it isn't.'

She laughed, delighted with the idea that she could be right even if she was wrong - just because she was having an expensive meal.

'It's just like on TV.' She was still whispering. 'Look at all these people, don't they look lovely?'

'I'm sure they do – but I'd guess that not many here are as smart as you are.'

She just shook her head at me and started reading the menu.

'What should I have? I don't know what all these things are.'

The suave man returned with a wine list. He must have heard Dao saying that she did not know what the dishes were. He bent down beside her and pointed out a couple of dishes and explained what they were. She listened attentively.

'Would it be all right if I have two small plates and not a big one at all? Is that OK?'

He assured her that she could have anything she liked. When Dao was eating her second starter and I was having my main course she leaned forward and said very quietly, 'There's a man looking at me all the time. Just to the left of you. I don't like it.'

I turned my head and met the eyes of a lean-faced grey-haired man in his sixties who quickly looked away.

'He thinks you're lovely, maybe he hopes you will smile at him. Just ignore people who stare at you – just look at them very briefly, don't smile – and then turn away. They will see you're not interested.'

He probably thinks she's a mail order bride - or something worse, I thought, but I don't blame him for staring. She's looking very exotic. A lot of people are looking at her, both men and women.

A short while later I noticed Dao's eyes tracking someone over my shoulder and then a familiar voice spoke next to me.

'Hunter – good to see you're back. Vivian said you were holed up in that cabin of yours.'

I looked up. 'Hi, Mark – how are you? I got back a while ago, but I've been busy. Susan, this is Mark Barton – we went to school together, a long time ago. Mark, let me introduce you to my friend Susan Johnson.'

Mark looked her over and clearly appreciated what he saw.

'Very nice to meet you. Are you new in town?'

Dao considered him seriously, took in the natty designer clothes, the spiky hair-style and his general air of stylish fashion and said politely, 'No, I'm not – I was born here.'

I added innocently, 'Susan is a new friend of mine, she's a mathematician. Is Maria here?'

Mark knew he was being sent back to his own party and grinned.

'I hope we meet again.' He smiled at Dao and left.

'Clever girl,' I said when he was out of earshot. 'He was fishing for information, and you kept him nicely at arm's length – well done.'

She picked up her fork. 'I thought maybe you didn't want him to know anything about me. And you never told me what story you told the man next door, so I had to say something safe.'

I went over the story I had told Nigel and she nodded.

'We have to say the same thing – even if it is a lie it's got to be right.'

A waiter appeared to take our plates and asked Dao if she had enjoyed her meal.

'I didn't like the second thing very much. But the first one was lovely – and pretty.'

Then she thought that she might have been rude and added naively, 'But please don't tell the person who cooked it, probably everyone else likes it.'

The waiter's expression was priceless, a comical mix of amusement and delighted surprise. You don't even know it, warrior girl, I thought, but you've got him in the palm of your hand.

It was late when we got home, and we headed straight upstairs. I went into the bathroom last and when I came out Dao seemed to be sleeping.

Once again I stood beside the bed looking down at her. I thought back to the day when I had found her in that shallow forest grave, cold and wet and starved, and how the first thing she had said when she was conscious was 'I don't need to eat, I am going to die'.

I lay down under the blanket that now lived permanently on my side of the bed and turned the light off. I was thinking about how the men in the restaurant had looked at her. I worried about her having to cope with all the attention she would undoubtedly get wherever she went. Her isolated years as Slave had deprived her of the time when most teenagers learn to distinguish flattering attention from bad intentions or end up in trouble as a consequence. She had natural caution, but she was not street smart. I was nearly asleep when her fingertips touched my shoulder just for a second, making sure I was there.

13

THURSDAY

Marcia called early the next morning. 'I just want to tell you that a senior sergeant called Benson from Organised Crimes will be in touch with you – probably this morning. I used to work with him before he got transferred and he's good. They want to ask a few more questions but I can't get your sister on the phone at the moment, so I thought I'd ring you first – just so you know what's happening. I'm out of this investigation because of the drug and gang connections.'

Willow called while we were having breakfast. 'I believe Marcia rang you? OK, Benson just wants a half-hour meeting. He's coming over to your place at eleven. I'll be there a bit before then – I hope. The twins are in a foul temper this morning – snotty and miserable. Synchronised teething – I'll leave them at the crèche for as short a time as possible – nobody will enjoy their company today. But I will be at your place on time, or nearly.'

I was just about to close the call when she remembered something.

'Oh yes – I forgot to tell you. Mum rang last night. I said you had the daughter of an old army friend staying – same story as before, just in case she got wind of it somehow. She

184

asked a lot of questions about who the parents are and why hadn't she heard about them before – you know the sort of stuff. She can't stand it that you never tell her things. I was pretty vague and said I hadn't asked for details.' She laughed. 'Tried to make her see it isn't anyone's business, but she's in one of her moods, thinks she has to know everything that goes on.'

'Well, that's fine. It's not as if she's likely to turn up on my doorstep to check it out, is it?'

'No, they're not planning to come for a visit, but you know how she is. If she had found out you've had a young woman staying with you for a while and she didn't hear until afterwards she'd straight away think you're up to something.'

Willow laughed again; she thinks our mother is funny in an absurd and maddening way, but it was no joke. Glenda can be relentless and intrusive about my personal life. I've often wondered if she's as inquisitive about her patients' lives as she is about her children.

'It didn't matter how many times I told her that Dao regards you as a favourite uncle. She was pretty full-on, but I said I didn't know a lot about it. I know it's evil to lie to my mother, but I couldn't tell her the truth. She would talk about it to Dad and then she'd tell Plum. And Plum would never be able to resist telling her friends such an exciting story. It would be in the papers before we could blink.'

I looked absently at Dao, who had a piece of toast in one hand and was doing something on the laptop with the other and thought maybe I should buy another laptop. The thought of my mother coming for a visit was a scary prospect. Glenda and Rob usually stay with me when they come to Auckland because I have lots of room, but at the moment I could think of nothing worse. Getting them involved in potential danger and our complex security would be more than I could cope with. Not to mention my mother's natural talent for interfering. I mentally crossed my fingers and hoped the situation would be well and truly over before their next visit.

Willow arrived shortly before eleven and we had barely started talking when the doorbell went. Benson was a short and slightly tubby man, the kind whose shirt is always coming un-tucked. He had penetrating grey eyes, a receding hairline and a very firm handshake He seemed friendly, but he had no time for idle conversation.

'Sorry to have to rush you like this,' he said. 'I just want to give you an update on what's been going on and ask a couple of questions.'

We sat around the table and Benson got an iPad out of his briefcase, put it in front of him and started talking.

'We raided the island – yes, we have decided to refer to it by your name,' he said, looking at Dao. 'It's a convenient name and the place doesn't have a name of its own anyway. Bramville was gone. There was no plastic barrel in the storage shed, but plenty of other evidence that forensics are looking at. We don't know if he took the barrel away or if the person you call the Boss collected it, but we found the boat. It was left where he parked his truck – on the beach at the end of the little road just to the north of the headland. Lots of leads to follow up. And we know his name – Bramville Newton – the local council gave us the name of the property owner, so we've been in touch with his landlord.'

He looked down at the iPad, then pushed it aside as if he had no idea what it was doing there and cleared his throat.

'Our problem now is that we have no leads at all when it comes to the Boss. We have to assume that his first priority is to make sure that we don't find Bramville. He's the only witness we have that links the operation to the Boss – apart from you, Dao. The tattoo on his arm is a good piece of evidence and we're working on that – searching our own database and those held by Customs and Immigration and the Corrections Department.'

So far I had kept quiet about the break-in at the cabin, but now I had to say something.

'I don't think I've told anyone yet – my cabin up there was

broken into just after we went back to town. Someone had a good look around, searched the place pretty thoroughly. The farmer down the road told me.'

There was silence for a moment. Benson looked hard at me, and I could tell he was annoyed and trying not to show it. 'Did you report it?'

'No, I didn't.' I tried hard to make it sound like the sort of reasonable decision anyone might make. 'At the time it hardly seemed worth the trouble. Nothing was taken and I thought it was just someone who came across the place and thought they'd have a look in case there was something worth taking.'

'And was there?'

'No, I never leave anything there that would interest a thief – it's all pretty basic.'

His face was inscrutable, and I knew I had better make it sound a bit more credible.

'After Dao told me about the notebook she took from Bramville we flew up there with a friend who has a chopper. Dao found the book and we gave it to Marcia. I didn't think of mentioning the break-in."

Benson had his eyes fixed on me and I knew he was trying to figure out if I was hiding something. 'OK, it's good to know. If he used those dogs of his to track Dao he might have broken in to see if there was anything inside to show if she had been there. Do you think he would have found anything?'

'No, nothing. We took the rubbish back to town and she had nothing apart from a shirt and a pair of jeans when I found her – and that bloody shackle. And I brought those things back with us. But he must have found out who I am from something in the cabin – and my town address.'

Willow spoke for the first time since we had sat down.

'I presume the crucial thing here is that Boss – or Bramville – sent someone to check this place too and we need to know if they think there's a link between Hunter and Dao. Has that man who broke in here said anything?'

Benson shook his head and frowned.

'Nothing - still claims he's just a common thief but I'm sure he was sent here. He can't explain why he had that sawn-off shotgun or why he broke in when it was as likely as not that someone was at home. We're working on tracing his connections, but my guess is that he's some little shit who'll do anything if you pay him enough. Or he owes someone a lot of money. And that's why I came. I need to find out exactly what went on and what he saw when he was inside the house.'

I knew we were on thin ice here. I did not want the cops speculating about me and the Remington. They might think I was just over the top cautious, or they might think I was armed all the time or that I had some involvement. Willow would say nothing about it and I hoped Dao would not either. Had she overheard the version of events I told the police who came to take the guy away? I mentally crossed my fingers – I wanted no interference from the cops and if they thought I was likely to shoot someone and claim self-defence they might take the gun off me for the time being. I had no idea if they could, but I was not about to risk it.

Benson looked at Dao. 'Did that intruder see you? Or hear you?'

She did not hesitate for a second, looked straight at him without letting her glance stray to my face first. 'No, he didn't. When the man broke the window Hunter shouted at me to keep out of the way, so I went into the kitchen. And then when he'd got hold of the man he asked me to do some things and when he talked to me he called me Paul. So the man wouldn't find out there was a girl in the house.'

'Did you see how Hunter got the gun off him?'

Aha, I thought, that cop who came here, the older one – he's told Benson he wondered about how I did that. But I can't reply, he's asking Dao. I was busy trying to figure out how I would explain it, if he found out I had been armed and ambushed the guy. The last thing we needed was for the police to think I had something to hide.

'No, I was in the kitchen, hiding – I was scared. I heard a lot of noise over there by the stairs.' She glanced at me and then back at Benson. 'I didn't dare look until Hunter told me to come and take the gun. Hunter was holding the man – he had his arm twisted up behind his back and one arm around the man's neck. He was bending him backwards. The gun was on the floor, sort of to one side of them. I just went up behind them and picked up the gun and took it back to the kitchen.'

She stopped talking and thought for a moment.

'And then Hunter put the man on the floor and asked me to bring him the bag of those black things and he tied him up. But he called me Paul again and the man never saw me. Then I went back and hid in the kitchen. Hunter rang the police and then he asked me to go down and open the front door. And then I hid again.'

Benson looked satisfied and I was too. The way Dao told the story it was very clear. I was surprised at the invented description of how I held the man, but it made the story very credible. Had Bramville held her in a neck hold when she got stroppy? I was glad Benson had not asked her if I was armed. She might not have been able to lie in response to a direct question and everything else fitted with what I had told the police at the time.

'I know Marcia has suggested that you move somewhere else temporarily,' said Benson. 'Would you do that? We have a safe house where you can stay.'

I hesitated now. When I told Marcia we would stay in the house it was because I knew how good our security was, but I had never asked Dao what she thought. I turned to her and made it clear that I was asking her, one to one, nothing to do with anyone else.

'Would you like to go somewhere else? We can go and stay

in a hotel somewhere, another town or even abroad – where you can feel safe? I'm happy to do whatever you want to do.'

'No, I want to stay here.'

She smiled at me and then she looked at Benson, talking to him as if they were alone in the room. I knew that focus and how it made one feel that she was very personal: serious and deliberate.

'I want to be here - I feel safe here. Scruff is a good guard-dog and Hunter has all sorts of alarm things so nobody can come in. And if they do he will tie them up or knock them down.'

Thank God she didn't say that I will shoot them, I thought.

'I thought that's what you would say,' Benson said. 'I bet it's nice to have a place that's like a home again. But you have to remember that the safest thing would be to go somewhere else for a while.'

Willow glanced at me, as surprised as I was. Somehow he did not seem like a man who would consider things from such a personal point of view. Dao gave him one of her full-on genuine smiles and said politely, 'Yes, it's lovely.'

The smile died away and she hesitated. 'But I want to ask you something. Did you find my mother? Her bones, I mean.'

'I'm sorry Dao, I should have said that straight off before we started talking about all this other stuff.' He seemed to be genuinely upset that he had forgotten to tell us. 'Bramville had covered her up again, but the search dogs found the grave. The forensic team has to finish their investigation first and they will be in touch as soon as they can. We have to find out all we can about how she died before she can be buried properly.'

Dao nodded, her voice neutral and seemingly calm. 'He hit her on the forehead – I saw the piece of bone that had been knocked out.' Her hands were clenched on her lap. 'He is very dangerous.'

Benson nodded, but there was something else going on in his mind. Willow noticed and so did I. He was debating with himself if he should tell us or not. After a moment he cleared his throat and looked around at all our faces.

'We also found another woman's body. Not far from where Dao's mother was buried, further down the slope. The rainstorm that started the erosion of that slope had washed the earth off the second grave too - the body was nearly on the surface.'

We all stared at him, and Dao said, 'Had he killed her too? Maybe that what the Boss meant, when he said, 'you've done it again, haven't you?' – he was really angry. I've been thinking about that a lot.'

'We have to presume he killed her too,' said Benson. 'She was hit from behind with something heavy. Her skull was cracked, and one arm broken. She was pregnant when she died – they found a baby's bones among her own.'

The room was completely silent now. Dao was looking down at the table, unmoving and silent. Neither Willow nor I could think of anything to say. In all our minds was the thought that this could easily have been Dao's fate.

To break the spell, I got up. 'Come with me, Benson – I want to show you the security systems I've installed. You might have some suggestions.'

We left Willow and Dao at the table and did a tour of the house. The first thing I did was take him down to the garage so I could give him the two pieces of the brass shackle I had taken off Dao's leg.

'Holy hell,' said Benson and turned the pieces over in his hands. 'I saw the photos you took of her leg and this thing, but my god – it's a nasty rough thing. How is her ankle?'

'Damaged for life, I think. It's like a branding. If I can find someone to remove the scar I will - or it will be a reminder forever of what was done to her.'

I showed him the various components of the alarm system and how I got alerts on my phone and computer.

'Very impressive,' he said when we finished. 'Must have cost you a pretty penny. These things don't come cheap.'

'Worth it, though. And when we go out Dao is always in the back of the wagon, under the luggage cover. She doesn't go near the windows, so nobody sees her at any time.'

'You have taken complete responsibility for Dao,' he said slowly. 'Do you mind telling me why?'

He studied my face with those sharp grey eyes, waiting for my answer, making sure he would miss no fleeting expression.

'Finders, keepers,' I said, but not flippantly. 'Willow says the Chinese have a proverb – if you save someone's life you are responsible for them forever. That's how it feels to me. She would have died, and nobody would ever have known what incredible strength of mind she has and how brave she is. I have to keep her safe, she is my responsibility now.'

He looked hard at me for another moment and nodded as if satisfied. He was a difficult man to second-guess, but I think he could see I was being genuine.

Benson and Willow left at the same time and when I came up the stairs after closing the door behind them Dao was back at the laptop and deep in concentration.

'Well done,' I said. 'I was hoping you wouldn't mention that I had him at gunpoint.'

'Of course not,' she said reproachfully. 'I didn't want you to get into trouble. And I don't want him to know you have a gun anyway in case he takes it away– just in case you have to kill someone, I mean.'

Her head bent over the laptop again. While I made us coffee and sandwiches I wondered again what had given her this pragmatic view of crime and punishment. Was it her harsh life, deprived of comfort and guidance, the hideous way she had been treated or was she just like that? And the dichotomy; that telling a social lie was a bad thing, but killing bad people was acceptable. A mind-boggling contradiction, but it certainly made for an interesting personality. The perfect profile for a warrior girl.

I put a plate and a mug beside her and saw that she was

reading about fractals again. It reminded me that I must get in touch with someone who could help us sort out what to do with her studies. And as I stood there thinking I decided on a new approach. Until now I had waited for Dao to tell me what was going on in her mind when she was upset, in her own time and without pushing too hard. But we had moved on and she had opened up about some pretty traumatic emotions. Now her retreat back into the world of fractals straight after Benson's revelations prompted me to speak.

'Did you think the same thing I did when he told us about the other woman and the baby? That it could have been you?'

She didn't look up, just sat very still and there was only a moment's delay before she replied.

'Yes, I did – like the other day when we said if you hadn't found me I would be dead.'

She shook her head as if to dispel the feeling and her voice was bleak. 'It's a strange feeling, Hunter. I did what I had to do to get away – it was difficult, and I was very scared nearly all the time, but I did it. And now I feel as if there's no more brave stuff left in me, I've used it all up.'

I had never seen any sign of defeat in her before. Black determination to die, yes, but this was different, and it touched me deeply. I put my hand on her shoulder.

'Of course, it's scary, but you're still the bravest person I ever met – and I've known some pretty brave people. The way you handled yourself when that guy broke in and when you took my gun and were ready to shoot someone – extreme courage. Being in serious danger can make you tired afterwards – depleted. All your senses and energies have been totally engaged and used up and you feel either over-the-top triumphant or flat somehow.'

Her shoulder was still rigid under my hand, and she made no response.

'Mind you,' I said, not sure how to get through. 'Don't get the idea you can ever grab my gun again – there will be a serious talk coming up if you do.'

She raised her hand and put it briefly on top of mine and then withdrew it and I felt her shoulders drop. I fetched my own lunch from the kitchen and went over to my chair by the balcony. We were quietly doing our own things at opposite ends of the room for a couple of hours and then the alert on my phone and the doorbell went, only seconds apart. Dao looked up in alarm.

'Who is that?'

I flicked the tablet screen to the security system and checked the camera at the front door.

'It's Vivian, the woman who rang when you answered the phone.'

She's come straight from school – this is going to be interesting, I thought, as I watched the expression on Dao's face. But it was only fair to give her a chance to absent herself. I did not want her hurt.

'Do you want to go upstairs? You don't have to meet her. She has never turned up like this before, so she's probably come to have a look at you.'

Dao looked me straight in the eye and said bluntly, 'I'm not afraid of her. I haven't done anything wrong.'

And as I walked towards the stairs she added, 'And I want to see what she looks like. You like her, don't you?'

Vivian greeted me with a big smile when I opened the front door; she had a bottle of wine in her hand. 'Sorry to come unannounced, but I think I was rude to your visitor on the phone. I've come to make amends.'

What could I say? There was no way I could avoid asking her in. I thought it was a good thing that Dao had dressed like a fourteen-year-old tomboy that morning. I wanted Vivian out of my hair and out of my life for a while instead of speculating and gossiping about my house guest.

Upstairs her eyes scanned the room and fastened on Dao, who was still sitting at the table immersed in some website. She looked up at us and I had no idea how she would handle this, but I was ready for anything.

'Vivian,' I said. 'This is Dao, who's staying with me for a while. She's the daughter of an old army friend.'

'Hi,' said Vivian brightly, scarlet lips smiling widely, no sign of embarrassment. 'I think I owe you an apology – I was a bit rude on the phone, wasn't I?'

There was no smile on Dao's face. 'Yes, you were,' she said bluntly.

I nearly laughed out loud. It was the last thing Vivian had expected and for a moment she was left without an answer. Then she shook her head. 'You're right, I was. But never mind, I've come with a peace offering.'

She turned to me. 'Perhaps we can have a glass of wine together?'

I fetched two glasses and handed her one. 'Let's go and sit over by the window. Dao's studying.'

Vivian looked at Dao at the table and then towards the armchairs at the other end of the room.

'Are you not going to join us, Dao?'

Dao's black eyes revealed nothing, and she said neutrally, 'No, thank you. I don't drink wine and I want to keep on doing this.'

'What is it you are studying? Is it interesting?'

I held my breath when I noticed the typical Dao look of assessing if the person she was talking to was likely to grasp what she was about to say.

'I think it's interesting.' A very slight emphasis on the word 'I'. 'It's an article from *Mathworld* about fractals.'

She did not wait for an answer, just shifted her attention back to the screen.

Vivian stayed for an hour and tried more or less subtly to find out more about Dao, but I side-stepped her all the way. When she commented that she had never heard me mention Dao before I said, 'Dao hasn't lived in Auckland for years, but she's come to stay with me for a while to see if she'd like to study here. Phil would like her to do maths at Auckland University.'

Vivian looked across at Dao with a thoughtful look on her face. The mention of university had made her re-assess Dao's age.

'I've never heard you talk about Phil, I don't think,' she said neutrally, trying to avoid turning the conversation into an inquisition.

'Well, we never talk about my life really, do we?' I said.

It was true, we hardly ever talked about anything from my past or things Vivian had no direct involvement in.

'I don't think you have met any of my old army buddies – apart from Charlie.'

'Oh yes – Charlie…' said Vivian.

Dao spoke from her listening post at the table. 'Hunter and I love Charlie – and Kristen.'

Vivian's head snapped around to look at Dao, but she was looking at the laptop screen and there was no expression other than concentration on her face.

One – nil to Dao, I thought. She's pretty much able to fight her own battles.

When Vivian left I saw her out, declined an invitation to a party and avoided making any promises about the near future.

Dao said nothing for a while, but when I was starting dinner preparations she suddenly turned up beside me by the kitchen bench.

'Sorry.'

'Why are you sorry?'

'I didn't like her. She said she had come to apologise but she only came to see what I look like. And I didn't like the way she said, 'oh yes, Charlie' – as if Charlie doesn't matter.'

She mimicked Vivian's dismissive tone of voice perfectly.

'I'm not worried, Dao. You and I like Charlie, it doesn't matter what Vivian thinks of her.'

She stayed right beside me, and I waited, knowing that there was something else on her mind. When I turned to reach for a saucepan she took a step closer. 'Are we still all right?'

'Of course, we are. You weren't directly rude – you were defending a friend. I didn't mind. Vivian should have watched her step.'

I filled the saucepan with water for the rice and said, 'And even if you had been rude I would still look after you and help you, so stop thinking about it.'

For some reason something she had said earlier popped into my mind; I remembered the context. 'Dao, remember a couple of days ago you told me how Bramville hung around and watched you all the time that awful day. And you said, 'even when I was fixing things in the generator shed'. What were you doing?'

'Just the monthly maintenance stuff – you know, air filter and oil and things.'

'How did you learn to service the generator?'

'I had to. Just after my mother died he gave me the manual and told me I had a week to learn how to do it.'

The implication was obvious and there was no need to say it. If she did not learn it in a week she would be whipped or beaten.

'You're a good girl,' I said, and we talked no more about it.

14

THURSDAY AFTERNOON

I was upstairs when Benson rang with an update just after dinner. Dao was in the kitchen, and I went upstairs to the bedroom to talk to him. God knows Dao did not need any more revelations sprung on her right now.

'We haven't found Newton or the Boss yet,' said Benson. 'But we've got some news about the guy who broke into your house. There's a rumour on the street that he owes money to one of the gangs that deals in drugs. Our source said, 'they own him, he does what they tell him to do or he's dead'. Sounds as if they hire him out and take the money for the job.'

Then he sighed; he sounded dispirited. 'Those gangs have a vast black economy of their own just under the surface of the legitimate world. But this guy won't be a direct link to the Boss. It's probably arranged at one remove, just like the traffic on the island. We got the banks to look at those accounts from the black book and they are Bramville's – under different names. Bits and pieces of cash going in over a period of years, a tidy fortune actually. We correlated the recent dates he deposited money with their security footage.'

'I would have thought he must have earned a lot – being the middleman in a dangerous operation like that? Do you think there's more somewhere else?'

Now Benson chuckled. 'He might have done that age-old thing and buried cash. He couldn't put too much into the bank – it would look suspect, cash always does. And people like him get scared someone will rob them. So they put money in glass jars and bury them. Or in zip-lock bags these days – modern things for modern scum. We've got a team out there now – digging and sweating and cursing me. My inspector – he's the one ultimately in charge of the case – he was involved in something a few years back where they dug up over forty thousand dollars in coffee jars, buried all over a back yard in Mt Maunganui – half of it so covered in mould it was useless.'

'And what about that tattoo the Boss has on his arm? Surely there are people on the street who would recognise it?'

'It's a pretty common thing for criminals to have tattoos of motorbike brands. And if he's not normally in short sleeves maybe not many have seen it. Don't worry – we'll find him eventually, but these things take time. We searched the computer files but nothing useful came up. What if he's not one of the obvious gang people? He might be some background guy with no form.'

I knew what he meant. 'Like the financier, the invisible partner or the businessman who has contacts in Southeast Asia or Central America? Maybe, he's not in a gang at all. He could be the man who organises the importation, distributes and sells the raw materials and never has anything directly to do with the gangs who deal the drugs.'

'Bang on,' said Benson. 'Exactly that kind of guy. He might wear an expensive suit and go to National Party fund raisers. Anything is possible. And that intruder of yours, he would have been lent to the Boss as a favour, by a gang or someone else – no direct connection, just a hired gun.'

'I thought of that when Dao told me about the Darth Vader helmet,' I said. 'If even Bramville doesn't know who the Boss is, then perhaps nobody does.'

'Possible,' said Benson. 'He seems to be very risk averse –

one degree of separation all the way down the chain. But he must be frantic by now – either he knows where Bramville is and he's found out that both Dao and the black book are missing. Or else Bramville's hiding somewhere, and the Boss doesn't know anything – only that Bramville and Dao have disappeared. What would you have done if you were Bramville, I mean after Dao ran away and took the black book?'

I tried to imagine myself in that situation. Tried to pull all the pieces together into some sort of pattern, look at it from Bramville's point of view. What would I do?

There was a moment's silence and Benson said, 'Well, what would you do? Any ideas?'

'I think I would have spent some days searching for Dao, hoping to find her and kill her and not have to tell the Boss she had escaped. And then, when I had to give up the search, I would have talked to the Boss on the radio. I would have told him about the dogs tracking Dao to the cabin, but I would have shut up about the black book going missing.'

'Exactly! And then the Boss orders Bramville to return to your cabin to check for traces of Dao and to find out who owns the cabin. And once he knows that he gets someone to try to establish if Dao is with you in town and if she is, to kill her. And that's the guy who's in custody. And now the Boss still has no idea if Dao is at your place or not.'

I was thinking ahead of him now.

'But that truck that went up to the cabin, it must have been Bramville's. Could you trace it? We know it is a white utility – my farmer neighbour saw it.'

'Yes, we've talked to him, but he was too far away to see any details. We're looking at CCTV camera footage in the places nearby – Bramville must have bought diesel for the truck and the generator somewhere nearby, and all the petrol stations have CCTV cameras.'

The way Benson was letting me into the investigation had

me slightly puzzled. Not that I had any experience of the police and how they work, but it seemed a bit unusual.

'Benson,' I said. 'I don't know if you trust me or if you think I can contribute, but there's one thing that I don't understand – and if you don't want to tell me that's fine. Why do you think he is still pursuing Dao? I mean, it's about two weeks since she escaped from the island. Wouldn't he think it's too late now? Either she's dead or she's told her story to someone already. And shown the black book to someone. What's the point?'

He sighed at the other end, and I imagined that pudgy face with a tired frown after a long day. 'You're right. We've been trying to imagine what his motives are too – there are really only two options. First up this one: he thinks she can identify him – or he knows that she can. And if that's the case he wants her out of the way, dead. I know Dao's been through hell but she seems like an exceptionally strong girl. Could you try to pick her brains about that day when the Boss came to the island, so we don't have to put her through another interview? And then if you come up with something we can get a formal statement about whatever it is.'

'Do you think there's something she hasn't mentioned yet?'

'Not deliberately - but there might be something she's not paid attention to, something that didn't register at the time. Not the tattoo on his arm – he'd realise afterwards that at least Bramville saw that – something else. I've read all the interview notes and I don't see any gaps. But what if there is something that he has realised is a threat to him, but she simply hasn't thought of?'

'OK, I'll talk to her. What's the second thing you think might motivate him to still go after her like this?'

'Revenge, pay-back – call it what you like. Some people will pursue someone for years just to get their own back. Some do it to show their associates what happens if you let them down. Doesn't seem reasonable to you or me, but it happens – frequently. It's about fear and control.'

I went downstairs and put my book and the phone on the table on my way to the kitchen to check I had put the left-over rice in the fridge. Dao had done it already. The kitchen was tidy and in the fridge was a bowl of rice wrapped in so many layers of cling film it looked like a mummy.

She really loves that stuff, I thought, better put it on the shopping list, we're going through miles of it. I reached for the pad beside the fridge and my phone rang again.

I was heading back to the table to pick it up when I heard her say, 'Hi, this is Hunter's phone' and then silence. I walked into the living room and found the phone lying on the table and Dao back in mathematics land.

'Who was that?'

'Nobody,' she said without looking up. 'They – whatever you call it, closed it down?'

I picked up the phone and checked the call log – a caller with their ID blocked. Who calls and says nothing and then hangs up?

In the back of my mind little warning lights were flashing. Had the fact that Dao answered my phone signalled something to the caller?

I showed Dao the call log. 'If you see this when a call comes through, don't answer. Just let it ring, do nothing at all.'

This got her attention, and she looked up at me, alarmed. 'Why? What does it mean?'

There was nothing to be gained by not being honest.

'If that was the Boss calling he would not want us to see his number and now he knows that there is a girl in this house. So if he calls again we don't answer.'

She considered this for a minute. 'He wouldn't know it was me. He's never heard me talk and he's only seen me from far away. But we'll have to be careful.'

'That's right, very careful. Remember I said to keep away

from the windows – no more standing by the window in your room like you do sometimes.'

A bit later I rang Charlie and talked quietly to her about the phone call while Dao watched something noisy on You Tube.

'Jesus, Hunter – this is getting worse all the time. I don't know what you can do that you haven't done already,' said Charlie. 'But tell the cops about the call – they might be able to check it with your phone company. I don't know how those things work. I'm glad you put that GPS tracker app on the phone for Dao – 'find my phone' or whatever the thing is called. At least if she gets snatched you can find her.'

It made my blood run cold, but she was right. Next I called Willow, but she was holding a screaming baby, so I said I would send her an email and put the phone down.

Willow

Dao answered my phone to a call from an 'unknown caller' with no caller ID – who said nothing and terminated the call. I don't have Benson's direct line or cell phone number. Can you please tell him that if he wants to check with Vodafone he has my permission – just in case it was the Boss or Bramville trying to find out if Dao lives here. Don't know if the phone company can 'see' the number in their system?

I got Dao a cell phone and I'll send you the number from my phone. Her phone has the 'find my phone' app on it and so does mine. Can I leave Dao with you while I do my errands tomorrow? I think it will be safe if she travels under the luggage cover and I back into your driveway so she can go round to the back of the house? Are you OK with this? If not she can fly co-pilot with Charlie who has an all-day job tomorrow with only two passengers.

Hunter

'Dao,' I said. 'Come over here and let me ask you something. Benson needs some help.'

She sat down beside me on the sofa; her shoulders looked stiff as they always did when she was braced for something unexpected.

'That day when the Boss came to the island – do you think there is something you might have left out. Some detail that you didn't think was important?'

'Why? Is something wrong?'

'No, nothing's wrong. But both Benson and I wonder why the Boss is still trying to find you. Think about it – you've been gone for a while, must be a fortnight since you ran away. And even if he doesn't know the black book is missing he must realise you've talked to people by now.'

'Or I'm dead.'

'Yes, but he doesn't know if you are. Why is he so desperate to find you? Is there any way he thinks you could identify him – apart from the tattoo?'

She was silent for a long time, looking unseeingly at the blank TV screen. I said nothing. After a while she said, 'I don't think so. He had that helmet on all the time, and he didn't know I was behind the corner of the shed. If he had seen me there he would have got me right away. But he must think ....'

She stopped abruptly and her eyes swung back to my face. She had remembered something. When she spoke again it was as if she was telling me a dream.

'When he left I was hiding behind the big bushy trees down by the end of the beach. He came out of the house with the helmet on and he was still angry - I could tell from the way he walked. He couldn't see me because those trees are sort of bent and bushy right down to the ground and you can't see under them – it's a really good place to hide. He pushed his boat out a little way with an oar and then he tried to start the motor.'

Her voice was getting urgent. 'And it wouldn't start. He

tried and tried. I heard him swearing. After a while he took the helmet off and put it in the bottom of the boat. He straightened up and rolled down his sleeve and wiped his face on it. Then he pulled the cord again and the motor started. The boat had swung around, so when he sat down to steer it away he was facing me. I saw his face! But I wouldn't recognise him – he was too far away. Just a red face, grey hair.'

She paused as if she was reluctant to tell me the next bit. 'There's a big gap between those trees on the side towards the sea. I was watching him and then the boat swung around.'

She was staring into my eyes, and we both knew that he had seen her, and he knew she had seen him without the helmet.

'But he didn't go back,' I said. 'He thought Bramville was going to do what he'd been told to and kill you.'

15

FRIDAY

W hile Dao was in the bathroom the next morning I called Benson. When I told him about Dao watching the Boss leaving in the boat he swore under his breath.

'That's it – he knows she's a crucial witness, the only one who links him to the island. Does she realise the danger she's in now? Is she upset?'

Once again I was surprised at his concern for her.

'Yes, she got it right away. She's very quick. Holding together, but more frightened than she was.'

'We've talked about her quite a lot, you know,' he said. 'Those of us who've met her are just blown away by her fortitude – unbelievable. I'd hate for anything to happen to her now.'

'It won't – not if I can prevent it. And she's not leaving my side until this is over. I'm not trusting anyone else to stop him.'

There was a long pause and I waited. I knew what was going through his mind. I had known it when I said my piece, but I wanted to hear how he would react. When he spoke his voice was serious, with an official tone to it.

'I hope that doesn't mean what I think it means, Hunter. I'm going to pretend I never heard you say that. And I must warn you – we're pretty sure you were armed when that guy invaded your house and that you confronted him with a gun. It all seems a bit too good to be true otherwise. Just be damn careful what you do from now on. I'd hate to have to charge you with threatening to kill – or something worse. You army guys who've seen combat – you're different from the rest of us, but the law still applies to you, just like it does to everyone else.'

I still said nothing, and he continued in a different tone of voice.

'But anyway – we've found Bramville on CCTV footage from a petrol station and a supermarket. He went a bit further afield to do his shopping than we had expected so it took a bit of time. The photo of him that you took from the helicopter was helpful – our technical guys played around with it and got his whole face quite sharp, even the top part that was shadowed by his hand as he looked up. And then we got CCTV images from the banks. We got the plate number of the truck and it's registered to Bramville Newton, just like his rent agreement was. But now we've discovered that's not his real name and there is no driver's licence in that name.'

'I suppose you got fingerprints from his house,' I said. 'Is he in your database?'

'Bang on,' said Benson. 'We did and he is. He was in prison under his real name sixteen years ago – for assault and possession of Class A drugs and having a weapon without a firearms licence. But we drew a blank with that phone call you got last night.'

I put the phone down. Vigilance had taken on a new meaning. The Boss definitely wanted Dao dead and alertness and preparedness were more important than ever. Dao was going to be right beside me day and night. Perhaps a safe hotel somewhere far away was the best solution after all.

Willow sent a text message to say it was all right for Dao to come around. I replied and told her Dao would not be coming and briefly explained why. Then I went upstairs to tell

Dao. She was standing in the bathroom with her back to the mirror and her T-shirt pulled up. She did not drop it down when I appeared.

'Look,' she said and turned around so I could see her back. 'I think those marks are getting better.'

They looked much the same to me, but I did not want to discourage her.

'They might be a bit smoother,' I said. 'And less bright red, perhaps. How often did he beat you?'

'All the time – sometimes he beat me for so long without stopping that he got all red and sweaty. He wanted me to scream or cry – he liked that. So, I didn't. I just thought of something else, really hard. Pain is just pain and you can think it away. Well, not all the time, but mostly.'

'What a warrior you are,' I said. 'The army would love you – but they can't have you. Don't you mind standing there with your T-shirt pulled up?'

She looked at me, surprised. 'Why – is it wrong? You took all my clothes off before – you know, when you found me and then when we got so wet, when I hurt my ankle. I'm not showing anyone else.'

There was nothing wrong with her logic. I was the one with the problem.

'God, not another phone call,' I said at breakfast when the phone rang again.

It was Willow. 'I got Dao an appointment with my doctor, this morning. I forgot to tell you – sorry! I'll take her.'

Dao was eating with one hand and turning the pages of a book with the other, oblivious to the conversation I was having.

'What is it about? Did I know about this?'

'We talked about it, when I mentioned that maybe she had been sexually abused. And that she needs the STD tests – she might be infected with something. God knows what that man might have passed on to her.'

I thought fast.

'Listen – we have to split this up according to what each of us does best. I'll get you to talk to her about what will happen at the clinic, but I will take her there. She's not going anywhere in public without me. OK?'

'Fine,' said Willow. 'Just get her to call me so I can brief her. She won't have a clue about what to expect and I don't want her to panic. And don't for god's sake take a gun to the doctors – it's where I go, and I don't want any problems.'

Dao was paying no attention to me. I put the phone down and tried to think about how to approach this. I remembered the way she had reacted when she realised that she could be pregnant. Would this trigger the same chaotic emotions, or was it less threatening? There was only one way to find out. I sat down opposite her and pulled my coffee mug toward me.

'Hey, Dao, there's something we need to talk about,' I said and waited. Nothing happened. 'Dao!' I said loudly. 'Are you there? Can you hear me?'

Now she looked up.

'Willow rang. I'm taking you to her doctor today, this morning. Willow thinks you should have some tests so they can check that Bramville didn't infect you with something nasty – some sexually transmitted disease.'

There was no way of telling what she was thinking, but she looked calm.

'If you call Willow she'll tell you what they will do at the doctor's. It can't be too bad – people have these tests all the time. But I'm taking you there, not Willow. Is this OK with you? We can cancel it if you really don't want to do it.'

To my relief she nodded and got up from her chair. 'OK, I'll go up and call Willow.'

She disappeared upstairs and I stayed where I was, wondering what Willow was telling her. Dao came down ten minutes later and went straight back to her book. She lifted her mug, looked at the cold coffee in it and put it down again.

'Did Willow fill you in? Are you OK?'

'She told me what they do,' she said. 'And I don't want to talk about it.'

And that was that. We tidied up after breakfast, got our jackets, armed the alarm system and went off to the clinic. The parking lot at the medical centre was nearly full. I reversed into the last empty space so Dao could get out of the far back without attracting attention. I had the Glock in the belt holster, positioned just in front of my left hip where I could reach under the jacket and pull it out fast with my right hand. Dao had seen me check it in the mirror before we left and made no comment.

I sat in the waiting room while Dao disappeared behind the scenes with a nurse. Ten minutes went by, then fifteen. Just as I was getting nervous that they had found something bad Dao appeared in front of me, waiting for me to get up.

'All done?'

'Yes, we can go now. The nurse said Willow had paid in advance. They will call me with the results in a couple of days.'

Her face was unreadable, giving nothing away. She got into the back of the wagon without anything being said. As I drove out of the car park I decided on a change of plan.

'I'm going to make a short stop at the shopping centre here. Are you OK? I won't be more than a few minutes.'

'I'm OK.'

I found a parking space, ran to the café, got two take-away hot chocolates and a bag of marshmallows, and asked for a cardboard transport tray. I opened the tailgate and put the tray beside Dao.

'Hold on to that, will you please? Scruff will tip it over if he gets near it.'

Ten minutes later I parked and opened the rear.

'You can come out now. We're having a hot chocolate break here and Scruff can have a run – it's one of the beaches where we can let him off the lead.'

We sat on a low stone wall in the sun and watched Scruff

chase sea gulls. We drank our no longer quite hot chocolate, and I showed Dao how to float the marshmallows in the mug. I told her why dogs are not allowed to eat chocolate and then there was silence.

After a while she said, 'I'm not going to talk about it Hunter. It was … sort of embarrassing. But at least I'll know if I've got one of those horrible diseases or not.'

I said nothing, just put my arm around her shoulders and let her lean against me. We sat there for a few minutes and then Dao turned her head and looked up at me and said, 'I love you Hunter.'

Bugger! I thought, here we go, now I've got to find the right words fast.

'I love you too, Dao. You're my favourite family member,' I said hoping this was a safe option. I knew I had to break the spell fast before this conversation went any further.

I dropped my arm. 'Let's have a look at the 'find my phone' thing and check that we know how to use it.'

We worked though it together each holding a phone.

'Can I have a look at yours?' said Dao.

I held my phone out and she nodded. 'It works,' she said. 'It says we're in exactly the same place.'

We sat quietly in the midday sun of a late winter day. The little beach was nearly empty and only Scruff's incessant barking and the screech of sea gulls disturbed the peace. It seemed unreal that there was someone out there waiting to kill one or both of us. It was a long time since I had been in a situation of real physical danger. It made me feel very alert, as if my focus had sharpened and everything I looked at was crisp and clear. The idea that we should leave town and go into hiding was beginning to seem like a sensible option. If something happened to her I would never forgive myself. I decided to tell her later.

If anyone set up a competition to find the most interfering mother in the country my mother would win it hands down. Glenda will never admit that her adult children are competent to make their own decisions. She makes Willow irritated in a mild sort of way, but she drives me mad. She called not long after we got home, and I figured she had a cancelled appointment and saw it as an opportunity to delve into my life for fifteen minutes.

'I hear you have a visitor,' she said breezily, and my blood pressure rose ten points. 'Who is she?'

'She's the daughter of an old army mate. She's here for a few weeks.'

Give her some unasked-for information I thought, keep it innocent and normal.

'Whose daughter is she? And why is she with you?'

'Her parents are posted overseas and she's here to check out if she wants to go to university here,' I said trying to sound casual. 'They have no family in Auckland, so I said she could stay here.'

'Willow said she's very pretty,' said Glenda. 'How old is she?'

Thank you, Willow, I thought. Was it necessary to tell Glenda that Dao is pretty? Or did Glenda make it up?

'She's twenty-one. How is Dad? Is his shoulder better?'

Rob had hurt his shoulder lifting a twenty-kilo block of clay in his studio a couple of weeks earlier.

'It's much better than it was, but he is still having problems,' said my mother. 'He can work nearly normal hours again, but he won't listen to me of course. He thinks he can stop the anti-inflammatory pills as soon as it starts feeling reasonably normal and then work eight hours a day as usual. So it never gets a chance to settle down properly. But you know what he's like, never listens to advice.'

She was off, as I had hoped she would be, and five minutes later I thought I could safely end the conversation. She means well, but I can only cope with her in very small doses.

'I've got to go, Glenda. I have a conference call with a client in a few minutes.'

'But Hunter, we haven't talked about this girl – I would like to know a bit more. I don't even know her name,' she said without any embarrassment whatsoever. 'I hope you're not getting into some kind of silly relationship with someone so young. And who knows what she might think she can get out of it when she realises what a catch you are. I know what men are like with pretty girls.'

I was getting really angry now; there was no way I was going to have a discussion with her about Dao. I managed to end the call a minute later without having told her anything more. Dao was listening with a worried frown on her face.

'My mother – Glenda,' I said in response to her look. 'Possibly the most infuriating woman in the country.'

'Was she asking about me?'

'She was – trying to find out who you are and why you are here. As you heard I lied to her, same lies that I've told everyone else. You just have to get used to living with a liar, I'm afraid. We might have to leave town for a while – not because of Glenda, just to keep safe.'

She stared at me, and I realised my voice still held a trace of the anger I felt against Glenda.

'Sorry, Dao, I didn't mean to sound so angry, but Glenda really winds me up. I just hope to God she doesn't suddenly decide a weekend visit would be a good idea. That's the last thing we need. If she does she'll have to stay with Willow and you, and I will go away somewhere.'

Early afternoon: we were studying the university website to see if we could identify who we should ask about Dao's education.

'I don't know how it works,' I said, and Dao looked surprised. I think she imagined that I knew everything except maths.

'I never went to university. I went into the army as a career and then I left the army and was asked to join the company in London as a consultant. I've never done anything else, so I know no more than you do.'

We had just sent an email to someone called the Special Admissions officer when I got a text message from Glenda. One look was enough, and I exclaimed 'Oh, fuck off!'

Dao looked at me, surprised and worried. She had never seen me lose my temper before. 'What is it? Your mother?'

'Worse than usual,' I said and smiled at her. 'She is doing her best to drive me mad today.'

I sent a brief reply to Glenda telling her, reasonably politely, to stay out of my business. But thinking of Glenda and her insinuation that Dao might try to take advantage of me in some way had given me food for thought. What would happen to Dao if the Boss killed me, and she survived? How would she manage – would she be able to study, or would she end up struggling through life, never realizing her potential? In the light of the current danger, I wanted to do something about it without delay. It would feel good to do something positive and constructive.

I sat down there and then and sent an email to my friend Simon. We've known each other since we were at primary school, and he has been my lawyer ever since he qualified.

Simon,

Can you please draw up a new will for me, asap. Two thirds of everything I own is to go to Susan Johnson, also known as Dao, and one third to Plum. If Dao predeceases me it goes to Willow and Plum. Their full names are Willow Mary Brimmer and Plum Charlotte Grant. I attach an electronic copy of Dao's birth certificate. My life has changed quite dramatically lately, and I need to make sure that Dao is provided for if anything happens to me. I want Willow and you to be executors of the estate. I will explain everything when I come in to sign the will.

Thanks, Hunter

PS In case you wonder: Plum gets a smaller share than Dao because she will also inherit from our parents. Dao has no family at all.

Simon replied nearly immediately.

Hunter

I presume you want Willow and Plum benefiting in equal shares if Susan predeceases you? It is a very simple will so I'll do it tonight. Can you come in and sign it tomorrow? I'm working tomorrow because I'm going away for a week on Sunday and there's work to be finished. My secretary will be here too so she can witness it. Who the hell is Susan Johnson?

Simon

That evening, when we were sitting in bed reading, Dao suddenly put the laptop to one side and said, 'Hunter, what is it your mother is so upset about – or angry or whatever she is?'

Probably best to tell her, I thought. It's insulting, but she needs to know so she understands what she's up against when she meets Glenda sometime in the future.

'Glenda interferes in everyone's life. She thinks we're all incapable of figuring out what's best for us – and that includes my dad. And now she's got this crazy idea that you're after my money or something. Ridiculous of course, but that's what she thinks. She doesn't know the truth about you, of course.'

Dao's eyes were riveted on my face. 'What does she mean – what money? Is it the money you earn from your job, is that it? And she thinks I'll steal it or something?'

That made me smile. I knew that for Dao money was the cash you had in your pocket; either you had some or you did not. I felt certain that savings and investments meant nothing to her.

'My job pays a very good salary, yes. And I have savings and money invested that earns me more money. But most of what I have was just luck, not something I particularly deserved or looked for.'

'What do you mean? Did someone give you some money?'

'No, but it was nearly like that. When I was in my early twenties an army friend and I won some money on a Lotto ticket – you know that lottery I explained to you in the supermarket the other day? It wasn't a huge amount, but we decided to invest it and we bought a biggish piece of not very good farming land north of the city, in an area that was really rural then. We thought we'd be able to sell it later on and get a bit more than it cost us. And it didn't involve any risk. And then we went off overseas with the army and more or less forgot all about it. But not long before I left the army that land became very valuable. The northern motorway extension had turned the area into what they call commuter country – some people like to live on large properties in the country and travel to work in the city. And our land had sea views, so it was even more valuable. We divided the land up into ten-acre blocks, sold them and got rich – or quite rich anyway.'

'OK, that's good,' said Dao and picked up her book again. 'But I don't want your money. I just want to be with you. If you didn't have enough money I would get a job too.'

'What would you do?' I said, amused by her attitude and trying not to show it.

'I could go and clean things, maybe at a café or someone's house? I'm really good at washing and cleaning. Perhaps I could do people's gardens? I don't know, Hunter. I only just thought of it.'

Over my dead body, I thought. You deserve something different and you're going to have it.

'It's lucky I have lots of money then, because I don't want you to do that sort of thing. I want you to study and become a famous mathematician or anything else you might want to be.'

Dao just shook her head and picked up the laptop again. "Can you show me the beach where we went today?" Nearly every day she looked something up on Google Earth. When I turned the light out she asked, 'Where is the gun?'

'It's here, on the floor beside my bed. And I've set the level one alarm.'

I lay on my back looking up at the skylight, thinking of Dao being provided for whether something happened to me or not. After a few minutes her fingers touched my hand very lightly.

'I'm still here, Dao.'

'I know. I wish I could be with you always.'

'You can.'

'No, I can't,' she said. 'You'll want to marry someone and then I can't be here too.'

I wondered what had made her think of it; Glenda's call or Vivian's visit perhaps.

'I don't think that's going happen. I'm thirty-eight and I'm very happy as I am.'

'I wish you would marry me. I love you, Hunter.'

I thought I had defused this situation already, this time I had to make it stick.

'You don't really love me, Dao – not like people do when they want to get married. You love me because I look after you and we're friends and you feel safe with me. Perhaps you feel I'm a bit like a parent. But you mustn't confuse that with the other kind of love. Everything that has happened to you has damaged you, even if you think it hasn't. It might be years before you can make a decision about a relationship.'

She said nothing more and it was a long time before I went to sleep.

16

SATURDAY

I half-woke in the early hours of the morning and found that Dao was no longer inside the bed, she was beside me under the rug and my arm was across her body. I lay still and thought hard. I had to get out of this fast and without any fuss and I had to come up with a plan to avoid a major incident. I thought back to the comment she had made the night before and decided that first things had to come first.

I worked my way slowly towards the edge of the bed and went to have a shower. Standing there with water streaming over me, I tried to understand what had led to this.

Had Dao understood my own feelings towards her and had that influenced her? Was it that saviour attachment syndrome someone had warned me about – or was it just that there had been nobody to give her affection for so long?

I came out none the wiser, worried about the impact it might have on our relationship and about how to resist this temptation laid out in front of me. I tried to think of arguments that would convince Dao and failed to come up with anything more than repetitions of what I had already told her. I went downstairs and got dressed in the living room and sat down to read my emails.

Dao appeared half an hour later, looking as if nothing

particularly unusual had happened, which left me dangling. Should I bring it up? She acted just as usual, and I avoided the subject until after breakfast.

'Dao, we have to have a serious talk. Please don't get up, the dishes can wait.'

The look she gave me told me that she was prepared for anything, contained and focused.

'We must never sleep together, like we did last night. You are a lovely young woman and I'm old enough to be your father, but my body reacts of its own accord. I don't want to wake and find I'm raping you in my sleep. It's not fair to you or to me.'

She listened politely and when she was sure I had finished she looked at me as if I was a little less than bright. 'Hunter, you can't rape me. I would let you f…, sorry, I would let you have sex with me – so it wouldn't be rape.'

'No, Dao – it would be wrong. You are not recovered from all the horrible things that man did to you and you can't make decisions about this sort of thing yet. Everyone would agree – my family, my friends, anyone you ask would say the same thing. If we had sex I would be abusing your trust.'

She looked mutinous. 'You're saying I can't make up my mind about what I do – it's like saying I can't think! I'm not a child, Hunter.'

'No, but it's recognised by most people that someone who is 'saved' by another person often develops this kind of attachment – the saved person feels such a strong attachment to the person who saved them that they think they love them.'

That look again; like an arrow flashing from her black eyes – a complete dismissal of my reasoning. 'But I do love you!'

'Fine, you can love me – like you would a parent or a brother. But not like you would a lover. I'm sorry, but it's wrong.'

'Who makes these rules? Is it Willow – or your mother? And is it supposed to be wrong forever?'

I was caught in hesitation, but I had to reply. 'At least until this situation is over – until you know that you can feel safe without me and don't need me – then you can make a decision.'

'Do you love someone else? I mean in a sex sort of way, another girl – or woman? Vivian?'

I knew that a lie now would make the situation easier, but I could not bring myself to do it.

'No, I don't.'

She stood up then and reached for my plate. 'Well, that's OK then,' she said quite casually, as if we had been talking about something completely unimportant. 'I'm not an idiot, Hunter – I know what I know but we won't sleep under the blanket together again.'

As she walked around the kitchen corner she looked back at me over her shoulder and said, in the voice of someone making a casual enquiry: 'Will you still let me sleep in your room?'

'Of course, we will sleep in my room. You are going to be right beside me every step of the way. I'm not letting you out of my sight until this is over. I will always look after you. As soon as this is over we'll start having a normal life – we'll talk to someone at the university and find out what we should do about your studies.'

She listened to me from the kitchen and returned with a damp cloth. She wiped the table and said in a tone of calm detachment, 'Perhaps sometimes people's bodies know more than their brains.'

She picked up my mug and returned to the kitchen, leaving me speechless. I had no idea how to respond. Her composure and calm unnerved me. She might seem like a child at times with her insecurity and ignorance of practical matters, but she kept me on my toes in an argument.

Simon called and said we could drive down the lane beside his office building and park under the building. 'Call when you're outside in the lane and I'll come down and let you in. Come when it suits you – I'll be here until late afternoon.'

'We'll be there as soon as we're organised. I have to bring Dao,' I said. 'I'll explain why when I see you, but she knows nothing about the will. Perhaps we can leave her with your secretary while I talk to you?'

I told Dao I had to see my lawyer about business, even though it was Saturday, because he was going away the next day. On the way into town Dao spoke from the far back of the station wagon.

'Can I say something about us? I just want to say it, I don't want to argue.'

I didn't reply straight away, and she added quickly, 'I just want you to understand something – just one thing.'

'OK, tell me.'

I tried to sound normal, but my mind was busy flicking through ways of defusing potential trouble.

'I know you like me, Hunter. And I think perhaps you love me – not just like a friend or a child or something. Real love – like you would love a woman. I think I can feel it when you touch me – or when I touch you. I've never felt it before but…'

Her disembodied voice coming from seemingly nowhere had a surreal effect on me. Normally when she was under the luggage cover we did not have conversations. I found it difficult to respond without seeing her face, so I said nothing. After a moment she continued.

'I just wanted to tell you. I'm serious and this won't go away. It doesn't matter if we talk about it now or much later. If you ask me when I'm fifty I will still say the same thing, that I love you. I'm not confusing it with something else. It's not going to change.'

My mind tried to bring up an image of what life would be like now. Trying to keep a lid on my own feelings, sleeping in the same room, continuing to be with her twenty-four hours a day – very difficult, the most emotionally difficult thing I had ever faced.

'OK,' I said. 'I believe you – you mean what you say. And we will talk about it again, later on.'

It was the only thing I could say to prevent an impossible situation. It was painful to dismiss her declaration so casually, but I felt I had no choice.

Simon came down to meet us and opened the gate to the parking area under the building. I wound the window down and he pointed down into the dusky space. 'Park over there, beside my car.'

His eyes swept the interior of the car, but he made no comment about my lack of companion.

I stopped beside his old Saab, got out and walked around to open the rear. Simon was coming towards me from the gate, but he stopped halfway and watched Dao getting out from under the cover. Calm and discreet as always he made no comment. I introduced them and Simon acted as if it was perfectly normal for his clients to emerge from the luggage compartment. We got into the lift, the doors closed, and Dao took a step closer and touched my hand. I looked down at her and saw her smile and guessed she had never been in a lift before.

Simon's secretary is a middle-aged woman who has been with him for years. She looked closely at Dao and tried not to show how intrigued she was.

'Rosie, this is Susan, also called Dao,' said Simon. 'Can you get her a cup of coffee or something? I need to discuss a few things with Hunter before he signs those papers.'

He had clearly briefed her before we came, but of course neither of them knew anything about Dao or the fix we were in. He started asking questions the moment he had closed the door of his room. 'This is very mysterious, Hunter. Who is this girl? And why the hell was she hidden in the back of your car like that?'

I needed to fill him in. Someone else apart from the police

and Willow should know what was going on. I trusted Simon completely; we had known each other from the age of seven. If the worst happened and Simon was going to look after Dao's interests he had to understand her background.

I told him the basics of the story, from the day Scruff found Dao to the present, but without too many details.

'Well, that's it. Willow and the police have the whole evidence file and Willow can fill you in any time if something happens to me. It's important for me to know that Dao is provided for whatever happens and that there's someone to advise her. She has no idea at all about how to manage money or property – she's brighter than ninety-nine percent of the population but she's also like a ten-year-old in some respects.'

'I think it would be a good idea if Willow sends me a copy of that whole file, don't you? And you need to tell the police I'm your lawyer. It all sounds incredibly dangerous to me, but I'm not like you. If this was about me I would go into hiding. You aren't armed now, are you?'

I nodded and he stared at me with fascinated horror. I doubt if Simon has ever handled a firearm in his life and the thought that someone was sitting in his office with a gun was like having a Martian in his visitor's chair.

He was about to comment, but suddenly he thought of something and picked his cell phone up.

'My god – now I know!' he said. 'I have to show you this, just wait while I find it. I got a message from Mark the other day.'

He searched his emails and grinned when he found it.

'This is what he said: *Went out for dinner with a group of people last night and saw Hunter with a stunning woman, very young, the complete package – gorgeous, exotic. Have no idea where he found her, she looked a bit Asian or something but goes by the name of Susan Johnson (!) and said she has always lived in Auckland. And he said she's a mathematician – but he might have been joking. Not to be found on social media or anywhere else. My darling wife is dying of curiosity along with some others who were present. Let me know if you have any clues what that devil is up to now.'*

Simon grinned at me across the desk and put the phone down.

'Of course, I said I had no idea who she was – but even if I had known I wouldn't have told him. That wife of his is a menace, a real mischief maker, so the less she knows about Susan the better. But what were you doing in a restaurant if you're trying to keep her out of sight?'

'I took her out for dinner as a reward for being so cool when that guy broke into the house with a gun. But please – be careful not to talk about her and warn Rosie not to. The fewer people who know about her, the safer we are.'

'And is she really a mathematician – or were you kidding?'

'She nearly is or will be soon. I think she's exceptional, possibly more intelligent than anyone I've ever come across – leaves me standing.'

We sat for a moment looking at each other and then Simon shook his head as if it was all too much and went to ask Rosie to come in to witness my signature on the will. I sat there thinking about what I had told Simon. Until now I had lived the story, but telling someone else from start to finish had clarified things in my mind. It nearly gave me an outsider's view of things and I knew that what I felt for Dao was a tightly woven blend of two things that would probably remain tangled for the rest of my life. I loved everything about her from her bright mind and her determination to her honesty and sense of humour. And running alongside this was an intense desire to protect her and help her to grow. I knew that for me it was the perfect mix, but it had to wait.

When Simon returned with Rosie, I got up and closed the door so we could talk. 'Rosie, it's very important that nobody finds out anything about Dao. Simon can fill you in with the basic details, but she is in serious danger and so am I. The most important thing for now is that she's not talked about. Nobody must know that she is with me.'

Rosie nodded, her expression struggling between curiosity and professional detachment. I thought of the secrets and scandals she must have been privy to over the years; she knew how to be discreet. I signed the will, Rosie and Simon witnessed it and then I was ready to leave. Rosie left the room ahead of me and came running straight back.

'She's gone!'

On the chair in the reception area where Dao had sat was a folded sheet of paper and two cell phones, hers and mine. The sight of her phone sent a surge of panic through my mind; it could only mean one thing.

Simon said, 'Where could she be? Check the toilets Rosie and I'll look in the other rooms.'

But I knew she had gone. I unfolded the paper and read her note; a scribble of sloping lines dashed down in a great hurry.

Hunter

I have to leave. You left your phone on the desk here. Read your texts. It's too dangerous. Find a way to make the Boss know I have run away so he doesn't burn your house. I can't stay. And the other things we talked about. Your mother is right – it would never work. People would always think I only say I love you because I want your money. I will always love you, but I cannot stay with you and use your money and not do anything to look after myself. Don't worry about me. I am not going to go somewhere and die. I will find a job and somewhere to stay. Please give Scruff a cuddle from me. Thank you for all the lovely things you did. You are the kindest person in the world.

Dao

I checked my phone. Two 'missed call' notifications, both from 'unknown caller'. I looked at my messages and found two new ones.

The first from the unknown caller: 'Tell us where she is or we burn your house down. Will call you later.'

And one from Glenda: 'I will call you again tonight. You must listen and be sensible. If you fall for this girl you will live to regret it, pls be sensible.'

I turned to find Simon and Rosie standing silently watching me.

'She's nowhere in the office,' said Rosie.

I handed the note to Simon and when he had read it I gave him the phone with the message from the Boss open. He shook his head. 'Jesus, Hunter, that's terrible – and where would she go?'

'I have no idea. How would she get out of the building on a Saturday?'

'There's a big sign at the gate in the parking area – with an arrow telling people they can open the gate from inside. There's a button beside that gate.'

I put both phones in my pocket and Simon followed me to the lift foyer. The lift was on its way up and the display showed that it was coming up all the way from the basement car park.

'What will you do?'

'I'll drive around and look. Can you ring Willow? She's in the directory as M and W Brimmer – ask her to inform Benson, he's the cop we're dealing with. Tell her I'll be in touch soon.'

The lift arrived and a rather bulky man with a huge scar down one cheek got out. He looked like everyone's idea of a film gangster.

'Hi, Simon,' he said and went to move past us, but Simon stopped him.

'Hey, Thomas – did you just come up from the car park?

Did you see a girl down there, a short, skinny girl in a grey hoodie?'

The man called Thomas stopped and looked searchingly at Simon and then at me.

'No, I didn't see anyone down there. I drove in and came straight up here so I didn't look around, but there are only three cars there – I would have noticed, I think. Can I help in any way?'

'Thanks, but no,' I said. 'I'd better go down and get in the car and have a look around the neighbourhood. Simon, don't forget to call Willow!'

'OK, doing it now,' said Simon and went back to his office.

Never had a lift been so slow. I should have run down the stairs. I had time to think of a hundred things that Dao would not know or understand. She had left her phone, so she had no access to Google maps. She had nobody's contact numbers, no way of getting in touch. Had she left the phone because of what Glenda had said about money or to avoid being found via that app we had installed?

I spent an hour circling Simon's office building, a block further out on each circuit, then back in towards the centre again but no sign of Dao. The whole time my mind was sifting through possibilities – where she would think was a good place to go, where she would start? Would she go for a familiar place or somewhere new where I would not find her? Probably somewhere familiar, not the centre of town. But how would she get over the Harbour Bridge if she had no money? The thought of her hitch-hiking drove me crazy with worry. My stomach was a tight knot of anxiety. I stopped before I got on the motorway on-ramp and called Willow.

'Simon told me,' she said. 'This is awful, Hunter – I can't imagine what she'll do.'

'I'm heading back over the bridge now. I'm going to my place – in case she decides to come back home. Did you talk to Benson?'

'He said he'll meet us wherever you think is best. I'll tell him you're on your way back.'

Then Dao's phone rang. By the time I found it under my jacket on the passenger seat it had stopped ringing. I checked the screen and saw that someone had left a message. It was the clinic: 'Your test results are fine, and you don't need another appointment.'

One good thing, I thought, but will she ever hear about it?

Next I called Charlie and asked her to come to my place as soon as she could.

'I'm on my way,' she said. 'See you soon.'

17

SATURDAY AFTERNOON

Waiting for them to arrive was torture. I knew there was nothing they could do, but against reason I hoped they would have practical suggestions I had not thought of. I sat on Dao's bed and looked at her pile of books and the red top Kristen had given her that was on a hanger hooked over the wardrobe door. I hadn't thought of it before, but probably she left it out because she liked looking at it. Not surprising for someone who had lived in a man's cast-offs for years; it might be the most beautiful thing she had ever owned.

Charlie arrived first. 'I was in the park,' she said. 'Left Kristen to watch the nieces and nephews playing cricket. Her brother will drop her home. Tell me exactly what happened.'

But I refused to start talking until I had them all in one place. My mind was busy filtering possibilities and options; I did not have the mental energy to waste on repeating the story over and over. Charlie gave my arm a pat and disappeared into the kitchen and I paced back and forth in the living room, trying to come up with ideas. Willow and Benson arrived about twenty minutes later. I introduced Benson and Charlie to each other.

'Charlie and I are old mates – she was a helicopter pilot in the army,' I said in explanation. 'She flew me over the island that day I took the photographs – and she took me and Dao up there to find the black book. She knows as much as we do.'

Benson looked as if he knew this already and probably a lot more.

'Have you guys had lunch?' asked Charlie. 'No? I made some sandwiches so we can have something to eat while we talk.'

We sat at the table with a plate of sandwiches and some biscuits and mugs of coffee. Benson looked at me, his face calm but with a hint of worry.

'Now then, tell us what happened, Hunter.'

Willow opened her notebook and wrote the date at the top of a blank page. They were all looking at me, but it was hard to get started. I made a couple of false starts and then I went right back to the conversation with Glenda the day before and took it from there. I explained that I had told Dao not to answer if someone with no caller ID rang my phone. I said nothing about why we were at Simon's office on a Saturday, just said there was some business stuff we needed to discuss before he went away. Last of all I handed Dao's note to Benson. He read it and passed it to Willow, and she gave it to Charlie. They all looked stunned and then Benson and Willow spoke at once.

'OK,' said Benson, pulling rank. 'I want a good description of what she was wearing and a photo so we can alert the patrol cars to be on the look-out. How tall would you say she is? About five foot three? I mean 155 centimetres.'

'Probably about that,' I said and thought of where the top of her head was compared to my height, just below shoulder level.

'But where on earth would she go?' said Willow. 'Let's say she had some money and got a bus over to the North Shore – would she head for somewhere familiar? Or would she deliberately go where nobody will recognise her?'

'She has no money,' I said. 'Probably she will keep away

from this place and yours, because she doesn't want anyone working for the Boss to spot her. She is familiar with some of the Takapuna shops, and we've stopped at a couple of other places, all east of the motorway – places where we bought clothes and gear for her and where we've picked up take-away food. I hope to God she didn't head south.'

I wondered if we all thought the same thing; if Dao had gone in a completely new direction there was little hope of finding her. South and west of the city lay vast expanses of suburbs.

'Had you two talked about how you could make the Boss think she wasn't here?'

Benson had picked up the note again and was looking thoughtful. 'I'm thinking of this part of her note where she says you could let him know she had gone. Or did she not base that on anything in particular?'

My mind brought up the image of Dao standing in the middle of the living room in her PJs and telling me she was going to leave.

'A few days ago, she decided that she would leave – so I would be safe. It was before the Boss started acting as if he knew for sure that she was here. She thought I could let his men in, literally say 'come in and look around, there's nothing here that belongs to a girl' – as a demonstration. I told her that was not an option, and I would prefer to look after both our safety rather than hand her over to someone else. That anonymous call – the one she answered – I'm sure it was the Boss. She probably thought that if he rang again I could talk to him and tell him she had gone.'

'We should divide up the suburbs between us and start driving around,' said Charlie. 'The chance of anyone connected to the island coming across her is minuscule, but I'm worried about her safety. She's very clever, but she's like someone who's been in cold storage since the age of ten – no idea of how things work and what the risks are.'

Willow looked down at the scribbled notes that only she

could read and added something short with an exclamation mark. Then she underlined it before she raised her eyes.

'I wonder what kind of place she would approach for a job? Shops and fast-food places, I suppose.'

'After Glenda's call she asked why Glenda was so upset and I just said she has silly ideas about money. Dao doesn't understand money at all – no idea about how much people earn or how anything works. She tends to think in terms of cash and perhaps savings. Investments are an unknown quantity to her – like a foreign language. She thought I might not have enough money to pay for her clothes and things – said she could get a job and earn money herself. She said she's really good at cleaning and gardening.'

Benson had been sitting quietly listening, but now he jumped in. 'Right, this is what I want, as soon as possible – both your phone numbers Hunter, yours and Dao's. We'll get the phone company to monitor things from now on. And as I said, I want a photo of Dao and the description of her clothes. And I want you to answer when the Boss calls – let's discuss what you should say so we retain as much control of this situation as possible.'

Charlie was the one who came up with something constructive and tangible that we could do ourselves. Ever since Dao disappeared I had felt powerless and frustrated. The only thing I had done was drive around looking for her, but it was too random. What were the chances of spotting her?

'Let's make a poster and put it up everywhere we can think of,' she said. 'A photo of Dao and your phone number and email address, Hunter – in the supermarkets and fast-food places. Print it on really bright paper, luminous yellow or something that stands out.'

She turned to Benson. 'And I think the police should issue a statement asking for the help of the public – it's a great way to tell the Boss she's not here. Not just a statement saying she's a missing person, but that you are keen to locate a person who is a vital witness in a criminal investigation and with the photo and the description. I'm sure everyone pays attention to those things on the news – I know I do.'

Three pairs of eyes focused on Benson. I was waiting to see how he would react to being given instructions. He needed only a second to make up his mind.

'It's a good idea. We kill two birds with one stone – we alert the public to tell us if they see her and we tell the Boss she's no longer here. So that sets the script for what you say when he calls you, Hunter – you can say she's run away, and you've contacted us and we're going to put out a public appeal to find her. Offer to meet with him, tell him to watch the news, show him you're devastated. Accuse him of having abducted her – anything you like.'

We dealt with the details of photos, phones and descriptions and then Benson reverted to an earlier issue.

'There are two things that I want to make clear before I go. One is that when we find Dao we're going to have to keep her strictly under wraps until we identify the Boss. She will have to go into the witness protection scheme for as long as it takes. I realise you don't want to let her out of your sight, Hunter – fine, you don't have to. We can organise a safe location for both of you to stay for a time.'

His expression changed from serious to one that said 'this is official' with no room to doubt that he meant it and I wondered what was coming next. For a short chubby guy, he had an impressive presence.

'And I warn you again – don't take the law into your own hands. Let us make the decisions about how to deal with things. If you have an intruder like you did before then protect yourself – but don't go after these guys – and don't kill anyone. And that goes for you too, Charlie.'

His eyes left mine and now he gave Charlie the full benefit of his penetrating gaze. He never missed a beat, that man. He had got Charlie's measure pretty quickly.

'Of course not,' said Charlie and tried to look as if she was shocked at the suggestion. 'I'd never do a thing like that.'

'Hmm,' was all he said, but it was clear he thought we were both likely to disobey his instructions and create problems for him. As he got up to leave he had another thought and stopped at the top of the stairs. 'We can have someone come in and take the call, pretend to be you – if you want us to?'

'No thanks, I'm quite capable of convincing him I'm devastated – because I am. If anything happens to her I'll never forgive myself.'

Willow touched my hand and said quietly, 'Hunter, we'll find her. And it's not your fault – you've done more than anyone could have to keep her safe.'

I saw Benson out and locked the door behind him. The last thing he said was, 'Watch the news – I'll try to get it on at six o'clock tonight.'

I went back upstairs and the three of us looked at each other, wondering what to do next. Then Charlie took charge. 'Willow, if you and Hunter create the poster I'll go and get coloured paper and then we'll draw up a list of where to take them and divide it up between us. And I think we should pull in Paul – he'd be useful and he's one of us.'

Willow stared, completely baffled. 'Who is Paul? One of us?'

'Paul is a really good mate of Charlie's from the army,' I said. 'And I know him too – very nice chap, sings while he works. He's out of the army now and runs a security installation business. He's the guy who did this house. God, it was only days ago.'

Willow nodded. 'OK, another pair of hands would be good. And you trust him?'

'Totally, we've known him on and off for years. And he met Dao very briefly when he came here. Is Matt back yet? We have to tell him and Plum – she knows nothing about what really happened to Dao yet and they've got to know before it's on the news. And Rob and Glenda, I suppose. Not that the police will mention my name, but still.'

Willow's husband Matt is one of a kind. She married him when she was twenty-one and still a student; he was forty-two or forty-three, I think. Our parents were against it, I had my doubts and the only person who really approved was Plum, who was seven and instantly fell in love with Matt; a relationship that has lasted right up to date. Over the years I have come to respect him more than most people I know. He's a serious-looking chap, an airline captain who says very little and has a dry sense of humour; seemingly quiet and not very interesting. But behind that façade of ordinariness lives a great guy who relates to everyone, young and old, with total empathy.

'I'll tell Matt and Plum as soon as I get home. You know, I only just realised that Matt hasn't met Dao yet. He was only just back when you set up the barricades around you. I have to tell Plum the whole story – we can't pretend any longer. And I'll ring Mum and Dad, so you don't have to. Even if there's no need for them to know it all right now, I think it's a good idea – saves a lot of grief later.'

Charlie knew the family well enough to understand the implications. 'I don't suppose the cops will tell the whole story on TV – just the basic fact that she's an important witness. But you're right, no point in trying to hide anything now.'

She headed for the stairs, then stopped and looked back. 'That Benson guy is OK. Did you notice that flicker when I said about getting it on TV? He'd thought of it already, but he was nice enough to let me think it was my idea. And another thing: do they actually know you had that intruder at gunpoint?'

'No, but he more or less told me they are sure I was armed. They don't like the general public acting like the Armed Offenders Squad, I suppose. I can see his point – sort of.'

The next two hours were busy. Willow and I created a simple poster. When Charlie returned with a pack of fluorescent yellow paper Willow went home to talk to Matt and Plum. I set the printer going and Charlie and I sat in front of my laptop with Google maps and composed a breakdown of shopping centres and other useful places where we could put up the posters. Willow called and said they were all coming over. They arrived with the twins, who instantly crawled towards danger, so we built barricades in front of the stairs and left them to chase Scruff around while we talked.

Plum, who normally talks most of the time, was completely silent. I wondered if she understood why we had not told her the truth about Dao. While the others were discussing the list of locations I pulled Plum to one side and put my arm around her.

'Are you OK? I'm sorry we lied to you, but at the time we tried to let nobody know the true story – it was the only way to protect Dao. It doesn't mean we don't trust you, it's just one of the basic rules when you're trying to keep things contained. Only tell people what they really need to know.'

'God, Hunter – I'm so scared,' she said, her chubby face scrunched into worried creases. 'I do understand. But poor Dao! She's the bravest person I've ever known. All those things Willow told me, it's like a nightmare. I never thought anything like that could happen here, not in New Zealand. You have to find her!'

'We'll try, Plum. I'm sure we will once that appeal has been on the news. A lot of people will be looking out for her.'

But I did not really believe what I was saying. Hideous scenarios played out in the back of my mind. My brain grabbed every opportunity to torment me.

Willow spoke from the other end of the room. 'Come over here, you two, and have a look at this and see what you think.'

The table was covered in printouts of maps and little piles

of posters. The twins were under the table picking up screwed-up sheets of paper and ripping them to pieces.

'One pile each for you, Matt Plum and Charlie,' said Willow, who had taken charge of logistics as usual. 'Charlie's got a bigger pile because she's going to share it with Paul – provided he can help. Sticky tape and Blue Tack for everyone to put the posters up with and one only flat-spread stapler to attach posters to wooden poles and things – thumb-tacks for the others. List of locations divided into logical areas for each of you to cover. I'll take the twins home and you can keep me informed as you go. Come back to our place when you are done, and I'll have a late dinner ready. And I'll record the news.'

18

SATURDAY EVENING

Half an hour later we all left together. Matt was dropping Willow and the twins at home, Plum had come in her own car and Charlie had hers. I was the last to leave and just before I set the alarms I thought of something. What if someone sent by the Boss was watching? What would he think?

I went back upstairs and wrote a note for Dao, but luckily I realised that my first attempt was fraught with danger. In it I asked her to go 'next-door to Nigel' which would have given the Boss the directions, so I wrote a new note, put her name on it and stuck it to the front door:

'Dao, if you come back please don't go away – just go to Nigel's place and wait for me to come home! We're all out looking for you. Hunter'

It was back-up confirmation for the Boss that Dao really had gone and the safest option I could think of for Dao if she did come back.

My phone rang before I was two blocks down the street, and I pulled over – caller ID unknown. I pressed Talk.

'Ready to talk?' said the voice I had been waiting to hear.

'Yes.'

'Give me the girl and save yourself some serious trouble.'

'She's gone. She ran away after that message you sent about burning the house down – you bastard.'

My hatred of him and what he stood for came through in my voice. It was easy; once I started it came naturally. Rage and frustration swirled in my mind.

'If you were here now I'd knock your bloody teeth out.'

'Why would she run away because I said I'd burn your house down? I'm not stupid – that's not it. I bet she's still there with you.'

'I have no bloody idea why that made her leave – none! But she's gone and I'm out searching for her right now – and so are a lot of other people, including the police.'

His voice had surprised me. I had expected something different. I remembered Dao telling me what he said to Bram and how furious he had been then. But now he sounded calm, educated and well spoken; certainly not rough. A slightly nasal voice, but pleasant.

'You can't possibly think I'm going to fall for that,' he said. He sounded as if he was enjoying himself, amused and superior. 'I'm reasonably bright and it just doesn't stack up.'

'You can think what you like, you bastard. Watch the news and you'll find there's a police appeal for her to be found. I'm not making this up. Ring the cops and ask them –if you dare.'

He did not rise to the challenge. All he said was, 'I will be in touch.' And then he cut the connection.

I rang Benson and told him about the call and carried on. I spent two hours putting up posters on supermarket notice boards and on the windows of little grocery stores and fast-food places. I stapled some to random power poles. I told everyone I met to watch the news and hoped they would tell others.

When I got back to Willow's the twins were in bed and dinner was ready. Charlie arrived just after me and stayed for the meal.

'I can't go home yet,' she said. 'We must compare notes, so we know what progress we've made. Kristen knows where I am. Paul met me at the first shopping centre I went to and he took half the posters. He's going to put them up tonight and tomorrow morning. And he's putting her photo on his Facebook page too – apparently he has hundreds of so-called friends and he's asking the ones in New Zealand to share it with their friends. He said if it goes viral it could reach tens of thousands.'

Plum got up from her chair and said with an expression of disbelief, 'God, I can't believe I didn't think of that right off! I'll get it on my Facebook page right now and get it circulating a bit further.'

We had dinner and a glass of wine. Matt turned the TV around so we could watch it from the table and played the recording of the appeal for help finding Dao. Then we played it again.

'Keep it,' I said to Willow. 'If we find her I want her to see it.'

Nobody would meet my eyes; they knew that we might never see her again.

The appeal came across well. The chief of the unit Benson worked for was filmed standing on Queen Street, just around the corner from Simon's office. He emphasised that there were serious concerns about Dao's safety.

'She is a crucial eyewitness in an important criminal investigation involving murder, drugs and enslavement,' he said, 'and she is young and knows few people in Auckland'.

He said nothing about her age and the picture made her look very young. It was the one I took in the parking lot at the shopping mall. She was wearing her new jeans and hooded jacket, the same clothes she wore when she ran away. Clever strategy, I thought, just what I would have done, play on the young look and don't mention her real age. He added that she was not suspected of any criminal involvement herself and they flashed her photo and description on the screen once again, followed by the police hotline number.

'Hunter, please don't get upset if I ask,' said Plum. 'But I just don't understand some of it. What does it mean – I mean what Dao said in that note and what Glenda had said to you? I've been thinking about it ever since Willow told me. Did Dao say she loves you and you don't love her? And what's Glenda got to do with it?'

Talking about it was hard. I'm not used to talking about my emotions and I felt I had failed Dao by the way I told her she could not, or did not, love me. But Plum deserved an answer.

'When we first came back from the cabin Dao was terrified of sleeping alone in her room. The way we had to prepare to defend ourselves that final night in the cabin, just in case whoever was out there came back – that was very scary for her. She was convinced from the start that the man she still referred to as Master wanted to kill her. The morning when she ran away from the cabin, when I said I would find someone else to look after her – she thought it would expose her to danger and she would rather run away to perish on her own, in her own way, than risk letting him catch her and kill her.'

Matt was staring at me, taking it all in. He had only heard these things second-hand and for him the story took on a new meaning.

'At some point Dao said to me 'I would rather let myself die anywhere and alone so long as I didn't have to die at that place' and I think she might have added 'or let that man kill me'. She just didn't want to give him the sadistic satisfaction.'

Plum was crying now, with her elbows on the table and her hands over her face.

I looked down at her, trying to collect my thoughts and my composure.

'So when we got back to town we both slept in my room. She was in the bed and I was on top of the duvet with a rug over me, on the side nearest the door, with the Remington handy. And then she did sleep because she felt relatively safe. But every time I moved she woke up and made sure I was still there. I was worried that she was becoming fixated on me. I thought that if I represented total safety she could easily confuse it with love. Like that saviour syndrome someone mentioned.'

Plum had stopped crying now. She still had her face hidden in the palms of her hands, but she was listening.

'When she said she loved me in that note she meant as a woman loves a man, she had made that clear to me when I tried to pretend I was not interested in her, so she would feel safe. She said 'I'm not a child, I know what I know. We don't have to wait until after all the police stuff is over. We can talk about it now, or next year or when I'm fifty – it will be the same whenever we do, I'll say I love only you, it can't change'.'

Matt said, 'From what I've heard of this extraordinary girl I would say that you have to believe her when she says a thing like that.'

Although Matt had still not met Dao he had heard a lot about her from Willow and Plum. With his innate instinct for people, he had developed a good idea of her character.

'I know,' I said. 'But how could I risk letting her think she loved me, at this point? Not that I didn't want to, I love her. But the state she's in now? When she has been through hell, she's being threatened by a killer – or two actually. What if she decided later on that she did not want me after all but felt obliged to have sex with me – like she had to pay that bastard what he used to call his fee? It would have been unforgiveable of me.'

I looked at Plum, whose hands had dropped away from her wet face, took a deep breath and tried to look calm.

'I hope she doesn't change her mind about 'not going away to die' – but most of all I hope nobody does anything dreadful to her.'

19

TUESDAY

Over the next three days I slept in short bursts at any time of the day or night when exhaustion overcame me. I spent most of the time in the car with Scruff beside me, cruising shopping malls and supermarket parking lots, parks and recreational areas. I showered once and only ate one proper meal sitting at a table, when Willow insisted. Everyone tried to provide what advice and support they could, but none of us could comfort the others; we were all on edge, apprehensive and exhausted.

On day three, Matt rang just as it was getting dark. 'Hunter, I've just had a call from a guy I talked to this morning at the Devonport shops. I was doing the rounds with her picture, just talking to random people and nobody recognised her, but I left both our phone numbers everywhere. And just now the man from a fish and chips shop there rang and said he's seen a girl on Cheltenham beach, and she fits the description. He said she was wearing dark jeans and a grey hoodie and white trainers. He had no phone with him, but he went home and rang me right away. So maybe you should head over there? Do you want me to come?'

I was walking towards the stairs, picking up my keys

while I listened.

'No, I'm fine; I'm on my way right now. Thanks, Matt – I'll call you as soon as I know something.'

It wasn't far but it seemed like the longest car trip I had ever made. I broke the speed limit the whole way and hoped I would not be stopped and delayed, but I was unable to keep my speed down. It was the beach where we had taken Scruff, the place where Dao had run along the water's edge with him beside her not long ago. I parked under the big trees where the street ends in sand and took my flashlight.

'Come on, Scruff! Where is Dao? Find Dao!'

Scruff ran towards the dark water, and I followed. Away from the street the beach was dark, and I saw nobody. The light from the houses further up did not reach down here. The tide was out, and the wet sand was firm under my feet. I set out making no noise and left the flashlight off to avoid ruining my night vision. I walked to the end of the beach along the water's edge, alternating between looking ahead and up towards the houses and the gardens. I saw nothing. I turned walked back, this time right up along the edges of people's gardens, with Scruff running back and forth. There was no indication that Scruff thought it was anything other than an unusual walk in the dark.

We passed the place where my car was parked and continued for five minutes in the other direction. It was much darker here: the houses were further up and the shore became rocky. And then I saw her just ahead of me and my heart missed a beat. A small dark shape sitting on a rock under a tree, just a vague outline against the dark background. Scruff had come back to my side after doing a long loop behind me and now he rushed towards her, jumping and barking with his tail wagging furiously.

Dao leapt to her feet, and I took four long strides and grabbed her with both hands. She was silent and I held her tight.

'Are you all right? I've been sick with worry. Never do this to me again, I was going out of my mind. Are you OK?'

Scruff was dancing around us, barking excitedly. Outside lights came on in a house just above the rocky bank where Dao had sat. A door opened spilling a path of light down the lawn and a man's voice called out, asking what was going on.

I pulled myself together and called back, 'Just a surprise meeting – no problems, but thank you!'

We stayed where we were for a long time. I held her against me with both arms to warm her up. She had not said a word since I found her. In the end I pushed her away from me and tried to see her face. 'Are you all right? Are you hurt?'

'No, I'm not hurt. I'm hungry and tired – nothing worse.'

We walked back to the car with Scruff sticking close to Dao's legs. When the lights inside the car came on I got a proper look at her. She was exhausted and she was thinner again. I refrained from questions, just started the car and drove back to the house. She was still not talking, and I got the impression that she was depleted somehow. As if her energy and vivacity had evaporated and left this quiet and tired shell of a girl.

In the living room I unzipped her jacket and pulled it off. She sank down on one of the dining chairs and I knelt in front of her and took her shoes off. Her face was still and serious; she was struggling with some emotion I could not read.

'Stay there and I'll get you a hot drink. And then you need to go to bed.'

She shook her head, 'I don't want a hot drink, I've had plenty of water – there's a tap in the toilets on the beach. I just need to sleep.'

I took her upstairs and she lay down on the top of my bed and closed her eyes; within seconds she was asleep. I got my phone out and sent a joint message to everyone involved: 'Found Dao, unharmed. Thanks Matt. Back home now, please don't call us, we need a long sleep.'

I pulled her jeans off and tucked her under the covers before I undressed and climbed in beside her.

20

WEDNESDAY MORNING

We woke up late with the light from the skylight casting a bright square of sunlight on the wall above the bed and Scruff telling me it was time to get up. I watched Dao open her eyes and look straight at me, still very serious. Then she wrinkled her nose and said, 'We stink!'

'I know – we're both filthy. I can't remember when I had a shower last. Get into the bathroom and I'll run down and let Scruff out.'

I unset the alarms and let Scruff out, returned upstairs and joined her in the shower. She was just standing there under the water, letting it fall over her, not moving. I reached for her and she leant against me and said something I could not hear over the noise of the water.

'I can't hear you.'

She raised her voice. 'I said I'm sorry.'

'Never mind, it's over now. Let's get clean and have breakfast.'

I pushed her away and washed her limb by limb, very carefully. I reached for the shampoo she liked, washed her hair and pulled her under the centre of the water to rinse her off. She stood a little to one side of the stream of water, leaning against the tiled wall and watched me wash. She looked absent-minded as if she was thinking of something else. It was the first time she had seen me naked and neither of us even noticed.

We sat just inside the balcony door where she could not be seen from the lane behind the courtyard wall and had coffee and toast. The sun was shining after a couple of grey and damp days. Dao was still silent and distracted looking.

'Dao,' I said, disturbed and worried. 'You are so quiet, and I still know nothing about where you have been. Did something bad happen to you? Did somebody hurt you?'

'No, nothing bad happened.'

She looked down on the courtyard garden where Scruff was asleep on the warm paving stones beside the table. 'I got very cold, and nobody wanted to give me any work. I tried a lot of places but once my clothes started getting dirty they didn't even listen to what I said.'

'Where did you sleep?'

'The last two nights I slept behind the toilets on the beach. It was out of the wind, and I thought I could lock myself in the toilet if somebody came. But I didn't get a lot of sleep.'

She still would not look at me. Having found her had resolved nothing apart from relieving my fear that she would come to harm.

'Was it really just those text messages that made you go?'

'Yes – but there was nowhere for me to go. The only thing I could do was to try to find some work and earn some money.'

'And now? Are you going to run away and leave me again?'

'I don't know what to do. I can't stay with you.'

She raised her eyes for the first time since we had come downstairs and looked directly at me. 'I must go somewhere else.'

I knew I had to push this conversation right to the edge and make sure we were both being completely honest.

'So, it's either find a job or 'go away to die again' – is that it?'

The silence lasted a long time. She was looking down at her hands, not moving; she seemed to barely breathe.

I broke the silence first. 'Is that better than saving my mind, making me happy and stopping me being miserable for the rest of my life?'

'I am not good enough for you – people will say I only pretend to love you. They think I'm just after money and that's what being a whore means.'

'But I know that you love me, Dao. I never doubted it for a moment. I don't give a shit what those people think – it's nothing to do with them, it's about us. If you don't stay with me my life really will be ruined. I'll be unhappy and lonely and constantly thinking of you and trying to figure out what I could have done to make you stay.'

'You said it wasn't allowed anyway – I mean even if people didn't think that I just wanted your money.'

'I know – I said what I thought was right. I was protecting you from the risk that you would think you had to sleep with me to pay me back for rescuing you – or something like it. And I couldn't risk that you would change your mind and decide you only liked me as a friend – but that I expected something else from you.'

She looked up again, surprised at the emotion in my voice.

'I ... I don't know. It's frightening that all those people might be saying nasty things about me.'

The unspoken word 'Glenda' hung in the air between us like a threat.

'I truly don't give a damn, Dao. I'll tell you what happened the day you disappeared,' I said. 'Everyone was out looking for you. Willow was beside herself with worry. Matt and Plum and Charlie and Paul too, and me – we all spent three days driving around handing out your photo and my phone number. Benson's boss was on the TV news saying that a crucial witness in a criminal case had gone missing –

they had your photo and Benson's phone number – which was good because not only might we have found you that way, but now the Boss really knows you're not here. Plum drove around too, when she was not at lectures, and she cried a lot. It was a man from a shop who recognised you on the beach and called us.'

She was staring at me, incredulous and listening to every word.

'So, do you think that sounds as if everyone is against us being together? I think it shows that everyone in the family and everyone who knows about you – apart from one person – thinks you're extra special and all they wanted to do was find you and help you and for you to come back to me.'

'Did they really do all those things? Even Benson's boss on TV?'

The phone rang and I got up to answer. It was Matt; after asking about Dao he said, 'If you don't mind I'll come over for a quick visit. Willow is really worried about you and Dao, she's fretting about it all the time. I think perhaps someone less involved might be able to put a different slant on the problem. Tell me if you'd rather I stayed away.'

It seemed as if providence had intervened just when I had run out of steam. Matt was the perfect person – if anyone could achieve clarity for Dao it would be him.

'Please do,' I said. 'I'm really stuck.'

When I turned back Dao was standing up and I could tell she was thinking about what I had told her. Now her precise mind was at work, separating emotions from facts and making sense of it.

'That was Matt – Willow's husband. I know you haven't met him but he's coming over to talk to you. I don't know what it is about.' I felt that a white lie was preferable to having Dao refuse to talk to him.

She walked up close to me and said, 'Please hold me – just for a minute.'

I knew that the rest of the sentence could be '...in case I decide to leave and never see you again.'

I wrapped both arms around her and held her tight against me. 'I love you.'

She raised her face and said, 'I have to think, Hunter. You know I love you, but I have to think it out for myself.'

There was nothing more to be said; we looked at each other and I dropped my arms and let her go.

Matt and Dao spent over an hour in her room with the door closed. I sat in my armchair with Scruff beside me and tried to relax, but it was difficult. Eventually Matt came down the stairs alone, said 'it's up to you now, Hunter' and continued without stopping, down the next flight of stairs and out the front door.

I stayed where I was, unable to think constructively about anything. It was easier just to sit there and do nothing. Scruff ran up the stairs and I was alone. I closed my eyes and rested my head against the back of the chair. Inside my head I replayed the day I found Dao and all that happened since. I wondered if she would let me go with her into witness protection or if she would just disappear from my life. There was a tight feeling in my chest; I wondered if people my age have heart attacks.

Then a hand touched my face and Dao said, 'Hunter, are you all right? You look very strange. Please open your eyes!'

I opened my eyes. Dao was beside me with one hand on my cheek and a look of concern bordering on serious worry.

'Are you going to leave me?'

'No, I can't. I didn't want to, and it would have broken my heart, but I didn't know how to sort it all out in my head. But Matt helped me.'

I stayed where I was, and she kept her hand on my face. 'What did he say?'

'He asked me lots of questions and then he sort of showed me how to make sense of things I didn't understand. Things about you and other people that I couldn't work out for myself somehow. He's very nice. He said I haven't had enough time to learn all those things. And that it doesn't matter what other people say – you were right. He said we can't live our lives to please others or to fit in with what they think. We have to remember we only have one life - this is it and if we don't make the most of it nobody else is going to do it for us. He told me how people thought that Willow was making a big mistake because he's so much older, but they are so happy and probably always will be. And he's right. He said 'if you live by what others think, you are giving them power over you' – and I think I know what he means. He's very clever.'

Good old Matt, I thought. He's just quietly saved the situation. Now all we have to do is deal with the Boss. Some things are meant to be and there is no point struggling against it.

After lunch I came up against a brick wall.

'But why can't we stay here?' said Dao. 'You got all these things installed and it's very safe. They can't even break in downstairs like they did before, not with the new glass.'

'But I promised Benson,' I objected. 'I said we'd go into some hiding place until the Boss is out of action.'

She looked hard at me. 'But you already lied to him and to that other policeman, and you always do what you want to do anyway. Does it matter that you said we'd go away?'

We had been through this twice before lunch. I was fine with the idea that we simply stay in the house, but at the same time I wanted to make a token gesture of compliance to Benson who had been very good about everything. But Dao was adamant, so we were debating it for the third time, and I was ready to give up. She would clearly rather be at home and take the risk than go and live somewhere else for an indefinite time.

I had called the others and told them that Dao was fine and not to worry. Plum sent a message and said she was coming over after lunch because she had no afternoon classes.

Charlie was flying an international VIP from the airport to the Kauri Cliffs luxury lodge in the Bay of Islands that afternoon. When I rang her she asked to speak to Dao, and they had a long conversation that I was not allowed to listen to; probably discussing my past. I heard Dao laughing from her bedroom a couple of times – God knows what Charlie told her.

I had hoped Matt and Willow would come over with Plum, but they were driving to Hamilton to visit Matt's ancient mother who lived on her own and was unwell. I was sitting there contemplating the call I knew I had to make to Vivian as soon as possible and trying to imagine what I could say, not an easy task. And neither would it be easy the next time I spoke to my parents. Glenda would not take it well and there was no remedy for that. If she decided never to talk to me again, well, I could cope with that too. So instead of doing the most unpleasant tasks first I rang Benson. He was less than pleased. 'I can't force you to leave,' he said. 'But I seriously recommend it. Can I speak to Dao?'

Everyone wanted to speak to Dao today. I handed her the phone and mentally wished Benson luck. He had never come up against Dao's unconditional-no-response and I looked forward to listening to this.

'Thank you,' said Dao. 'I'm sorry I was so much trouble, but there were things that I couldn't cope with.'

'Did you? I don't know what that means – I'll have to look it up.'

'Thank you.'

'Really?'

'No I don't. I like it here and it's so safe now with that wire glass downstairs and all the alarms and things. Hunter will look after me. If they break in somehow he will sh....'

'No, no! I was not going to say he'll shoot them! Of course, not – he wouldn't shoot anyone. I didn't mean to say that. But he would beat them up – he's allowed to do that, isn't he?'

'OK, I promise. No, I really promise, I'm not tricking you. I hide been under the luggage cover every time we go out in

the car and I get in the back before we even open the garage
door. Nobody can see me.'

'Yes, I promise. I never go close to the windows now.'

Then she giggled.

'Having a shower! I was really smelly and it's my
favourite thing.'

Now she was blushing. 'Yes, of course. I just didn't want
to say it.'

She said goodbye and handed the phone back to me.

'That was very interesting to listen to, Dao,' I said. 'I think
you could make Benson believe anything you tell him.'

She smiled and looked a bit embarrassed. 'He's really nice.
I didn't know that he had read the note I wrote for you at
Simon's office. He said some very nice things.'

'You said 'of course' to something and 'I just didn't say it'
and then you blushed. Am I allowed to know what that was
about?'

The temptation to tease her a little was irresistible. I had
never seen this side of her before and it was very encouraging
to watch her react just like any other girl when teased.

'He asked what the best thing was when I came home.
And I said having a shower. So, he asked if being back with
you wasn't the best thing of all.'

'And what's the word you must look up?'

'Integrity –do you know what it means?'

Plum arrived, full of smiles, hugged Dao and me and then
hugged Dao again. I had dozens of emails backed up again
and a new client London wanted me to liaise with; another
powerful man who needed a private army. I should start the
process of getting Dao a passport so I could take her next time
I had to go on a site visit for a client. Everything had piled up
again and I needed to start sorting and prioritizing.

'I'll leave you girls to talk,' I said and picked up my phone
and the laptop. 'I'll go and sit at the desk in the bedroom and
get some work done. Block off the stairs again please, so I can
set the ground floor alarm.'

I worked for a couple of hours and managed to sort out most of the things that needed immediate answers. The new client was in Kuala Lumpur, and I would need a lot of information before there was any point trying to decide whether I had to visit before putting a proposal together. Our kind of client never tells us everything first up; they keep the worst things close to the chest and sometimes crucial information only emerges very late in the piece. They don't seem to realise that we need to know absolutely everything, if we are going to be able to put together adequate protection for them. I spent fifteen minutes scrolling through the names of so-called security personnel in our database to check who was available; mercenaries are an international commodity, and the London office spends a lot of time updating the database details as best as they can.

Late in the afternoon I went down for a cup of coffee. Plum and Dao were sitting in opposite corners of the big sofa with their legs pulled up, eating chocolate biscuits and drinking something in the big breakfast cups that I never use.

'What are you two drinking? I'm making coffee if you want some.'

'We're having a special tea,' said Dao. 'With flowers in it – very pretty. Plum brought it with her. Come and see.'

I admired the flowers in the tea, wondered vaguely what they had been talking about, made a cup of coffee and went back upstairs.

By six Plum had gone and we were talking about dinner.

'I really don't know what we have,' I said and went to have a look in the fridge. 'Nothing useful – not a damn thing. We ate the only good stuff for lunch. We have a bit of stale bread, half a bottle of old milk, two squishy tomatoes and some lamb chops that are going off. That's what happens when you're out searching for people all day – no time to shop. Either we starve or we get pizza or something. I can't take you into the supermarket and I'm not leaving you in that huge parking lot while I shop.'

'Let's go and get pizza. You can park right outside and see the car the whole time. Take the gun.'

'We could order from that bigger place in the mall, they deliver,' I said. 'But their pizzas aren't as nice as the ones from the little Italian place. What do you think?'

'Let's have the nice ones like last time, from the little shop – with anchovies.'

Dao had recently discovered anchovies and liked them. We went upstairs to get our jackets. I washed my hands, Dao decided to clean her teeth. She enjoyed cleaning her teeth nearly as much as showering. I looked at her in the mirror.

'You and Plum had a long conversation this afternoon. Was it OK?'

'I told her everything that had happened on the island.'

'Everything? You mean really everything? About being raped and all the rest – really everything?'

She nodded. 'Yes, I did – everything. I know that it will come out anyway if there's a court case. But I wanted to tell her now, so she knows we trust her – you know, after we told her those lies before. I don't want her to always be the last person to hear things.'

She put the toothbrush back in her mouth and watched me steadily while she brushed her teeth. I looked back at her with a feeling of having been caught unprepared. She had talked to someone else about the most traumatic things that had happened to her, and no doubt about her decision to die too. I felt a brief flash of something like resentment, as if she had decided she no longer needed me. She had reached a level of security that I had thought might take months to achieve. And integrity was precisely the right word to describe the reason she had done it.

21

WEDNESDAY AFTERNOON

I backed out of the garage, let the door down and paused to set the alarm. Scruff was in the back under the cover with Dao for the first time. I drove around the block and some way off in the wrong direction before I headed for the pizza place. Just taking precautions.

'I've just made a detour to make sure nobody is following. Are you still OK back there? Is Scruff a problem?'

'I'm nearly asleep – I'm so tired again,' she said, and I could only just hear her. 'It's nice to have Scruff in here. We're cuddled up together.'

It was only when I parked outside the pizza place that I realised I had only brought the Remington and not the Glock. I briefly considered going back for it, but perhaps the most acute danger point was going in or out of the house, in which case I might as well stay where I was. It was a bit early for most people to buy take-away food and there was only one customer inside. The two guys who own the shop were both behind the counter talking to him.

'I'll go inside now and place the order and then I'll come back and sit in the car.'

'OK – can I have one of those ice creams in a little plastic bowl, please – like we had last time?'

256

Ice cream was a close third after showers and cleaning teeth on Dao's list of things of importance and enjoyment.

I placed our order, paid and said I would wait outside. The man asked if I wanted to take the ice cream now and I said I would take it when the pizza was ready and went out to the car. Fifteen minutes later they signalled through the window that my order was ready. I balanced the boxes on one arm with the ice cream tub in my hand, pushed the door open and fished in my pocket for the car keys. A pickup truck with a double cab had arrived while I was inside. It was parked just to the right of the door, facing out.

I took a couple of steps towards my car and two men came around the truck very fast, one in front of me and one from behind. In a second they had me trapped between their bodies and the truck. One grabbed my right arm, the other tried to get his arm around my neck from behind but he was too short. The boxes went flying as I wrenched my arm away from the guy on my right and swung my bent arm hard into his face. He was the perfect height; my elbow connected with his nose, and he staggered back against the truck.

I turned fast to deal with the other one and came up against a knife pointing at my stomach; about five centimetres away. I knew I could not take it off him. He was holding it with his arm slightly bent and his hand curled upwards around the handle. He would have stabbed me with an upwards motion before I could reach around to grab his arm. I kicked his shin to create a diversion and then went for the knife hand; off-balance he slashed sideways and got my left arm.

Now the other one came back into the fight. Blood was pouring from his broken nose and dripping off his chin. He was furious and in serious pain. He smashed his fist into the side of my face and literally rocked me on my feet. He was short but powerful and that upward punch nearly over-balanced me. For a moment I saw stars and then they were both on me. They hauled the truck door open, bundled me in and jumped into the front seats. I reached for the door handle and had my left foot ready to kick the door wide open and jump out, but the handle was out of action. They had the childproof function on, and the door would only open from the outside. I lunged forward and pushed my arm around the driver's neck, but the headrest made it hard to get a good grip. I gave up when the knife appeared again, pointing at the side of my face. There was blood everywhere, from the flattened nose and my arm. The nose guy was swearing loudly and the other one kept saying 'shut the fuck up' over and over. It was not a happy trip.

In my head I tried to work out my chances. They obviously had no idea Dao was in my car so for the moment she was safe. But what would she do? Did she have her phone with her? She must have heard the fight; she would get out of the car and see the pizza boxes on the ground. The pizza guys must have heard it or perhaps seen it. Were they calling the cops? Did they have CCTV in the parking lot?

I checked my pockets. I had my wallet in the back pocket of my jeans, my phone in the right-hand front pocket and the alarm system remote in the left. Nothing in my jacket pockets. I would have to rely on my size and my fists. I worked the phone out of the pocket and pushed it inside the waistband of my jeans. The Remington was in my car and the Glock was at home. I cursed myself for not taking it; I would have had total control of the situation if I had brought it.

It was half dark already. We were heading north through the suburbs into unfamiliar territory. I thought of trying to send a text message to Benson but getting the phone out was a risk. If they caught me at it they would take it off me.

We turned into an empty parking area beside a playground and stopped. Nothing was said. Five minutes later a large grey van pulled in beside us. A tall broad-shouldered man got out. He was wearing a Darth Vader helmet.

The guys in the front seat got out of the truck and closed the doors. The man with the helmet handed over something small, possibly an envelope. Now was my chance; climb over into the front seat, get out on the far side and run. It would take a minute to scramble over the front seats. I half stood up and turned sideways to get my leg between the seats. But my two new friends opened the door beside me and dragged me out before I had a chance to make my move. Darth Vader had a pistol in his hand now. The two thugs each took hold of one arm and marched me over to the van. One of them tied my hands together with a cable tie and tightened it with a vicious jerk. Helmet man pointed at the open side door with the gun, and I got in. The back of the van was empty apart from two seats just behind the driver. As they fastened my ankle to the metal undercarriage of the seat blood from the shorter guy's flattened nose dripped on my jeans. I could feel his fury like vibrations in the space between us. His DNA might be in the police database, I thought, if I survive this and can tell someone.

Before they climbed out again the nose man threw a straight left punch at me and hit me in the cheekbone with brutal force.

Helmet man said, 'Steady, man! I want him conscious and talking.'

That educated, slightly nasal voice; it was unmistakable. The doors closed and the Boss got into the front seat, reversed out and drove us away. Those heavies were not his, they were the hired help; the kind who will do anything if you pay them enough.

He drove carefully; I was sure he was keeping under the speed limit. Being stopped by the police would have ruined his day. Within a couple of minutes, he slowed and pulled over to remove the helmet and then we started up again. I checked if I could reach the side panel and kick it but my leg on the side closest to the wall was the one strapped to the seat. My cut arm was seeping blood at a steady rate, but there was nothing I could do with my hands tied together. Taking the phone out in the dark van was not an option. If he glanced in the rear vision mirror the light from the phone would stand out like a beacon. There was nothing I could do until we got to our destination. I leaned back, closed my eyes and thought hard.

The van stopped. I opened my eyes and waited in the darkness. The Boss opened the side door and stood there, without his helmet. He was very sure that I would not be around to identify him once I had told him what he wanted to know. There was little ambient light, and his face was just a featureless oval shape; so far I had not got a decent look at him.

He had it all planned in meticulous detail. Nothing left to chance or impulse. First he reached in and attached a long rope just below my knee. The rope had a dog collar on the end and he pulled it tight and tucked the end tidily into the little holding loop. I could have swivelled in the seat and brought my fists down on his head, but it would have achieved nothing. There was no way I could knock him out from the position I was in. Next he leaned in and passed me a very small set of hobby scissors with plastic handles. No points on the blades, just rounded ends; useless as a weapon.

'Cut the cable tie around your ankle.'

He was very calm and sure of himself; there was no anger or animosity in his voice.

I did what I was told; bent down, tried to get a grip on the scissors with my fettered hands, cut the ankle tie after some strong sawing and stood up when he told me to. Bent over, moved towards the door and got out. He backed away, one step back for each one I took forward, the rope never slackened. I stretched and looked around me. We were in a yard among large buildings, factories or warehouses of some kind, industrial. To one side of us there was an ordinary-sized door, no windows. There were two trucks parked on the far side, but it was too dark to read the sign writing. I thought of running straight at him and knocking him over, but he had the gun, and my hands were tied. I decided to wait for a better opportunity.

'Throw the scissors into the van and close the door.'

I did what I was told. 'Walk towards that door, then along the wall to the left,' he said. 'Stop when the rope is tight.'

I obeyed and stopped when I felt the rope go taut. Now he was by the door, and I was further along the wall. He pushed a piece of wood aside with his foot and bent down, picked up a key. He unlocked the door and walked backwards, motioning to me to walk back along the wall towards the door. We went in, still in the same formation, me first and him at the end of the rope, keeping it taut. I noticed he took the key with him and locked the door from inside. He knew the place even in the dark; a quick flick and a row of fluorescent light tubes along one wall came on. The place was huge, long and very high. There were machines in rows, long work benches and chest-high dividing walls here and there splitting the place up into separate areas. Electric cables and hoses came down from high above us in several places. I looked up. Way up there a gantry system ran along both sides with cross beams in a couple of places. Something was suspended from a hook high up, further down the length of the building. Whatever they did here involved very heavy things.

He pointed. 'Go on, walk ahead of me till I tell you to stop. I have the gun in my hand and if you turn around and try anything I'll shoot you.'

'Good luck with that – perfect place for a ricochet,' I said, deliberately flippant and wanting to annoy him.

The whole space was full of steel pillars and beams and pieces of machinery. Firing a weapon in here could end up like being inside a deadly pinball machine. We walked down the left-hand side of the building, with a chest-high separating barrier on our right. There was nothing I could grab, but I saw plenty of potential weapons on workbenches and tool trolleys in the central space.

'Stop here.'

We were level with an opening in the low wall. 'Turn right and then left and stop beside the table.'

I followed his instructions, stopped and waited. The thing he referred to as a table was a huge waist-high box shape. I had no idea what it actually was. It was very large, and the surface was about twenty centimetres lower than the edges and made up of slats of some kind, looked like narrow metal ribs quite close together.

'Turn around.'

He was standing on the far side of a piece of machinery, about as tall as he was, not very wide. Hoses and a cable hung down from up high and were attached to it. To one side was a small shelf with a keyboard and a computer screen.

We looked at each other. There was no way to reach him fast; I would have to get around that piece of whatever it was, and he had a gun in his hand.

'Turn away from me.'

His footsteps passed behind me and then he returned to the machine.

'Turn back to face me.'

He had tied the end of the rope around a steel post on the side away from him, making it impossible for me to lunge at him.

'Now we talk.'

'OK.'

Now that I could see him I had a niggling feeling that I had seen him before and not that long ago. Long, lean face, short grey hair, bushy eyebrows – about sixty. Tanned in that tropical holiday kind of way that never looks quite natural. I tried to picture a context, but nothing surfaced. Perhaps he just reminded me of someone I had seen on TV or in a newspaper.

My arm was bleeding less but my hands were beginning to feel numb. Even if I got the cable tie off my wrists I would be pretty useless in a fight. I moved my wrists against each other trying to relieve the pressure and allow blood to circulate.

'So, talk,' I said, never taking my eyes off his face. Whatever happened now I wanted him to know I was not scared of him and I was not about to cave in.

'I want the girl. As I said when we talked – I think she's been moved. That appeal on the news was a hoax.'

He smiled, an arrogant and self-assured smile. 'But the appeal was useful, now I know exactly what she looks like - I'll know her when I see her.'

We had used the photo I took of Dao in her new clothes, the one I sent to Willow; it was a very good likeness.

'It wasn't a hoax. She ran away and I have no idea where she is.'

At least this last was true. I tried to inject a bit of emotion. 'My family and I have been searching for days, we're devastated. I told you before – she ran away on Saturday when we were in a lawyer's office in town. She's got no money and she left her phone behind. God knows what's happened to her.'

His eyes never left my face; he was looking for a false expression, some sign that I was lying.

'Tell me why you think she would run away. She was with people who protected her, I know you're armed, and you can defend her. Why would she run?'

'The cops were moving her into the witness protection system, with a family in a small town. She didn't want to go. She wanted to stay at my place and then you threatened to burn the place down.'

'No, I don't believe you.' His reply was calm and without emotion. 'No way, it doesn't add up. She'd run into the unknown with no resources, just to avoid being in a safe place? Rubbish!'

More time would be good; I must stall him. I had no idea how he planned to make me talk, but I was fairly sure he had something effective lined up. This guy was methodical and cold, he would have thought it out in advance.

'You know she saw you, don't you?' I said, deliberately taunting him. 'When your motor wouldn't start at Bram's place? You stuffed up and took that stupid helmet off.'

'Yes, I know.' He frowned, irritated with himself. 'It was a very unfortunate coincidence that she was watching just then.'

His vocabulary and the way he spoke – he was used to communicating. Very clear and concise. Lecturer, schoolteacher, lawyer?

'If she hadn't been there to see me none of this would be necessary. She has caused me a lot of grief.'

The idea that it should matter that Dao had caused him grief made me furious and I had to make an effort not to show him how angry I was. I had an idea and I hoped it would work. Getting him off-balance, making him angry or frustrated while I kept my cool might give me an opportunity to tackle him somehow.

'She's a good little artist, did Bramville tell you?'

His eyes flicked to the left and he turned his head fractionally. Something had triggered a reaction, but what?

'What do you mean – artist? What's that got to do with anything?'

'She draws people really well. It's been very useful.'

I paused as if we were having a leisurely conversation about a common acquaintance, all the time in the world.

'Not bodies so much – she gets the proportions a bit wrong but faces – she's very good at likenesses.'

Now I had his attention. A couple of vertical frown lines had appeared between his eyebrows. His voice had a slight edge to it, the first sign of tension.

'So she's been drawing things for the police, has she?'

'Yeah, spent hours doing it. Everyone she ever saw at that place, years of memories. As I said, she's a clever girl.'

I smiled as if I remembered something particularly pleasing, something he did not know. I could sense his irritation increasing like a tiny rise in temperature.

'Not only is she good at drawing, but she has a fantastic memory too.'

'Such as?' His voice was a notch higher now, more intense. I was slowly getting under his skin. But could I make him lose his self-control? I pretended to think.

'Well, details of boats for example. She can recall the exact details of every boat that came to visit since she was ten – and their names. Faces, what kind of boots people wore, their little identifying marks, like tattoos. All sorts of useful things – quite exceptional.'

His eyes flickered again, this time slightly down to the left. He was wearing a long-sleeved grey sweatshirt, but that split-second involuntary reaction was easy to read.

I decided provocation might be a good idea, now that he was a bit unsettled already. 'She drew your left arm tattoo – the Norton logo – so exactly that even that swirly line was precisely as it should be. And she'd only seen it once. The cops love it.'

Now he was getting angry. I could see veins on his temples where before there had been nothing. In some distant corner of the place something cooled and contracted in the night air – a couple of metallic clicks, silence and another little cracking sound.

'Never mind! It won't matter whatever she draws.' He was speaking faster, a few degrees less in control of his temper. 'I have no convictions, no links to any gangs. My life is as clean as it can be. And nobody's seen my face.'

I laughed. 'Don't kid yourself – the girl saw you and I'm looking at you now. That's two for a start. And the cops have your portrait – and I can see now that it's a good one. I recognised you from it.'

'No matter,' he said decisively. 'They have nothing on me, even if that drawing rings a bell. But enough of this – we're wasting time. You are going to tell me where she is or something very unpleasant will happen. Have a look over there.'

I wondered why he thought his face might ring a bell with the police; there must be a link. If he wasn't in the crime database it must be some legitimate connection. My mind was working on two levels; calculating and observing and waiting for an opportunity to take him down and at the same time trying to figure out who and what he was.

He turned and pointed at the far end of the box structure beside me. At the end of it, about three metres away, was a lump of something resting on the slats. I looked closer; it was a boot lying on its side with the heel end in my direction.

'OK, looks like a boot.'

He smiled; satisfied that he had the upper hand, arrogance restored.

'Quite right, it is a boot and there is a foot inside it – Bram's foot.'

I stared at him, not sure if he was trying to intimidate me with a lie or if it was true. Had he cut off Bram's leg and left the foot there?

'And where is Bram? Hopping around on crutches?'

He frowned. Levity and sarcasm were not on his agenda tonight, at least not from me. My attitude was really beginning to bug him. He pointed upwards and away towards the end of the building.

'See that thing hanging there? It's Bram, inside a big thick vinyl bag with a zip and strong handles. Large sails come in those when you buy them from some companies – very useful things, those bags. I have two more.'

I looked at the bundle hanging in the shadows way up under the roof, five or six metres from the floor. It was suspended from a hook on the gantry, big enough to hold a body and it looked as if it had something body-sized in it. There was no reason to doubt his word. If the foot was down here on the table it was because he had cut it off and left it there to convince me to cooperate.

'This place is full of convenient machinery,' I said. 'You have useful connections, or do you own it?'

'The company is in liquidation. You can get access to anything if you pay enough. Or if you know things that people don't want you to tell. I know a lot of bad stuff about a lot of people.'

His vanity and arrogance were king-size. He saw himself as someone with infinite resources, who knew how to use them; used to having the upper hand. The pieces were slotting together like a jigsaw puzzle in my mind. He was a barrister who knew a lot of criminals. It explained his connections to drugs and gangs, people he could blackmail or hire to do things he would not do himself. I decided to push things a bit further, see if I could ruffle his feathers.

'I know you from somewhere,' I said casually. 'Are you famous?'

He smiled, certain of his superiority. His memory was better than mine; he was invincible.

'We were in the same restaurant not long ago.'

The scene snapped into place: The man in the light grey suit, admiring Dao and then looking away when I turned. But then he had not known who I was, or realised who my date was. Now I held an ace, but he did not know it – yet. I smiled straight into his eyes, said nothing, waited.

And then it struck him, and his face turned red with fury. It was his first out-of-control moment and my smile drove him crazy.

'Shit! That was her – in the restaurant!'

I laughed, mocking him. 'Yep – the girl herself. Getting a special treat for being so cool when that fucking idiot you hired to kill her broke into my house.'

He was furious, took a step forward, wanted to hit me. He

restrained himself with a visible physical twitch. The word mistake was not in his vocabulary.

Come closer, you bastard, I thought, and I'll smash my forehead into your face. I can knock you out cold with little damage to myself if you get close enough. If I wasn't tied up I could kill you with my bare hands.

'And now you're going to start cutting parts off me like you did with Bram, are you? To make me tell you where she is? Did you get nothing out of Bram, or did you kill him as punishment for losing her?'

No way was I going to use her name in conversation with this monster. He was calmer again and he had something nasty up his sleeve, some secret he was keeping to the last.

'Do you know what this is?' He gestured at the box structure and the machine beside him.

'No.'

'It is a very powerful cutting machine – it uses a very fine jet of high-pressure water. The jet is only a millimetre wide. This one uses powdered garnets as an abrasive. The jet cuts through anything: granite, steel – anything. Cutting bone is like slicing cheese, effortless.'

I studied the box shape beside me that he had called a table earlier. There was water below the slats. If you put something on the slats and cut it, the water from the jet would drain through and leave the object dry. I wondered if they recovered the abrasive particles from the bottom of the tank or if garnets were cheap; I nearly asked him.

'This is the cutting head,' he said and put his hand on the tall structure beside him. 'It's computer guided and it will cut the exact shape or line that I programme into it. I could cut a heart shaped hole through your chest, right through you.'

Now I noticed the robotic arm with joints where it could bend and swivel, and at the end of the arm the cutting head with the jet nozzle. He was watching my face. Then he reached over and lifted something heavy from the bench beside him. Held it up so I could see it. A cube of metal, each side about fifteen centimetres, with a hook-shaped tunnel right through it.

'See this? Mild steel – they cut a new tow-hook for a big truck out of it. Took a while apparently, but it tells a story, doesn't it?'

It certainly did, it painted horrific visions in my mind of parts of my body being sliced off while I watched.

'Must be very high pressure?'

I wanted to keep him talking, wanted to find another weak spot or some way of winding him up. He had recovered his poise and it left me at a disadvantage.

He gazed fondly at the cutting head. 'I think it's about seventy thousand psi or thereabouts. I know the jet has to go through a hole in a diamond or it would eat away whatever it passed though.'

He liked lecturing, having the facts, controlling his audience. I could just imagine him in a courtroom, performing like an actor. That measured manner, the smooth appearance. He would be a real star in front of a jury.

'You're a lawyer,' I said. 'Criminal cases, defending scum. I bet you're good at it.'

His eyebrows went up a notch and then he smiled. 'Quite right, that's what I do and yes – I'm very good at it.'

He was not worried about my having identified him, he knew he was safe. And he enjoyed this conversation – perhaps it was the first time he had ever had an opportunity to show off, to tell someone how clever he was, how he could get away with anything. And he only risked it now because he was going to kill his audience.

'Back to business,' he said suddenly. 'Are you going to tell me where she is, or do we crank up this little beast? You can't save her – she has to die. But you can save yourself.'

A stupid lie: even if I told him he would kill me. 'I've told you already – I have no idea where she is. I can't tell you what I don't know.'

'Rubbish!' he said impatiently. 'You're lying, I can see it – I

can nearly smell it. You're an arrogant bastard, but this thing
will make you talk. You physical chaps are all the same, you
think that brawn makes you kings of the world. Move closer
to the table and lean over the edge and I'll show you who
holds the aces.'

22

WEDNESDAY NIGHT

I moved right up to the side of the table and bent forward, and he realised that he had made another mistake. My wrists were tied together in front of me, and the table surface was so much lower than the edge; the only part of me that I could rest on the slats would be either my head or my chest with my arms between me and the slats. He could chop my head off in that position or cut into my back, but he wanted slow torture, not instant death. It was a stand-off.

For the first time he completely lost his cool. 'Fuck, fuck, fuck!' he shouted, furious with himself and with me for witnessing it. It was a serious blow to his perfect plan and his self-esteem.

I straightened up and waited. Smiled as if amused, but inside I was jubilant. A serious blow indeed – he would have to improvise, but would he be any good at it? His forte seemed to be planning, not ad hoc solutions.

He was silent for a couple of minutes, stood still and stared at the table. Whatever he decided would be well thought out, but would it be good enough? Finally, he worked it out.

'Stay there, I'll have the gun aimed at you all the time. Face away from me.'

I heard him walk further away; things were moved around, probably stuff on one of the work benches. Things were picked up and put down again, metal knocking against metal. Then he came closer again.

'I'm going to give you something to cut the cable tie with. I'm sure you can manage if you hold it between your hands and sort of cut backwards.'

He was way over to one side of me, the gun was in his right hand and he reached over with his left and placed a saw blade of some kind on the slats. He moved away again, and I picked the thing up. A replacement blade for a hack saw; a straight blade, not very wide and about a foot long, holes both ends. I manipulated it awkwardly with my numb fingers and it was clear that there was no way I could exert a sawing motion against the plastic tie around my wrists. I let it drop to the floor.

He watched closely and had to accept that I could not do it.

'OK, that won't work. Turn around again.'

He spent a few minutes messing around with things and returned; this time he sounded confident.

'This should do it. Turn around, hands out in front of you and stand still.'

He was nearly within my reach. He had the gun in his right hand still and in his left a box-cutter.

'I'm going to cut it – but don't even think of trying to attack me. I'll shoot you instantly. I'm a good shot and the safety is off.'

I nodded. He was right; trying to tackle him from this angle would be a sure way to get shot. He reached out, standing sideways with the knife blade just reaching my hands and started cutting though the cable tie. It took a few seconds. He was careful not to put his weight too far forward. The angle was awkward, but he did it.

The tie fell to the floor and my hands dropped like dead weights. Pins and needles, agony as the circulation got going.

My slashed arm bled steadily. My hands would be useless for the next ten minutes at least.

He stepped back and smiled, satisfied that at last he had me where he wanted me.

'Turn around and lean forwards. Put your upper body on the slats, face sideways – right arm straight out from your shoulder. I have the gun in my hand, so don't try anything.'

I did what I was told. I heard him grunting with effort behind me and then something very heavy dropped hard across my upper back. I had no idea what it was, but it effectively anchored me to the table. The raised edge of the table cut into my ribcage and breathing was difficult. I heard keys tapping; he was starting up the cutting machine. Then he said 'Right!' in a satisfied voice. Out of the corner of my eye I saw the machine swing its multi-jointed arm towards me and start to lower the cutting head. He had a remote-control unit in his hand, and he was going to cut my right arm off. With a high-pitched scream the jet of water cut into my arm just below the shoulder.

Now I had no choice; I would rather be shot than cut to bits. With a huge effort I lifted and twisted my torso and toppled the weight off my back. It fell to the floor with a reverberating clang of metal on concrete, the shockwaves bashed against my eardrums. I straightened, skin twitching in anticipation of the shot I felt sure would follow. The scream of the water jet stopped.

At exactly that moment someone started to sing. The sound soared towards the high roof and floated like threads of gold through the dark space. There was a slight echo effect. Someone was singing 'Amazing Grace' very beautifully, a slightly mezzo voice with clear diction. I stared at the Boss. His eyes were wild, his expression outraged.

'What the fuck?' It came out as a shout. He swung around and his right hand swung with him, but before I could move he collected his wits and turned the gun on me again.

The cutting head was moving slowly back to its original

resting position, the robot arm neatly folded its joints and pulled itself into place. Then the gantry crane started up high above us. We both looked up and saw the big sail bag gliding slowly along the overhead track, coming towards us out of the gloom at the end of the building. The singing continued.

It was like being in a surreal French art movie – eerie and chilling. The bag approached and lowered as it went, until it stopped right above us. The singing stopped and there was total silence. The heavy bag rocked gently back and forth, and we stared up at it, mesmerised. I looked down at my arms; blood was dripping from my numb hands. I tried to pull my mind together and figure out what to do next.

The Boss turned this way and that, tried to see in all directions at once, then back to focus on me. His voice was half strangled with fury and panic. 'Tell me where she is – right now or I shoot you, you bastard!'

I tried to keep my eyes on his face, but at the edge of my field of vision I had seen something that nearly made my heart stop. Just to the right of his shoulder, and no more than four or five metres away, stood Dao. She was in the twilight area between the well-lit patch where we were and the dark depths of the building. Her stance was that of a discus thrower; both hands at shoulder level, one further back than the other and her upper body twisted sideways. I could not see what she was holding, but it looked heavy. I had a momentary impression of someone else moving in the deeper shadows, way behind her.

The Boss either saw my eyes move or perhaps my expression changed. His head turned very fast. The gun swung towards Dao just as she made a gigantic effort and threw the heavy circular blade from an electric saw hard and fast, like a large Frisbee.

It came towards us in a slight curve and on a nearly flat trajectory. I threw myself away from the arc of the approaching disc and crashed down between the cutting table and the barrier. Two shots very close together, the sharp ping of a ricochet off metal and then silence.

I got to my feet, clumsy and slow. My arms were nearly useless, falling on them had done them no good. The leg rope had come loose from where it had been tied to the beam.

Dao was staring at the Boss with a look of horror. He lay on his side on the floor beside the machine. A gaping tear in the side of his neck pumped blood into a rapidly spreading pool. His left arm was twitching convulsively, but he was not going to get up – not with that wound. If it had gone any further around, his head would have come off. The gun was safely out of reach.

Dao was rooted to the spot with her eyes fixed on the Boss. I walked around his body, careful not to step in the blood. The rope dragged behind me. I could not touch her; both my hands were covered in blood.

'Are you OK?' My voice sounded as if it belonged to somebody calm and collected, a man who would take control and sort things out. But my heart was beating like a drum and adrenaline coursed through my body. We had very nearly lost.

'Yes, I think so,' she said absent-mindedly, as if she was thinking of something else. I recognise shock when I see it; pretty soon she now would either start to cry or sit down on the floor and lose focus.

I said sharply, 'Look at me, Dao! Now – look at me!'

And she did. Her eyes moved to my face and then slid down to stare at my arms and at the blood dripping on the floor.

'Hunter – you're hurt,' she said, still speaking slowly. 'Let me have a look.'

'Not yet. I'm OK for the moment. There's someone else in here.'

I started in the direction of where I had seen movement before she threw the saw disc. I rounded a barrier set up in front of a workbench with a drill press on it and stopped in shock.

On the floor in front of me lay Paul, nearly flat on his back with one arm flung out, his eyes open and sightless. There was a semi-automatic rifle just to one side of his legs. I knelt beside him, wondering what I could do with my useless arms. Dao appeared. She drew in a sudden breath and knelt beside me.

'Oh no, it's Paul! Is he dead?'

Her voice was more like her normal voice, and she was speaking at normal speed. I peered at him, there was very little light there, but my eyes were adjusting. There was a hole just above his left eyebrow, so close it was hardly noticeable.

'Touch his wrist, see if you can feel a pulse,' I said to Dao. 'My hands are useless. Do you know how to do it?'

She shook her head, and I talked her through it. She tried both Paul's wrists and his neck without success.

'I think he is dead,' she said, tears running down her cheeks. 'His skin feels sort of limp. Poor Paul! What happened to him?'

I bent and pointed at the hole on his forehead and drops of my blood fell on his cheek. I took a fast step back.

'A bullet hit him there and it's either gone right through or it's inside his head somewhere. The Boss must have fired just as you threw that metal Frisbee at him. But why the hell was Paul here and how did you get here? I don't understand any of it.'

'Charlie is outside,' said Dao. 'She was waiting for Paul to arrive when I climbed in.'

None of it made much sense to me. I was bleeding at a steady rate. Blood was running freely down my right arm and dripping from my hand and the knife cut on the other arm was bleeding too, though not as much. It was very messy and painful. I looked at my right arm and noticed in a detached sort of way that the water jet cutter had made a very neat job of slicing through the sleeve of my jacket.

Apart from being soaked with blood the edges were as straight and crisp as if a tailor had cut a long gash across the fabric.

'Come,' said Dao urgently. 'Let's go outside and tell Charlie we are all right. She can tell you about it. I don't know what to do with your arms, but she will.'

She took my bloodied hand and led me towards the door where I had come in with the Boss. We had only taken a few steps when all hell broke loose.

Doors were smashed open and rapid footstep approached from two directions. Voices called out to drop all weapons and put hands on heads. The call to stand still and put weapons down was repeated, someone said, 'over there' and booted feet moved fast in our direction. It was a full-blown invasion. We stayed where we were and waited.

Men from the Armed Offenders Squad were all over the place. Black-clad men in Kevlar vests and helmets, with rifles at the ready, spread through the big space. The man in front of me stared at my bloodied appearance through his goggles and then at Dao. He had not spotted Paul who lay where he had fallen, a few metres behind us.

'This is Hunter,' said Dao, before he had a chance to speak. 'He's the one they took away – they were going to kill him. It was Charlie and me who rang for help. She is outside.'

Over his shoulder I saw Charlie coming towards us accompanied by the unmistakable outline of Benson. I was very glad to see them.

'These two will be able to explain,' I said to the AOS guys in front of us. 'They know me. I need to sit down.'

I perched on a stool and rested my arms on a workbench and listened to Charlie, Benson and Dao all talking at once. Blood was now dripping from my elbows. Dao led Charlie to one side to where Paul lay and I heard Charlie's voice, raised in distress.

'No, no! That's terrible – he only came along to help us.'

Her distress stabbed me. Between us we had involved

someone who really had nothing to do with all this and now he was dead.

Benson made a signal to someone behind me and then turned his attention to me. His eyes ran over me, taking in the blood and the rope around my leg.

'You're injured, Hunter. How bad is it? There seems to be a lot of blood everywhere.'

I tried to smile at him. 'I don't think it's too bad. I got knifed when they took me outside the pizza place and then that bastard tried to cut my other arm off with the water cutter. He just got started and then Dao threw the saw blade at him, and I got away.'

I could see that it was not making a lot of sense, but I was feeling incredibly tired suddenly. Starting at the beginning and explaining it all while in this state was a boring proposition. Charlie was coming back to us with Dao and heard what I told Benson.

'Let's have look, Hunter,' she said. 'Let's get that jacket off and see what the damage is.'

She pulled the jacket off my arms very slowly, one arm at a time. She tugged the edges of the cut in my sweatshirt sleeve and looked at the knife cut first.

'You need stitches, definitely – quite a few, and it's still bleeding.'

'I'll get the medics over here,' said Benson. 'We've got a couple of ambulances on stand-by outside.'

Charlie put my left hand down to rest on my thigh and walked around to the other side. Dao watched every move Charlie made and took a step close to Benson. She whispered something I did not catch, and he nodded and gave her a smile.

'Shit!' said Charlie. 'This is a really nasty cut – looks as if it's deep into the muscle.'

I heard Dao suck in a shocked breath. I did not look too closely myself; I already knew it was bad. Benson whistled and raised his arm at someone, and a paramedic came up at speed carrying a large case that he put on the floor. 'Right then – what have we got here?'

He sounded relaxed and casual, nearly cheerful and Dao's eyes shot black arrows at him. Before she could launch an attack I said, 'I've been knifed on the left side and cut into with that damn water cutter thing on the other.'

I turned to Benson who was looking perplexed and tried to explain.

'The water has ground-up garnets in it as an abrasive – very effective. And the blood on Paul is mine – we were checking his pulse.'

God knows what was going on in my mind. Random information seemed important at the time. Benson put his hand on my shoulder for a moment and then took a step back.

The paramedic was moving my arms around and cutting the sleeves off my sweatshirt, but I was focusing on the other end of the building. There were a lot of people there now, setting up bright lights and reeling out crime scene tape. From the semi-dark space where we were it looked like a film set. The big white bag hung over the cutting machine, still now, like a mystic presence watching over the proceedings.

'Christ, look at that!' said the paramedic. 'Did you know you've been shot as well? Or that's what it looks like. Look, just below that big cut.'

I shook my head. He looked at the back of my arm and said on a note of triumph, 'Yep – exit hole at the back, quite neat.'

'I'm glad someone is pleased,' said Charlie coldly.

Things were happening all around us now. There was a cluster of men beside Paul's body; someone found the switches and all the big overhead lights came on. Suddenly the entire place was brightly lit and for the first time I saw the extent of it; big enough to house a passenger jet or two.

'Let's get you out of here,' said Benson. 'I think we need a stretcher.'

'I can walk – nothing wrong with my legs,' I said but the paramedic would have none of it.

'Sorry, mate. You're not walking. If you fall and split your head open I'll be in trouble.'

Outside there were flashing lights, police cars, big vans and a couple of ambulances. The place looked like some crazy over-the-top drama on TV.

Benson came out with us and watched while they loaded me into the ambulance. Dao got in too and I heard Charlie say to Benson, 'I'll give you my number. I'll be at the hospital if you want to talk to us.'

The doors shut and we moved off. The emergency department nurses were very efficient. In no time at all they had me in a cubicle and stripped off. A doctor arrived and Dao was taken away to wash the blood off herself.

Charlie said, 'I'll go and sit in the waiting area. Kia kaha, mate.'

What followed was painful and slow and brought back memories of the field hospital in Afghanistan. They used a lot of saline to rinse the cut the water jet had made to get the abrasive out of the wound. Painkilling injections went into both arms before they started stitching everything up. First the knife wound which was easy. On the other side, where the water jet had cut me, they stitched the muscles first and then the skin, then the two holes just below that where the bullet had gone in and then out on the other side not far above the elbow.

'You're lucky it didn't nick the bone,' said the tired-looking doctor who was doing the stitching. 'It missed the humerus so it's only tissue damage – it will heal in no time.'

I love the way medical people minimise everything and make it seem so normal. I suppose it is normal to them, but having both arms full of stitches and wrapped up in bandages did not feel normal to me.

When they opened the door I sat up and swung my legs

over the edge of the table. 'Thank you. Are you finished – can we go home now?'

'We'll give you some painkillers to take home. You'll need them when the anaesthetic wears off in a couple of hours. But you can't drive, and I'd advise you not to drink alcohol.'

Fat chance, I thought. If I ever needed a drink it's tonight. Charlie and Dao were outside in the corridor.

'I'll drive you home,' said Charlie. 'We all need something to eat – dinner never happened, and a beer would be good.'

'We've got no food,' I said, remembering how all this had started. 'That's why we were at the pizza shop. There's literally nothing to eat at my place. And now I think of it, where are my keys and my dog – and the car?'

I had nothing on apart from jeans and shoes. My bloodied jacket and sweatshirt had gone into the rubbish, but I had checked that the garage remote was still in my left front pocket. My phone was gone.

'Bugger! I pushed the phone under the belt on one side so he wouldn't take it off me and now it's disappeared. God knows where it is, maybe in that van.'

'I've got your car keys,' said Charlie. 'Dao found them on the ground – she locked your car and left it there. Scruff is outside in my car, but I've no idea where your phone is.'

Dao had been looking down while we were talking and now she held her phone up and smiled.

'Your phone is still at that place, where we've just come from – that factory.'

'Someone will pick it up,' I said. 'Or we go back and find it tomorrow.'

'See,' said Dao, 'I told you that you should have that find-my-phone app on your phone too – and I was right.'

'I never doubted it,' I said. 'You are usually right. We'll ask Benson to get his guys to find it.'

'Did you see the Boss?' I asked Charlie.

'I did – and good riddance.'

Dao shuddered. 'That was horrible.'

She raised her hands as if to cover her eyes and I noticed her hands. 'Hey, what happened to you? Look at your hands!'

We all looked at Dao's hands. Cuts on her palms, skinned knuckles and a patchwork of scratches and bruises.

'It was when I climbed in that window. And that round thing I threw – I had to get a good grip on it to throw it, it was heavy – and very sharp around the edges.'

Charlie looked at me across Dao's head and shook her head in amazement; she was about to tell me something.

'Later,' I said. 'We'll get the full story when we get home.'

A nurse turned up with a bottle of painkillers and we went outside. It was cold and felt like rain coming on. Scruff danced around my legs while Charlie found a jersey in the back of her car, not big enough for me to wear but she draped it across my shoulders.

'What on earth happened to your back? Did they check this out? Christ, Hunter – you are such a mess. And do you have to be so tall?'

'What's wrong with my back?'

Dao went behind me to have a look.

'There's a big scratchy area right across.' She touched it lightly. 'I can't see properly in this light, but it looks as if there's going to be a big bruise.'

'Must have been that bloody thing he dumped on my back to hold me down. Let's get in the car – I'm freezing. I'll tell you later, when we are back at the house.'

On the way home Charlie's phone let out the manic laughter ring tone she uses for text messages. 'We'll check it when we get home,' she said and drove on. 'I sent out a general update to those who need to know. If it's questions they'll have to wait.'

She fumbled around in the compartment between the seats and handed me my bunch of keys.

'I hope you can turn that alarm system off without your phone or we'll have to go back to my place for the night.'

That reminded me of Paul and those who must be informed about his death. 'Did you tell Benson who Paul is?'

'Oh, yes – he's got all the details. And he knows Paul's van is outside the factory. He said they'll organise everything.'

'Did you call him for back-up before the cops came? I didn't think he was the type to have a gun.'

'He wasn't – that's my gun. I had a rifle and the other Glock in the chopper when I took that VIP guy to the lodge, so when Dao rang I was pretty much equipped to deal with anything.'

I felt guilty that I knew so little about Paul in civilian life. You should know everything about a man who has died for your sake. The relief of being rid of the Boss had been diluted with sadness and I knew the feeling would be with me for a long time.

'Was Paul married?'

'No, he had a girlfriend, but they didn't live together. I suppose there are parents and maybe siblings.'

We sat silent and exhausted until Charlie stopped outside a row of late-night fast-food outlets.

'Pizza, hamburger or chicken?'

We got back to the house just after midnight and I struggled to get the garage door remote out of my pocket. My arms felt as if they belonged to somebody else. I opened the garage door and managed to punch the code into the keypad before the twenty seconds were up.

Dao and I went upstairs to the bedrooms while Charlie organised food and drink. Dao helped me out of my bloody jeans and into clean gear. Her own clothes were covered in dust and dirt. She put her PJs on and then looked at her hands.

'I must wash my hands again,' she said. 'Even touching my clothes has made my hands filthy.'

While she did that I fished around in the bathroom cabinet and found some disinfectant and sticking plasters.

'Stand here,' I said and pointed. 'I don't like the thought of how much dirt you must have got into those open cuts. Let's fix you up a bit.'

'OK, let's eat while it's still warm,' said Charlie when we came downstairs. 'Go and sit somewhere comfortable, Hunter - I'll bring you a plate and a glass. I took the Remington out of your car at the pizza shop. I've put it in the corner there by the stairs.'

We sat with plates on our knees and wine and beer within easy reach. When the doorbell went we looked at each other in surprise and Charlie ran down. She came back with Benson and a younger man following.

'I'm glad to see you're being fed,' said Benson. 'What happened to you, Dao?' He was looking at her hands.

'She threw a circular saw blade, a very large one,' said Charlie. 'Very hard to handle – but she did it.'

Benson nodded and said neutrally, 'She certainly did.'

Nothing more, but I knew that to him it was potentially a murder weapon. The danger this posed should have occurred to me earlier. I had no idea if Dao realised that everything would depend on how she described what had motivated her to throw it. Having her on a manslaughter or murder charge was the last thing we needed.

'Would you guys like some beer – or wine?' said Charlie. 'Are you still working, Benson? Or is this a private visit?'

He smiled. 'I'm not officially on, but they got me in for the raid. They knew I'd want to be there. Steve here can't have one, he's on duty and he's got to drive me home. A beer would be good. We'll take formal statements tomorrow when everyone has had a sleep.'

Charlie got a glass for Benson and a coffee for Steve, whoever he was. He wasn't in uniform, so I supposed he was a detective of some kind.

'Now then, Charlie,' said Benson. 'Let's find out what happened tonight. What you told the emergency centre when you called them was very sketchy. All I got told was that you were at that factory with Dao and that Hunter was inside with the Boss and there might be firearms involved. And then you cut the call – but I imagine you had other things on your mind at the time. Perhaps we should start with Hunter and get the whole story in sequence.'

I told them what had happened from the time I got jumped by those two heavies outside the pizza shop. When I got to the part where the singing in the factory started I paused and looked at Dao.

'That was the most surprising thing I've ever experienced. That lovely voice suddenly singing in such an unlikely place and when we had no idea there was anyone else in the building. Surreal is the only word for it – like some French film. And then that gantry crane starting up – I can tell you it startled the hell out of the Boss – and me.'

Charlie and Benson looked at each other; until now neither of them had heard about this.

'Imagine this,' I said, looking forward to their surprise when they realised what I was talking about. 'There we are, the Boss and I, thinking we're alone in that huge space – only half-lit and echoing. He started cutting my arm off and I've just managed to heave that weight off my back and stand up – we're at a stand-off. And out of nowhere someone starts singing 'Amazing Grace', very beautifully. We have no idea what's happening – who is there or why. And a minute later the gantry crane starts, and we both look up and see that white bag coming slowly closer and descending as it comes. Very unsettling – I was mesmerised, and the Boss looked as if he had been struck by lightning.'

Dao said, 'Good!' and I laughed.

'And then Dao appeared out of the gloom a few metres behind the Boss. I must admit my heart missed a beat then. I was terrified he'd see her and shoot her, because that was his whole aim. He wanted her dead – I was just a bit player, a way to get to her.'

Benson nodded. 'Exactly right.'

'I realised she was going to throw something,' I said. 'The

way she stood like a discus thrower, holding something. I couldn't see what it was, and I didn't dare look properly at her in case I alerted the Boss. But he did see her and fired. When that damn saw disc came flying through the air like a mega-Frisbee I just threw myself to one side to get out of the way.'

The guy called Steve said, 'Awesome!' with great relish. Benson cast him a quelling look that shut him up. Probably showing enthusiasm for unusual methods of killing people is not approved of.

'You next,' said Charlie to Dao. 'I don't know all of it either – tell us, please.'

Dao looked around at four faces waiting for her to start and said nothing.

'Come on, Dao!' said Charlie. 'Start at the beginning when you were in Hunter's car. We really want to know.'

'Well, it was strange – scary,' said Dao. 'I was in the back under the luggage cover and the windows were closed and the car was locked, so I couldn't hear exactly what happened. But I knew something bad was going on. I heard some shouting and noises and doors slamming shut – then a car left very fast. So I waited a minute and then I got out and the men from the shop were standing there staring at the pizzas lying on the ground. One of them said he thought they should call the police. I don't think they noticed me getting out of the car. I had climbed over into the back seat and got out the door on the far side from them because I wasn't quite sure at first who they were. They were so busy talking – they never looked at me.'

'Why didn't you call us and wait until we arrived?' said Benson.

'I had to find Hunter, of course – right away,' said Dao. 'I ran around the car as soon as the men went back into the shop, and I saw the pizzas and the keys. So, I picked the keys up and locked the car and then Scruff and I ran around to the far side of the shops and started walking. That's when I rang

Charlie, because Hunter put her number in my phone, and he said if anything ever went wrong she would know what to do. I knew we'd find him because of that app – the 'find my phone thing'. We both have it on our phones.'

Charlie looked at Benson and tried to sound apologetic. 'I had come back from a job at the end of the day – I was on my way to a friend's place where Kristen was when Dao rang. I was in the perfect spot, about fifteen minutes from where she was so I told her to get working on that app and find out where they were taking Hunter. I rang Paul while I was driving and asked him to come to back me up, told him I might need help and said I'd call him as we went and tell him where we were heading. Paul and I were great mates for years.'

She stopped for a moment and looked into space with a frown between her eyebrows. 'And then I picked Dao up from the end of the block where the shops are and went back and had a quick look at the car. By the time I got to Dao she knew where they were heading, and I could tell Paul. I'm sorry, Benson - I know we've broken all the rules. It was totally my call not to tell you guys until we knew where they would stop, it seemed pointless. But I rang you as soon as we got to that factory.'

Benson's face spoke volumes, but he restrained himself. 'OK – and then what happened?'

'We stopped on the road outside the factory,' said Charlie. 'We went into the yard at the back and saw that large van by the door and a couple of trucks parked up on the far side. Nobody around, but you could vaguely see light in some windows high up. I tried the door, and it was locked so we went right around the building, but the only possibility was a small window that was open, fairly high up on the yard side of the building. Probably a toilet?'

She looked at Dao, who nodded, and Charlie continued.

'I didn't think that even Dao would fit through – it had four bars across it. But we had to try. The idea was that if she could get in she would creep around and open that door into the yard so I could get in. And then she was supposed to go outside and let me deal with it. I told her she must not go anywhere near the Boss and if she couldn't get to the door she should hide somewhere and just stay quiet. She climbed on to my shoulders and could just reach to get a grip on that window frame, and somehow or other she hauled herself up and wriggled inside. '

'Were you armed, Charlie?' said Benson, as if he already knew the answer.

She looked hard at him. I thought she was about to tell him not to play silly games. 'I'm sure you've researched me since we first met. I have the appropriate license to carry a handgun. Because it was a VIP that I had flown from the airport to a luxury lodge in Northland I had a couple of guns with me – one handgun and a rifle. I always do when I fly people from the Middle East or somewhere politically tricky. No way is anyone going to be assassinated in New Zealand on my watch.'

Her eyes challenged Benson to interrupt or start an argument. He said nothing.

'And that guy today was from Israel, some big shot in government – and his wife and some kind of heavy-duty companion. Anyway, Paul arrived just after Dao climbed in. We waited for a few minutes, but she didn't come to the door, and I was getting worried.'

She took a sip of her drink and sighed. 'So, Paul climbed on the roof of his van to see if he could hear anything and he found that those bars over the little window were rusted and not very secure, so he managed to rip two of the four out of the old brickwork – made the opening wide enough for him to climb in. He was supposed to just have a look and listen. But he climbed right in before I knew what he was going to do and then he refused to come out and said to pass him the rifle – and disappeared. I wish I could have gone in myself! So I never used a gun tonight. The other one is still here.'

She patted her jacket that she had flung over the arm of the sofa.

'What is it?' said Benson, professional interest interrupting the story.

'A Glock, the light one with the small magazine, short recoil.'

He nodded and turned to Dao again. 'OK, so now you're inside the building, Dao. What happened next?"

'There were no lights where I got in, so I had to feel my way. I was worried I'd trip over something and make a noise. But I found a passage with a door just a bit open at the end and I saw the lights were on out there – so I tiptoed down to the door and had a look. I had to see where they were before I tried to find the door to let Charlie in.'

Charlie and I were both leaning forward slightly, our eyes fixed on Dao's face. Neither of us had heard her side until now.

Dao looked at Charlie. 'Sorry! I forgot to go back and open the door for you. I had to try to do something right away when I saw what was going on – I knew it couldn't wait. At first I couldn't see Hunter and the Boss, but I heard their voices. So, I followed a low sort of wall and I had to get about halfway to where they were before I could hear what they were saying.'

She looked at me and her face told me something that I was sure the others would not pick up. I knew that look – Dao trying to control tears. I smiled and she blinked and managed to smile back.

'I just kept going closer, very quietly. I heard the Boss say that Bram's foot was in his boot, and I didn't understand what he meant. But then he started talking about big bags with zips that sails come in and something 'up there'. And I looked up and saw a big white bag hanging from a hook way up there under the roof – towards the other end.'

She stopped again and looked at me. 'Did he really cut off Bram's foot?'

'Yes, he did. It is lying on that cutting table, still in his boot. Bram's body is in the bag.'

Benson turned to Steve. 'Christ – get on to the team out there and make sure they know about the bag, will you?'

'Dao,' I said. 'I know you realised I was in danger and that the Boss had killed Bram. But I can't understand how you managed to start the crane. It totally distracted the Boss – and me for that matter. We both looked up and that damned bag came sliding along towards us. It was the spookiest thing. I had goose bumps and the Boss nearly wet himself. How did you do it?'

Steve came back from the other end of the room and sat down again. Benson said, 'Did you really start the gantry crane up? My word, I've never heard of anything like it – how did you know what to do?'

Dao looked embarrassed, as if she had been caught doing something bad. Sitting there, in her grey PJs with pink butterflies and her fingers covered in sticking plaster, she looked like a harmless child. 'I don't know – it just happened. I don't know anything about factories. I was so scared that man would cut Hunter to bits. He was trying to use that machine. And Hunter had made him angry, I heard it.'

She looked at me. 'You were making him angry on purpose, weren't you?'

'Yes, I was. I wanted him on edge and not so sure of himself – in case I got a chance to tackle him.'

Dao nodded. 'I thought that was what you were doing. But it seemed very risky to me. Anyway, I was really close to them by then and where I was standing there was a little space with walls around it, just low walls, as if they had made a little place for some special thing. And there was a thick cord hanging down from the ceiling with a thing like Hunter's garage remote on the end, but much bigger and bright yellow. Just a few buttons – one was bigger than the others, red. I could just see the colours. And then four black buttons with arrows like on the laptop.'

She paused and drank some orange juice.

'Hunter got that big slab of metal off his back and stood up. I started singing 'Amazing Grace' because it was my mother's favourite song. I used to sing it on the island, when Bram was away, and I was chained up in the shed. It made me feel better. And I thought it would get the attention away from Hunter. Because the Boss didn't know I was there. Anyway, I decided to see what that remote would do, start something up or … whatever. Just to make something happen. I had no idea what it was. So, I pressed the red button and I heard a motor starting, not beside me – somewhere further away. Then I pressed the button with the arrow pointing down and that bag started moving towards our end. I kept my finger on the button and the bag came closer and closer. There were two more buttons below those arrow ones. One said Up and one said Down. I pressed the Down button too and the bag came down lower as it slid along. I thought I would drop it really low when it was just above Hunter and the Boss. I was going to try to hit the Boss with it.'

We all stared at her, stunned by how chance and the simplicity of the gantry remote and Dao's presence of mind had worked together to create the perfect diversion. Benson shook his head in silent disbelief.

She looked at us just sitting there, mutely contemplating her and said, 'What's wrong?'

Charlie started to laugh. 'Nothing's wrong, warrior girl – it's just bloody incredible, the whole thing.'

Benson got us back on track. 'So, both Hunter and the Boss were surprised and a bit spooked. And then what did you do?'

I was worried about this next bit, really worried. But I could do nothing to help her out, just hope that she would put it in a way that made it acceptable. If she said she had planned to kill him she would be in trouble. And with Dao's propensity for suggesting lethal solutions, she could well come out with something that would be impossible to explain away.

'I saw that round metal thing lying on the next little bench, just past where I was standing, and I had an idea. I thought I would grab it and throw it like a Frisbee, you know those plastic things? I had one when I was little, I was really good at it. I used to be able to hit nearly everything I aimed for. So, I went closer and picked it up and sneaked closer and closer and just when I was close enough Hunter saw me. I threw it at that machine – I was hoping I could break it and then Hunter would be safe and maybe the Boss would drop his gun if he got a fright. But I missed, it was very heavy, that thing – it hit the Boss.'

She looked apologetically at Benson.

'I am not going to pretend I'm sorry because I'm not! But if the thing hadn't been so heavy I would have hit the machine, not the Boss. His gun went off at the same time that he fell down and Hunter threw himself in the other direction. And that's how my hands got into such a mess. That saw thing was very sharp around the edges, but I had to get a grip on it and throw it before the Boss did something. I'm sure I missed because I couldn't hold it right.'

Well done, warrior girl, I thought. You're out of the risk zone now, perfect explanation – and I'm never going to ask you if it's true or if you really aimed at the Boss.

'But hang on,' said Charlie. 'There must have been two shots fired. One hit Hunter and one killed Paul.'

I had been thinking about that. There had been two shots and I had been trying to figure out how it had happened and in what order.

'I think the Boss hit Paul by mistake. He would have been aiming at Dao because she was the only person he could see when he swung around. Paul was further back, but roughly in line with Dao. I think Paul's shot ricocheted off something – I heard that distinctive hard metal ping – and it hit me. Perhaps he fired as he was hit himself.'

We finally got to bed about half past two in the morning. Charlie left soon after Benson. She turned on the doorstep and pretended she was going to punch me in the arm like she always does and grinned when I flinched.

'I wouldn't – just kidding. And just think, now you don't need to have a gun beside the bed tonight, Hunter.'

'Wrong,' I said. 'It's going to stay beside me until I know that every single person linked to this has been arrested – both those boat guys are still out there, and they'll be getting worried. I'm not relaxing yet.'

'Fair enough,' said Charlie. 'And I replied to those text messages when you were upstairs – I told Willow to hold off until morning and let you sleep. See you!'

We retrieved Scruff from the courtyard where he had been since we got back, set the alarms again, took the Remington with us upstairs and went to bed.

23

THURSDAY

A call from Willow woke me the next morning. I was bleary with sleep and my arms were giving me hell. I rested the phone on the pillow and turned my cheek into it to avoid having to hold it. Dao was curled up with her back to me, sound asleep. She never stirred while I talked to Willow.

'I won't go into the details,' I said very quietly. 'It's a long story and I don't want us to have to tell it more than once – how about we come for coffee or lunch or something? Then we can tell you all at the same time.'

'But Hunter, who were the two people who got killed? It was the top story on the news, but they mentioned no names, not the victims' names or yours. And Charlie didn't say – she just said you and Dao were OK, but you had been injured. On the news they said one of the people killed was the hostage taker – was it the Boss or Bramville? How badly are you hurt?'

'The Boss was killed last night – the other one was Paul.'

'No! Not that nice quiet guy who came and helped when we were searching for Dao?'

'I'm afraid it was. Charlie called him in as back-up. I can't go into it now – we'll tell you later. I haven't got my head around it yet, we're all in shock I think. But Bramville is dead too, the Boss had already killed him.'

As soon as I put the phone on the bedside table it rang again.

'Good morning!' said Benson brightly as if he was rested and fit for anything. 'Have you got time to make formal statements today? This afternoon, perhaps?'

'Yes, fine. What time?'

'Hunter, I can hardly hear you, can you speak up?'

'No, I can't.'

I turned away from Dao and spoke slightly louder. 'Dao's asleep right beside me and I don't want to wake her up.' I didn't care what he thought about it – it was no business of his. I was not prepared to wake Dao for anyone.

'That's good,' said Benson. 'I did hear you then. How about half past three at the station?'

'OK – we'll be there.'

But he was not finished. 'I'm going to tell you something that hasn't been released yet – so keep it in the family for now. The Boss was a very well-known barrister called Wilfred Beckinsale. I'm sure you've heard of him. Quite famous – he's defended gang bosses and other scumbags in the courts for decades. Very wealthy and very successful. Seems he had links to crime in a different way than the obvious one. We won't release his name until his family has been informed, so mind you keep it quiet.'

With some difficulty I managed to turn on my side. I reached out slowly and put my right arm over Dao and pulled her tight against my chest. She mumbled something in her sleep. I tucked her head under my chin and tried to get back to sleep.

We arrived at Willow and Matt's for a late lunch. Plum had stayed home from classes so she could be there, and Matt was on his last day's leave before another long trip to Europe.

'I saw you through the window,' said Plum when she

opened the door for us. 'Why were you in the back under the cover, Dao? I thought it was all safe now.'

'Not quite,' I said. 'I'll explain when we're all in one place. I'm all talked out. Perhaps Dao can do the talking.'

Willow came out and went to hug me and then stopped and considered. 'God, Hunter – are you huggable? I think I'll just go for Dao.'

Over lunch we told the whole story again. They all had the same reaction that Dao and I had felt the previous night; something threatening and ghastly was behind us but our relief was tempered by grief over Paul. Last of all I told them that Benson knew who the Boss really was. Willow was stunned.

'I can't believe it! Not that I knew him well, but I've talked to him in court. He was always so suave and charming, expensive suits, perfect haircut. I think he was a great ladies' man too - I've heard rumours about him. Fancy him being a crime boss!'

Dao and I left at three and when we got to the central police station I stopped Dao before we went in.

'This is important, warrior girl – be very careful what you say now that it's a formal statement. They will record every word. Say exactly what you said last night about what you were aiming for with that mega Frisbee of yours. Don't give any indication that you aimed for the Boss or that you wanted to kill him, OK?'

She flicked me one of those Dao glances that makes you aware that something's going on in her head, but you have no idea what it is.

'Of course, not – I thought of it last night so I made sure he understood I aimed for the machine.'

So, I still had no idea if it had been intentional or not and neither did I know if Dao intended to leave me dangling. Not that it worried me either way.

We went inside and spent two hours going over every single detail. By that stage I was on auto pilot and had it all lined up in chronological order, easy to tell in a straight line. The questions about details took up most of the time. Finally, it was over, the recorder was turned off and I thought we were leaving, but Benson stopped us in the corridor outside the interview room.

'Come back to my office for a minute,' he said and turned without waiting for an answer. He closed the door behind us and sat down behind his desk.

'Now – two things, or maybe three. I didn't want to talk about it with the constable in the room, but I'm deadly serious. I could make this warning official, Hunter, and believe me – I will if I think I need to.'

I said nothing, but I knew where this was going.

'I saw your gun by the stairs in your living room last night. I know you had that intruder at gunpoint when you disarmed him. I'm certain you've been driving around with a loaded gun all over town ever since you knew the threat Dao was under – and you have probably been carrying a loaded handgun too – you have such useful friends.'

Those grey eyes drilled into mine, making sure I was taking him seriously.

'And I have no doubt at all that if you thought it was necessary you would shoot to kill. So here's the warning – or the ultimatum if you like. You can hand your guns over to me now or you can promise me to stop having them with you in the car, loaded. To me you are a potentially dangerous person –based both on your army experience and from what I have learnt about you since this started, the sort of things you have done. And what I know you are prepared to do if you think it's necessary.'

He paused for a moment and looked briefly at Dao before his eyes swung back to me.

'The other option is that you go away for a while until we get those guys from the boats who know that Dao can ID them. It won't be long – we know a lot more about those boats now and it's just a question of locating the owners.'

He meant it. It might have been irregular and unofficial, but I knew he could have me stopped and searched repeatedly, anywhere and at any time, to check if I was carrying the loaded gun in the car or on my person. But his motivation was a bit of a mystery.

'Why is this so important to you?' I said, sounding as reasonable as I could. 'I would only use the gun if it was them or us – I'm not an idiot, Benson.'

He looked blandly back and then he smiled. 'I don't give a damn about you, Hunter – I like you a lot, but if you choose to kill someone and get yourself locked up it wouldn't ruin my life. But it would probably ruin Dao's life – and that's another matter altogether. So, there it is – your choice. Those injuries can be checked by any hospital anywhere. Go to Queenstown or some distant place and have a break, show Dao a bit of the rest of the country.'

'All right, we will. I can work from anywhere. But you've got to let us know when we can come back.'

Now he smiled a genuine, friendly smile. He got up and came around to our side of the desk; hand out to shake on the deal.

'Of course, I will let you know. And I hope you have fun – you both deserve it.'

I thought about the various details he had not touched on. Paul's family that I needed to talk to, the funeral and other things that must be attended to. But as he had said, first things first. I would find a way of doing what had to be done.

When we got back to the car Dao said, 'But what about Scruff? Can he come on a plane, or do we have to go away in the car?'

'I don't know if I can drive very far for a little while, but we could do short stages and spend a night here and there. We could take him on the plane, I'm sure they take dogs. Let's talk about it when we get home.'

'OK,' said Dao. 'Let's go home now.'

MANY THANKS

We hope you've enjoyed reading this story and would consider leaving a review on your favourite review site, or with the retailer you purchased from.

These are not only much appreciated, they also help other readers discover new authors.

For more about other titles in this series, please read on.

ALSO BY TINA CLOUGH

THE GIRL WHO LIVED TWICE

What would you do if you woke up one morning and found that time had rewound exactly a year? Would you revisit your past mistakes and try to do better? Would you try to get revenge on those who had wronged you? Or would you use what you knew to get rich? When Mia finds herself in her own past, she must decide how best to use her pre-knowledge of one year's worth of events and personal issues.

When Karen's flat-mate Nick is gunned down in front of her in the street her life is turned upside-down. Everything she thought she knew about him turns out to be a lie. She becomes a suspect in the police investigation and drug bosses think she knows where Nick has hidden a large sum of money. When her life is threatened, she decides to leave town and disappear.

Karen becomes Cara and creates an anonymous existence, severs all links to her past and adopts a cash-based way of life that leaves no electronic traces. But despite her careful planning danger still stalks her and she is forced to make dramatic choices in the face of threats and brutal violence.

Can she trust the man she is attracted to, or has he been sent by the killers to gain her confidence and find the money they believe she has?

Book 1 - Hunter Grant Series

Army veteran Hunter Grant thought he had left war behind in Afghanistan – a conflict that left him with physical and psychological scars.

But finding an unconscious girl in the Northland bush and gradually untangling her story involves him in warfare of a different kind in his own country.

Hunter sets out to find and punish the man Dao calls Master, but he soon finds there is more to this story than enslavement. Before long he himself is being hunted by the overlord of a drug empire whose sole objective is to kill Dao because she knows too much.

Protecting her and waging war while trying to keep the police from stifling his enterprise takes all Hunter's ingenuity and determination and puts him in deadly jeopardy.

Book 2 - Hunter Grant Series

Journalist Hope Barber disappears two weeks after returning to New Zealand from an assignment in Pakistan, leaving her front door open and her bag and phone inside. The police are tight-lipped about their reluctance to act, and Hunter Grant and Dao agree to help Hope's brother Noah find her. Details about Hope's time in Pakistan gradually emerge but only raise more questions.

Was Hope under surveillance?

Was she linked to terrorists?

And who is the man Hope called 'my stalker'?

Book 3 - Hunter Grant Series

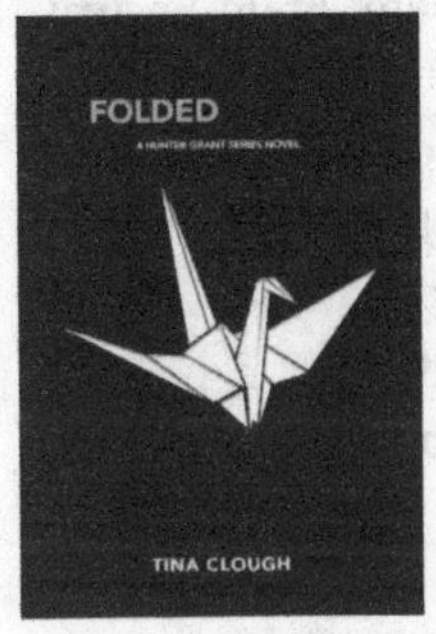

First notes asking for help and folded into tiny origami shapes are found outside a city apartment building, then a physics textbook with tiny writing between the lines and then the woman who found them abruptly resigns and disappears. Are the notes asking for help real or is it a game? Hunter Grant, ex-army and with a pragmatic view of justice, reluctantly agrees to help find the missing woman.

Things get complicated when a high-powered lawyer arrives form the US, and shortly after his meeting with Hunter and Dao, a "cease and desist" letter arrives from the Cayman Islands. Inspector Bakker - a woman, who in Hunter's words "looks as if she would be useful in a brawl, provided she was on your side" - takes instant exception to his involvement and threatens to arrest him for interfering in an investigation.

Dao sets out alone on a dangerous mission, driven by a compulsive need to find out what has happened to the girl who wrote the notes, and Hunter looks death in the face when he decides to risk everything to put an end to the Darknet forces that threaten their lives.

It is 2026 and individual freedoms are severely curtailed, with state surveillance everywhere. State Security has a Watch List, and being on it means that nothing you do or say escapes the authorities, but does the Kill List really exist? And if it does, how would you know if you were on it?

Coded messages on a found burner phone, top-level government corruption and a shadowy mastermind who calls himself The Broker. In this climate of state control, three unlikely friends start quietly looking for connections and set in motion a deadly game of hide and seek that will change their lives forever.

Trying to uncover the truth means risking your life, and nothing is more dangerous than searching for evidence of government corruption.

ABOUT THE AUTHOR

Tina Clough grew up in Sweden and now lives in New Zealand; dividing her time between writing fiction and translating and editing medical research papers.

Between working and writing she looks after an acre of fruit trees, vegetable gardens and roaming hens.

Apart from reading her interests include photography, wine, growing organic vegetables, making jam and kayaking.

https://lightpoolpublishing.com